The Legend of the

Night Nurse

By

John Avanzato

KCM PUBLISHING
A DIVISION OF KCM DIGITAL MEDIA, LLC

CREDITS

The Legend of the Night Nurse by John Avanzato

ISBN-13: 978-1-939961-94-5
ISBN-10: 1-939961-94-7

First Edition

Publisher: Michael Fabiano
KCM Publishing
www.kcmpublishing.com

Cheryl

Dedicated to the nursing staff and administration of Auburn Community Hospital who embraced a stranger with open and welcoming arms. In particular I would like to recognize Veronica Ruggiero RN, Melissa Marie Dennis RN, Cynthia M. Purington RN, Sandra J. Rabuano BSNRN, Karen S. Cummings RN, Mary O'Neill RN and Jennifer Young RN for their hard work, professionalism and devotion to patient care. The world needs more people like you.

A special thanks to Mr. Scott Berlucchi FACHE, NHA, President and CEO of Auburn Community Hospital and Dr. John Riccio, Medical Director and Chief of Pathology who came into my life like a breath of fresh air through an open window. Through act and deed they restored my faith in a system I had thought irreversibly broken and showed me that you can run a hospital and still be nice guys.

To my special friend in the Bayou, Tracy Ambrose. Thank you for your support and advice.

Other Novels in the John Cesari Series

Table of Contents

Prologue

"**M**ake haste, they come," she whispered nervously.

The children scrambled through the field toward the forest's edge, barely awake but trying to keep up with their mother. There were thirteen of them, all born on the same day seven years ago and conceived on a night just like this one. Katrina looked up at the cloudless sky and felt a surge of energy run through her body. On Halloween night with a full moon her powers were at their greatest, but even she couldn't withstand the overwhelming advantage of her pursuers and guarantee the safety of her family. Despite her qualms, she felt exhilarated to be out and about on this special evening. The Dark One would not allow harm to come to his offspring.

The year was 1799 and they were fleeing their home in Sleepy Hollow with witch hunters hot on their trail. Most of the clan had scattered east and west, but she had chosen to go north. They had been surprised in the middle of the night by the screams of their neighbors as they burned to death in their beds. She and the children had narrowly missed the same fate. Where was Brom? She feared for him. He hadn't returned home from his hunting trip, but that wasn't unusual.

If he fared well, he would find them. For the moment she was on her own.

Their escape was slow and laborious hampered by the young age of her brood and the fact that at least half of them were shoeless. Twelve girls and one boy and she loved them all equally. Though not quite of age, the girls had already exhibited signs of the great potential that coursed through their veins, but still they were mortal and if caught, they would perish just the same by rope or by flame. Even worse would be the inevitable torture by their inquisitors if caught alive.

Stumbling through the dense woods and bramble and moving impossibly slow, she realized too late that she'd made an error, possibly a fatal one. In the distance ahead she saw the flickering light of torches and heard hounds barking. Breathless and alarmed, she halted her band to assess the situation. The hunters had circled around them and were now closing in from the front and the rear.

With no choice but to alter course, she ordered them all to silence, grabbed two of the nearest children by the hands, and veered due west toward the river bank, showing great poise in a moment where most would have been frantic and stricken with panic. As a mother of thirteen she had learned to be disciplined as well as nurturing in their upbringing. The result was that there was no whining or dissent as they followed her unquestioningly.

Entering a clearing, less than fifty yards from the water's edge, her heart sank. Anticipating her escape route, the hunters had outflanked her. A score of them waited on horses and foot at the shoreline with muskets, bayonets and ropes. When they discovered her presence, they began a methodical approach fanning out as they did. She looked back and saw more emerging from the tree line behind, their torches flickering brightly. They were fierce men with hatred in their eyes and determination in their hearts. Glancing down at the two girls at her side, a tear slid slowly down her cheek. Letting go of their hands, she turned to her troop and bid them all to sit in a circle close to her.

The baying of approaching dogs disquieted them and with her voice quivering ever so slightly, she comforted them as best she could. "Fret not my children. Close your eyes and do not open them again until I bid you so."

Dutifully, they sat in a tight ring around her with their eyes closed, and with all nearly lost she decided she had no choice but to defend her family by any means possible. She raised her face to the moon and slowly began to chant verses taught to her by the unholiest of teachers.

"Foul beast who doth live in hell
Rise from the hole in which doth dwell.

Come forth from where ye hide
To aid and succor your master's bride.

For this purpose I command thee live and breathe
To slay mine enemies and on thy flesh do feed.

On Satan's behalf I do now summon thee
To surround us all in death and misery."

When she finished, she raised her arms upward and let out a bloodcurdling cry. The oncoming men froze. They were just ten yards away, their animals snarling and straining at their tetherings. Several of the children began to sob and all clutched the hem of her dress for solace.

Momentarily fearful, the hunters looked in every direction but saw nothing. The closest one regained his courage and called out, "Witch! Yield ye to the righteous?" he demanded. "Spare ye not I will but perhaps thy spawn if they be put to the test and proved pure."

Seeing the lie for what it was she said nothing. The wickedness of the man may not have been obvious to the ordinary but for Katrina it glowed like a beacon illuminating his black soul.

He shouted out angrily, "What be thy answer, whore of Satan?"

Defiantly she replied, "I yield not to ye or any man nor shall ye harm a single hair on the head of any of these innocents."

"Then let it be. All must die."

"Sadly, that is so," she countered with great confidence.

He hesitated unsure of himself, then said, "Kill them all, sever the heads and put the bodies to the flame"

As he finished, a deep, ominous, rumbling sound ensued. She knelt and begged the children to keep their eyes closed. The men glanced around nervously. The sound went away and was replaced shortly by a trembling of the ground beneath their feet. The men began to step back slowly, uncertain of what was happening.

In between Katrina and the witch hunters the soil began to sputter and spew upward like a fountain. Slowly at first, and then faster with increasing violence like a volcano spitting earth and rock in all directions. The ground shook terribly, the horses neighed, and the dogs growled. Men on all sides began stumbling and retreating in terror and consternation. From the center of the eruption rose a thing of nightmares. So monstrous and fell a demon its mere visage could cause madness.

Katrina embraced her children as they gathered closer to her in an ever-tightening cluster, their eyes shut tight. She whispered consolingly, "Fear not little ones. To thee no harm will come."

Night Nurse

Chapter 1

The Boys

Cesari pulled into the hospital's parking lot ten minutes ahead of his scheduled noontime appointment. He'd driven four and a half hours to get here and was a little road weary. The second-hand Porsche was six years old and had made a funky sound the last hour of the trip. The check engine light had blinked ominously, but he couldn't afford to waste time to stop and have it evaluated. He straightened out his hair in the mirror and buttoned the top button of his shirt before adjusting his tie. Grabbing his leather briefcase from the passenger seat, he got out and made a bee line for the elevator.

A muscular six feet tall, with rugged features and thick, dark brown hair and olive, Mediterranean skin, Cesari cut a striking figure in his navy-blue suit and tie. He was north of thirty-five and south of forty but looked younger because of his life-long obsession with exercise and firm belief in moderation in all things. He wore brand new black wing tip dress shoes and they pinched a little as he strode through the lot.

The entrance to the hospital was one flight up and he walked quickly, glancing at his watch. It was an inexpensive model he had picked up at Walmart. He had been attracted to it because the advertisement said it could be submerged in up to thirty feet of water without damage. Not that he ever planned to test it out, but it was a great hook. It glowed in the dark and had all sorts of other features that he would never use but it got the job done, and more importantly, kept him from fumbling around for his cellphone all the time, a nasty habit of the modern era. He was a punctual guy and dreaded being late for anything, let alone a job interview. It had been a few years since he'd been on one and he was just a tad apprehensive.

An older woman with a 1970's hairdo greeted him at the information desk. Her voice was raspy, she was overly made-up and looked like she desperately needed a cigarette. Pleasant enough though, she directed him to the administrative offices, and a minute later, he inhaled and knocked on the CEO's door. He was exactly one minute and thirty seconds early.

A forty-year-old blonde secretary named Jamie, introduced herself and ushered him into a boardroom inviting him to take a seat at a long oval table. She was very nice and said, "Mr. Bardolino and Dr. Rizzo will be in shortly. May I get you a cup of coffee, Dr. Cesari?"

It was noon and he was famished and starting to get light-headed. He'd eaten a couple of slices of toast before he left Manhattan but that was it. He'd made the entire trip without even stopping for a bathroom break. He nodded gratefully, "Yes, thank you. Black, please."

"I'll be back in a moment."

Cesari took a seat and looked around. Neither new nor old, the room had the appearance of a typical boardroom featuring a table seating ten or twelve with audiovisual equipment at one end and several phones placed here and there. On a credenza to one side was a metal serving tray with multiple bottles of various distilled spirits resting on top. Cesari thought that a little out of place. Usually you kept that stuff hidden out of sight in a cabinet.

Alcohol was the lubricant that all businesses used to facilitate deals and debates and restructuring and job interviews, but it generally was not flaunted openly like that. He had no problem with it per se but it was not usually the first thing you wanted visitors to see. It tended to make a lasting impression.

The chairs were cloth not leather and the carpet a little faded. The hospital's finances had seen better days but what else was new? Every health care facility in the country was struggling for financial survival, and he would have been shocked if it were any different here, but usually it wasn't the executive meeting room where you figured that out. He had worked in hospitals of similar size before and some very large hospitals and the one vice they all seemed to have in common no matter what their economic fortunes were ostentatious boardrooms designed to impress the community, board members, and philanthropists. The boardroom was where you tried to send the subliminal message to the world that despite the turmoil swirling around healthcare, we were doing all right. You were safe here. You were right to put your trust in us.

As he examined his surroundings, he noted that this was probably the smallest boardroom he'd ever been in. For some reason he liked that and thought that the guys who ran this place must be down to earth. He'd gotten a hint of that from the headhunter who had randomly solicited him one week earlier for the job opening. The guy had been persistent about the merits of working in a place such as this and had convinced Cesari to at least give it a look. The timing was right for him, so he figured it couldn't hurt to give it the once-over. He'd worked in a rural upstate hospital like this several years ago but had never been to this particular hospital or this town before.

The door opened, and two guys entered, one large and the other larger. Both wore dark suits with crisp white shirts and power ties. Except for the smiles, they could have been FBI. The bigger of the two stepped forward with hand outstretched. Cesari rose to meet him. He was in his mid-fifties, six feet three inches tall and close to three hundred pounds but carried it well as if he had been an athlete back in the day. He had a full head of jet-black hair and a ruddy complexion. His grip was strong and Cesari sensed he was the alpha dog. He had a disturbing right-sided facial tic which gave the impression that he was winking. He spoke with a pronounced Boston accent.

"Dr. Cesari. Welcome to upstate New York. It's a pleasure to meet you. So glad you could come all this way on such short notice. I'm Sal and this is Dr. Rizzo, our Medical Director and chief of pathology."

The other guy was maybe a year or two younger, six feet even and about two hundred and forty pounds. He wore wire rimmed glasses and was graying at the sides. Cesari sensed he was under more stress but exhibited no facial tics. He extended his hand and as they shook, he said, "The name's Richard but everyone calls me Dicky."

"Dicky?"

"As in 'Tricky Dicky'… Don't ask. The guys in my fraternity at Yale labeled me with it and it stuck."

Sal said, "Don't be shy, Dicky. Dicky is a big fan of Richard M. Nixon, and the boys at Yale used to ride him hard about it. He even did his senior thesis praising President Pariah. It nearly got him thrown out of school. C'mon, Dicky. Say it loud and say it proud."

Dicky laughed, "I don't mind. He was one of the greatest presidents we ever had despite everything."

Nixon's troubled presidency was before his time but Cesari studied history. He asked, "Didn't he leave the White House in disgrace; Watergate, the Christmas bombings of Hanoi, lying to Congress?"

"Total bullshit," said Dicky, "by today's standards he'd be considered a choir boy."

Cesari raised his eyebrows, "Well, it's nice to meet you both. Please call me John or plain old Cesari will do just fine."

The secretary came in with Cesari's coffee and handed it to him. He said, "Thank you."

"You're welcome. Will there be anything else, Sal?"

"I think we're good, Jamie." She walked away and Sal turned to Cesari and asked, "Have you had lunch, doctor?"

Cesari shook his head. "No, I haven't. I just arrived minutes ago."

"How about we take a short ride and grab a bite. Dicky and I have been in painful budget meetings all morning and need to see the sun. I heard it's a beautiful day out. What say you, Dicky?"

"I never turn down food, Sal," he replied jovially with a broad smile.

"Or booze," Sal laughed at his own joke and added, "… or anything wearing a skirt."

Dicky chuckled but didn't offer any protest. Cesari glanced back and forth not sure if it was appropriate to join in on such an inside joke as that. So he let it go and smiled politely.

Sal clapped his hands together and said enthusiastically, "C'mon, we'll need to hurry before they run out of bourbon. You're going to love this restaurant, Dr. Cesari."

Sal grabbed a manila folder from Jamie's desk on the way out and waved goodbye to her. She was on the phone and waved back. They hopped in a brand new green Jaguar parked in the doctor's lot outside the emergency room in a space marked, *I'm the CEO & You're Not!* On either side, the parking spaces were blocked off by orange construction cones to protect the Jaguar from dings. Maybe the hospital's finances had seen better days, but Sal was apparently doing just fine.

The restaurant was actually a bar called A.T. Wally & Co. and was only a five-minute drive from the hospital. Sal swung the Jaguar into a *No Parking Anytime* zone like a Formula One race car driver coming in for a pit stop. They got out and Cesari looked at the *No Parking* sign and then at Sal and Dicky, who didn't seem to notice. These guys were starting to amuse him.

As a matter of due diligence, Cesari said, "Are you sure you want to leave it here? It's an awfully nice car. It might get towed."

Sal chortled and said mostly to Dicky, "Listen to him. He's worried about my car." Then, mostly to Cesari he said, "Thanks for your concern, but I'd be more worried about the guy who tries to tow me. This is a small town, Doctor, and I'm...how do you say... Dicky help me out here. What am I?"

"You're the big fish, Sal."

"That's it. I'm the big fish. C'mon, let's eat."

Inside, the bar was quite civilized with leather chairs, ornate wood trim and row upon row of George Dickel small batch Tennessee whiskeys locked in individual cages lined up floor to cciling throughout the entire room. They sat at a small table, ordered sandwiches and of course, three glasses of Dickels, neat. They could have ordered another type of whiskey or bourbon or scotch or even wine for that matter, but it would have seemed gauche.

As they waited for their food, the waiter placed their drinks in front of them. They were the largest pours Cesari had ever seen, filling up half of each tumbler. He guessed at least four but possibly as much as six ounces. The glasses were deceptively large.

Dicky sipped his whiskey and said, "So, John, tell us about yourself. We reviewed your resume. You grew up in the Bronx. What was that like?"

"Like a headache that won't go away."

Sal downed half his drink in one gulp and they both grinned at Cesari's response. Dicky continued, "It must have made you tough though?"

"Tough?" Cesari thought about all the street fights, near death experiences and mobsters he knew growing up. He said, "Tough is relative. I mean if you're nice to me then I'll be nice to you. I'm pretty straight forward like that. I try to avoid trouble when I can even if it means swallowing my pride."

"But what if you can't avoid trouble?"

Cesari hesitated and replied honestly, "Well, if I absolutely can't avoid it. Then I generally try to make sure that I'm always the last man standing no matter what it takes."

Sal finished his whiskey with a second swallow and murmured his approval. He asked, "Is this your first visit to Auburn, Doctor?"

"It is. I went to medical school in Buffalo and practiced for a year in a small town just south of Rochester. Other than that haven't spent a lot of time north of New York City, and please call me John or Cesari. Doctor sounds so formal."

Sal signaled for a refill as he said, "Well you're going to love Auburn Cesari, especially in the autumn. October is a great month. My favorite time of year. You must have noticed the fall foliage is spectacular, and there's a briskness in the air. Not to mention, Halloween is just around the corner."

Cesari smiled, "Halloween?"

"You heard right, Halloween. It's a big deal around here; parades, parties, costumes, candy. The whole town gets into it. The hospital throws a gala for everyone."

"A gala?"

Dicky explained, "It's a huge costume party the hospital sponsors for the town. Everyone's invited. We usually get several thousand people in attendance. You'll have a great time if you're here, but a costume is required."

They were both quite excited and Cesari was tempted to laugh but controlled himself. He looked at Sal and then at Dicky, saw they weren't joking and said, "That sounds like lots of fun. I haven't really been to a Halloween party since I was a kid but I'm game."

Inwardly, he shook his head and chalked up their enthusiasm to small town quaintness. There was nothing wrong with Halloween, but it was mostly for children, maybe young adults too, but middle-aged businessmen and doctors getting all revved up about it? He didn't see it. The waiter brought their lunches and placed a turkey panini in front of Cesari. Sal tackled his second whiskey with just as much gusto as the first. Dicky said, "We're quite impressed with your background and experience level, but you were kind of sketchy about why you're available at such an odd time of year."

Cesari took a sip of his Dickels. "That's easy. I had a one-year contract at St. Matt's in Manhattan which comes up for renewal the first of January. The hospital made it known to me that they would be declining to renew our agreement and wished me well in my future endeavors. Apparently, they are flush with gastroenterologists and I got the short straw. In any event, they told me that if something came up, they would let me out of my contractual obligations early." He paused and added, "A head hunter serendipitously called me about this opening."

Sal, who was nearly finished with his second glass, said, "That seems reasonable."

Dicky nodded in agreement and ordered another Dickels for himself. "We haven't done a full background check yet, but we'll need three professional references. Are we going to find any surprises about you on the New York State physician's website or with the Office of Professional Misconduct?"

"I don't think so."

He'd had some run-ins with the law and actually had a non-medical related felony conviction for which he had served community service and a period of probation, but that was over a year ago and last he checked it hadn't made its way to the state's website thanks to a variety of legal maneuvers performed on his behalf. His lawyer was a cutthroat who charged him six-hundred dollars an hour whether he called him about legal advice or asked him to come over and watch the ballgame together, but he was worth every penny. He hated and loved him all at the same time. It was funny how that was. Everyone hated lawyers until they needed one.

"What about your personal life? You married? Kids?" asked Sal.

"Single, no kids. I've been seeing someone casually in New York, but nothing too serious. We're not tied at the hip."

"No roots?"

"No roots." For some reason, Sal and Dicky seemed pleased by that. Cesari felt it was his turn to ask a few questions. "So what's the situation here in terms of endoscopy?"

Sal said, "We have five general surgeons, a colorectal surgeon and two other GI guys. They all scope. We have four endoscopy rooms that pretty much run all day every day. We use Olympus brand equipment, and it's relatively new. We purchased it two years ago. If you need anything special, we don't already have, just let Dicky know and we'll get it for you as long as it's within reason. You'd be in an on-call rotation with the other guys so one in nine weekends. That sound fair?"

Cesari agreed. "It does, but when the head hunter called me, he said there were three GI guys here?"

They glanced at each other quickly and Dicky explained, "There *were* three until several months ago, but now we're down to two. One of the guys left unexpectedly. We had contracted with that particular recruiting service nearly a year earlier and hadn't updated our status with them. As a matter of fact, we hadn't heard from that headhunter in so long that we had already contracted with another."

Sal added, "The important thing is that we feel there is enough volume for four gastroenterologists, so you should be pretty busy."

Neither one had bothered to expand on what had happened to the last GI guy and Cesari didn't feel compelled to inquire. Guys up and left positions all the time. He was about to do the same.

He nodded. "Anything else?"

"When can you start?" Dicky asked.

"When do you want me?"

They smiled, and Sal passed him the manila folder he had brought with him. It contained an employment contract. Sal said confidently, "Auburn Community Hospital welcomes you to the family."

Cesari grinned and perused the document. "I appreciate that, but we haven't discussed salaries, benefits, and stuff like that. You know...details."

Dicky looked concerned. Sal looked for the waiter with his empty whiskey glass raised high in the air. Dicky said seriously, "Go over the contract with your lawyer. It's all spelled out. You'll find our compensation package is in the ninety-fifth percentile for gastroenterologists in New York State with full benefits, health insurance, 401-K, malpractice coverage, opportunity for a significant end-of-year bonus, CME stipend, four-weeks vacation, and moving expenses. If you think we've missed anything let us know."

"Sounds good. When do you want my answer?"

"As quickly as possible."

"Well, today is Thursday. I have tomorrow off so I'll see if I can have my lawyer read it. You'll have my answer Monday. Is that quick enough?"

Sal said, "That'll do. Now c'mon, Doctor, drink up."

Two hours later, they were still drinking and Cesari was getting concerned that he wasn't going to be able to drive back to New York. The boys were on their fifth and sixth Dickels respectively. Dicky had started off a little slow but was rapidly catching up to Sal. The chatter had taken a decidedly social turn and Cesari concluded after only two and a half whiskeys that he honestly liked these guys.

Dicky had no children, but four ex-wives made up for that in terms of keeping him busy and spending his money. They all lived in town to keep a watchful eye on their alimony payments. Ever the romantic, he had married wife number five three years ago and was working on his commitment issues although he had hinted that he was banging an ICU nurse half his age and thought that Cesari would be pleased with the local talent. Tricky Dicky had a minor drinking problem but a stint in rehab and several rounds at Alcoholics Anonymous hadn't seemed to slow him down.

Sal was more complicated. A graduate of Harvard's MBA program, he also had been unlucky in love and was now on his third marriage to a woman named Lola, whom he had met in Vegas and had said at least twice that he wished he had left her there. Apparently, it had been a whirlwind romance fueled by alcohol and a gambling triggered endorphin rush.

Sal and Dicky had been running the Auburn Memorial Community Hospital now almost ten years together and the financial sheets were in excellent condition. The inpatient beds were filled to capacity, the OR schedules were always maxed out, and the state's regulatory agencies had given them a thumb's up with every inspection. Every day was a struggle here as everywhere, but these guys seemed to have tamed the dragon.

By 5:00 p.m., Cesari had counted five whiskeys for himself and lost track of what the boys were up to. His stomach juices began to rumble and incredibly he was starting to think about dinner. He had passed a couple of motor lodges and three-star hotels when he drove into town and he was now planning on staying the night, thankful he didn't have to work the next day. He had to use the bathroom and tried to stand unsuccessfully. In fact, he wasn't sure that he could even feel his legs anymore. He grabbed the arms of the chair and with a mighty effort, hoisted himself upright and wobbled unsteadily to the men's room. Dicky and Sal laughed loudly as they watched him veer across the room and stagger into the lavatory.

He didn't remember much else after that.

Chapter 2

Lola

Cesari's headache was epic. It felt like he was being stabbed in the temples with icepicks. His mouth was parched as if someone had poured sand from the Sahara Desert in it, and no matter how hard he tried, he couldn't open his eyes. He had to pee and wasn't sure if he was dreaming but he heard music. Actually, he heard someone singing, off key and very badly. The bed was soft, and he didn't want to get up.

A door opened, and the singing got louder as the voice got closer. His head throbbed, the sound waves hammering unmercifully at it like a blacksmith on an anvil. He opened his eyes a sliver and spotted a girl at the foot of the bed glaring at him. She was young but old enough to know better. Maybe in her early twenties, she wore a red terry cloth robe and her short brown hair was wet. She had just come out of the shower, and he was quite sure he'd never seen her before. She was angry or maybe she was happy. Women confused him like that.

"It's time to get up," she said curtly with a frown. She was thin, cute, and clearly out of sorts, but why? What had he done?

"Who are you?" he whispered in a raspy, hoarse voice. His throat hurt.

"That's none of your business. Just put on your clothes and go."

His eyes opened fully at that and his head started to clear. Looking around, he had no idea where he was. He lifted the covers and peeked underneath. He was in his underwear but had no recollection how that had happened. He asked, "Where am I?"

"You're in my bed, in my room, and I want you out... now."

He was still having trouble connecting the dots. "Did we...?"

She rolled her eyes. "God no...You're so old...Eww. Just leave, please."

"Where are my clothes?"

"They're on the floor here."

She pointed downward, but just stood there waiting and he asked politely, "Could you give me some privacy?"

Looking like her head was going to explode, she rolled her eyes. "For God's sake...fine."

She stormed into the bathroom and slammed the door closed. He groaned and rolled out of bed, found his crumpled suit and got dressed while trying to piece together the night before. He remembered the whiskey bar and then...they were hungry... They spent the whole afternoon drinking and Sal suggested they find a restaurant for dinner. Some Italian place...Osteria something. Sal and Dicky knew the owner, a Mexican guy from Brooklyn who had grown up working in Italian restaurants and pizzerias since the age of ten. Cesari vaguely remembered the fried calamari, red wine and music, but that was it and now he had the worst hangover of his adult life.

He tied his shoes and tucked his crumpled shirt in his pants just as she came back out of the bathroom. Finding him dressed and ready to vacate the room hadn't taken the edge off her. She said sarcastically, "Are you still here?"

"I really need to use the bathroom…please?" he begged.

She was profoundly offended. "No effin' way. Use the one at the end of the hallway. Oh my God."

His mind was too muddled to worry about her attitude and he left the room. The bathroom was indeed at the end of the hallway and after relieving himself he splashed cold water on his face. It helped. He came out and appraised his surroundings. It was 10:00 a.m. He was on the second floor of what appeared to be a very large house. There were five other rooms on his floor not counting the one he had woken up in and he presumed they were also bedrooms. The central staircase leading down to the main floor was lined by eight-foot wide steps which led into a fifty-foot-wide living room highlighted by a Yamaha grand piano in its center beneath a massive crystal chandelier. Floor to ceiling, paned windows lined one of the walls and provided a beautiful panorama of some lake.

He followed the scent of fresh coffee and passed through a swinging door into a spacious, modern kitchen complete with granite counters, professional six burner gas stovetop, an elaborate overhead exhaust, designer tilework. A pot of fresh coffee sat in its cradle within a very expensive and very complicated looking Italian-made automatic, bean grinding, multi-purpose, espresso, cappuccino, latte and regular coffee machine. Most dramatic of all was the curvaceous black woman standing at the sink with her back to him wearing a short peach-colored chiffon, see-through house coat. With low heeled slippers she was easily as tall as Cesari with long wavy hair and gold hoop earrings. He tried not to notice her thong, easily visible through the house coat.

He cleared his throat and knocked gently on the door to announce his presence and she turned abruptly. Her breasts were huge and without a bra, they bobbled frenetically as she turned to face him. With difficulty, he tried to ignore the sight of her interactive anatomy. She was in her thirties, gorgeous, and gave him a big smile.

She said, "Good morning, sleepy head."

She seemed to know him. That was good, but he had no idea who she was. "Good morning," he replied. "I'm afraid you have me at a disadvantage. Have we met?"

Laughing she nodded, "Sal brought you home last night, Dr. Cesari. He practically had to carry you up the stairs. You boys really went at it hard. Would you like some coffee? It's a fresh pot, and there's a Danish ring in the refrigerator."

His stomach wasn't ready for food. "Just coffee will be fine…black."

He came a few steps closer as she poured him a cup in a large ceramic mug. He took it, watched the steam rise off the top for a few seconds, inhaled its aroma and took a sip. It made him feel good. Letting out a deep contented breath, he said, "Thank you."

"Have a seat at the table, honey, and I'll join you."

He sat down as she poured herself a cup. There was a place mat on the table in front of him which read, *I'm the CEO and You're Not!* Cesari smiled. That must be Sal's credo. She sat opposite him and he said, "I'm sorry, but I don't remember a whole lot from last night. Your name is?"

She said, "I'm Lola. Sal's wife."

Cesari tried to control his surprise. As she spoke, he noticed how large her hands were. He nodded, "I see and who was the girl I met upstairs? She threw me out of her bedroom."

Lola looked concerned. "Oh dear. That's Bobby Jo. She's Sal's daughter from his first marriage. She's attending Syracuse University Law School and lives on campus. She came home unexpectedly last night and was quite upset that Sal put you in her room. I apologize if she was rude. She can be quite a handful, and…she's had a difficult time accepting me into the family. Sal and I haven't been married that long and she hasn't quite adjusted to me. I'm sure that and finding a stranger in her bed pushed her over the edge."

"I can understand that and I'm sorry about your strained relationship with her. I'm sure she'll come around one of these days. It's not unusual for grown children to feel a little threatened in a situation like this. It's a complicated dynamic." Cesari rubbed his aching temples and asked, "You wouldn't happen to have any aspirin, would you? I have a terrible hangover."

"Sure, I do."

She rose and walked over to one of the kitchen cabinets and fumbled around in it until she found a bottle of ibuprofen. She handed it to him with a large glass of tap water.

He said, "Thank you."

"Drink the whole glass. It'll help, but you should know that. You're a doctor."

She was standing right next to him and he couldn't help staring at her cleavage. She noticed, smiled politely, and went back to her seat as he gulped four of the little pills and drank the whole glass of water in one long draught.

"Are you sure you don't want something to eat, Doctor? I could make you some eggs and we have bacon. It would be no bother."

"No, thank you. My stomach's a little off and I really have to get going. I don't even know where I am. How far is the hospital from here?"

"We're on Owasco lake and just over a mile from the hospital but don't worry. Sal told me to tell you that he's taking care of everything and to meet him in his office whenever you're ready."

"He's taking care of everything?"

"That's what he said. You can use my car to drive to the hospital."

"But I'm a mess. I need to clean up."

She looked at him sympathetically. "Then go shower in the master bedroom upstairs. All of Sal's toiletries are there. He won't mind you using his razor and there are a couple of new tooth brushes in one of the drawers. If you give me your clothes, I'll give them a quick press. I'm pretty good at that kind of thing."

"Really?"

"Just leave everything outside in the hall on the floor and I'll take care of it. It's the room with the large double doors. You can't miss it. The doors have the letters B and F on them."

Cesari looked puzzled and she added. "Big Fish."

He grinned, gulped down his coffee and went back up the stairs to clean up, passing Bobby Jo on the way. She didn't make eye contact or say anything, so he let it go.

When he came back out of the bathroom thirty minutes later, he found his clothes hanging on the doorknob outside the room. He dressed, came down the stairs and thanked Lola. The iron was cooling off on its board nearby as she handed him the keys to a Corvette.

"Red, I hope?"

She smiled. "Of course. It's brand new so don't scratch it up. It's in the garage out back. I already opened the door."

He put the key in his pocket and furrowed his brow. He searched his pants and then his jacket pockets and looked troubled.

"What is it, darling?" she asked.

"I can't seem to find my own keys." He hesitated and added, "And there was a manila folder that had my contract in it. They must still be up in Bobby Jo's room."

"Oh, I'm sorry. I should have mentioned that Sal has them both. He told me to tell you he'll explain everything when you see him."

Cesari was bewildered. Why would Sal take those things? It didn't matter. He felt much better now that he had showered and shaved. Even his clothes felt fresh. "Okay. Well, I'll be on my way. Thank you so much for your hospitality. What's the best way to go to the hospital?"

"Turn left out of the driveway. That's Lake Road. In about half a mile you'll reach a light. Make a right and follow the signs. Park next to Sal's Jaguar and I'll have Bobby Jo drive me to pick it up later."

"Thanks."

He left out the back door and spotted Bobby Jo sipping coffee on the patio staring out at the lake. She was curled up on a deck chair wearing shorts, sun glasses and a pullover Syracuse University sweatshirt. It was a beautiful autumn morning and the sun gleamed over the gently rolling waves of the lake as a warm breeze drifted in. The deciduous trees along the shoreline were dazzling with their fall colors. He was tempted to ignore her but felt that he ought to say something.

He stopped three feet away. "Great day, isn't it?"

She didn't say anything, so he continued, "I'm sorry about the misunderstanding."

"Please..." she said with disgust dripping all over her voice.

Cesari sucked it up and tried to empathize with her. "I mean it. I didn't choose or request to come here last night let alone to sleep in your room."

She looked at him over her sun glasses. "I could give a rat's ass about anything you have to say. All right? You saw what's going on in there. I have much bigger problems than some geezer doctor sucking up to my father for a job."

Ouch! She was hard for someone so young. Despite his better judgement, he smiled, "I'm not that old."

"Are you going to force me to talk to you?"

"Nope. I'm leaving. I just wanted to apologize for inconveniencing you last night and this morning, and for the record, Lola seems really nice. Maybe you should give her a chance?"

"You can't be serious?" she said drolly and then started to laugh.

"What's so funny?"

"You are... You don't get it, do you?"

She was thoroughly amused. He said, "Get what?"

"Oh my God. You really don't."

She turned away from him signaling an end to the conversation, and as Cesari walked to the garage he could still hear her chuckling.

Well, at least he'd made her laugh.

Chapter 3

Welcome Aboard

It was almost 11:30 a.m. when he walked into the administrative offices looking for Sal. Jamie was sitting at her desk busily engaged with piles of paperwork, two computer monitors and a screeching phone. She wore a pair of reading glasses and her hair was tied back in a business-like manner. In Cesari's experience, every hospital had a Jamie. They were always women, usually middle-aged or thereabouts, detail oriented with super-efficient work ethics. No matter how much of a clown the guy in charge seemed, you could always tell what kind of a ship he ran by spending a few minutes with the serious-faced woman standing by his side holding a legal pad taking notes. She made the hospital run and by extension, he had learned to treat the 'Jamies' of this world with great deference lest they make his life unnecessarily difficult, like forgetting to submit vacation requests or accidentally misplacing his malpractice renewal forms. There were a vast array of techniques at her disposal to torment him. It followed that although there were very few people whose ass Cesari would willingly kiss, administrative assistants were on top of that list. Very close runner-ups were OR nurses.

So although he was in a rush to find out what was going on, he also recognized the need to get his relationship with Jamie off to a good start should he agree to work here. With that in mind, he stopped briefly at a coffee shop he spotted on the way to the hospital and grabbed a couple of large French roasts and a chocolate-filled croissant. He stood there now waiting for her to acknowledge him. She played the game well ignoring him only enough to bring a humble smile to his face but not long enough for him to be genuinely annoyed. Apparently, she had made the determination that he was a keeper and had begun his training in earnest. Yesterday's civilities were just that; a thing of the past. She answered two more calls and read several more e-mails before finally looking up at him.

She said, "Hello Dr. Cesari. How may I help you?"

"Good morning, Jamie, or good afternoon actually. I brought you a cup of coffee and a croissant. Are you interested?"

She smiled, pleased at his tribute. She knew the dance and accepted his opening gambit. "Thank you."

"Is Mr. Bardolino available?"

"He's in a meeting with the board and won't be available for at least another hour. Is it an emergency? I can buzz him out."

"No, don't do that. It can wait. What about Dr. Rizzo? Is he around?"

"Yes, he's in his office. Down the hall about a hundred feet and then make a right. You can't miss it. Just follow the signs to pathology. Oh, and before I forget…"

She reached down into a drawer and came out with a thick manila envelope stuffed with paperwork and handed it to him. "What's this?" he asked.

"Everything you need to work here. Applications for privileges, hospital by-laws, New York State rules and regulations, permission to do background checks etcetera, etcetera. Just fill them out the best you can. Sign everything in the appropriate places and I'll go over it all in detail and make sure you didn't miss anything. There's a hospital ID badge in there as well. It will also serve as your electronic key to get through all the secured doors. We used the picture you sent us on your application. I hope that's okay."

He hesitated not wanting to spoil the moment by telling her he hadn't actually made up his mind yet but decided against it. She was doing her job and if he told her that he wasn't one hundred percent sure about whether he was coming here or not she might interpret that as a criticism.

He said, "Thank you."

He walked over to Dicky's office where he found him sitting at his desk with his eyes glued to a microscope. There was a half-eaten pastrami sandwich with a dill pickle sitting on a paper plate next to him. A can of diet Mountain Dew with a straw sticking out was next to the plate. He knocked politely on the partially open door. Dicky looked up, stood, and greeted him warmly.

"Johnny, how are you feeling today?"

"A little bit older."

Dicky laughed, "Yup. I know what you mean. It never gets easier. Have a seat. Are you hungry? I've only eaten half of the sandwich. It's great but too much. There must be a pound of meat on that thing."

Cesari shook his head. "No, thanks. I'm good, but I wouldn't mind the pickle."

Dicky picked up the plate and placed it close to Cesari saying, "Help yourself."

Cesari snatched the pickle, took a bite and washed it down with black coffee. "Thanks."

They both sat down, and Dicky said, "So how was your night at the boss's house? Beautiful place, huh?"

"Oh yeah. I had a great night's sleep. He has an amazing view of the lake." Cesari hesitated for a moment before continuing, "Say, Dicky…I had quite a bit to drink last night. I hope I didn't make a fool out of myself?"

He shook his head grinning. "Not a chance. You did better than the last guy we interviewed. We had to bail him out of the drunk tank the next day. You didn't even throw up or have a seizure. You're good. I'll give you credit for that."

Cesari raised his eyebrows. "You interview everyone like that?"

"No, not intentionally anyway. Sometimes circumstances spiral out of control… Did you meet Lola?"

"Yes, she was very nice. Quite beautiful."

Dicky nodded and then looked past Cesari into the hallway. He stood, walked around his desk and closed the door to the office. He retook his seat and looked at Cesari choosing his words carefully.

"Yeah, she's quite a gal. I don't know how much you got to talk to her, but she loves to cook."

Not sure where this was heading Cesari was noncommittal. "I can't say much about that but I can attest to the fact that she makes a great cup of coffee."

That made Dicky chuckle as he nodded in agreement. "I'll bet. Keeps a great house too. She moved in a year ago and redecorated the whole place."

"She did a fantastic job from what I saw of it."

"It's too bad she can't have children though. I know she'd like one or two, but they can always adopt."

Cesari was silent for a moment contemplating that last. Clearly Dicky was leading him along some predetermined path. He said, "There's nothing wrong with adoption."

Dicky cleared his throat. "There's probably something you should know lest you step on a landmine accidentally."

"What's that?"

He hesitated and then said, "Completely confidential, understood?"

"Of course."

"Sal and I went to a conference in Vegas a little more than a year ago and we…well you know…we partied pretty hard." He took a deep breath and let it out. "Well, we went to one of those shows…"

Cesari shook his head. "I'm not sure what you mean. What kind of show?"

Reluctantly, Dicky added, "The kind of show where men dress as women."

Cesari suppressed a laugh because he saw how serious the conversation had turned. "I see. That kind of show. A drag queen review."

He nodded. "Yeah, that kind of show. Well, we were pretty bombed, even worse than last night. It kind of got hard to tell who was legit and who was…"

"A drag queen?" Cesari interjected.

"Exactly."

"Interesting."

"You know, Johnny, some of those guys…they look like the real thing. I don't even think their own mothers could tell the difference when they're all dolled up like that."

"So what happened?" Cesari was getting curious.

"The next morning Sal woke up in the bridal suite of the Bellagio with a wedding band on his finger and…Lola laying across his chest."

Cesari's eyes went wide. "Wow…"

"Wow is right. It's been interesting ever since to say the least."

"Couldn't he get the marriage annulled or something like that?"

"Naturally he tried to do just that, but the wedding was videoed as well as the wedding night."

"You're kidding?"

"I kid you not. The Bellagio performs that as a service. A lot of people these days really like that."

Cesari thought that over before saying, "Is Lola holding that over his head?"

"Yes, and I saw the videos. Sal needed for me to know what's going on so I could run interference for him. Besides, I was in a portion of the video, so it could affect me too."

"Why were you in the wedding video?"

Dicky cleared his throat again. "Well, apparently I was his best man and the maid of honor was my date if you get what I mean. He…she was all over me. I have to admit Lola made a beautiful bride. The gown was awesome, and then there was the lingerie…" He let out a low whistle.

Cesari looked at him but didn't say anything. Dicky continued, "It's a little worse than just straight blackmail. You see, Lola is actually head over heels in love with Sal. I know it seems crazy, but she really is. She's threatening to commit suicide if he leaves her and then have someone deliver the video to the local press and copies to every LGBT organization in the country as well as to our board."

Cesari almost couldn't believe his ears and uttered, "Jesus, Mary and Joseph."

"Yeah, so tread lightly on the subject of Lola. I'm sorry to burden you with this but I like you and would hate to see you commit a faux pas by saying something out of turn in front of Sal. I've known him a long time and I don't think I've ever seen his feathers as ruffled about anything as they are about this. Besides, I thought you'd figure it out on your own. You seem pretty worldly."

"Thanks. I thought she had big hands for a woman, but I had a hangover and her breasts were kind of distracting."

"Great ass too," Dicky said with almost too much enthusiasm.

Cesari raised his eyebrows at that and then out of curiosity asked, "So what's the deal over there. They just pretending to play house?"

"Something like that. Only a handful of people know the truth. He sleeps on a roll away cot in his bedroom to keep up appearances. I guess once was enough for him. He doesn't want the word to get out. The board's pretty straight laced and might crucify him. Interracial is one thing. They even kind of like that. Makes him look well-rounded, but this is a whole different ball game."

Cesari nodded. "Man, this is crazy."

Dicky said, "You're telling me…What's that package you got there?"

He indicated the manila envelope with the paperwork Jamie had given him. Cesari said, "It's the application for privileges and other stuff I need to work here. I was going to ask you about this…"

Dicky smiled and interrupted him, "Good. Get cracking on that right away. Sal and I will muscle you through the credentialing committee this afternoon, so everything will be in order…" he glanced at his watch, "…by five tonight when your call starts. Let me be the first to say, welcome aboard."

"What are you talking about?"

Dicky looked confused. "You agreed to take call this weekend."

"No, I didn't."

"Sure, you did."

"I couldn't have."

"What do you mean?"

Cesari was getting upset. "I'm not sure what's going on here, Dicky. How can I take call starting tonight when I haven't even agreed to work here yet? Besides, I never would have agreed to start working here just like that. I have obligations at the hospital I'm working at already. I have a full panel of patient's waiting for me next week. For crying out loud, all my stuff is in New York. I don't even have a place to stay."

"But you agreed to. Last night, I told you we were short-handed, and you volunteered."

"I don't remember that."

"You really don't remember?"

"I don't remember anything after the calamari."

"Well, I'm sorry about that but last night you told us that you didn't need to think about it anymore and that you wanted to come work here right away, as in immediately. You signed your contract and everything. I think that was right before we rented the limo."

"Limo?"

"Yeah, we went to a strip club in Syracuse to celebrate. You got some moves, boy. I'll tell you. It takes a big pair to pole dance in a suit like you did."

Cesari stared at him in disbelief. "This is bullshit. I was drunk. How could you let me sign a contract? Is this why they call you Tricky Dicky?"

"Hey, take it down a notch. There's no need to get personal. You're a big boy and we were just as drunk as you. Besides, what are you complaining about? You were about to be canned at the other place anyway. This is a win-win for everybody."

"I don't believe this."

"I think we should talk to Sal."

Cesari didn't say anything for a whole minute. He just sat there with steam coming out of his ears. Finally he said, "Are you going to eat the rest of that sandwich or not?"

Chapter 4

Jasmine

"That's your signature, right?"

Cesari nodded in affirmation. He was looking at the employment contract he had signed in three different places over dinner the night before. He, Dicky and Sal were sitting in the boardroom going over the particulars.

Cesari said, "Yes, it is."

"And who's signature is underneath yours?"

"It looks like yours."

"And underneath that, next to the official seal?"

Cesari looked up at Dicky. "It's Dicky's. You're a notary?"

Dicky smiled. "I wear many hats."

Sal continued, "In addition, you received a ten-thousand-dollar advance on your salary which you signed a receipt for here."

He slid another piece of paper in front of Cesari which was also signed and notarized. Cesari looked very confused and Dicky said, "If you check your wallet, you'll find a check made out to you from Auburn Memorial for that sum."

Cesari took out his wallet and saw the said check folded in half. He looked it over and said, "What if I don't cash it?"

Sal replied, "It's your money. You can do whatever you want with it, but I urge you to turn to page eighteen of your contract. There's a clause that stipulates that if you break any part of this contract you will be subject to liability of fifty thousand dollars in punitive damages in addition to refunding any pre-paid monies with interest."

Cesari flipped to page eighteen of the thirty-page document and read the paragraph. He looked glum. "But guys, I can't work here just like that. I have obligations elsewhere."

Sal smiled, "All taken care of. I took the liberty of calling the medical director of St. Matt's this morning and explaining the situation to him. Harvey Goldberg or something like that. He was happy you landed on your feet and said he'll make arrangements with the other doctors to cover your patients and that you shouldn't worry about anything."

"His name is Arnold Goldstein and he said he was okay with this?" Cesari said with incredulity in his voice.

"More than okay with it. He was sorry to see you leave and confirmed your story about being down-sized. He said he'd be happy to be one of your references and that he vouches for your abilities without any reservations. He's a good guy. I liked him…Now look, Cesari, if I recall correctly, it was your idea to move things along as quickly as we did…" He looked over to Dicky who nodded in agreement. "…but having said that, we don't want you or anybody else here to be unhappy. If you would prefer, we could just tear up the contract and pretend we never met. We can do that, but I can't promise that the offer will still be there a week from now. I'm not an overly sensitive guy by any means, but something like this could potentially injure our relationship. Am I an overly sensitive guy, Dicky?"

"No, you're not Sal. You're a rock."

"You see, Cesari? So do I tear up the contract?"

Cesari thought it over. This wasn't quite the way he had hoped things would work out, but it seemed that he had brought most of it on himself. The truth was that he needed a job in a few months anyway and it sounded like Arnold Goldstein had just accepted his resignation effective immediately without any rancor. Dicky and Sal were colorful and despite the presumptuous nature of their negotiations he thought they were basically sincere. He looked again at the check before placing it back in his wallet. Certainly, the numbers seemed reasonable.

Letting out a deep breath, he said, "That won't be necessary."

Dicky and Sal smiled broadly very pleased at the outcome. Sal said, "Great news. Dicky will show you around and introduce you to people."

Cesari asked, "What about my stuff in New York?"

"Already taken care of. I took the liberty of borrowing your keys and sending a courier to your apartment in Manhattan. I used the address you gave us on your employment application and hired a moving company to collect anything that's not nailed down. They'll have it up here by Monday and place the big stuff in a storage unit on Grant Avenue just outside of town. Your clothes and anything else you want they'll bring directly to where you're staying. I also did a quick google search of the area. I don't know what condition the apartment is in, but the location is prime. You shouldn't have any trouble subletting it if that's what you want to do."

"Where am I staying while I'm here?"

"Wherever you want of course, but until you find an apartment to your liking, I reserved a room for you at the Dulles House on South Street. It's an historic inn about a half a mile from here that rents rooms by the weekend, the week or the month. It's a very high-end place. You'll love it. To ease your pain, I'll pick up the tab for the first three months or until you find some other place."

"I'll need my car keys."

Sal reached into his pocket and slid the Porsche keys over to Cesari. "It makes a knocking sound and I think the clutch is on its last legs. You should have it checked out. Use my mechanic. He's pretty good with high end cars. Tell him I sent you. He'll take good care of you."

He slid a business card over to Cesari with the name and phone number of the mechanic. Cesari said, "You drove my car? How'd you even know what car I drove or where I parked?"

Sal laughed. "Look at him, Dicky. Wants to know how I know things. You talk in your sleep Cesari or maybe you just told me last night you were having car problems on the way here and what make and model you drove and where you parked? I can't be sure. Anyway, I moved it from the dent center known as the visitor's parking lot to the physician's lot where the spaces are at least a foot and a half wider as a courtesy."

"Thank you."

He looked at his watch. "Dicky, why don't you take Cesari on a quick tour of the hospital and introduce him around. Be mindful of the time, the credentials committee meets at 3:00 p.m. sharp. His paperwork won't be complete, but we'll grant him temporary privileges. All right, Cesari. Call us for any problems. You have both of our numbers."

Cesari nodded and they all rose. He shook Sal's hand and left with Dicky still not sure if he was an employee or a hostage. They stopped in the OR first where he met the unit manager and several nurses and secretaries. He was assigned a locker, given a key, and shown where the surgical scrubs, bathrooms, shower stalls and coffee machines were. The next stop was a tour of the endoscopy rooms where he was introduced to the senior nurses, Karen, Sandy and Cindy. He performed a brief inspection of the equipment and asked a few questions. It was the middle of the day and everyone was too busy to spend more than just a few minutes in chit chat. They all seemed very nice though. Cesari was encouraged by that as he informed everyone that he was on call with them and hoped he didn't have to bother anyone. He met several of the surgeons, but the two other GI guys weren't around. Both were in the office seeing patients.

By 2:00 p.m. Cesari needed food and another cup of coffee. The half of a pastrami sandwich he ate in Dicky's office was good but not enough to hold him until dinner, so they went to the cafeteria on the second floor of the hospital where he bought a tuna melt and a cup of black coffee. Dicky got a Greek yogurt. As they roamed the nearly empty cafeteria for a table, they were accosted by a loud voice with a profound New York accent.

A stocky man in a white lab coat approached them. He spoke quickly and knowingly as if he was very important. "So who's this guy, Dicky? You guys never tell anybody what's going on. Does he know the score yet?" He took a quick breath and turned to Cesari. "So what's your deal? Are you one of them or one of us?"

Dicky raised his hand. "Take it easy, Herb. This is John Cesari. He's GI and it's his first day. Cut him some slack, will you?"

"That depends on him whether I cut him slack or not." Herb put out his hand and Cesari grasped it. The guy said, "Herb Funkelman. Ortho. You need anything you call me. Don't let these guys brainwash you. We doctors got to stick together these days. We're getting screwed big time. I'm forming a PAC to lobby on our behalf in Washington. You should join it. I'll tell you more about it over drinks. I hope you're not one of these guys that just comes to work and wants to bury his head in the sand."

Herb Funkelman was a sixty-year-old orthopedic surgeon with a full head of curly brown hair occasionally speckled with gray. Pugnacious and animated, he looked like he was always ready for a brawl and spoke as if he had just left one. Cesari said very politically, "Well, I'd like to get oriented to my clinical responsibilities here before I get involved in anything else. Patient care comes first."

"That sounds like a cop-out to me, but whatever. We'll talk more when the gestapo aren't listening in if you get my drift." He nodded at Dicky as if his statement wasn't entirely clear. "Here's my card."

He reached into his pocket and handed Cesari a business card. Cesari said, "Thank you."

"You should thank me. It's guys like me that do all the heavy lifting while the rest of you reap the benefit, but I don't care. Somebody's got to do it. I'll keep you posted... Look, I got to go. There's an old lady in the emergency room with a compound fracture of her left hip. They tell me she's also having a heart attack. I told them I don't give a shit. She needs to go to the OR like now. You know what I mean? You can't just leave her with a broken hip. Now anesthesia's giving me grief because they're scared she's too unstable. I told them to grow a pair of testicles. This is the kind of crap that goes on around here."

Dicky said, "Herb, take it easy. We're in the middle of the cafeteria for Christ's sake. This isn't the place for this."

"I don't care where we are. Look, I gotta go. Call me, Cesari."

He turned abruptly and stormed away. Cesari felt bad for whoever was going to be next in his path. He had worked himself into quite a lather. Once he was out of sight, Cesari and Dicky sat down in a booth to eat.

"Does anybody know there's a bulldog running around without a leash?" Cesari quipped.

Dicky laughed. "He's quite the character. That's for sure. You were very tactful."

Cesari took a bite of his tuna melt. "Thanks. Is he always like that?"

"He's usually worse."

Cesari grinned and Dicky continued, "I have to say, John. I'm extremely impressed. You handled yourself very well not just now but with Sal earlier too. Things could easily have gotten out of hand in both situations."

"Well, I know when to hold'em and I know when to fold'em."

Dicky nodded, "Exactly... Were you okay with the endoscopy equipment by the way?"

"Yes, I used the same scopes in New York and the nurses here seem very professional. I think I'll be fine. I'll just need a list of phone numbers for whoever's on call with me and for consults like surgery and radiology."

"I'll get that to you before call begins. I promise."

Cesari finished most of his sandwich and signaled that he was done. He threw his trash out and placed the tray in its holder. With coffee in hand he followed Dicky out of the cafeteria.

"Where to now, boss?"

Dicky glanced at his watch. "I'm running late for the credentials committee. I'm going to have to pass you off to someone else to show you the on-call room and teach you about our electronic medical records. You'll be given a temporary password until you're fully matriculated into our system. Come with me."

They walked down the hall to an office with a sign on the wall next to the door which read, *Nursing Administration.* Dicky let himself in and was greeted by a robust woman of about fifty.

"Hello, Dr. Rizzo. What can I do for you?"

"Anne, this is Dr. Cesari. He just joined our staff and has graciously agreed to take call this weekend to fill an opening in our schedule. He'll need someone to show him the on-call room and a few other things, but most of all he'll need a crash course on how to use the electronic medical records."

"Oh, if it's the EMR he needs help with then come with me. I got just the person you need."

They followed her down a short hallway into the inner depths of the office and found a large room with multiple computer work stations. A woman in her early thirties sat at a monitor clicking away at the keyboard. She had strawberry blonde hair, big hazel eyes and a beautiful face. Cesari's heart skipped a beat.

Anne said hello to her as they walked into the room. "This is Dr. Cesari. He's just joined our staff and will need…"

Cesari stepped forward with outstretched hand and finished her sentence. "…lots of personalized attention."

Smiling, she stood to greet him. She was a perfect five feet four inches tall and was wearing a conservative blue skirt and white top. Cesari liked what he saw and suddenly wasn't as put out at being stuck in this town as he was an hour ago. The strawberry blonde with big hazel eyes took his hand politely, delicately and held his gaze.

"I'm Jasmine."

"I knew that the minute I entered the room."

Puzzled, she asked, "What do you mean?"

"Jasmine is a rare and beautiful flower."

She blushed just a little. "Not that rare and not that beautiful, but thanks."

Dicky said, "I guess you'll be all right if I leave you with Jasmine."

Cesari turned to him. "You could say that."

Chapter 5

The Night Nurse

Jasmine Van Tassel was a thirty-one-year-old native of Auburn, New York and an RN who specialized in information services. That was as far as Cesari got before they settled down to the business at hand. He sat next to her in the computer learning center staring at the screen in front of him. There was a lot of pointing, clicking and typing and then try-it-again type of stuff. She walked him through practice reports and how to look up labs and medical records. He wrote down his temporary username and password for the system and she gave him her cellphone number in case he ran into a technical problem over the weekend. After two hours of taking notes and trial and error, he felt he had at least a fighting chance when the action started. Jasmine was a very good teacher, and this was her primary role at Auburn, to train and re-train nurses and physicians in the electronic medical records system.

At 5:00 p.m., he looked up and said, "Don't you have to leave now?"

She glanced at her watch and seemed surprised at the time. "Well that went quickly." She had a gentle nurturing voice and smiled a lot when she spoke. "Technically, my day is over, but we still have a few things to review and I have to show you where the on-call room is."

"And the ER," he added.

"And the ER."

"You really don't have to stay although I appreciate the offer. I think I can handle it from here. How hard could it be to find them on my own?"

"I don't mind at all."

He really didn't want her to leave. "Are you sure? I wouldn't want your husband or your boyfriend getting upset if you're late. They might yell at you," he said in jest. He hadn't noticed a wedding ring and was quietly hopeful on that score.

His lack of subtlety wasn't lost on her. She grinned and shook her head. "There's no husband and no boyfriend to yell at me."

Having given him the slightest of openings, he dove right in. "I'm new around here. Is it normal for extraordinarily beautiful women in this town to be unattached?"

Now she laughed out loud. "Thank you for the compliment but I'd have to perform a survey to answer that question."

Laughter was always a good sign. Happy women sometimes just fell out of their clothes without even realizing it. He said, "Well, they're overrated anyway."

"What are?"

"Boyfriends and husbands."

She nodded. "I agree. What about you? Is somebody waiting to yell at you?"

"No, I'm as free as a bird… What a coincidence? We're both free as birds and here it is, dinner time."

There it was hanging out there, a gentle lob over the net. An invitation to be gentle with his heart. She hesitated briefly and said, "How about we finish our work?"

Not unkindly or with any hint of a rebuke. Just matter of factly. 'How about we finish our work?' Not a total rejection, but more of a *I hardly know you so let's keep this professional* kind of thing, at least that was his interpretation. Women were never direct. They never said things like, *No, I wouldn't date you if you were the last man on earth because you repulse me so much I'd rather drink a gallon of lye than let myself suffer your touch.*

They used a lot of body language, innuendo, and words that sometimes meant the opposite of their strict definition. Women were more evolved than men in many ways but mostly in their communication skills. You had to pay careful attention to their inflection and facial expressions during conversations or you could find yourself in a world of trouble. With that in mind, he decided not to push it any further. Cesari was as famous for his flirting as he was for his colonoscopy skills. And being the master at both activities he had learned to read in-between the lines as well as to go with the flow, so he shifted his libido back into neutral and turned back to the computer screen.

Thirty minutes later, they wrapped up the lesson as she felt he had enough basic skills to make it through the weekend. She suggested they continue on Monday.

He agreed, and she said, "Okay, then. Let's go to the on-call room. The emergency department is on the way."

He looked at his watch. "That won't be necessary, Jasmine. You've done more than enough. It's already 5:30 p.m. I really appreciate your help, but I feel bad about keeping you so late."

"It's no problem at all. C'mon let's go."

"Are you sure?"

"I'm sure."

They left the nursing office and walked down the main corridor with Cesari glancing in every direction to get his bearings. They passed the emergency room, and at the very end of the hall, almost two football fields away from the main entrance, they came to a set of old doors.

Cesari asked, "Where are we now?"

She said, "This is the old hospital. It was abandoned fifty years ago. They built the new hospital next to it. The on-call room for the physicians is actually a patient room that has been renovated."

"Seriously?"

She nodded and pushed open the door which groaned loudly in desperate need of oiling. He followed her through a dark and dusty corridor and was surprised that the lights were still on in this section, but then he saw some offices and realized that parts of the building must still be in use. About a hundred feet in they came to a small elevator with drab gray doors and old-fashioned black buttons. She pressed one and they waited as it noisily approached. The doors opened, and they boarded going up to the third and top floor. The elevator came to a stop and the tour began in the dark.

She explained, "To save money on electricity, the lights are generally kept off on all the floors but the first. So the first thing you have to know is where all the switches are. To keep it simple, there are a set of hallway light switches just to the right of the elevator as you exit." She reached over and flipped on the lights. The long hallway suddenly illuminated. "Try to remember to turn them off when you leave. There's another set of light switches just outside your room."

"Wouldn't it have been more efficient to put the lights on a timer and some sort of sensor, so they'd turn on and off automatically?" he asked reasonably.

She looked at him and said, "You should get out while you can. You're way too smart to work here."

That made him laugh. "I gather I'm not the first one to float that idea."

"Only every doctor I show around, but I have to admit, you came to it quicker than most. You can drop it in the suggestion box outside the administrative offices. I'm sure they'll file it with all the others. C'mon, follow me."

The bleak and deserted corridor was painted a drab industrial puke green with fluorescent lights running up and down the center of the ceiling. The old tiled floor was worn and chipped in places. Cesari guessed he was looking at 1940's or 50's architecture and décor. There were multiple doors on either side of the hallway and exposed painted pipes running across the ceiling at points where there were breaks in the lighting.

"Are all the rooms up here being used as on-call rooms?" he asked.

"No, just the one I'm about to show you. The others are vacant. There really hasn't been a need for more than one. Most of the physicians live in town and prefer to go home to their own beds. We provide this room for those just in-case times. You know, when it's very late and you're too tired to drive or if you're expecting to get called in again for some reason. If you do decide to sleep up here, you should let the switchboard know. It will prevent conflict in the unlikely event another physician desires to use the room at the same time. It's first come first serve and as a rule it's never been a problem however, we do have a backup plan if you forget to notify the switchboard."

Fifty feet from the elevator they reached their destination, and as she mentioned, there was a panel of switches just outside the door. She opened it, turned on the room light and then turned off the hallway lights.

He nodded. "I got it. So what's the backup plan?"

She smiled and pointed to a *Do Not Disturb* sign that was hanging from a hook on the back of the door. She said, "Just put that on the outside door knob."

He grinned. "Low tech but it should work."

The room was large and used to house four patients but now was a single spacious, well-decorated apartment. In stark contrast to the building, it was modern, well-furnished and inviting. There was a king bed, a full bathroom, a comfortable recliner, a desk with a laptop, and a flat screen TV on the wall. The windows looked out at the rear of the new hospital and there was even a treadmill off to one side. What more could he want?

He said, "I'm a little disappointed. I thought there would be a mini-bar."

She smiled, "Like I said, there's a suggestion box… Any questions?"

Cesari stepped into the center of the room and glanced around observing the pleasant wall paper and window dressings. This was nicer than any on-call room he'd ever been in. He said, "I'll take it. How much?"

She liked that and for a moment they stood there looking at each other. He said, "You're pretty brave."

"How so?" she asked furrowing her brow.

"You're up here alone in a deserted building with a man you just met a few hours ago. I could be a serial killer."

She stepped closer and lowered her voice. "Maybe you're the one who's brave?"

"How so?"

"Maybe the reason I don't have a husband or a boyfriend is that I killed them. Brought them up here to a deserted, isolated place so I could take my time... enjoy myself. Maybe I'm crazy and after I leave you, I'm going to rip my clothes and tell everyone that you attacked me? Everyone knew we were alone. Poor little me. Who wouldn't believe it?"

Her delivery was deadpanned and Cesari's eyes went wide in apprehension. He instinctively took a step back. She had obviously given that a lot of thought. She laughed and said, "Well, I guess you're not a serial killer."

He relaxed. "I guess not and you... are you crazy?"

Side-stepping the question, she looked at her watch. "It's almost 6:00 p.m., I really do have to go now."

"But we were having so much fun..." he said with just a twinge of whininess in his voice.

She looked at him and grinned. "Is that what we were doing?"

"It felt like it."

She hesitated, and he could feel her resolve wavering. She said, "One slice of pizza."

He smiled from ear to ear. "In the cafeteria?"

"God no. There's a place on Genesee Street called Angelo's. It's been there forever. It's not much to look at but it's great."

"I wish I knew where Genesee Street was."

She shook her head, "I can't believe I'm doing this... I'll drive."

They walked to the parking garage and found her Honda Accord. It was a black two-door coupe with leather seats. The pizzeria was a five-minute drive and reminded Cesari of every pizza shop he had ever been in back in New York City. There was a long counter with swivel seats and small laminate tables for two dotting the narrow room. Toward the back it opened up into a larger area with a round table for eight. There were multiple photographs and memorabilia hanging on the walls from various high-profile visitors including the governor of New York who had passed through the town a decade earlier and a couple of well-known sports figures. The owner, Angelo D'Angelo, was a Brooklyn transplant and had opened the shop sixty years ago. He now had several people, including his son-in-law, running the place but he was on site wearing a white apron supervising every single minute of every day even at ninety years old.

They ordered diet Cokes and pizza topped with mushrooms and sausage. Sitting at one of the small tables, Cesari said, "The pizza's great."

"It is. Angelo knows what he's doing."

"So tell me about yourself, Jasmine."

"What would you like to know, Doctor?"

"First of all, Doctor is for the ordinary people. Special people call me John, or to be honest, I prefer just plain

Cesari. So many people call me Cesari I feel like it's my first name anyway."

"Well if you don't mind, I'll call you John. It's a nice name and I like it. So I'm special, John? How is that possible? We've just met."

"I have an instinct about these things, and I predict that you will easily achieve special status."

She smiled at that. "I'm going to be very honest, John, because I do kind of like you and I don't wish to mislead you, but I do not, emphasis on not, date people from the hospital. I know from experience how unwise that can be."

He swallowed a bite of pizza and dabbed his lips with a napkin as he searched for the right response. He said, "Fine, I'll hand in my resignation tomorrow. I'm glad we found an easy fix for that one. I thought we were going be here all night arguing about it."

Laughing she said, "You don't stop, do you?"

"I don't want to die a virgin. That's all. That happened to friend of mine and it was awful."

She shook her head and said wryly, "Yeah, right. I just bet you're a virgin."

"It's true. A lot people look at me and they think…Oh boy, look at that guy; incredibly handsome, smart, knock-out smile, great personality, bedroom eyes, killer body. He must be getting it hand over foot, but that couldn't be further from reality."

She sat back rolling her eyes at the show he was putting on for her benefit. "Oh my goodness. Where did they ever find you?"

"The truth?"

"That's always a good start."

"Your boys Bardolino and Rizzo got me drunk last night and had me sign a contract I hadn't even read yet... Here I am."

"You can't be serious?"

"Oh, I am, but it's not as bad as all that. I was looking for a job anyway, and now there's you, so I can't complain."

She looked at him for a long moment before saying, "Thanks, but I can't believe they did that to you."

"I'll get over it."

"I hate to change the subject, but did anyone tell you about the old hospital we were just in?"

"No, what about it?"

She leaned forward suddenly very serious. Her eyes gleamed as if she was about to share some sort of deep, dark secret like *I know who really shot Kennedy*. She said, "It's sort of a local legend. Almost everyone who grew up here knows it. About fifty years ago, a terrible tragedy took place there. It used to be a privately-owned psychiatric facility..." She hesitated unsure of herself. "You know, maybe I shouldn't say anything."

His curiosity piqued, he insisted, "C'mon, you can't just start a story like that and not finish it."

She glanced around at the other customers. No one was paying them any attention. Cesari found her antics amusing. She lowered her voice. "There was a guy, Levi Blackburn, he was the Night Nurse on the third floor of the hospital back then."

"The third floor? Where the on-call room is?"

"Yes. Well anyway, one night he completely lost it and killed all the patients on that floor. There were six of them. He went into their rooms one at a time and strangled them."

Cesari sat back fascinated. "Really? So what happened?"

"The next morning when the day shift arrived, they found Levi hanging by a rope from one of the metal pipes in the hallway. There was a pentagram painted on the floor below him in one of the patient's blood."

Cesari whispered, "You can't be serious?"

"I am."

"And I have to sleep up there?"

"You don't have to. I told you most of the doctors don't… I'm sorry. Did I frighten you?"

"That's twice now in the last hour but who's counting? Did you just make that up to scare me?"

"I scared a big guy like you?" she giggled, pleased with herself.

"I hate spooky stuff."

"I found your weak spot. That was easy."

"You made that up."

"No, I didn't. Ask anyone. Do a Google search or go to the library here in town and look it up. They probably have a whole section devoted to it. At the time, it was a really big deal."

"I bet, and just why did you feel compelled to share this with me when Dicky and Sal didn't?"

She got serious. "To be fair, it happened so long ago it may not always be the first thing on people's minds… Look, I'm not trying to start trouble between you and administration, but I just don't think it's right to tell somebody that's where they're sleeping and then withhold that kind of information. Most people would want to know."

He nodded. "You're right about that and don't worry, you're not starting trouble."

"So what do you think you're going to do?"

"In terms of…?"

"Are you going to sleep up there?"

"Hell no… There's no way I'm sleeping up there now." He let out a deep breath. His romantic inclinations suddenly thwarted for the moment. "You know, Jasmine, I just wanted to have a pleasant conversation with a pretty girl, and now look what you've done."

"Did you stop thinking about sex?"

"Well yeah…"

She laughed. "Mission accomplished."

"You think you're funny, huh?"

"A little."

"You know, you didn't answer my question when we were in the on-call room earlier."

"What question?"

"I asked you if you were crazy."

"John, we're all a little crazy."

Chapter 6

The Inn

In the early part of the twentieth century, the Dulles House on South Street was home for a brief time to the family of James Foster Dulles, the Secretary of State for Dwight D. Eisenhower, the 34th president of the United States, and for whom the home is named. While in office, Dulles developed colon cancer and due to failing health resigned from office in April of 1959 dying a month later at Walter Reed hospital at the age of seventy-one. When hearing the story, one might think he died of natural causes as a consequence of his age and disease. Not so. He was pushed out of a window of the hospital for reasons unknown and his murder to this day remains unsolved although heavily laden with conspiracy theories.

For several decades after the Dulles family moved out, the house was the residence of the Superintendent of the Auburn Correctional Facility. Constructed in 1817 as the Auburn Prison, it was the second state prison in New York after New York City's Newgate prison established in1797. The Auburn Correctional Facility's big claim to fame was that it was the site of the first execution by electric chair in 1890, and the namesake of the 'Auburn system', a correctional system in which prisoners were housed in solitary confinement in large rectangular buildings and performed penal labor under silence that was enforced at all times. The prison is one of the oldest in the United States.

It was further rumored that the superintendent of the facility used prisoners as slave labor at the mansion and that many of them were never heard from again. In any event, the abuses were quietly swept under the rug and the home discretely put up for sale. It was then acquired by the Van Brunt family, in whose possession it has remained ever since.

The three story, ten-thousand square-foot, federal-style brick house on ten acres had only recently in its history been converted to a ten-room upscale inn. Financial difficulties had led the owner to make the conversion from a private residence to a commercial property about ten years ago and it had been doing fairly well since, steadily gaining prominence as a culinary and vinicultural destination.

Cesari parked his Porsche in the lot in back and followed the signs around to the front of the inn to check-in. After Jasmine had dropped him off at the hospital, he picked up some surgical scrubs from the OR, checked in with the switchboard to make sure they had his number, and drove to a Walmart to buy toiletries, jeans, a couple of shirts and underwear to tide him over until his belongings arrived on Monday. It was now 8:00 p.m. and dark out.

The foot path in the front of the house was a solid one hundred feet long from the sidewalk to the wrap-around wood porch and was lined with carved pumpkins and other Halloween type lawn decorations. The porch was beautifully adorned with lanterns, rocking chairs, bench swings and witches on broom sticks hanging from hooks. The old wood double doors were large with brass handles and knockers. He rang the bell, let himself into the foyer and was impressed.

The décor, woodwork, and furnishings rivaled any five-star hotel he had ever been. The grand staircase directly ahead led to the second floor with railings curving off to either side. A massive antique chandelier with numerous candles dominated the center of the room and as he walked in, he strained to see what was above.

A burly man in his early thirties approached him. He was Cesari's height but about twice as wide and solid. He had the appearance of a weight lifter who spent most of his time inside a squat cage and the rest of it eating raw meat. He was Nordic in appearance with long blonde hair, blue eyes, and a mustache that drooped over the sides of his lips to his chin. Broad in the shoulder and a powerful grip, he clenched Cesari's hand tightly as if testing him. Cesari held on for dear life and tried not cry uncle. The man liked that and eventually let go.

"You must be Dr. Cesari?" he asked.

Cesari had called ahead to confirm the reservation but had spoken to a young woman. He discreetly shook his wounded hand and replied, "Yes, I am."

"I'm Brom Van Brunt, the owner of Dulles House and your host. It's a pleasure to meet you. I am so glad you decided to check-in tonight. When Mr. Bardolino called us, he hadn't specified when we might see you."

"Well, here I am."

"Please follow me to the desk and we'll go over things. Do you have any luggage?"

He held the Walmart bag in one hand and the surgical scrubs rolled tightly under his other arm. "No, my belongings will arrive Monday."

Off to one side of the massive room was an ornate mahogany desk whose legs were carved to look lion's paws.

Cesari signed in and was given two keys to a room on the third floor. Brom led him up the stairs although he pointed out there was a small elevator by the side entrance of the home if he so chose. On the second floor they had to walk around to the other side of the building to find the next flight of not quite as impressive steps and a minute later Brom let him into a large two room suite.

Cesari flung the bag and surgical scrubs onto the four-poster king bed, peeked inside the bathroom, and took in the expanse of the living room. He turned to Brom and said, "This is very nice."

Brom was pleased. "Thank you. All the rooms are air conditioned and come with Wi-Fi and cable television. There's a small refrigerator with complementary water and a bottle of prosecco. Breakfast is served in the dining room from 7:00 a.m. to 10:00 a.m. daily and there is a self-serve coffee machine in the kitchen available 24/7. Dinner is from 6:00 p.m. to 11:00 p.m. A word of warning: the restaurant is small and open to the community and frequently fills up. So, if you plan on dining with us, please call ahead to reserve a table. I encourage you to read about the history of the inn and to mingle with our other guests. There is a full-service bar downstairs with a bartender but if you go at an odd time feel free to help yourself."

Cesari glanced at his watch. "Is anyone there now?"

"Certainly. I'll take your leave, but if there is anything you need please let me know."

"Great, I'll freshen up and check out the bar... Actually, there is one thing. Is there a dry-cleaning service nearby? My suit's a mess."

"Just leave everything outside your door and I'll have someone take care of it for you."

"Thank you."

"Ciao."

After he left, Cesari showered and put on the new clothes. Placing his suit on a hanger, he hooked it on the outside doorknob to the room. He then laid down on the bed and called Vito Gianelli, a mobbed-up friend of his in New York, to fill him on recent events. Vito was a notorious gangland figure in lower Manhattan and ran certain neighborhoods in the Little Italy area like an African warlord. They had been close since childhood and in some ways, he was the only real friend Cesari had despite their vastly different life trajectories.

After a few minutes of listening, Vito whistled, "This guy Sal really rolled you good, Cesari." His voice was deep and raspy from too many unfiltered cigarettes. "Are you sure you're okay with it? I could come up there and unroll you if you want? Most guys become reasonable again after I talk to them."

"Thanks, I appreciate the thought, but now that it's happened, I think it might be for the best... Besides, I met a girl."

Vito laughed loudly into the phone. "You met a girl? One day... only one effin' day and you met a girl. Cesari, you are a public menace. Jesus... only one day. I can't believe it."

Cesari smiled. "It's not what you think. Nothing's happened."

"You mean nothing's happened yet."

"Anyway, I just wanted you to know where I was and what's going on."

"What about your apartment in the Village?"

"Not sure yet. I still have a year and a half to go on the lease. I was thinking maybe of subletting it."

"I'll rent it from you."

"You? Why?"

"I need another place. I'm starting to outgrow the building I'm in now."

"You mean the feds have found your other safe-houses and are bugging all of them?"

"Do you want the rent money or not?"

"Fine, but don't leave any dead bodies up there."

"Fine. Mail me the keys. When will you be coming down again?"

"I don't know. All my stuff's on the way up here. My car's here. Most everything else I can handle with a few phone calls. Maybe a month? I don't know? I can barely see straight right now so much has happened in the last twenty-four hours."

"All right keep me posted. Maybe I'll come up there. Isn't there a casino somewhere near Auburn?"

"Actually, there are several but the big one is a place called Turning Stone. It's about forty-five minutes from here. You'll pass it on the way if you come up. It's just off the thruway. It's run by the Indians."

"You mean native Americans. Columbus never found India, Cesari."

"Great."

"Well, now I got a second reason to take a trip up there."

"What's the first reason, to see me?"

"No, to see this girl that's sending you into a tailspin. She better be hot."

"Goodbye."

Downstairs, he found the bar and lounge area. It was elegant and neatly stocked with high end liquors. There was a large fireplace with leather chairs and sofa as well several very comfortable looking bar stools. He didn't really want any alcohol as he was still recovering from the night before, but he liked the atmosphere of bars in general. You always met interesting people there.

An older couple sat on the sofa near the fireplace sipping cocktails deep in conversation as Cesari greeted the bartender and ordered a club soda with a twist of lime. The bartender was young and tall, dressed in black and sported a man-bun.

He said, "Are you sure you don't want a cocktail? It's on the house."

"I'm sure but why is it on the house?"

"Open bar is included in your room fee."

"Really? I didn't know that. Well maybe some other night."

He handed him his club soda and Cesari stepped over to the fireplace and took a seat facing the couple on the couch. He said, "Hi."

They both smiled and said hello back. They were in their seventies and well-dressed. The man was grotesquely overweight with thinning white hair and a bushy handlebar mustache. He was threatening to bust every button on the vest he was wearing. He sipped sherry from a crystal glass and said, "Good evening, young man. I'm Balthazar and this is my young bride, Hannah."

The woman laughed, "Oh Balthazar. You can be so silly sometimes."

Hannah was delicate almost frail. She wore so much jewelry, Cesari thought they might own a diamond mine. He smiled politely. "My name is John Cesari and I don't think he's silly at all. When I came into the room, I thought that maybe you were his granddaughter."

Balthazar chortled, and she laughed some more. "You men will be the death of me, but for heaven's sake don't stop."

Balthazar asked, "What are you drinking, John?"

"A club soda."

He snorted and said, "None of that. You must join us with a serious libation. We are celebrating fifty years of wedded bliss." He called out to the bartender, "Timothy, bring us a round of the house mead. I wish to make a toast."

Events out of his control, Cesari fell back to his default position of go with the flow. Timothy brought the honey-wine over to them in Waterford glasses and they each took one.

"Have you ever had mead, John?" Balthazar asked.

"No, but I've heard of it. It's wine made from honey, right?"

"Yes indeed, and Brom's mead is the finest I've ever had."

"Brom makes wine here?"

"No, Brom makes honey here and brings it to a local winery whom he contracts with to make the mead."

"Brom is a bee-keeper?"

"Oh yes, but not just an ordinary one. He is a major producer of honey and has nearly nine hundred hives scattered across the county with more than a hundred of them in the back of the property here alone along with the honey-house."

"Honey-house?"

"The place where he extracts the honey and purifies it. It used to be the carriage house for the estate generations ago until he decided to put it to better use."

"That's very interesting, and the mead here is very good you say?"

"Not just good, lad. The best, and I should know. I taught a course on the art of making mead at Cornell and have travelled the world over studying the subject. Brom's mead has a distinct flavor that simply can't be reproduced anywhere else. There's some plant around these parts that he's been unable to identify that the bees must come across as they gather pollen which gives it a flavor unlike any other… Well, how about that toast?"

They raised their glasses and Balthazar said, "To my beautiful wife, Hannah. May the next fifty years be as much fun as the last."

Cesari said, "Hip hip!"

The mead was good. Whether it was great or not Cesari couldn't say because he had no reference point to compare it. Whether it was wine or not was also a debatable point. It seemed like some sort of hybrid between beer and wine. It had a peculiar smell, familiar but unusual. He couldn't quite place it. You could taste the honey but there was something else flavoring it. Balthazar was right. It was very different from anything he had ever had.

He nodded his approval and Balthazar smiled, pleased with himself. Cesari said, "Brom must be a busy guy. Running an inn and making mead must be very time consuming."

Balthazar's countenance changed. He suddenly seemed melancholy. Hannah too. Balthazar said, "He is very busy and quite successful financially, but as they say lucky in cards, unlucky in love…"

There seemed to be a backstory so Cesari waited patiently sipping his mead. Hannah said, "There's no need to bore the young man, Balthazar."

Balthazar said, "Are you married, John?"

"No."

"Ever been?"

"No."

"Are you in love?"

"Sometimes when I pass a mirror, I get all tingly."

The old couple guffawed at his joke. Balthazar said, "I like a man with a sense of humor. I wish Brom had more of one."

"You sound like you know Brom well?"

"Only his whole life. He's like a son to us. We live just a short distance from here and were close friends with his parents may their souls rest in peace. Anyway, our Jasmine and Brom grew up together and we all had high hopes of a union, but it wasn't meant to be."

"Jasmine?"

"Our daughter. She's a nurse at the hospital."

"I think I met her today. I'm a new physician there. She trains the doctors and nurses?"

"That's her."

"She's very nice."

Hannah smiled, "What a small world."

Balthazar glanced in all directions to see if anyone was within ear shot. Timothy had left the room momentarily and there was no one else around. Still, the old man hunched forward in his seat and lowered his voice. "Anyway, Brom has been in love with her since the age of five, but unfortunately she doesn't reciprocate his feelings. I don't think he's ever accepted her rejection, and the poor girl, she's been just as unlucky in love as Brom."

"What do you mean?"

"Neither Brom nor she have ever married. Brom hasn't even tried to find anyone else as far as I know, and poor Jasmine has had the worst possible luck." Nearly whispering he continued, "She's been left at the altar once and two others have just up and run-off without explanation. They all seemed so nice too. The latest of her romantic disasters was with one of your kind."

"One of my kind?"

"Yes, a doctor at the hospital. Of all the people I wouldn't have expected to be such a coward... a man of letters."

Hannah shoved him gently, "Baltus, don't... You've had too much to drink. The doctor doesn't want to hear this, and I'm not sure it's wise to discuss it here of all places. What if Brom were to overhear?"

"Oh Hannah, I'm tired of all the secrecy."

"You don't have to tell me any family confidences... although I'd be lying if I said I wasn't curious." Cesari gently coaxed them. He was now dying to hear the story.

Balthazar stood up and went to the bar's entrance and looked both ways in the hallway outside. Satisfied the coast was clear of eavesdroppers, he said, "It's not that much of a secret, only to certain people. Our Jasmine was dating a doctor at the hospital. His name was Dave Pullman. They had been dating for about six months and according to Jasmine they seemed to be getting along quite well. Then one night about three months ago he pulled up stakes and left town. Didn't even say good bye to her. A 'Dear John' letter came in the mail several days later. How rude was that?"

Cesari agreed. "That's awful."

"Yes, but since it wasn't the first time, Jasmine took it in stride. The sad part is that I think she's starting to accept this kind of thing as her fate."

"Really? That's hard to believe. She's so nice and quite beautiful too."

"Thank you and we totally agree, but it is what it is. She's becoming quite discouraged. A girl can only take so many emotional blows before she starts to blame herself as if the rejection were somehow her fault."

"Well, that's too bad... Not to change the subject but why isn't she here now celebrating your anniversary with you?"

Hannah explained, "Our anniversary was actually last night, dear, and we did have dinner with her, but at our age it can't hurt to stretch out the celebration for as long as possible. We're hoping to have dinner with her again tomorrow night."

Balthazar said, "Why don't you join us, John? I'll arrange to have a mirror set up by the table for you."

Cesari laughed, "Sure, why not? Where?"

"Right here. Best food in town. Say around 7:00 p.m.? It will be a wonderful surprise for Jasmine."

"I'll be there."

After an hour more of pleasant chatter, Cesari said goodnight and left them there to quietly enjoy the fire in romantic solitude. Cesari felt a twinge of jealousy. He had never crossed the finish line with any woman and he was starting to wonder if the fault was his. Maybe he just wasn't the marrying kind?

Then there was that whole story about Jasmine. Very strange, he thought. On the surface, she seemed like quite the catch, pretty, intelligent, quick-witted, but you never really knew who a person was until you got close. And what was all secrecy stuff about?

As he walked to his room, he passed a large mirror.

Chapter 7

He's Coming

At 2:00 a.m. Cesari's phone buzzed. He groaned, reached over and looked at the screen, but didn't recognize the number.

"Hello."

"Is this Dr. Cesari?"

"Yes, it is."

"This is Jeremy Taylor one of the emergency room physicians at Auburn Memorial. You're on call for GI?"

"Yes, I am Jeremy," he responded, instantly snapping to attention. Years of being woken up suddenly in the middle of the night to care for seriously ill patients had conditioned his mind and body to hit the floor running when called upon. "What can I do for you?"

"I'm sorry to bother you at this hour. We have a guy here with an esophageal meat impaction. He's sixty and in pretty good shape. Says he was having prime rib at Lasca's at around 8:00 p.m. when he noticed a piece got stuck. Long story short he's been trying to gag it up at home ever since. He finally got exhausted and his wife drove him here. He can't swallow anything and is spitting up saliva. He's pretty uncomfortable. Says it's the first time this has ever happened.

I got some labs and have a chest film cooking. I don't think this can wait until morning."

Cesari sighed. Great. His first night. He said, "No problem, Jeremy. I agree with you. I'll be there in about twenty minutes. Could you do me a favor and call the endoscopy nurses in for me. I'll meet them in the OR. By the way, I'm new in town. What's Lasca's?"

"Lasca's is a restaurant, Italian-American food. It's an Auburn landmark. You should try it sometime. Big portions if you're into that. Most people rave about it. Well, thanks, for being so agreeable. I'll take care of the nurses."

Cesari hung up, dressed quickly and splashed water on his face. He laced up his dress shoes and kicked himself for not buying sneakers when he had the chance. His feet were already sore, and he had a blister, but he ignored the pain and focused. Brom had given him a key to the front door in addition to his room key. He made sure he had both before leaving. In the hallway, he was greeted by a dim orange glow from electric wall sconces with small orange bulbs flickering like candles. They took Halloween very seriously in this town. The main floor was deserted and the fire in the bar area was down to glowing embers.

The night air was cool and moist and there was a light, annoying drizzle. His Porsche was parked in the back of the house and he made his way there quickly, guided by the moon and ambient street light. The Porsche started but not without a fight. The knocking sound was much louder than it had been and more frequent. Cesari shook his head. Just another thing to deal with. Five minutes later, he was parking in the doctor's lot near Sal's space.

The emergency room was busy and noisy. Every room was filled room with apprehensive patients and their families. Harried nurses scurried back and forth, phones rang loudly, and an occasional police officer glanced casually in his direction. It took him a while, but he eventually located Jeremy, the ER physician who had called him. Supported by a small army of nurse practitioners and physician's assistants, he was the only doctor there. He looked overworked and stressed. He wore a blue cotton shirt with a stethoscope wrapped around his neck. Sweat stains under his arms were very unattractive. He was in his thirties, sported two days growth of facial hair and wore glasses. Cesari felt sorry for him both professionally and personally.

"Hi, I'm John Cesari. We spoke on the phone."

They shook hands and Jeremy said, "Hey, thanks for coming in so fast. The guy's in room 8. His name is Peter Eckert but there's been a development. Ten minutes ago, he barfed up the meat and says he feels better in that regard. I was just about to call you back and tell you not to bother coming in when he started having chest pain. I'm sorry, but I got distracted. I think he's having an MI now. We're running an EKG on him and I've just sent off some cardiac enzymes. You can still see him if you want."

"He's not having any more problems swallowing?"

"Nope. Right now, his only problem is the elephant sitting on his chest. I gave him some morphine and slapped an inch of nitro-paste on him. He's a little better."

"I'll say hello just to make sure I'm not needed. Did you call my nurses in?"

"I never had the chance. I've been swamped and now this guy is crapping out."

"Well, I'm sorry you're having such a bad night. Nothing else for me as long as I'm here?"

"No, you're good to go."

"Okay, call me if you need anything."

"Thanks and once again, I'm sorry that I got you up."

"Don't worry about it."

Cesari found Peter Eckert looking fairly uncomfortable sitting up on a gurney in room 8. He was grimacing as a technician placed EKG leads on him and a nurse adjusted his nasal oxygen cannula. Cesari had witnessed this scene many times and knew that Peter was in trouble. His color was way off and there were tiny beads of perspiration on his forehead. The machine monitoring his heart rate and oxygen saturation beeped rhythmically, thankfully indicating he was stable for the moment, but that could change literally in a heartbeat. If he got through the night, he most likely would wake up in a cardiac catheterization lab feeling worn out but glad to be alive. If he had to have an endoscopic procedure in the middle of an acute myocardial infarction his risk of a complication just shot through the roof.

Cesari nodded at the patient. "Mr. Eckert?"

The man looked up. "Yes."

"I'm Dr. Cesari, the gastroenterologist on call. The emergency room physician called me in about the meat stuck in your esophagus. He just told me that you brought it up and are feeling better."

"Yes, much better but then I started having chest pain. They think I'm having a heart attack."

"Unfortunately, that may be the case. I'm sorry you're not feeling well so I'll be brief. I just want to make sure you're swallowing okay before I leave. So what happened? You were eating steak somewhere?"

"Yes. Prime rib, at Lasca's but it was my own fault. I was drinking and talking and bit off too big a piece. Then someone told a joke and I started to laugh. I didn't chew the damn thing. Practically swallowed it whole, but I'm better now. I brought it back up a few minutes ago. Damnedest thing that's ever happened to me except for what's going on now."

"I'll bet. How do you feel right now in terms of your swallowing?"

"I'm fine. They gave me a glass of water just a minute ago with an aspirin and I had no problem with it. Swallowed it right down. I can tell everything's back to normal. If I didn't feel like my chest was in a vise, I'd walk out of here."

"Well, I'm glad the swallowing is better anyway. That's one problem out of the way. Hopefully, it was just a one-time thing. Chew your food well from now on, okay? If you have any further problems, they'll call me back. The doctors and nurses are going to take good care of you. I hope everything turns out okay."

"You and me. Thanks."

Cesari left the ER and ran to the Porsche. It was raining hard now, and he got soaked on the way. He turned the key and the ignition made a grinding, impertinent sound and wouldn't start. He waited a few seconds and tried again. It still wouldn't start.

Shit.

Several more unsuccessful attempts left him frustrated and he sat there trying to decide what to do. He was still exhausted from the previous night's escapades and needed to sleep. The Dulles House was more than a half mile away.

The idea of walking that far at 3:00 a.m. in dress shoes with a blister on one foot in the rain was not very appealing. What were the odds of there being an all-night taxi service in a town as small as this? Probably not very good.

He ran back to the ER splashing through puddles. Thoroughly drenched, he ran into a nurse and introduced himself. She confirmed his fear that there was no taxi service at that hour. She offered him a hot cup of coffee and blanket to dry off with. He accepted, thanked her, and moments later, walked out of the ER into the main corridor of the hospital sipping black coffee from a styrofoam cup with a blanket wrapped around his shoulders. He realized he must have been quite a sight.

Looking right and left, he thought about his options. The only people he knew were Dicky and Sal. He was sure he could call them for a ride but how lame would that be to call your boss because your car broke down on your first day of work? He cancelled that idea almost immediately. Jasmine had given him her number in case he ran into any technical problems with the EMR. He was quite confident that his car not starting didn't fall under that heading. Besides, a call from him at this hour would creep her out as it would almost any woman he wasn't already in a relationship with. So what to do?

The on-call room actually had been rather pleasant, and better than any he had ever used elsewhere. That story Jasmine had told him about the murders was unnerving but starting to fade into memory and he now felt a little foolish for his less than manly reaction. As fatigue overcame him, the sillier he felt.

Making up his mind, he went to the end of the hallway and entered the old hospital, found the elevators and went up to third floor. As the doors creaked opened into blackness, he became uneasy again, but shook it off and gingerly reached around to find the light switch. They flickered and came on buzzing eerily the way fluorescent bulbs did. Carefully, he stuck his head out into the hallway glancing back and forth. He laughed quietly to himself when he saw there were no bogeymen and walked quickly to the on-call room.

He closed the door behind him, deadbolting it from inside, leaned back against it and breathed a sigh of relief. Jesus, he hated creepy night crawler stories. He was going to give Jasmine a piece of his mind for doing this to him. He might even call her an old-maid… Well, maybe not that, but certainly he'd call her mean for scaring him. Definitely, he would call her mean. Peeling his wet clothes off, he draped them over the chair and bathroom door to dry. Then he got under the covers and found the remote to the television before turning off the night light. He was tired but now a little wound up. A few minutes of C-span ought to put him right to sleep, and it did. He dozed off with the TV on.

An hour later he woke to the sound of someone turning his doorknob. His heart raced, and he held his breath as he sat bolt upright. The TV was still on but there was no image just static. He flipped on the overhead light and watched the doorknob as it turned back and forth slowly at first and then picking up speed.

He kicked himself for not placing the *Do Not Disturb* sign out as Jasmine had cautioned him and called, "Who is it? The room is occupied."

There was no answer, and the knob turned and jiggled insistently with more urgency. Cesari broke out into a sweat, his imagination running full steam ahead. If it was another physician looking for a place to crash for the night, why wouldn't they say something? Besides, the door was locked. Wasn't that enough evidence there was someone inside even without the *Do Not Disturb* sign? He stood up and approached the door, apprehensive and ready to fight. Against what, he wasn't sure, but fight he would. That was his nature.

He repeated more forcefully, "I said the room is occupied!"

No response just the relentless rattling of the knob and then he heard a sound from behind him. Cesari swung around quickly but saw nothing. He was getting nervous bordering on panic. Whoever it was started banging on the door. He glanced around the room in search of a weapon and noticed the TV screen had gone blank. He stared at it for a second or two trying to digest what had happened. As he looked at it, words suddenly appeared on the screen in glowing red letters.

He's coming!

Cesari woke up panting, his heart pounding, drenched in sweat. C-span was droning on the TV. He turned on the lights and splashed water on his face in the bathroom. Staring at himself in the mirror, he thought, *Jesus Christ, Cesari, get a grip.* It was 4:30 a.m. and he was on the verge of collapse. He turned the TV off and got under the covers and tried to go back to sleep, but now he heard a faint, intermittent electrical sound. He looked up at the TV. It was off, and he listened carefully. The sound was coming from out in the hallway.

He got up again, determined not to let his imagination get the best of him this time. Opening the door briskly, he was surprised to see the hallway lights flickering on and off. He was sure he had turned them off when he had entered the room earlier. He reached for the switch and found that it was in the on position and he flicked it off. Cesari wasn't happy as he closed and locked the door again getting under the covers or more accurately, hiding under the covers. Dawn couldn't come fast enough as far as he was concerned.

At 9:00 a.m. Cesari woke to the sounds of men working in the hallway. The sun shone brightly through the window and he squinted as he glanced around making sure he wasn't dreaming again. He shook his head and was amazed at what the power of suggestion could do to a person. Miss Jasmine was going to catch heat about this for sure.

He dressed and left the room. Down the hall he spotted two maintenance men staring into a utility closet. There was a metal ladder set up in the middle of the corridor and a large toolbox on the floor next to it. Looking past them into the room he saw a fuse box, a lot of wires, a mop, plastic buckets and basic housekeeping paraphernalia. The fuse box was the focus of their attention.

He introduced himself. "Hey, guys, I'm Dr. Cesari. What's going on?"

The senior guy turned and said, "Oh hi, doctor. Were you in the on-call room? I hope we didn't disturb you."

"Not at all. What's up?"

"What's up is that a tree blew over in the storm last night and knocked out a transformer. It sent a surge through the hospital and we're playing catch up today."

"Oh okay. Well, be careful."

"Thanks."

Cesari left them, relieved that he had an adequate explanation for the flickering lights. His spirits bolstered, he picked up a coffee in the cafeteria and went to see his car. The lot hadn't quite dried off and he skipped over small ponds of water to the Porsche. It still wouldn't start, and he resigned himself to having it towed. He called Sal's mechanic and an hour later a fat guy in overalls named Ralph was hauling the Porsche away for an evaluation. As he stood there watching the tow truck leave the lot, Sal's Jaguar sailed into its spot with Dicky riding shotgun.

Great.

Chapter 8

Colonoscopy is a Mitzvah

Sal was in a chipper mood. "Cesari, glad we ran into you."

"How was your first night on call?" Dicky inquired.

"Uneventful. Thanks for asking. It's Saturday, why are you both wearing suits and ties?" Cesari said, noting their formal attire.

Sal laughed, "You have a lot to learn about running a hospital, Cesari, but I'll tell you what. I'll give you your first lesson for free. Come with us and I'll show you what guys like us go through while you practitioners are playing golf and screwing your girlfriends when your wives are out of town. Have you eaten breakfast yet?"

"I haven't even brushed my teeth yet. I came in to see a patient last night and my car broke down. I just had your mechanic tow it."

"You slept here?"

"Yeah, but since I wasn't planning on spending the night, I didn't bring an overnight bag. Hence, the unkempt, un-shaven look."

"No worries. I keep a spare tooth brush and electric razor in my office for late nights. I told you there was something wrong with that car. It's probably the transmission or the clutch but possibly both. I don't know what the guy who sold you that car got, Cesari, but he should've gotten life." He laughed at his own joke and then added, "Man I crack myself up, but don't worry, Ralph will take care of you. Come with us."

He placed a massive arm around Cesari's shoulder and dragged him back toward the hospital in a bear hug. Cesari said, "Where are we going?"

Sal said, "To the boardroom. The state's coming for a surprise inspection of the hospital. They called me at 6:00 a.m. and said they'll arrive at 10:00 a.m. Can you believe that? They could care less if you're dying in bed from pneumonia. You know what they told me? Picture this, I'm barely awake and lying there in my underwear and they tell me, 'Be there and be ready to undergo a prostate exam without lubrication.' Can you believe that? Real jokers."

Cesari replied, "They really said that?"

Dicky added, "You can believe it, John. They have no respect for little guys like us and the harassment never ends with them. You can kiss their asses from morning till night and come sun up there will be someone new and even more aggravating to take their place."

"Have you met your partners yet?" Sal asked.

"Partners?"

"The other GI guys?"

"No, I was swamped yesterday, and they were in their offices."

"Maybe we'll see one of them today. I know Henry likes to scope on Saturdays."

"Henry?"

"Henry Katz, one of the other GI guys. He's a real work horse. Scopes seven days a week."

Turning to Dicky he asked, "Seven days a week? Where was he yesterday? They told us he was in his office when we came by."

"He starts at 6:00 a.m. sharp and finishes up at about 1:00 p.m. and then goes to the office to see patients. We didn't get there until 2:00 p.m., but he'll be there now." Dicky looked at his watch. "Look, if the state hasn't arrived yet, you go over there and meet him and then come back here. We're having coffee and bagels brought up from the cafeteria."

Sal added, "The razor and toothbrush are in the private bathroom in my office. Make yourself at home."

The state hadn't arrived so Cesari went to Sal's office and cleaned up. There was even some aftershave there which he splashed on. Feeling fresh, he proceeded to the OR which to his surprise seemed to be running on all cylinders as if it was just another day. There was a full complement of staff and it was crowded with patients coming and going. He found the endoscopy room where Katz was working and knocked on the door.

A nurse opened it a crack. It was Karen, one of the nurses he had met yesterday. She greeted him, "Hi."

Cesari said, "I just wanted to say hello to Dr. Katz. I didn't get to meet him yesterday."

"Come on in," called a high-pitched male voice. "We're almost done."

Cesari entered the dark room and said hello to everyone introducing himself to Katz. "I'm John Cesari. Mr. Bardolino sent me over to say hello. I just started yesterday."

Standing next to Katz assisting with the colonoscopy was Cindy, another nurse he had met yesterday. A nurse anesthetist named Jennifer was positioned at one end of the bed monitoring the patient, an elderly female who was sound asleep. Katz was a little guy with glasses, in his mid-fifties, pudgy and very soft-looking. He wore blue surgical scrubs and hat. He said, "I'm Henry Katz. I heard through the grapevine a new guy had replaced Pullman. Where are you from?"

"I'm from New York."

"New York? Whereabouts? I'm from Long Island."

"No kidding? Well, I grew up in the Bronx, but I've been working in Manhattan at St. Matt's... Did you say I'm replacing a guy named Pullman?"

"Yeah, Dave Pullman, the previous GI guy. One second please... Cindy, I want to biopsy that."

Cesari glanced at the screen and saw a small area of irritation in the rectum which Henry biopsied and said, "Karen, call that nonspecific, mild inflammation of the rectum."

He pulled the scope out, thanked everyone for their help and said to Cesari. "Come with me. I only have five minutes before the next case."

Karen said, "Hold on... Were there any other findings?"

"No."

"What about hemorrhoids?" she asked.

"Yeah, small ones. Grade 2 internal and external."

"And diverticulosis? I thought I saw some on the way in."

"I saw some too," Cindy added.

"Okay fine. Diverticulosis. Is there anything else?"

Karen said, "No, I don't think so."

Cindy agreed. The lights came on and he walked away. Cesari followed him to a small dictation room and they sat opposite each other on swivel stools. Katz said, "I'm not sure what they told you but they're all pathologic liars. Would you like some tea?"

He started playing with a Keurig machine and fumbling for a K-cup in a desk drawer at the same time. Cesari said, "No thank you. Who are?"

"Administration, that's who. They couldn't pass a lie detector test if you asked them their own name. They're that bad."

"I'm not sure what you mean."

"Hold on a second." He positioned the green tea K-cup into the machine and pressed the *Brew* button. He then opened a small package of individually wrapped graham crackers and began nibbling. In between mouthfuls he said, "I got low blood sugar. Did you know these are kosher?"

Cesari shook his head. "I had no idea. Are you orthodox?"

He glanced around nervously. "Yeah, I am. What are you, some kind of undercover rabbi?"

He laughed. "No, but I trained with a lot of Jewish guys. I thought you couldn't work or operate machinery on the sabbath?"

"This isn't work, Cesari. It's charity. I'm saving people's lives one colonoscopy at a time. Just remember that. It's a mitzvah, a good deed. Every time I remove a polyp, I'm doing the work of God… So what did those clowns in administration tell you about this place?"

Raising his eyebrows at that very interesting interpretation of the Torah, he said, "They told me there was plenty of work and that everybody was making money hand over fist."

Katz nearly spit up his tea. "Do yourself a favor, Cesari, and get out of town before the ink dries on your contract. There are barely enough cases for the guys that are here now. I got six kids and they're all suffering from malnutrition. I'm this far away from chapter 11 myself."

He placed an index finger about a half inch from his thumb to show Cesari how desperate his financial situation was. Cesari was thoroughly amused. He'd heard this sad story from every GI guy at every hospital he'd ever worked. He said tactfully, "Well, I'm sort of locked in at this point, but I'll do my best not to get in your way. I hope that we can have an amicable relationship."

"Oh, don't misunderstand me. I'm sure we'll get along fine. I just don't want you to be upset when you're pulling pud with nothing to do."

"Thanks for the warning. Say could you tell me about that guy Pullman and why he left?"

Katz was shocked. "They didn't tell you about Pullman? I don't believe it. These guys are sick."

Cesari leaned forward, curious. "What happened?"

"What happened is that something or somebody scared the living crap out of the guy and he took off like a jackrabbit. He didn't even bother to pack or say goodbye to anyone. I've never seen…I take that back…I've never even heard of anything like it. He was on call one night, did a routine case at around midnight and the next day he calls to tell me he's already left town and never coming back. He had a moving company get his stuff. He wouldn't say what happened or where he was going. Tell everybody I said goodbye and that was it. Don't call me, I'll call you. The call lasted no more than thirty seconds. I tried calling him back multiple times, but he turned his cellphone off right after that."

Cesari was fascinated by this. "You don't have any idea whatsoever as to what happened?"

"Look, Cesari, between me and you, Pullman probably had a few loose screws to start with and something just tipped him over the edge. That's usually the way it happens. In his case who knows?"

"But you said you thought something frightened him?"

"I don't know for a fact and as I said the call lasted all of thirty seconds, but there was something in his voice that made me think that. Maybe I'm just trying to rationalize why somebody would leave a six-figure job like that. He didn't even pick up his last paycheck."

"Was he on drugs? Could he have had a nervous breakdown?" Cesari asked reasonably.

"I doubt it about the drugs, but you never know and the other… anything's possible, I guess. When I asked him where he was going all he would say was far away. Me and everybody in the office watched the news for weeks waiting to see if he would show up in the trunk of some car or running naked through a schoolyard but it never happened." Katz looked at his watch. "Jesus, I'm running behind. I still have to do my note, drink my tea and say my prayers."

"Prayers?"

"I'm hedging my bets in case I'm wrong about this being a mitzvah. Here's my number, Cesari. Give me a call if you need anything."

He scribbled his cellphone number down on a scrap of paper and handed it to Cesari who took his cue and left him to do his thing. He walked through the recovery room and stopped briefly to introduce himself to the nurses there. They were polite and receptive but also very busy. Sandy, one of the endoscopy nurses he had met yesterday, showed him the breakroom and offered him a cup of coffee which he accepted. Another nurse, Melissa, was already in the breakroom in heated discussion with someone on her phone. Sandy had a few minutes, so Cesari decided to sit and be sociable. He considered time spent like this an investment in future relationships since OR nurses were going to run his life for the next year or two.

They got to know each other for a few minutes while Melissa berated the person on the other end of the line. When she finally hung up, Sandy made the introductions. Melissa was in her late forties and very frustrated about something. She sighed deeply, her mind a million miles away.

Cesari showed concern and asked, "Is everything all right?"

Sandy rolled her eyes. "Never ask her that question, Dr. Cesari. She's got chronic man problems."

He grinned and noticed Melissa didn't deny it or object to the invasion of her privacy.

Sandy continued, "She robbed the cradle and now she's upset that he acts like she's his mother."

He said, "I'm sorry to hear that, Melissa."

Melissa was clearly unconcerned about revealing the private details of her life to a total stranger and said, "It's my husband. I don't know what I'm going to do. He's next to useless around the house."

He said, "That's too bad. Have you been married long?"

"A year."

"That's not very long. He's still well within the window of trainability as we say."

"You sound like you know a lot about this stuff," she laughed.

Cesari was enjoying this. He'd met a lot of nurses and a lot of Melissas. He sipped his coffee and nodded. "Well, I don't mean to speak out of turn, but maybe I can help. It sounds like this cowpoke needs to be house trained. When I was in medical school, a lot of the other students used to come to me for relationship advice. I was known as the doctor of love and I took my responsibility seriously."

Melissa smirked. "Oh really?"

"True story."

Sandy said, "Well, if that's the case, Doctor, you're going to be busy around here. That's for sure."

Melissa said, "Well, what's your advice for a man that comes home from work and does nothing but lie on the couch playing video games until two in the morning. I come home from a twelve-hour shift, have to stop at the grocery store, prepare dinner, clean up after dinner, load the dishwasher, unload the dishwasher, vacuum the house and do the laundry."

Cesari thought about that. "Okay, well full disclaimer. I've never been married, nor do I perform miracles, but the way I see it all relationships are two-way streets. The fact that you got married suggests you are in love or at least care very much for each other. Am I warm?"

She said, "You're warm."

"Sandy said you robbed the cradle. May I ask how much older you are?"

"I'm forty-nine and he's twenty-nine."

Cesari whistled. "That's the problem. That's quite a difference. Most men these days aren't adults at twenty-nine. I'm not making excuses for him. I'm simply making an observation. Women mature faster and act ten years older than they really are while most guys behave ten years younger. He's still acting like he's in college."

"You're telling me?"

Sandy said, "Shut up and let the man talk."

He said, "You need to set boundaries with him and once you set those boundaries you need to keep to them. So you need to say, 'Look, I work hard too and I need help around here. I'll make dinner Mondays, Wednesdays and Fridays. It's your responsibility Tuesdays and Thursdays and we'll wing it on the weekends' or something like that and the same thing for the other household chores. But once you do that you have to keep to it. No going back if he forgets. It's his job and that's that. Now here comes the tricky, and for many women, the extremely difficult part... Are you ready?"

They were both ready, listening eagerly and very tickled. He said, "You need to be nice when you speak to him not threatening, hysterical or angry. Many women have difficulty keeping an even keel in these situations and approach the task with too heavy a hand. If he cares about you, he will be devastated to learn that you're upset and disappointed in him as a man and a partner in life and will want to improve himself in your eyes. There's absolutely no need to call him names..."

Sandy interrupted him, "Like asshole. She calls him that a lot, Doctor."

87

Melissa chuckled, "Well, he is."

Cesari cleared his throat. "Well you see Melissa, if you come flying at him like a bat out of hell in a full frontal assault, he will instinctively defend himself and do just the opposite of what you want."

Sandy said knowingly, "That's Melissa, a bat out of hell."

Melissa shook her head. "Shut up, Sandy."

He continued, "Okay, keep in mind that the goal is to repair not destroy the relationship. No spite work, no pettiness, no tit for tat, all right? Make him come to understand that if he makes you happy, you will make him happy…very happy." Cesari winked at her. "You getting my drift?"

"Yeah, I'm getting your drift."

"Good. One last thing. In any successful relationship the most important ingredient is compromise. You give a little, you take a little. You don't draw up battle lines with someone you love, and most of all learn how to forgive and forget. Ben Franklin used to have a saying regarding this… eyes wide open before marriage and half closed after."

They both liked that and laughed. Sandy said, "Man, you're going to be busy for sure with these girls. Do you charge consultation fees?"

Cesari smiled at her. "No, it's a service I've always provided for the betterment of mankind. Okay, now it's my turn. I'm sure you both knew Dave Pullman, the last GI guy. Can you tell me what happened to him? I was told that he was on call one night and then no one's heard from him again."

At the mention of Pullman's name, Sandy's demeanor changed completely. She shrank back with a look of horror on her face. Melissa said, "Oh boy. You shouldn't have brought that up."

Before he could ask why, Sandy said, "I was here that night doing recovery. I told him not to sleep in the on-call room. I warned him, Dr. Cesari, but he was tired and laughed at me."

Katz didn't tell him this. He said, "He slept in the on-call room that night and you think something happened to him up there?"

"I don't think it. I know it. He went there to sleep and the next day he was gone. Wouldn't even come back to get his belongings. Had professionals do it for him that's how frightened he was. That place is haunted. I told him so."

Melissa intervened, "Oh Sandy, please... You're always going on about that. Doctor, no one really believes it's haunted. I don't know what happened to Dr. Pullman but I'm sure we'll find out a rational explanation one day."

Sandy had a conniption. "I'm telling you, Doctor, if Dr. Pullman had taken my advice, he'd still be with us today. That place has evil spirits in the walls. Mark my words." She pointed a bony finger at him. "They came for him. That's what they did."

Melissa shook her head in frustration but didn't say anything. She'd obviously heard this rant on more than one occasion.

Cesari said, "You think it's haunted because of what happened there long ago?"

She nodded her head. "Of course. So you know the legend?"

"Yes, I've heard about the murders."

"Yes, but have you heard about the legend?"

Cesari was confused. "I'm not sure what you mean by the legend?"

"Levi Blackburn wasn't just a deranged murderer, Doctor. He was a devil worshipper and practiced satanism in its extreme form. He didn't just kill those poor people up there. He sacrificed them in ritualistic manner in order to conjure up his master, the Dark Lord himself. He didn't commit suicide either…"

Melissa had enough and was becoming visibly upset. "Sandy, stop. I hate this kind of stuff, and no one has any idea what happened that night."

"Well, I believe that's what happened," Sandy affirmed. "And Dr. Cesari has a right to know before he goes up there."

Cesari finished his coffee thoroughly amused. This was the second person that felt he had the right to know. Interestingly, the more outrageous the story got the less inclined he was to believe any of it. "Sandy, if he didn't kill himself then what happened?"

"The devil took him away as a reward for what he'd done. The pentagram drawn on the floor below him was a portal for his soul to pass through into hell. Satan drew it himself after he hung Levi from the pipe."

Melissa quietly waved goodbye and left the room to go back to work or because she couldn't take it anymore. He couldn't blame her. Supernatural stuff like this struck a primitive chord in most people including him, but unlike many, he had the ability to work past his fears.

"That's not all," she continued. "It's said that the evil inhabiting that building becomes more active as the anniversary of the murders comes close, and this being the fiftieth year something big is expected to happen."

"Like what?"

"Like the devil himself, that's what. He's coming and he's looking for more sacrifices."

Jesus, she was nuts. Time to go. "Well, thank you for the coffee Sandy, but I really should get going. I'm late for a meeting. I'm really looking forward to working with you."

"Mark my words, Doctor," she repeated her warning in dramatic fashion. "Don't sleep up there if you know what's good for you."

"Thanks, Sandy, I'll keep it in mind." He didn't see any point in telling someone so fanatical that he already had slept up there. It might make her head spin. "By the way, when is the anniversary of the murders?"

"Halloween, Doctor."

Chapter 9

The Bureaucrats

The meeting had already started when Cesari entered the boardroom. There were three bureaucrats from the state sitting on one side of the table, two men and one woman. They were middle-aged, dressed in dark suits with ID badges and had stern looks on their faces. The woman in charge looked particularly severe and unforgiving. She sat between the two men and across from Sal and Dicky. To Cesari's great surprise, Jasmine sat by herself at one end of the table almost as if she were the moderator. She had a yellow legal pad in front of her and was jotting down notes. Sal introduced Cesari to the state people as a representative of the house-staff and he took a seat next to Jasmine.

There was a platter of assorted bagels, thinly sliced lox and condiments in the center of the table. Cesari grabbed a sesame bagel, smeared a gargantuan dose of cream cheese on it and poured himself yet another cup of coffee. Jasmine grinned watching him.

Sal said to the bureaucrats, "Feel free to go wherever you want and talk to whomever you wish, however, please be mindful that although today is Saturday, our hospital is fully operational, including the OR, and people are trying to do their jobs. I must insist that patient care comes first at all times and not be compromised by your presence which might serve as a distraction to the staff."

The woman made a face appearing insulted, as if he were deliberately talking down to her, which he was. "Naturally, we will be respectful of the fact that patients are being cared for. We will not interfere with your staff, but we do expect their full cooperation."

"And you will get it within reason, but I will not allow or tolerate any disruption of their clinical duties."

She narrowed her eyes until venom oozed out the sides. He was rattling her cage and she didn't like it. This was a well-seasoned team of hospital inspectors and Sal was talking to them as if they were children taking a tour of the Louvre, but he had a point. It was very disquieting for nurses to be stared at and grilled while they're trying to concentrate on caring for very ill people.

The 'within reason' part seemed to be the main sticking point of the discussion and occupied the bulk of the next thirty minutes as Sal defined what his thoughts on the subject were. New York State's idea of reasonable meant everybody should stop what they were doing and bow, kneel and grovel before them. Governmental authority in healthcare had reached the point that they actually thought they were not only an important part of the process but *the* most important part of the process. They had no idea that guys like Sal and Dicky and every nurse and every doctor and every janitor in the place would like to see them disappear like Jimmy Hoffa.

Sal and Dicky sparred with them like that while Jasmine took notes and Cesari watched in silence eating his bagel and sucking down coffee. He felt like he was watching two heavyweights throwing jabs to test each other's defenses, patiently waiting for just the right moment to deliver a knockout blow. Eventually he got bored, took a pen out of his pocket, borrowed Jasmine's legal pad and wrote her a note.

What are you doing here?

She wrote back.

I'm their tour guide/minder. I'm supposed to keep them out of trouble once the meeting ends.

Cesari read it and smiled. A full hour later, just when he thought the proceedings might never end, they got suddenly heated when the bureaucrats suggested they be allowed to interview patients in the emergency room. Sal slapped the table declaring that inappropriate, even unethical, and possibly illegal, given HIPPA laws and the amount of stress patients were under as they waited for evaluation and treatment. The state backed down at the mention of HIPPA violations as that was a beast of their own creation and wouldn't serve them well to be on the wrong end of that accusation. Mercifully the meeting adjourned shortly after that exchange, everyone shook hands and Jasmine led them off to the various departments. Before she left however, he slipped her one last note on the legal pad to which she nodded her head.

Call me when you're done. I'll be waiting.

Jasmine and the state nerds filtered out of the boardroom leaving Sal, Dicky, and Cesari alone. Sal loosened his tie and Dicky chewed on a second bagel loaded with lox. They were noticeably upset.

Sal looked at Cesari. "Do you see what I mean?"

"I do."

"These guys got the power to shutter us up and they know it. The only chance we have is to stand up to them, look them right in the eye, and say bring it on."

Cesari said, "I though you did well. I was surprised at first by your tone but then I realized you were playing a game of brinksmanship with them."

Sal turned to Dicky, "This guy catches on quick. I like that." He turned back to Cesari. "You don't even know the worst part."

"What's that?"

"These guys are nothing. They're simply a scouting party for the state looking for anything big…sizing us up for weaknesses. The real gorillas will be coming in a couple of months. Ten of them… I repeat ten of the biggest assholes you ever met crawling all over the place for three straight days not just looking but hoping to find something wrong."

"I don't envy you. So what's their game plan today?"

"They'll sniff around, review a few charts, scare a few nurses, but their real purpose is to put us on notice for the big review coming down the pike, so we have a chance to put our house in order. See, Cesari, the problem with this system is that they know as well as we do that they can't afford to shut us down. It would make them look bad as well as us. This hospital services a city of fifty thousand with a catchment area of three or four times that. The next nearest hospital is almost an hour away. You close our doors and you'll have nearly a quarter of a million people screaming bloody murder to their state representatives in Albany. Furthermore, we've passed every inspection for the last ten years. How bad would it look if suddenly they declared us unfit? They'd look pretty incompetent, so all of this is just smoke and mirrors, but we have to play the game. Like tonight, Dicky and I have to take these guys out to dinner to show them there are no hard feelings, the way the state department wines and dines foreign dignitaries even though they might hate them."

"It's a tough business."

"You're telling me. So how was Henry?"

"Katz?"

"Yeah, Katz."

"He seemed fine. We only chatted for a few minutes but I kind of liked him."

"You liked Henry?"

They both snorted at once. Cesari defended himself. "From what I saw, he seemed all right."

Dicky smiled, "Did he tell you how much he hates us."

"The subject never came up," Cesari lied.

"Trust me. It will. The guy's making three quarters of a million a year and you'd think we're screwing him the way he's always complaining."

Sal asked, "Do you want to join us for dinner tonight? If you thought this meeting was bad just wait until you have to spend a couple of hours in a restaurant with this crew. Dollars to donuts their idea of fine dining involves some form of all you can eat buffet."

"I would have loved to, but I already have dinner plans."

Sal laughed, "Listen to him, Dicky. He's only here two days and he already has dinner plans. Did you meet a cute nurse, Cesari? Because if you did, you'd better keep her away from Dicky. Isn't that right, Dicky?"

"You got that right, Sal," Dicky laughed.

Cesari said, "No, nothing like that. There's an elderly couple I met at the inn last night. They're celebrating their fiftieth anniversary and invited me to join them for dinner. I couldn't say no to that and they would be very disappointed if I begged out."

"All right, Cesari. I'll let you off the hook this time. Well, Dicky and I have some homework to do. Hopefully, these guys aren't teetotalers. If you change your mind come over to the whiskey bar at around 3:00 p.m. Remember the place?"

"A.T. Wally & Co. on Genesee Street?"

"That's it. We'll be pre-gaming it with them before dinner."

Cesari suddenly felt bad for the bureaucrats. "I'll keep it in mind. Thanks."

They left, and he hunted for the doctor's lounge on the second floor across from the cafeteria. He had passed by it several times on his tour with Dicky and then with Jasmine. It was a small room maybe fifteen feet long and slightly wider. There was a comfortable old brown cloth sofa with several recliner chairs, a coffee table, several computer stations and a bathroom. He sat at one of the computers and logged on.

Once the main screen popped up, he went to the google search page and typed in Levi Blackburn. In seconds, up came numerous hits most related to the notorious murders fifty years ago. He read carefully and was even more surprised at the heinous nature of the crime as several eyewitnesses gave vividly gruesome descriptions of the scene; bulging eyes, purple faces, incontinence, wall-to-wall blood splattered in one of the rooms, and Levi's neck stretched almost six inches from his chin to his shoulders because of his great weight. The whole nation was shocked and the state, for political reasons, was forced to close the hospital down.

The building was privately owned and under such financial strain, the banks eventually foreclosed, but due to the scandalous cloud surrounding the event they were unable to unload the property. With time, memories began to fade and a need for a general hospital in the community grew. A group of outside entrepreneurs bought the structure and the surrounding property thinking to renovate and modernize it. Word spread however, and the stories revived, stoking superstition and fear once again throughout the community. The new owners soon realized they had a public relations nightmare on their hands and compromised. The new hospital would be built from the ground up attached to the old one which would be used only as a storage facility and for certain administrative offices. They had to promise never to house patients there, and so Auburn Memorial Hospital sprung up from the ashes of devil worship and death.

"Nice town you landed in, Cesari," he muttered under his breath to no one.

Reading on he discovered that Levi Blackburn actually did belong to a little known but fanatical sect of devil worshippers known as the Order of Nine Angels, which was considered by law enforcement to be one of the most extreme and dangerous of the Satanic cults because of its belief in human sacrifice and black magic.

This guy Levi Blackburn really was a maniac, and Sandy the OR nurse, may have been more right than wrong about what happened that night. Cesari let out a deep breath and googled up Satanists in the U.S. He discovered that Lucifer was alive and well and not just in New York State. Accurate statistics were hard to come by because most people were reluctant to admit they were devil worshippers, but having said that, there were over half a million acknowledged Satanists spread across the country. Most groups seemed to be harmless gatherings of hedonists bent on celebrating life in the pursuit of ritualistic mass orgies and pot parties. Nonetheless, the more serious groups although small in number like the Order of Nine Angels were considered a clear and present danger to the public good and were hounded relentlessly by the authorities wherever they found them. There were numerous reports of murder, retribution against ex-members, and human sacrifices performed on behalf of Beelzebub.

Great.

Getting a headache, he rubbed his temples. His research was interrupted by the sound of loud, angry voices outside the door to the lounge. He turned as Jennifer, the nurse anesthetist he met in Katz's room earlier, walked in. She was red in the face and clenched her teeth as she took off her OR cap and flung it into a trash can. Shaking out her shoulder length brown hair and barely acknowledging him, she stormed into the bathroom where he heard her sobbing.

Cesari stood and walked to the doorway to see what happened. The top half of the door was glass and he saw Herb Funkelman disappearing quickly down the hallway into the cafeteria. Cesari wanted no part of this and went back to the computer to log off. His plan was to leave before Jennifer came out of the bathroom. He wasn't fast enough however, and the bathroom door opened just as he stepped away from the computer desk to leave. She stood there in front of him, red eyed and teary.

He looked at her and she looked at him. He was uncomfortable and didn't know what to say. She blurted out, "Do I look like I need testicles?"

She was young and cute with big eyes. He said, "God no. Don't even talk like that."

"That's the second day in a row that jerk, Funkelman, told me to grow a pair. What the hell is wrong with him?"

"A lot I suspect... I'm sorry."

"Some days I feel like killing him."

"Not today please. New York State inspectors are roaming the halls looking for minor deviances from standard of care."

She allowed herself the tiniest of smiles and said, "I have to go back to work. I can't let him get to me like this."

"No, you can't."

"But I still want to kill him."

"Give me a chance to leave the building first."

She laughed. "I'll try."

Cesari watched her walk out the door and breathed a sigh of relief. He was getting a whirlwind introduction into Auburn Memorial politics and was not necessarily the better for it.

Chapter 10

Giddyup

Cesari caught up with Jasmine a few minutes after one in the lobby of the hospital. She looked good in blue jeans but was obviously frazzled from her experience with the state people.

He said, "Hello there."

She said, "Hi, how's your day going?"

"Better than yours, I'm sure. How'd the pencil pushers treat you?"

"They were brutal. I hate them."

He grinned. "Were the bad people mean to you?"

Laughing she nodded. "Yes, they were. Would you beat them up for me?"

He nodded. "If that's all it takes to get on your good side, consider it done."

She added, "Especially the bitch lady in charge. I want you to hurt her good. She was totally out of control. She's still up in the ICU torturing people. I had to leave. I couldn't take it anymore."

"She had that look. I could see it a mile away. Let's go slash her tires."

"We should. She was awful. She left two young nurses in tears up on the second floor because they forgot to wash their hands when they came out of a patient's room. I know it's important, but she made them feel like the hospital was going to close because of them and that it was all their fault everyone was going to be out of work. She was horrid."

"That's inappropriate. There's no need to be cruel like that. Did you tell Sal?"

"Not yet, but I will… in great detail."

"So who's watching them?"

"I called Dr. Rizzo and told him I had enough. He laughed and said I could leave and that he would take over. He didn't mind because they were taking them out to dinner later somewhere in town."

Cesari smiled. He knew where they were going and what was about to happen. They weren't going back to Albany tonight. That was for sure. More than likely, Sal would be bailing them all out of the drunk tank tomorrow morning. Serves them right. He said, "What about you? Have you had lunch?"

She gave him a shy look and hesitated. "No, I haven't."

"Perfect, where are we going?"

She hesitated and said, "I'm not sure lunch would be smart."

"Why is that?"

"I don't want you to get the wrong idea. You know what I mean? We talked about this."

"What kind of wrong idea?... Oh please. C'mon, give me more credit than that. You said what you had to say. I get it. You don't date guys from the hospital. You don't have to keep beating that horse because…hello…he's already dead. I don't see why we can't be friends. Friends eat together sometimes, don't they?"

She shook her head laughing. "Fine. There's a pub on State Street called Curley's. It's pretty good. I'll meet you there. You just turn right when you leave the parking lot. It's less than a quarter of a mile from here."

"Can I bum a ride? My car wouldn't start this morning and I had to have it towed. Probably won't be fixed until Monday afternoon unless they have to send out for a part. Then, who knows?"

She looked at him for a moment. "You're not making this up just to get in my car again?"

He made a face. "Why would I do that? I don't even like Hondas."

"Because some guys don't take no for an answer."

"Not me. No is my middle name. John…No…Cesari. My mom took a lot of flak for doing that to me."

She giggled. "I bet. C'mon, let's go."

They entered Curley's pub a few minutes later and grabbed a table off to the side. It was a pretty standard bar-restaurant, and a peppy waitress with her hair up in a bun took their orders. He ordered a cheeseburger with fries and a Coke. She ordered a Caesar salad with grilled chicken and bottled water.

He smiled at her. "Our second date."

She frowned. "Don't start. I told you I don't date people from the hospital. You said you were going to be good."

"I don't remember saying that."

"It was implied."

"Is that dating rule, hard and fast, or something we can discuss over dinner tonight?"

"It's a hard and fast rule and not open to negotiation."

He was quiet for a moment and chose his next words carefully. "You know, Jasmine, just because you've been hurt doesn't mean you should harden your heart."

She looked up at him with a serious expression. "And just what is that supposed to mean?"

"It means bad news travels faster than the speed of light and that, my beautiful friend, is pretty darn fast."

She was silent for a minute and then said, "You heard about Dave?"

"Yes, I heard about Dave."

"How could you possibly have heard about Dave?"

"It's a small town," he replied coyly not wanting to blow her parents in as the blabber mouths.

She rolled her eyes. "You've only been here two days and you heard about Dave? I can't believe it."

"I heard that you two were pretty close."

"Then you must certainly understand how I feel?"

"I do although I hope you realize how lucky you are to have escaped from a man of such weak moral character. One way of thinking about it is he did you a favor."

"Oh he did me a favor, did he?"

"It's one way of thinking about it."

"I don't want to discuss this anymore."

"That's okay with me. I just want to be friends and if you need someone to talk to then I'm your man."

She softened up. "Thank you."

"When you fall off that horse you have to get right back on."

"Enough already."

He hesitated and then said meekly, "Giddyup."

She glared at him as their server placed their food in front of them. They started eating, and after a couple of bites he looked up and said seriously, "Did I tell you how much I hate you?"

She put her fork down and looked sad. "Please don't be like that."

"I'm not talking about that. Geez, you're obsessed. I mean that story you told me about the Night Nurse and the murders in the old hospital. I wound up sleeping there last night because of my car and had a terrible time. My imagination ran roughshod over my ability to reason."

He told her about what happened. She couldn't help herself and laughed. "I'm sorry. It wasn't my intention to do that to you."

"Well, you did and now I hate you."

"You don't really hate me, do you?"

They held each other's gaze for a moment and he smiled. "No, I don't really hate you."

She smiled back. "How are you planning to manage without a car?"

"Hopefully, it will only be for a day or two. I don't really have any place to go although I do need to pick up a pair of sneakers. I've been wearing dress shoes for two days straight and my feet are killing me."

She thought it over for a bit and said, "I'd be honored to drive you to a sporting goods store or wherever it is you would like to buy men's footwear as compensation for telling you that scary story."

"Thank you. I'd appreciate that. If you really mean it then maybe we could go after lunch? I'd love to put my feet into something more comfortable."

"No problem... So the place really spooked you?"

"It got under my skin for sure and one of the OR nurses really compounded it."

"Sandy?"

"Yeah, you know her?"

"Everyone does. She's a real conspiracy theorist and black arts fanatic. There's nothing that has happened since the dawn of man that she doesn't believe the Free Masons are behind."

Cesari thought that was funny. "I sensed she was little out there, but she did mention something that you didn't; that Levi Blackburn was a raging Satanist who was trying to conjure up the devil that night. I did a little research on old Levi and he really was a devil worshipper. He belonged to some cult called the Order of Nine Angels."

She shrugged. "Yeah, I've heard that story. Everyone has. What difference does it make? I mean, no matter how you cut it, he snapped. Does it really matter whether some voice in his head told him to do it or if he was trying to conjure up the devil? I mean who cares? Unless you're going to sit there and tell me you honestly believe that Satan came for him, like Sandy does."

She made a good point. He said, "I guess you're right. Either way he was nuts although..."

She finished her salad and dabbed her lips with a napkin. "Although, what?"

"According to what I read, he was found hanging without a chair or trip stool nearby. That's a little hard to explain, and the blood on the floor… I read about it all afternoon. It was a perfect pentagram without any smudges. If he drew the pentagram and then hung himself directly over it, he would have smeared the blood at least a little, and even more interesting. Only one account mentioned this but there was no blood on Levi's body when they took him down."

"So he washed his hands before he hung himself."

"No blood at all; not his hands or his clothes. Not possible. Multiple eyewitnesses say the victim from whom the blood came was butchered badly and blood had splashed all over the room. There's no possible way he could have avoided getting some of it on himself."

She shook her head. "I see Sandy got to you. Look, it was fifty years ago. Forensic science was still in its infancy. There's no way of looking back now and being sure of anything that happened that night including that they performed a careful inspection of the crime scene. You add that to a gullible society that wanted to believe in a supernatural explanation then almost anything would seem possible."

"I feel like you're trying to talk me out of something."

"I am. I'm trying to talk you out of getting sucked into conspiracy theory hell where you'll spend the rest of your life peeking out the side of your window shades at night like Sandy."

He laughed. "So you're not buying it?"

"No, I'm not."

"What about lunch?"

"What about it?"

"Are you buying that? I mean, as long as it's not a date…"

She pursed her lips in a wry little smile. "Fine, but I'm charging you for gas and for wear and tear on my tires and suspension system."

"Fair enough."

The waitress came with the check and he grabbed it quickly taking out his wallet. She said, "No, I want to pay."

"Then you should have moved faster."

"Are you always like this?"

"Like what?"

"Difficult, and it's still not a date and you still owe me for gas," she said with a big smile.

"Maybe it's not a date now, but one day when I'm telling our children the story of how we met I'll want them to know how nice I was to you despite your being so mean."

She snorted. "Oh my God… Where did they ever find you?"

Chapter 11

You still got it, Cesari

After they stopped to pick up a pair of sneakers, Jasmine parked her car along the curb about a half block away from the Dulles House. Cesari thought it odd that she didn't bring him right to the front of the inn but didn't mention it. Instead he said, "Thank you for being so nice, Jasmine. You didn't have to chauffeur me around like this. I really appreciate it."

"I didn't mind. I didn't have much else to do today. Besides, I have to admit, you make me laugh."

"Laugh?"

"Yeah, you're funny."

"You think I'm funny?"

She thought about that for a moment. "Sure, very funny. Why?"

He groaned, "This is so bad."

"What is?"

"Women never sleep with guys they think are funny."

She laughed. "You see. There you go. You said you weren't going to bring it up again."

"I did?"

"Yes, you did."

"I can't help it. I think I'm in love."

She rolled her eyes. "That's sad because there are at least ten guys ahead of you in my cue."

"Ten guys ahead of me? You didn't tell me that."

"I didn't want to hurt your feelings."

"Ten?" he repeated.

"Maybe one or two more. I lost count."

"You know what this means?"

"What?"

"I'm going to have to step up my game."

Grinning she said, "I'll say."

He smiled at her and changed the subject. "Do you live in town?"

"Not too far away... You didn't tell me you were staying at the Dulles House."

"You didn't ask. Does it matter?"

"No, it's a nice place. I know the owner."

"Brom?"

"Yes, we went to school together."

Cesari knew the backstory but didn't let on. "Well, he's done quite well for himself."

"Yes he has, financially anyway."

Cesari let that pass. "I heard he's got quite the apiary in the back of the house."

"Quite... He's the largest producer of honey in this county and his mead wins awards every year. It's even been mentioned in *Wine Spectator*. The inn also gets a nod in TripAdvisor every year as an upstate destination. The current chef has won the James Beard award for culinary excellence."

Cesari was impressed. Without mentioning his chance encounter with her parents, he said, "I've heard a lot about the mead already. I even had a glass last night. Pretty good stuff. For a bee-keeper, Brom's doing all right."

Unconsciously, she glanced around nervously for a second. Cesari asked, "Is everything all right?"

"Please don't ever call him that to his face."

"What? Bee-keeper?"

"Yes, he hates that. He feels it's demeaning. He prefers the term apiculturist."

Cesari found that amusing. "I'll keep that in mind. Say, would you like to come in for a minute? There's a great lounge area with a fireplace. I know it's early, but we could have a club soda. The bartender's a friend of mine."

"You make friends fast." She hesitated and added, "I would love to... but I can't."

"If it's the whole I don't date people from the hospital thing again, I wish to reassure you that I'm over it... Just a club soda between two... co-workers."

She sighed. "It's a little complicated. I hope you don't mind, and I do have to get back to work."

"It sounds like there's a story somewhere in there..." he said hoping to persuade her into telling him more.

"There is..." Very reluctantly she added, "Brom and I... Well, we..."

She was obviously uncomfortable, and he decided not to push it. She had opened up the door a little. That was enough for now. He said, "You and Brom have a history. I get it. You don't have to say anymore. I understand."

"Do you?"

"I do."

"It's not that I never come here. It's that if I were to come alone with a man like this... it might... upset him."

"Understood. I'll let you go. Thanks for the ride and also for the pleasant company." He looked serious and said, "Number eleven in the cue? I'll have to remember that."

Giggling she said, "Actually, you might be number twelve or thirteen. I'll have to do a recount."

"Do me a favor. If there's a cancellation, please move me up the list."

"Oh I will. That's a promise."

She drove off and he felt a little bad about not mentioning that her parents had invited him to dinner tonight. Jasmine was obviously damaged and not ready for an overdose of Cesari. He needed to take baby-steps and let her gradually become accustomed to him hanging around. He had the feeling that if he had told her, she might not show up.

As he approached the inn, he decided to take a walk around to the back. He was curious about the bee hives and honey-house, so he ambled along the paved driveway at the side of the building. It led to the rear guest parking lot and then another one hundred yards back of the inn were all the hives, which were three-foot-long rectangular boxes stacked neatly on each other. Each box was about six inches deep and each hive was comprised of four or five stacked boxes. Cesari approached to within about twenty feet and held his ground. There were at least a hundred such hives and in the middle of a beautiful day they were very active with bees gathering the last bits of pollen in preparation for winter.

He wasn't afraid of bees per se but had a healthy respect for them. Several came near him and he gently shooed them away. The honey-house nearby was about the size of a two-story home. There was an open garage door with a large pickup backed in with the front cab sticking out. The structure was very old and had been painted and renovated several times. All things considered, it was in pretty good shape from what Cesari could see. He heard activity coming from within.

Walking up to the entrance, he peeked inside. The smell from the ancient honey-permeated wood nearly overwhelmed him with its fragrance. It was almost like being in the cellar of a winery only with a sweeter, lighter scent. He saw a shirtless Brom with his back to him lifting heavy honey combs from the back of the pickup and placing them on a conveyor belt that slowly moved toward what looked like a gigantic washing machine which in turn rotated slowly on its horizontal axis.

Brom was a beast made of solid muscle and sweat dripped down his bulging sinews. There was a lot of un-tainted Viking blood in this guy, Cesari thought. Brom had an odd tattoo across his broad back, *ONA*. It was three simple letters written in old English. Cesari had no idea what that meant. He thought about politely knocking on the door and asking for a tour. He was curious to learn how things worked here but something told him not to disturb Brom while he was toiling, so he discreetly backed away and returned to the inn.

Outside his room, hanging from the doorknob wrapped in plastic was his suit and dress shirt, dry cleaned and pressed, looking like new. He would wear that tonight at dinner with the Van Tassels, but first things first. He looked at his watch. It was 3:30 p.m. He let the water run in the bath tub as he called Arnold Goldstein, the medical director at St. Matt's hospital, his previous place of employment.

"Good afternoon, Dr. Goldstein."

"Cesari, I was wondering when you would call. I hear you've been very busy."

"I have been Arnie, and I might add that I'm a tad insulted at the way you threw me overboard."

"What are you talking about?"

"Some yahoo from upstate calls you out of the blue and tells you I'm not showing up to work Monday and you say no problem we've got it covered? Geez, I didn't realize I was that unimportant."

"Oh, quit you're crying. I did you a favor and I'm glad you found a decent job. Your new CEO sounds like a great guy. Funny as all get out. He had me in stitches on the phone. Did he tell you he offered me a job as a hematologist up there?"

Arnie was the chief of Hematology-Oncology at St. Matt's as well as its Medical Director for life. Cesari wasn't surprised. He was already getting used to Sal's over-the-top way of doing business. "He didn't but I'm not shocked. He tends to make snap decisions. Did you say yes?"

Arnie chuckled, "No, but I was tempted. The guy's a real schmoozer. I might come up for some winter fishing with him. He's got a cabin in the Adirondacks."

Cesari couldn't believe his ears. "I'm glad you like my new boss. Look Arnie, what do I have to do to wrap things up down there?"

"Send me an email with your formal resignation and at some point, you'll have to figure out a way to sign off on any of your incomplete medical records. Some of it you can do remotely but some you may have to drop by in person to sign. If you can't come by in person, I'll arrange to have them mailed to you. I'll leave your username and password active for a couple of weeks, so you can tidy things up."

"Thanks."

"No problem. I hope things work out and if they don't, check back with us again next year. You never know how the wind is going to blow with these things."

"I'll keep that in mind."

He hung up and placed the phone down next to the porcelain tub. The water was perfect, so he stripped down and got in. After a few minutes, he was so relaxed he felt like closing his eyes but then a thought crossed his mind and he smiled as he picked up the phone again.

He searched for the nearest florist and dialed the number. It wasn't quite 5:00 p.m. and they were still open. A young woman answered and he said, "Hi, could I have a dozen of the most beautiful long stem red roses you have delivered to the Dulles House?"

"Sure thing. Would you like them boxed or in a vase?"

He thought it over and said, "I'd like them in a bouquet, so I can hand them to someone special."

"Sure thing. Can I have your name please?"

"Dr. John Cesari."

"How would you like the card addressed?"

"That won't be necessary. I'll handle that. I'm in room 7 on the third floor."

"They'll be there in an hour."

"Thank you."

He gave her his credit card number and expiration date which he had committed to memory. The cost surprised him as it was half of what he would have expected to pay in New York, an unexpected perk of country living.

An hour later, he dried off, flexed in the mirror and thought, *You still got it, Cesari.* Putting on a robe, he walked into the living room and noticed someone had slipped a card under his door. It was an invitation to a Halloween party next weekend right here at the Dulles House in the main ballroom downstairs. Costume required.

Sure, why not. Go with the flow. If everyone in this town wanted to go nuts over candied apples and playing dress-up, why should he rain on their parade? There were much worse things people could do in their spare time. According to Sal and Dicky, he could expect to see many parties going on all week leading up to the weekend and culminating in the big hospital gala next Saturday on Halloween night itself at some placed called the Emerson Pavilion located on the lake. There would be a five-piece band, cocktail party, buffet dinner and open bar all night. Thousands were expected to attend. The party at the Dulles House on Friday night would surely be a much smaller, refined affair he had no doubt.

He tossed the invitation down onto the bed and finished dressing just as the flowers arrived at fifteen minutes past six. He tipped and thanked the delivery guy and placed the flowers on the dresser. He needed to do one more thing before he was ready. Along with the basic toiletries he had picked up at Walmart was a bottle of inexpensive after-shave, Drakkar Noir, his signature scent. It was a dangerous move, but he felt he needed to roll the dice with Jasmine. Drakkar Noir blended with his particular body oils in such a way that caused havoc with most women's hormonal systems rendering them helpless or occasionally insanely aggressive sexually. He splashed some on and grinned at his reflection.

Now he was ready.

Chapter 12

The Honey-House

Cesari waited in his room until 7:15 p.m. The reservation was for seven but he wanted to be fashionably late. He was sure Mr. and Mrs. Van Tassel wouldn't say anything to Jasmine about him because they wanted it to be a surprise, and he was just as certain that had she known she would have said something earlier. He straightened out his blue tie one last time, picked up the bouquet of roses and went downstairs.

The dining room was on the other side of the main entranceway across from the bar. As far as restaurants went, it was small with fewer than two dozen tables, half of them for four and the other half for two. The lights had been turned low for mood and intimacy. Linen table cloths and bees wax candles in pewter holders were lit in the center of each table giving rise to a romantic ambience. What it was lacking in size it more than made up for in elegance and charm. There was a twelve-foot-wide brick fireplace with a six-foot long log in its center burning slowly, rendering an earthy smell and feel to the room. The pine wood floors and roughhewn timber lined ceiling spoke to the age of the house and shimmered in the soft warm glow of the fire. Over the wood mantle was a large oil painting of an older couple. She was a full-bodied woman with shoulder length gray hair pulled back and very expensive taste in jewelry. The man was large and bald with bushy old-fashioned sideburns. They both had stoic, puritanical expressions on their faces.

Cesari spotted the Van Tassels sitting at a table near the hearth talking to Brom. Brom wore a tuxedo with a white bowtie and was in the process of greeting them as he handed out menus. Cesari approached and everyone looked in his direction. Jasmine's eyes went wide as did Brom's, but the elder Van Tassels smiled warmly. Balthazar stood to shake his hand.

Balthazar said to Jasmine, "I took the liberty of inviting this young man to join us. He told us last night that he worked with you at the hospital and I thought this would be a nice way of welcoming him to town."

Jasmine stood as well but was nearly speechless. Brom was apprehensive and eyed the bouquet of flowers suspiciously. Cesari said, "Hello everyone. I'm sorry I'm late."

Balthazar said, "Nonsense. We've barely just arrived ourselves. Do join us."

Cesari nodded at Brom and turned to Jasmine. "Hello… You look very nice." Her hair was made up and she wore a dark green, knee length dress with a braided gold necklace, matching earrings and modest heels. He added, "The color of your dress complements your eyes well. I've always been partial to hazel for some reason."

Blushing, she tried to suppress the surprise in her voice. "Thank you… I… I didn't even know you and my parents were acquainted."

Hannah said, "We met him last night over drinks, dear. Such a lovely young man. We thought we'd surprise you with his company."

Brom got down to business. "Would you like something to drink, Doctor? Everyone ordered a round of martinis just before your arrival."

"A martini would be fine; vodka, shaken not stirred with a twist of lemon, but first things first. I have a bouquet of the most beautiful red roses money could buy and I'd like to present them to one of the most attractive and vibrant young women I have ever met."

Jasmine turned scarlet again and held her breath as Brom's eyes flashed. Cesari held out the bouquet a little and just as Jasmine moved ever so slightly to receive it, he brushed past her to Hannah and placed it in her arms saying, "Happy fiftieth anniversary, Hannah. I wasn't at the wedding but judging from your daughter's beauty, I am sure you were the envy of every girl in town."

Balthazar glowed, "She was indeed, Dr. Cesari…and still is."

"What a sweet thing to do. Thank you so very much, Doctor," gushed Hannah. She sniffed the flowers with a satisfied look and rose to give Cesari a hug saying again, "Thank you so much."

Jasmine was embarrassed at having thought the flowers were for her but recovered quickly. "That was tremendously kind of you, John."

He responded, "Fifty years is quite a milestone and should be recognized."

"I agree," added Balthazar. "What about those drinks, Brom?"

Brom who had been frozen in place watching the scene unfold said, "I'll place the order right now."

He turned to leave but Cesari stopped him. "One moment, Brom. Certainly, we'll have cocktails, Balthazar, but only after we've toasted you and Hannah properly. Brom, could you please bring us a bottle of your best champagne?"

Brom's features had darkened considerably since Cesari's arrival. He didn't appreciate being upstaged in his own playground and he didn't like the way Jasmine seemed captivated by the newcomer.

He said, "Certainly. Will Dom Perignon be satisfactory?"

"If we were in the middle of a desert and on the verge of dehydration, yes, but since this is a very special celebration, I'd prefer Bollinger1988. Extra Brut if you have it."

Brom's eyes went wide and the color rose in his cheeks. He nodded and murmured something about checking. Tail between his legs, he backed away and Hannah called out, "And Brom please have someone place these lovely roses in a vase for me. I'd like to look at them during dinner."

"I will take care of that promptly, Mrs. Van Tassel."

She thanked him, and they all sat down, boy girl, boy girl. Cesari looked across at Balthazar's rotund features. The man was grinning ear to ear and said, "Lad, you certainly know how to make an entrance."

Cesari smiled, "That's nothing. Wait until you see me make an exit."

Balthazar guffawed, and the women laughed. Jasmine said, "I don't know too much about champagne but that sounded expensive."

"Not to worry. We'll drink half the bottle and then send it back. We'll tell Brom it had turned to vinegar and he should comp us the entire meal for our trouble or we'll call TripAdvisor."

Jasmine put her hand over her mouth to suppress her giggling. Balthazar guffawed again, and Hannah couldn't stop smiling. Balthazar said, "I think Brom would have a heart attack."

A waiter set champagne flutes down in front of them, and another placed the vase of roses in the center of the table. Brom came out seconds later with a bottle of champagne and leaned over to whisper something in Cesari's ear.

Cesari nodded and looked disappointed. He said, "That will be fine. I'll get over it."

Brom opened the bottle and filled their glasses. After Brom left Jasmine asked seriously, "Is everything all right?"

"Not really. They didn't have the 1988 Bollinger only the 1996. It was a good year just not a great year."

Balthazar exclaimed, "Heaven's sake! What's the world coming to when a man can't even get decent bottle of champagne in upstate New York."

They all laughed again and then they toasted Balthazar and Hannah. By the time they finished the bottle, martinis were set in front of them with their appetizers and Brom was opening a bottle of mead in anticipation of dinner. Cesari noticed the nasty glances in his direction and was a little taken aback by it. He hadn't been that rough on the guy, and he had assumed that whatever went on between Jasmine and him was in the remote past. He had his own share of childhood crushes and knew how painful they could be, but everyone needed to grow up including Brom, so all things considered, he had no sympathy for him.

Dinner was arguably the best venison Cesari had ever had, sautéed in a mushroom cream and cognac sauce, with roasted root vegetables and house-baked French baguette smothered in a honey butter rosemary mixture. The mead went well with the meal but Cesari felt a California Russian River Pinot Noir would have paired better. Dessert was a honey flavored crème brulee and by the time they finished they were all ready to loosen their belts a notch or two.

After dinner, Cesari and Balthazar fought politely over the bill and Cesari only yielded when Balthazar challenged him to arm wrestle for it. They left the restaurant at around 11:00 p.m. tipsy and exhausted. Cesari walked them to the parking lot and helped Hannah into her seat. He spoke to Balthazar for a few minutes to make sure he was sober enough to drive. He was a big man, and this wasn't his first rodeo. Cesari felt he was okay and let him go.

Jasmine and Cesari stepped back and watched them drive away. She had driven herself and they walked to her car. When they reached it, he found she was in no hurry to leave so they leaned back against the Honda taking in the night air.

She said just a teeny bit sarcastically, "You are quite the charmer, aren't you?"

"Me?"

"Please… you had them eating out of your hands and you know it."

He laughed. "I'm sure I don't know what you're talking about."

"I'm sure you do, but just so we're clear…nothing's changed."

"It wasn't my intention to change anything. Besides, I'm only number thirteen on the list. I'm prepared to wait for my turn."

She smiled and nodded. "That's good. Anyway, I think you made an enemy out of Brom tonight. I'm sure he sees you as a rival now."

"Brom? From our conversation earlier, I wouldn't have thought he was even on the list."

"He isn't, but I'm not sure he sees it that way."

"Well, he'll get over it. They always do."

"They always do? Who are they?"

"The lesser males, of course."

She shook her head in exasperation. "Let's take a walk."

He liked where this was going. "Sure, where to?"

"The honey-house. I'll give you a tour."

"It's awfully dark there," he said looking over her shoulder toward the back of the property.

She opened the car trunk and reached in coming out with a twelve-inch mag-light and a pair of sneakers. Cesari smiled as she took off her dress shoes and put on the sneakers. She explained, "You never know when you're going to break down on a dark country road and might have to walk a mile or more to find help."

He nodded, "Smart. Plus, a flashlight that size is a pretty good weapon."

"I'm glad you noticed. I'd hate to have to use it on you… C'mon, let's go."

They walked along a narrow path to the honey-house. The night air was cool and the ground moist. Crickets chirped noisily along the way. They reached the hive area and examined several of them up close. The bees were resting quietly inside, and she said, "Get close and listen."

He did and heard a low rhythmic humming. "What's that sound?"

"The bees keep warm by contracting and relaxing their wing muscles. It generates heat. They are able to dislocate their wings, so they stay in place, but with so many bees the vibration still makes a little sound."

"Interesting."

"In the dead of winter, they form a ball and the center can reach ninety degrees Fahrenheit. They rotate their positions periodically, so everybody stays warm."

"Like Emperor penguins in the Antarctic?"

"Exactly."

"They don't hibernate?"

"No, that's why they make so much honey. It's what they live on during the cold months."

Cesari nodded. This was all new to him and he was fascinated by it. Jasmine signaled him to follow her to the honey-house. The door was locked, and she searched around eventually finding a spare key hidden under a ceramic turtle placed aesthetically near an evergreen bush.

She turned to him. "I haven't been here in a while but Brom has always been a creature of habit when it comes to things like this. If you ever forget your key to the front door there's a spare one under the door mat."

"Practical, but not very clever."

"Not at all."

They went inside. "You know what all this equipment is?" he asked glancing around at the array of machinery.

"Oh yeah, I've been here many times. In fact I practically grew up here, and Brom proposed to me the first time right over there." She pointed at the conveyor belt he had seen earlier. "I was helping him unload the honey combs at the time and place them on the belt."

Pretending not to know the story he feigned surprise. "Brom proposed to you?"

She sighed. "Yes, many times but the first time was right here in the honey-house. It was right after his parents disappeared and he took over the inn and apiary. We were barely twenty-one years old."

"His parents disappeared?"

"Yes, a little more than ten years ago. He had just graduated college and I had just started working at the hospital. They were quite the intrepid world travelers and went on an expedition to explore the Amazon. They never returned. It was awful."

Cesari nodded in agreement. "That's terrible, and no one knows what happened?"

She shook her head. "No, the whole exploration party including the guides vanished. They were deep in the rainforest and hundreds of miles from even the vaguest semblance of civilization."

"Was that their portrait hanging over the mantle in the restaurant?"

"Yes, it was. They had it commissioned less than a year before the tragedy. The portrait is so life-like that sometimes it feels as though they're still with us. They were good people. Brom was devastated."

Cesari let that sink in before saying, "Brom wasn't the love of your life, I gather?"

She took a deep breath and let it out. "No, he wasn't. We were childhood sweethearts and dated throughout high school and most of college. It took me a while to understand my feelings. I tried to let him down easy, but he didn't take it well. It was a very difficult time for everyone. Our families have known each other for generations. Everyone in town expected us to marry and with his parents gone, he felt that I had abandoned him when he needed me most. While there have been other men in my life, I have tried not to flaunt it in his face. However, I also refuse to live my life in fear of offending him."

Cesari nodded, "Good policy... Out of curiosity, just how upset would he be if he found us here now?"

"Good question. I don't know. He only proposes to me once a year now, so we've made progress in that area."

"You're kidding?"

She shook her head. "Unfortunately, I'm not. He feels it's our destiny."

"I'm very sorry to hear that. This has to be very difficult for you."

"It used to be much worse, but I've developed a thick skin and have simply accepted my fate. I suppose I could have moved away and maybe I will one day. To further answer your question about how Brom would feel about us being here you should know that I have come here many times before without asking his permission to show the honey-house to other nurses and their children. Brom told me long ago that I could do so anytime. He felt it was good for public relations and therefore good for business although I suspect his real reason was that he felt it kept us close. It's been at least a year since the last time I came. Realistically speaking, I doubt that he would let on he was upset but it's rather hard to believe he wouldn't be deep down."

Changing the subject Cesari asked, "Where does that pipe lead to?" He pointed to a metal pipe at the bottom of the washing machine-like device he saw earlier. It led through the floor boards into the level below."

"That's the honey extractor. The combs go on the conveyor belt there and are fed into the extractor. The extractor turns slowly allowing the honey to drain out by gravity. It collects in the funnel below and flows down that pipe you pointed to into a collecting vat in the cellar. Let's go downstairs and I'll show it to you."

They walked down an old rickety staircase and at the bottom, she flipped a switch, turning on a series of incandescent bulbs attached to the ceiling. Three of the four walls were field stone giving the room a damp, eerie feel. The fourth and far wall was made of old brick, stained, faded and crumbling in places, in desperate need of pointing. There were bits of wax, dried honey, and dead bees all over the floor. The smell of honey was almost overwhelming in the confined space. In the center of the room was a large rectangular metal box twenty-five feet long by ten feet wide by six feet deep. It rested on the concrete floor and was connected to the honey extractor upstairs at one end by the pipe he had seen. The side of the container had a set of dials, gauges and spigots.

He commented, "Pretty tall ceiling for an old basement."

"Yes, but this used to be the carriage house for the estate years ago and those old carriages were quite large. Before that it was possibly a barn. I believe they may even have kept horses down here at one point before they sealed the wall up. Whatever, I'm sure they had their reasons. People back then were very practical and rarely did things without a purpose."

Lined up neatly along one of the walls were many rows of glass jars of various sizes and shapes to pour the honey into for sale, and finally, there were large metal drums that were used to transport the raw honey to the wine-maker for mead production.

Duly impressed, Cesari asked, "How many gallons does it hold at once?"

"Filled to the top over ten thousand gallons, give or take."

"That's a lot of honey."

"Yes, it is."

"What are the hoses for?" Cesari asked, noting a garden hose hanging on the wall.

"Twice a year, Brom cleans out the honey vat with a good hosing. There's a dry well and sump pump in one of the corners to clear the water out."

Cesari walked close to the metal box, studying it. In the front was a three-step metal ladder leading to small platform to allow someone to look and work inside the vat comfortably. Along the outside perimeter at the upper edge was a series of metal clasps. He assumed that once undone the top would lift off, probably with some difficulty, but Brom looked like a strong guy.

There was a wood bench against a wall and Jasmine went over and sat down, patting the space next to her as an invitation. He followed and sat beside her. She studied him quietly for what seemed like a long time. Eventually, she said, "That was a mean trick you played on me with the roses. You knew darn well I was going to think they were for me."

He let out a little laugh. "I agree. It was kind of mean. I'm sorry. I'll get you some tomorrow."

She giggled, "It's not necessary… It was a nice gesture. My mother loved it." She hesitated and sighed. "What am I going to do with you?"

He looked into her eyes and lowering his voice said, "Whatever you damn well want to."

She liked that. "I want to kiss you."

"I promise not to defend myself."

"I can't with the lights on."

He laughed. "You're one of those?"

She smiled and nodded so he walked over to the stairs and flipped the overhead lights off. Turning the flashlight on she guided him back to the bench, and as he sat, she turned the light off and nestled in close. He put his arm around her and their lips met. They kissed longingly…slowly…ardently. He was surprised by her passion.

She tasted like…honey.

Chapter 13

Fettucine Bolognese

Cesari woke up Sunday morning feeling better than he had in a long time. It was 9:00 a.m. and he was famished. He looked at his phone and saw two missed calls and a couple of texts from Jasmine. The last text from an hour ago read, *How about Breakfast?*

He called her immediately, but she didn't answer so he texted her to come and get him if the offer still stood. Jumping in the shower he cleaned up quickly and threw on jeans. As he came out of the bathroom, he saw another text from her to meet him outside on the front walk.

Twenty minutes later, they were drinking coffee in an old run-down diner on Main Street waiting for buttermilk pancakes and local maple syrup. She wore black leggings and a red top. It was a blue-collar joint that specialized in grease fried in more grease. Overweight locals in flannel shirts sat hunched over large mounds of eggs and bacon and hash browns. Cesari noticed that a house specialty was a thirty-two-ounce chocolate malted milk shake, waffles, and fried chicken. As far as he was concerned everyone in the place ought to see a cardiologist right after they finished their meals.

Paint peeled here and there, and the drop ceiling had water stains, but Cesari and Jasmine were too busy smiling at each other to care about the décor or lack thereof. She giggled, "I feel so silly."

"Why?"

She cocked her head smiling, and said, "Really? Making out in the honey-house at midnight…in the dark? Kind of high schoolish, don't you think?"

"Making out? I haven't heard that expression in a long time. I don't even think kids today say that anymore. Besides, making out is a bit of a stretch. We kissed once. That's all."

"We kissed twice…and hugged."

"It was more of an extended first kiss with a follow up chaser and how are you supposed to kiss without hugging?"

She laughed. "Still, it felt…"

"Felt…what?"

She got quiet as she pondered him almost as if for the first time and sighed. "It felt good."

"Yes it did feel good…very good."

"Well, I hope you don't think I bring guys to the honey-house for that purpose as a routine."

"It never entered my mind until you just said that, and before this gets blown out of proportion, you didn't do anything to be ashamed of."

"Thank you, and I have to admit. Considering the circumstances, you were a real gentleman."

Laughing he said, "And I have to admit. I can't remember the last time all I got from a girl was a kiss and didn't feel short-changed."

"Well, I'm glad for that, but…"

She was suddenly very serious. "But what...?" he asked.

She took a deep breath and let it out. "I shouldn't have done that...kissed you. I don't know what came over me. I drank too much."

He rolled his eyes. "Seriously? You're going to blame it on the mead and the champagne?"

"We did have quite a bit."

"You don't have to hide behind the alcohol, Jasmine."

"I just don't want you to think of that kiss as a...promissory note."

He laughed and then said just a little bit more loudly than necessary, "Hey everybody, this girl gave me a promissory note and now she's trying to renege on the deal."

She glanced around quickly, her cheeks crimson. "Shhh...lower your voice." No one noticed his antics and she continued, "Stop, it's just that I'm so embarrassed."

"Why?"

"I don't know. I just am. You're so different."

"I hope you don't mean different as in requires certain types of calming medications."

She grinned. "I meant different as in really nice different."

"That settles it then. I want no more talk of honey-house kissing and embarrassment. However, I would like to add that I think you, Miss Jasmine Van Tassel, are one very special person and I am truly looking forward to getting to know you better."

She didn't say anything for a moment and he thought she might cry. She didn't and whispered, "Thank you."

"I also wish to reassure you that I have not misinterpreted last night's show of affection. Placed in proper context, it was merely a symbol of your gratitude for the kindness and generosity I showed your parents."

The waitress placed their food in front of them and they patiently waited for her to leave before they continued.

He said, "So what now?"

She seemed relieved at his attitude. "I don't know. I certainly think I would like to get to know you better too, but as long we agree to move slowly."

"I agree to the terms and conditions as set forthwith. I guess a celebration is in order. What can we do on a beautiful fall day like this in Auburn?"

"We can go for a walk by the lake and take in the foliage."

"I'd like that. Is that slow enough for you?"

She laughed. "Yes, it is."

As he sipped his coffee, his phone rang. It was the hospital. He answered and spoke for a few minutes asking questions and waiting for answers. When he hung up, he looked unhappy.

He said, "I have to go into the hospital and see a patient. It shouldn't take too long."

"Aw, that's too bad, but it'll be nice all day. We can go for that walk when you're done. Should we get the bill or do we have time to finish breakfast?"

"No, we can eat. It's not that urgent. There's a patient who's been in the hospital since last Wednesday with anemia and somebody finally noticed."

She looked concerned. "Really? It took them almost a week to realize they needed a consult?"

He nodded. "To be fair, he's an old guy and had a bunch of other things going on which took priority. The doctors are just working their way down the list of problems."

"And they figured it all out on Sunday morning?"

He smiled. "It's like this everywhere. Some doctor takes over a case on the weekend and decides he has to clean up whatever mess the doctor before him left behind. I'm used to it…These pancakes are amazing by the way, light and fluffy the way they should be all the time."

"They really are."

He watched her eat. "I know it's not appropriate for me to say this, but you really have quite a healthy appetite."

Smiling she said, "You mean for a girl?"

He nodded, "Yeah."

"How am I going to finish eating now? You just made me self-conscious," she said playfully.

"Here's a big head's up. Women have been known to develop eating disorders because of my big mouth."

"I'll bet, but don't worry. That won't happen to me. I love to eat and cook, and I don't care what anybody thinks about it."

"Good for you. What do you like to cook?"

"Everything, but Italian is my favorite."

"Seriously?"

"Oh yeah, I make my own pasta and everything."

"Somebody pinch me. I think I just died and went to heaven."

She was pleased with herself. "You like that?"

"You're never going to get rid of me now. That was a tactical mistake from which you may never recover."

"Ha."

"So what's your favorite dish?"

"There are so many."

"How about your best one?"

"That's easy," she replied. "Fettucine bolognese hands down. I can make it for you sometime."

"I would love that."

"Tonight?"

"Moving kind of fast, aren't we?"

She giggled and looked away.

He continued, "How about tomorrow night when I'm not on call? I'd rather not take the chance on having to walk out in the middle of a great home-made meal."

"You're on."

"How do you stay so thin if you like to cook and eat so much?"

"I run… a lot. I ran five miles this morning already."

"Really? Weren't you tired from last night? I could barely wake up this morning."

"I was exhausted." She cocked her head at him and smirked. "After you and I…you know…kissed, I couldn't even sleep I was so wound up. By 5:00 a.m., I had to blow off some steam, so I went for a run."

"I see," he said, finding her candor refreshing. Most women, in his experience, didn't usually let it all hang out like that. "I feel kind of bad. I fell asleep without a problem."

"Thanks for telling me that. Maybe it wasn't your first trip to the honey-house?"

He grinned, "That's right. There was this honey-house in the Bronx where I grew up. I took so many girls there they installed a revolving door for me."

"I had a feeling."

They finished breakfast and she drove him to the hospital. She got out and walked with him to the entrance. "Where are you going?" he asked.

"To my office. I'm supposed to write up a report about the time I spent with the state people yesterday. What happened, what kind of questions did they ask, what did I tell them? That kind of stuff."

"How long will that take?"

"An hour tops."

"I'll come to your office when I'm done."

"I'll make sure to wait."

"Then I'll make sure to come."

Once in the hospital they walked awkwardly, side by side, not too close and not too far apart. They tried to keep up an air of professionalism, in case anyone saw them, but he was afraid the grins on their faces would tell the whole story. One look at them and any self-respecting American female would know they had kissed in the honey-house. There was something about those kinds of kisses that left an indelible imprint on a person's face.

When they reached her office, they both gave out a sigh of relief at having arrived safely without running into any hospital busybodies that might have thought it peculiar seeing the two of them there together…alone…on a Sunday morning. Both were experienced enough in hospital gossip to know how fast and furious rumors spread, became exaggerated to larger than life proportions and how damaging and hurtful they could be.

She unlocked the door, stepped over the threshold inside and turned around to face him. They locked eyes and he desperately wanted to lean down and kiss her, just a quick one, but that would violate their agreement to move slowly.

So they stood there staring at each other. She said, "I'd ask you to come in but if somebody were to find us in here alone…"

She let it hang out there and he understood perfectly well the consequences of such reckless behavior. He glanced in both directions down the long corridor, saw no one, made a snap decision and stepped over the threshold into the room with her. She closed the door quickly behind him and started giggling. With complete and utter disregard for their guiding principle of 'going slow' with their new found friendship, they wrapped their arms around each other.

Chapter 14

The Old Man and The Sea

Cesari wandered onto the medical floor in search of the patient he was asked to consult on, his head reeling from thoughts of Jasmine. He had left her in the nursing office in a similarly confused state and he doubted she'd be able to get any work done.

At the nursing station he read the patient's chart. His name was Santiago Cortese and he was a sixty-year-old man with emphysema, hypertension, diabetes, heart disease, prostate cancer, status-post prostatectomy and radiation therapy five years ago, who smoked like a chimney and drank like a fish and couldn't care less what anyone thought about it. At least that was the message Cesari got from the admission note. He was married, had a grown daughter and was a retired truck driver.

He came in a week ago with bronchitis and had improved on antibiotics. His admission hemoglobin was on the low side but had continued to drift down even lower and his stool tested positive for blood. The consulting physician would like to know if the patient would benefit from a colonoscopy as he hasn't had one in ten years. Cesari thought that was funny. It was a running joke in his specialty that everyone would benefit from a colonoscopy whether they needed one or not.

He found the room and knocked gently on the door as he entered. The man's excessive lifestyle and medical problems had taken their toll on him and he looked much older than sixty as he sat in a chair wearing a robe, staring into a book. The bags under his eyes and his weathered, tobacco-stained skin told Cesari more about the man in one glance than any chart ever could. He was reading *The Old Man and The Sea*, by Ernest Hemingway, and Cesari wondered if there was some sort of metaphor here. He had an IV running into one arm and a tray nearby with an open carton of milk and an empty pudding container. It was a private room and he had a nice view of the parking lot.

Cesari said, "Mr. Cortese?"

He put the book down and brushed back his wispy silvery gray hair with his hand. "Please come in. How may I help you?"

Cesari walked up to him and extended his hand. "I'm Dr. Cesari, a gastroenterologist. Dr. Patel asked me to see you because of the blood in your stool."

"Dr. Patel you say? I never heard of him."

"He's the hospitalist doctor taking care of you."

"I'm telling you he's not my doctor and I've never heard of him. All I ever see in this place are nurses."

Cesari let out a deep breath. "I'll make sure he drops by this afternoon to say hello… May I sit down?"

"You're a pretty big guy. Do I look like I can stop you?"

Feisty but nothing he hadn't encountered before. Cesari sat on the edge of the bed and crossed his legs. Cantankerous patients weren't that uncommon in this setting. A week in a modern hospital was strenuous and very confusing for any-body. On any given day, multiple people came to visit every patient. The list was long and included rotating medical staff, nurse practitioners, physician's assistants, respiratory and physical therapists, social workers, billing agents, patient right's activists, and dieticians not to mention an army of nurses and nurse's aides. You could easily lose track of an individual in that mass of humanity.

Cesari said, "I would just like to ask you a few questions if I may?"

"Sure, and I'd like to ask you a few questions too if I may?"

"You're the patient. You get to start."

"Who's this Patel guy because he's not my doctor."

"I promise you I'll look into it."

"Fine, your turn."

"Have you noticed any blood when you move your bowels?"

"Yes, I've been telling them every day since I checked in. The only one who hasn't heard is that Patel guy because he's never been here."

Cesari smiled. The guy was growing on him. He decided to change tactics. "You like Hemingway?"

"How would I know? I never met him either."

Jesus!

"I meant are you enjoying the book you're reading?"

He lifted it up. "This? Yeah, I guess so. Have you read it?"

"Yes, I have. I thought it was quite powerful and thought provoking."

"I agree." Then he chuckled and said, "It's about a cranky old man like me. His name is even Santiago."

Cesari smiled. "You may be cranky but you're not that old."

He laughed, "You speak your mind. I like that, but I feel old. I should have taken better care of myself. Anyway, I enjoy reading about Cuba and Cubans. I'm Cuban you know."

"I didn't know. Were you born there?"

"No, I was born on a fifteen-foot-long refugee boat in the middle of the Atlantic Ocean. My mother fled the island when that bastard, Castro, took over. He shut down the airports to prevent people from leaving and everyone who could jumped onto anything that could float. That's how wonderful communism is. They caught my father trying to hock my mother's wedding ring, so we would at least have some money when we got to the U.S. They detained him for three years on a sugar plantation. Nearly worked him to death; beat him regularly, starved him, told him my mother drowned… all because he had some funny notion about freedom. And now these morons in Washington expect me and the others to forget all that because they want to start building casinos there again. Not a chance. They can all kiss my ass."

The bitterness in his voice was thick. Cesari had struck a chord and went with it. "What happened to your father?"

"They finally let him go. He was too weak to work, and they didn't want to waste anymore food on him. One day they put him in the back of a pickup truck, drove to some rural village, and rolled him out onto the center of the street and left him there. Some compassionate people took him in and nursed him back to health. He snuck onto a boat a full year later and in the middle of the night arrived on the shores of Florida. My mother, God bless her, never gave up hope. She stayed in Miami and checked the refugee camps every day looking for him. I was four years old when I first met my father, and I cried when I saw the whip marks on his back… Think about that. I was only four years old and I still remember it like it was yesterday."

He bowed his head, overwhelmed by the memories. Tears ran down his face and Cesari reached out to hold his hand. He said, "I'm sorry."

"Don't be. He wasn't. They never broke him. He never gave up his hope for a free Cuba and neither will I. Nor will I ever forget what they did to him."

Cesari nodded and was impressed with the man's fervor. Santiago said, "Now what is it you really want? Make it short and sweet, and in a way I can understand and we'll get along."

"You're losing blood somewhere and we need to take a look in your colon and your stomach to make sure you don't have an ulcer or cancer. You had a coloscopy once a long time ago, according to your records."

"I remember… Fine, then let's do it because I'm not ready to check out of this world yet."

"I'll take care of scheduling it. You'll have to drink some medication tonight to clean everything out but I'm sure you'll have no problem doing that. I know you had breakfast and that's fine, but don't eat anything else today."

"I'll do whatever it takes. What about pain? Is there going to be any?"

"We'll give you a light anesthetic, so you'll be asleep and comfortable during the procedure, but there are no guarantees. Do you want to hear all the possible complications?"

"Just the top three."

"Death…"

"That's enough. Just schedule it."

Cesari said goodbye to him and went to the nursing station where he took a seat with the chart. He wrote a short consult note and recommended both colonoscopy and upper endoscopy for evaluation of the man's anemia. Then he wrote nursing orders for the preparation. He introduced himself to a nurse, handed her the chart and summarized what needed to be done.

She said, "I can take written orders, but at some point you'll need to make an electronic entry for confirmation."

"I will as soon as I learn how. I promise. I'm still a little wet behind the ears when it comes to the EMR. I can look things up, but charting consults and orders is a bit more complicated."

"No problem, but you're lucky this hospital still does paper. I came from a place that was one hundred percent electronic... I'll flag it for medical records and they'll send you a triage about it to remind you. They won't let you forget to do it."

"Thanks." As he turned to leave, he hesitated and said, "Do you know Dr. Patel?"

"Of course, he's one of the hospitalists. I believe he's here today."

"Would you tell him that Mr. Cortese would like to meet him sometime if it's not too much trouble."

She gave him a knowing look. "I'll be sure to pass that along."

"Thanks."

He left and realized he wasn't too far from the cafeteria and decided to pick up a couple of coffees for him and Jasmine. As he paid for the beverages, he saw Herb Funkelman holding court with two other people in a booth. Herb caught Cesari's eye and signaled him to join the group. Cesari paused momentarily, not wanting to get caught up in politics or keep Jasmine waiting but concluded that a few minutes spent wisely might stave off the idea that maybe he was aloof or unfriendly. Once you got labeled like that, it was hard to shake it off. He was very new here and didn't want anyone to get the wrong impression...even Herb Funkelman.

He sat next to Herb and observed the two physicians across from them, one man and one woman, middle aged, wearing white coats with stethoscopes around their necks. They looked very generic. Herb said, "This is Cesari, a new gastroenterologist in town. This is literally his first weekend here. Cesari, meet Sally Webster and Max Jensen. Sally runs the rehab unit and Max is an ER doctor."

They all shook hands and smiled. Herb continued, "What are you doing here, Cesari? Got a case to do in the OR?"

"No, I had to do a consult for a hospitalist named Patel. Has anyone seen him by the way? I need to talk to him."

"Why don't you just call him?" offered Herb.

"I wanted to meet him. You know, new guy in town kind of stuff, but if it comes to it I will."

Sally said, "He's probably catching a smoke in the parking lot."

"Probably. He's a pretty bad chain smoker," Max concurred and then asked, "Are you on call all night?"

Cesari nodded, "Yeah, until the morning. You got something going on?"

"Not right now, but that could change in a heartbeat."

"Ain't that the truth."

Cesari sipped his coffee. Herb said, "Max and Sally think we have to take a stand too."

"What kind of stand?"

"C'mon Cesari, don't you listen? I told you the other day when we met. I'm forming a PAC to lobby in Washington for physician's rights."

"Physician's right's or physician's pay?"

"It's the same thing isn't it?"

"I don't know about that. The right to take care of my patients without having the albatross of an over-reaching government around my neck and in my jock strap isn't the same as expecting to make a lot of money."

"True, but since you're never going to get rid of the albatross you might as well make a lot of money."

"Define what a lot of money is. Because what a GI guy thinks is a lot of money may not be what an orthopedic surgeon thinks is a lot of money."

"Whose side are you on, Cesari?"

"I'm on the patient's side, Herb. Look, the day I got into medical school was the best day of my life. It was a dream come true, and as poor as I was, money never entered the equation. I wanted to become a physician to help people. I never thought about how much I was going to make or what I was going to do with the loot. The problem right now with healthcare isn't so much that physicians aren't being compensated adequately it's that we can't take care of our patients the way we ought to because of government intervention, insurance company shenanigans and regulatory agencies strangling us. They're forcing us to practice the way *they* think we should and not the way we learned. I don't have a problem with money, Herb, but if that's the focus of your PAC then you can count me out."

Sally and Max stared at him. She slowly raised her hand and pointed her index finger at Cesari. She said, "I want him to represent me in Washington, Herb, not you."

Max seconded that emotion. "Me too. If he represents us then I'll write you a check tomorrow, Herb."

Herb said, "Shit."

Cesari looked at his watch and said, "I got to go now. Somebody's waiting for me."

"You throw me under the bus and then you leave?" Herb said wryly.

"I didn't throw anybody under the bus..." he turned to the others, "...and although I appreciate the vote of confidence, I'm not going to Washington. I just want to be left alone."

"That's it?" Herb questioned incredulously.

Cesari stood to leave. "Yeah, that's it. It was nice meeting you both. See you around, Herb."

Herb said, "Shit."

Chapter 15

Nobody Fornicated with Anybody

Cesari found Jasmine standing on a chair in the nursing office hanging Halloween decorations and humming to herself. On the floor next to her was a large box of witches, goblins, ghosts, hanging spiders, and orange and black streamers. He stepped close just in time to assist her in positioning a large pumpkin on the wall.

She smiled. "You took too long. We were going to do this tomorrow, so I figured I'd get a head start."

"I got detained. I'll help you."

"Great. You finish this wall and I'll do the other. It'll only take a few minutes. I got most of it done already. We're way behind schedule with this stuff. Usually it's the first thing we do in October, but we've been swamped."

Thirty minutes later they wrapped things up and she put the box away. As they readied to leave the office, she gave the room one last satisfied inspection and said, "How was your patient? You didn't say."

"He's fine. I scheduled him for a couple of procedures tomorrow, but I'll need your help with entering the orders into his electronic record. The nurse accepted the hand-written ones for now."

"Let's do that now. It'll only take five minutes."

She fired up one of the terminals in the office and walked him through the process. He thanked her as he signed off.

"That was pretty easy," he noted. "But I'm still not sure how this works with the guy I saw. Do I scope him tomorrow or do one of the other guys? All I got was a quick meet and greet Friday. Dicky was a little short on details and I don't want to step on anybody's toes."

She looked at her watch. "There won't be anybody in your office now. Even Katz has shortened hours on Sunday. I guess you'll have to wait until tomorrow to meet Linda Lu. She'll explain what you need to do."

"Who's Linda Lu?"

"You haven't heard? Linda Lu is the office manager."

He was troubled by her tone. "The way you say it sounds as if I should be concerned."

"No, I don't think you have anything to worry about. You have the right set of genes."

He glanced down at his pants. "She likes clothes from Walmart?"

Laughing she shook her head. "No, silly. Not those kinds of genes. The kind that are inside the pants."

"I see."

"I don't think you do. You'd have to be a woman to understand. She's got that alpha female thing going on and takes no prisoners, but if you're a guy...man, you got it made in the shade especially if your last name begins with a K, ends with a Z and has an AT in the middle."

Cesari didn't say anything for a while trying to decipher her meaning. Finally, he said, "You mean...?"

"That's the word on the street."

"Isn't he married? He told me he had six kids."

She raised her eyebrows. "He does, and she has three."

Cesari whistled. "This place is like a soap opera."

She smiled and said with exaggeration, "You ain't seen nothing yet, brother."

As they left the hospital through the ER, Cesari spotted a guy in a white coat leaning against a wall smoking. He was Indian, mid-thirties and neatly groomed. He had no doubt it was Patel, the hospitalist he was looking for. He said, "Give me a second, Jasmine. I need to talk to this guy about the patient I saw in consult."

She waited as he walked over and greeted him. He extended his hand and said, "Hello, I'm John Cesari, the GI guy. Are you Dr. Patel?"

He looked up and smiled. "Yes, I am. A pleasure to meet you, sir."

"I just saw your patient Cortese, on the second floor, the one with anemia you called me about, and please call me Cesari."

Patel shook his hand and blew a puff of smoke out of the side of his mouth. "Thank you for seeing him so promptly. What do you think?"

"It's probably a slow bleed from somewhere. I scheduled him for both a colonoscopy and upper endoscopy in the morning. I wrote all the orders and spoke to the nurses. If you have any problems or questions about him later, I'm available."

"Once again, thank you, sir. Are you new?"

"Today's my second day."

"Welcome aboard."

"Just to let you know. That guy, Cortese, is telling everyone that he's never met you. You might want to spend a little quality time with him before he files a complaint or something."

He raised his eyebrows. "But I see him every day."

Cesari raised his hands. "You don't have to defend yourself to me. I'm sure you do, but sometimes we're so busy we forget the little things like making eye contact instead of hiding behind a laptop or maybe spending an extra sixty seconds to ask a man about his children or his life. You know what I mean? He's reading *The Old Man and The Sea*. Did you know that?"

He shook his head, "No, I did not."

"Well, he is. He's Cuban. You should ask him about that sometime. He's an interesting guy."

He nodded. "I most certainly will, sir. Thank you for the head is up."

"My pleasure."

Cesari went back to Jasmine and they walked to the Honda. As they got in, she asked, "Where to?"

"Still want to go to the lake?"

"Sure, but would you mind if I stopped at my parent's house for a minute first? I was supposed to go to church with them this morning, but something distracted me." She flashed him a big smile. "I just want to check on them. They're getting on in years and don't like to admit it. Especially my dad. If you leave him alone too long he'll start doing things like climb up a twenty-foot ladder to clean the gutters."

Cesari nodded although he had trouble picturing a man of Balthazar's great weight and age on a twenty-foot ladder. "I wouldn't mind at all."

They pulled into the driveway of the two story, white clapboard, colonial home with a pitched roof and a brick fireplace on either side. They were on South Street four long blocks away from the Dulles House. Cesari remembered Balthazar telling him that they lived nearby. The front lawn was large and covered with wet multicolored leaves from giant oaks and maples that lined the street and adorned the property.

Vibrant mums and seasonal lawn decorations lined the brick path leading up to the front door. There was an old-fashioned straw broom and faux cauldron on one side of the front door and a large pumpkin on the other. As they approached, they heard impassioned voices in animated exchange coming from within. Jasmine glanced at Cesari and opened the door. Brom was standing in the living room wagging his finger at Balthazar and Hannah. He was angry about something.

They all turned to look at Jasmine and Cesari. Brom's eyes burnt holes through Cesari's clothing. He turned back to the elderly couple. "I said what I had to say. Now I'll leave."

He brushed past Cesari and Jasmine in a rush without saying anything. His massive shoulder grazed Cesari just enough to tip him off balance into Jasmine. Cesari didn't react and watched the large man slam the front door as he left.

Jasmine asked her parents, "What was that about?"

Visibly shaken, Balthazar walked to a liquor cabinet and poured himself a scotch. Hannah seemed exhausted and sat on a sofa. Cesari waited patiently for some type of explanation.

Balthazar sat next to Hannah, and Jasmine said again more forcefully, "Well?"

Her father said, "Please sit, Jasmine. Welcome to our home, Dr. Cesari."

There were two wingback chairs opposite the sofa and a mahogany coffee table in between. There was a black cat sitting on one of the chairs taking them all in. He had big yellow, inquisitive eyes. Jasmine said sternly, "Get off the chair, Ichabod. You know better."

The cat immediately jumped down to the carpet and meandered off to someplace safe. Cesari was mildly surprised and said, "Ichabod?"

"It's a long story."

"He's a very well-behaved cat. I didn't know they responded to commands."

"He's very intelligent. I agree." She sat down and signaled him to join her which he did, cat dander notwithstanding. Cat lesson over, Jasmine returned to the matter at hand and gave Balthazar and Hannah a demanding look. She said, "I'm sorry I didn't make it to church with you this morning. Now tell me what's going on."

He said, "Brom is...upset."

"I could see that much, Father. Upset about what?"

Hannah said meekly, "About you dear."

"Me? What did I do?"

Both her parents were silent for a moment before Balthazar said, "It's about last night. He feels that you having dinner with Dr. Cesari in his restaurant was a direct slap in his face."

Jasmine said, "But I didn't even know John was going to be there. I thought that was plainly obvious at the time. Did you explain that to him?"

"We told him emphatically that Dr. Cesari was our guest, not yours. He didn't believe us. He thinks we put a show on for him last night about you not knowing he would be there."

Cesari said, "This is ridiculous. Jasmine and his relationship ended long ago. He has no right to comment on who has dinner with who in his restaurant. It's open to the public."

"Be that as it may, that is how he feels, Doctor. I suppose we could have celebrated our anniversary with you elsewhere."

Jasmine was irate. "You're telling me he came over here personally to berate my elderly parents over who I had dinner with?"

Balthazar said, "No, he came over here personally to tell us that we'd better make sure you don't ever see John socially again."

Jasmine turned red. "What?!"

"That's what he said."

Cesari was upset as well. "I can't believe I'm hearing this. What right has he got to do that?"

"The right of the morally outraged I'm afraid," Balthazar explained as he looked away toward the fireplace.

"And just what do you mean by that, Father?"

"Daughter…"

Hannah said, "Brom says you were seen going into the honey-house late last night after we left…"

Cesari and Jasmine glanced at each other. Hannah left an important part of the sentence unfinished but Cesari saw where it was going. He said, "Thank you for being polite Hannah, but we both know that I was with Jasmine. She was just giving me a tour at my request, just as she had to others."

Both Hannah and Balthazar looked down, nodded, and seemed for some reason to be thoroughly defeated. Jasmine said, "Father, Mother, you can't be serious. So I showed John the honey-house? As he said, I've shown many people the honey-house. Brom told me I could do so anytime. You know that."

Both of them sat there quietly before Hannah cleared her throat and said, "Do you always sit in the dark in the base-ment of the honey-house with people you are giving tours to, dear?"

Jasmine and Cesari were taken aback by that and his stomach started to churn waiting for the other shoe to drop. Jasmine was speechless and stared at them not sure how to counter the accusation without telling a bald-faced lie.

Balthazar added, "Brom had a security camera installed in the honey-house six months ago because of vandals…"

Cesari groaned almost inaudibly and Jasmine's throat tightened. Finally regaining her composure, she said indig-nantly, "I'm an adult and I refuse to be treated this way."

Balthazar said reassuringly and calmly, "Of course you're right, my dear."

"Then what?"

"Well, should you not do what Brom says and end any relationship you might have with the doctor then he will…"

"He will what?"

"He says that he will have no choice but to tell the other parishioners in our church."

"Tell them what? That I sat in the dark for a few minutes with a man?"

Balthazar glanced downward unable to make eye contact with his daughter. "He is going to tell the parishioners that you are…"

"Spit it out, Father."

He couldn't so Hannah said, "He's going to tell them that you are a fornicator."

Cesari's eyes went wide. He stood and felt blood pounding through his very pissed off carotid arteries. "That did it. I'm going to break his neck."

Jasmine jumped up and touched his arm. "John, please let me handle this. I know you're angry. I am too, but I've known Brom his whole life. I know what this is all about," she turned to her parents, "as do you."

Balthazar said, "That we do, daughter mine, but I have to ask you a very difficult question and I would like an honest answer."

"Go ahead."

"Is it true?"

She was really, really angry. Cesari thought her head might spin around. "Father, Mother, I love you both with all of my heart and there is nothing I wouldn't do for either one of you, including sacrificing my life. So remember that well when I tell you from the bottom my soul that it is none of your or Brom's business who I choose to fornicate with. John, let's go."

Her parents were shocked, and Cesari couldn't believe what she just said. Why not just defuse the situation with the truth? All they did was kiss. He was pretty sure there wasn't a religion on earth that had a problem with that.

He said, "Now wait just one minute. This is getting out of hand. Nobody fornicated with anybody. Nothing happened in the honey-house. We held hands and kissed once maybe twice, but that's all. I swear. Absolutely no fornicating of any kind. Everybody needs to calm down. Brom has got some nerve to come in here and try to make hay with that. I have a mind to find the pastor of your church and tell him what a scoundrel Brom is."

Balthazar said, "Good luck with that. He is the pastor."

Cesari felt like someone had just gut-punched him. "What kind of a church has a pastor that blackmails its parishioners?"

"Call it what you will. The fact remains that it would be a scandalous revelation in a church in which we have been members our whole lives. It's a very small community. I can already hear the old women clucking. There have been so many rumors swirling around Jasmine's inability to settle down. This will fan the flame even more that she is a wanton woman and that men flee from her like the Israelites from Egypt. We'll be ostracized."

Jasmine glared at him, "I can't believe what you just said, Father."

"Those were Brom's words, Jasmine, not mine, and he plans to shout them from the pulpit with fire and brimstone."

Cesari sat back down in the wingback chair looking as defeated as Balthazar and Hannah did a few minutes earlier.

Jasmine paced back and forth across the plush oriental rug, steam coming out of her ears. "I refuse to allow him to dictate who my friends are. This is worse than when we were in high school. I tried to tell you then what he was like, but you didn't believe me. He's a good boy, Jasmine. He comes from a good family, Jasmine. He'll make a good husband, Jasmine."

She was on a roll and her parents listened passively and dejectedly at her rebuke. Cesari said consolingly, "Okay look, I'm not sure what the right thing to do here is, but certainly an easy first step is for me to move out of the inn. Maybe if he doesn't see me every day he'll cool off?"

Balthazar said, "Well actually, if you left now, it would be like pouring gasoline on a fire. He said to tell you that you should *not* leave the inn because he wants to know where you are every night, and that if you do move out, he will go straight to the congregation and condemn us."

Cesari was stunned. "Are you telling me I'm under house arrest or else he'll tell everyone in town Jasmine's a whore?"

"Not everyone. Just the members of our church."

Cesari shook his head in exasperation. "I don't believe this."

Jasmine suddenly stood bolt upright in the middle of the room, her hands clenched into tight little white-knuckled fists at her side. Her rage boiling over, she closed her eyes and arched her head backward. Cesari thought she was going to scream. She grimaced, and her face contorted but she uttered not a sound.

Suddenly the room began to shake.

Chapter 16

Ichabod

Cesari clutched the arms of his chair reflexively as the room vibrated for a full ten seconds. He was concerned, even alarmed, but not necessarily frightened. It wasn't a violent shaking but enough to knock wall paintings askew and cause a framed family photo to tip over. Certainly enough for people to notice which is why he found it odd that no one did.

When it was over, Jasmine seemed to regain her composure and looked at him. He looked back and then at her parents who sat in silence on the sofa. They were shaken up. He wondered if there had been an underground explosion, maybe a gas line. If he had been in the Bronx, he might have thought an elevated train had just passed by close to his apartment. No one said anything which seemed even stranger.

Finally, he said, "What was that?"

Balthazar replied, "What was what?"

Jasmine interjected, "Don't be silly, Father. John is obviously referring to the tremor we all just experienced." She turned to face Cesari more fully. "Auburn is on a fault line and once in a while we will experience low grade tremors like that. Generally, nothing serious. I hope you weren't alarmed."

"Are you telling me that was a mild earthquake…in upstate New York?"

Balthazar regained his confidence stating, "Yes, as Jasmine says. We're so used to them that sometimes we barely take notice. It's the occasional tornado that that is of most concern."

Cesari asked, "Tornado?"

"Very infrequent and nothing like they experience in the Midwest. It's all this climate change, I'm afraid. It's upset the natural order of things."

"I don't know too much about climate change," Cesari said, "but changing weather patterns didn't cause fault lines in upstate New York. That would have had to have happened millions of years ago."

Jasmine said, "Well, it's over and no one is hurt and that's what's important." She bent down to pick up the family photo that had tipped over. "I'll come back later to help you straighten out the paintings. I don't want you two climbing on any chairs or ladders. Right now, I promised to show John the lake and personally, I need some fresh air to think things through."

Hannah rose and gave Jasmine a hug. "We love you so much, Jasmine. Always remember that. I'm sorry we had to tell you this."

Balthazar joined in what now became a group hug. "Of course we love you with all our hearts, Jasmine. We're on your side no matter what."

Cesari took a few steps toward the door. He needed some fresh air himself. Jasmine said goodbye to her parents and as she walked toward him she called out, "C'mon, Ichabod. Let's go for a walk."

The cat came running from somewhere behind the sofa and positioned itself patiently by the door the way a dog would have. Jasmine pushed the door open and they all left together.

Cesari asked, "You walk your cat?"

"Sure, he likes the fresh air, and now that you know his name, I advise you to use it. He doesn't like to be referred to in the third person."

Cesari gave her a look, not certain if she was serious or just being eccentric. He continued, "Is it wise to let him run free without a leash or harness?"

Ichabod had been walking quietly by their feet and meowed loudly, and Cesari thought, somewhat angrily. Jasmine said, "He didn't like that."

Cesari grinned and decided to go along with the gag. It was her cat. If she wasn't worried about him running away or climbing a tree, then he shouldn't. "I apologize, Ichabod."

The cat didn't respond, and they piled into Jasmine's car and drove to the lake. A few minutes later, they parked and found the entrance to a path that wound around the entire lake. It was lined with willows, maples and birch trees alive with brilliant fall hues. It was late afternoon, and they pretty much had the park to themselves.

Ichabod walked slightly ahead and in between them. He showed no interest in chasing birds or exploring the trees. The lake was quiet, and a few boaters were out enjoying the nice weather, perhaps the last of the season.

Cesari sensed Jasmine's mood. "Are you okay?"

"If you had to guess, what would you think?"

He chuckled quietly, "Please tell me you don't own any firearms."

That brought a smile to her face. "Good guess. I can't believe this is happening, and I'm sorry you got dragged into my sad, pathetic life."

"I don't think it's that sad and it's certainly not pathetic."

"What would you call it?"

"Complicated."

She agreed, "Very complicated."

"And I didn't get dragged into anything. I'm happy to be here. That kiss was worth any repercussions that might follow."

Now she laughed and seemed jovial again. "It was two kisses, remember?"

"Two kisses."

"And it was definitely worth it."

She slid her arm around his waist and he put his arm around her. Ichabod stopped, turned around and looked at them. Jasmine said, "Mind your own business and keep walking."

He turned back and started walking again. Cesari was puzzled. It was illogical that Ichabod actually understood her to that degree. Yet, his response was perfectly timed and appropriate to what she said both in the house and here. Cats were smart but not that smart. Maybe it was her speech pattern and inflection, he thought. He put it aside for the moment. There was still the issue of Brom.

"So what are we going to do?"

"I don't know yet."

"Would he really humiliate your parents publicly like that?"

She glanced at him. "Oh yeah, and at their age, it would be devastating to be denounced like that. Except for me, the other parishioners are all they have."

"I suppose beating him up is out of the question?"

She grinned. "You're in decent shape, but seriously, you wouldn't have a chance."

He was crushed at her lack of confidence in him. She saw that he was hurt and added softly, "John, you don't understand. I've seen his abilities against men much larger than you. There's a fight club in town. It meets once or twice a month and Brom always wins. I've been there and seen him in action. He is not to be trifled with, believe me. Please, for your sake and mine don't attempt to get physical with him."

Cesari was astonished. "The pastor of your church belongs to a fight club? Who is this guy anyway?"

"Just stay clear of him until I come up with a plan, all right? Fighting isn't the answer. Besides, he needs to be dealt with in a much more permanent way. I've been too soft on him all these years because of the way he felt for me and because of what happened to his parents, but I think it's time for everyone to move on."

"And how is that going to happen?" He was still smarting from her assessment of his physical skills. Cesari had never backed down from a fight and never concerned himself with the odds. The idea that someone else didn't share his confidence was upsetting to say the least.

"That is what I have to work on. For the time being, we need to do what he says. I'll stay away from you and you do the same. Remain at the inn and keep a low profile. I'll figure it out one way or the other."

"Great. So I can't see you anymore?"

"I didn't say that, but keep in mind that Brom has lots of eyes and ears in this town. He'll undoubtedly spread the word for them to keep a lookout for me and you."

"Should we even be here right now?"

She laughed. "I think we can consider today a freebie. He just left my parent's house an hour ago. He'll need time to cool off and start making phone calls to his spies."

As they chatted, a man walking a Doberman came toward them along the path. At about fifty feet the Doberman spotted Ichabod growled and lunged in his direction. The owner yanked backward but the leather leash was old and snapped. Distracted in conversation, Cesari and Jasmine didn't notice at first because the Doberman charged in silence intent on only one thing, the total destruction of his feline brother. His owner frantically chased after him yelling out the alert.

Ichabod didn't react or panic but simply watched like an old friend was approaching. At twenty-five feet, Cesari's heart skipped a beat, the next move uncertain. Outrunning a Doberman was out of the question. Jasmine said calmly, "Ichabod, now."

In one smooth, catapulting leap, Ichabod jumped onto Cesari's shoulder and then nimbly climbed on top of his head and sat there meowing. Just as he reached them, Jasmine inserted herself between Cesari and the dog. The dog abruptly halted, growled, and barked his disapproval. Jasmine put her hand out for him to sniff. Cesari held his breath. Putting a hand near a frothing Doberman didn't seem like the smartest thing to do. He was wrong. The dog sniffed her and then licked her and then whined to be petted, so she obliged him and began stroking him gently as the owner arrived out of breath.

A panting fat man nearing forty in tight sweat pants and a windbreaker apologized profusely, "I'm so sorry. He's not usually so wild. Is everyone all right?"

Cesari and Jasmine nodded as the owner grabbed the dangling remnant of the leash and wrapped it tightly around his hand. Jasmine said, "We're fine. He's a good boy. He didn't mean any harm. He just got a little excited."

"Thank you for being so understanding. Damn, I almost had a heart attack."

Cesari said, "Relax. Like she said, we're okay. No harm, no foul."

"Well, have a nice day. C'mon, Rocky. You need another trip to obedience school."

They watched him and Rocky walk away and then they faced each other. She looked into his eyes and he looked into hers. She said, "You want to say something?"

"How did you do that?"

"Animals are very instinctive. If they sense you mean them no harm, then they warm right up to you. In many ways they are like children. All they really want to do is play and be hugged."

"Maybe that will work with Brom."

"I doubt it."

"Um, Jasmine?"

"Yes?"

"I don't know if you noticed, but there's a cat on my head."

Ichabod reached down and tapped Cesari gently on the nose. Jasmine laughed, "I told you not to refer to him in the third person. He doesn't like it."

"Am I missing something here?"

Ichabod leaned down over Cesari's forehead, and upside down, looked him in the eyes and meowed.

Jasmine said, "Apparently... Ichabod, c'mon down. Enough playing."

She reached up, grabbed Ichabod and placed him on the ground. Cesari said, "Is the offer still open?"

"Which offer?"

"You said something about a home-cooked meal this morning. I declined because I was afraid I might get called in, but I suddenly don't give a damn and since tonight might be the last time we might be able to socialize without risk..."

"I think that would be a splendid idea, but we'll have to stop at a grocery store first."

"Are you okay with that, Ichabod?" Cesari asked.

Ichabod meowed and rubbed his head against Cesari's leg.

Jasmine said, "I think he likes you."

Chapter 17

Hocus Pocus

After a trip to a local supermarket for ingredients, Jasmine drove them back to her parent's home. She opened the trunk and handed Cesari a grocery bag. She took a second one and they walked around to the side of the house with Ichabod right behind. Cesari thought it was her intention to have dinner with her parents, and although he was disappointed at having to share her, he'd take whatever crumbs came his way. As they reached the side entrance he asked, "Why didn't we go in through the front door?"

"Because this is where I live. The house is quite large as you may have noticed, and my parents partitioned off an apartment for me."

"You live with your parents?"

She put the key in the door. "Not *with* exactly. More like side by side."

"Close enough."

Ichabod scooted through the open door. "And you have a problem with this?"

"Not at all. Will they be joining us for dinner?"

Sensing his concern, she said, "Not if I can help it. I want you all to myself."

He liked that and smiled. In the kitchen, they unpacked the groceries on the table and Jasmine retrieved a sauté pan and a stock pot to boil water. She handed him a bottle of Sonoma chardonnay to open while she turned on some music.

"Is Perry Como okay for you?"

"More than okay. By the way, that was one heck of a grocery store."

"Wegmans? Yeah, it's quite the upstate phenomenon. They've taken grocery shopping to another level. I'm sorry we don't have time to make home-made noodles, but their fresh pasta is pretty darn good… I hope you don't mind the slight change in menu, but I simply don't have time to make fettucine bolognese."

"No worries. Spaghetti alla carbonara is my second favorite pasta dish."

"Mine too, and it's so much quicker to make than bolognese, but we'll do that too one day when we have more time."

Ichabod had jumped onto the counter and was watching Cesari decant the wine into two glasses. He said, "I have to say, Ichabod, you are incredibly well-behaved. I've never seen anyone of your species ride around in a shopping cart before."

Ichabod meowed and Cesari said, "Did I say something wrong again?"

Jasmine laughed as she took out a cutting board and started chopping onions. "No, that was a happy meow, but that species thing was too close to call. I wouldn't do that again, but at least your learning."

Pretty soon the smell of pancetta rendering its fat in a pan with onions filled the room, and with water coming to a boil and wine bolstering their spirits, they soon managed to put Brom behind them.

After dinner, they sat on the sofa in her living room with the last of the wine. She said, "How about a movie?"

"Sure, you pick one."

She picked a DVD out of a box, slipped it into the player, turned on the TV and returned to the couch. With the remote in her hand, she snuggled into him. The movie started and Cesari chuckled, "*Hocus Pocus*? You can't be serious? A Halloween movie?"

"It's my favorite movie, especially at this time of year. You said I could pick. Have you seen it?"

"A long time ago. What is it with everyone up here and Halloween?"

"It's a fun time of year. Think about it, candy, parties, costumes, ghosts, graveyards and hay rides. How much fun is that?"

"You forgot witches."

"Don't you like witches?"

"I adore them."

She smiled. "I'm glad to hear that."

"You do realize that this movie is all about witches either eating or sucking the life out of children?"

"Relax, it's a playful Disney movie. Besides, everyone knows witches don't eat children… They prefer grown men. They have more flavor…gamier if you will, especially after two servings of spaghetti carbonara."

She poked a finger gently into his stomach and he laughed. "I never heard that, but it sounds legitimate. How do you know so much about witches?"

"Ten years working with women disguised as nurses helped educate me."

He nodded. "A lot of women in the same building might be difficult I would imagine."

"You have no idea."

"But then you throw men into the mix and you have sexual harassment. I don't know which is worse."

She snickered, "Oh please. Women harass each other all the time and they can be brutal, even worse than men. We just haven't figured out a name for it yet, but they will some-day… How about we watch the movie?"

Thirty minutes into it, he commented, "I have to admit, I do like the idea of going to a Halloween party. I was invited to two already, one at the Dulles Inn and another at the Emerson Pavilion."

She paused the movie. "Are you planning on attending?"

"Sure, why not? The gala sponsored by the hospital sounds is if it might be crazy fun and the other maybe a little toned down in comparison but still a nice way to meet people. That is if Brom doesn't withdraw the invitation."

"He won't. That's not his style. He'll want to put on the front that all is normal between you two. It wouldn't suit his image if everyone thought he was acting petty. Well, I'm glad to hear you're going. I was definitely going to the gala but was sitting on the fence about Brom's soiree, but if you're going then I think I will too."

"I wonder how Brom will react to that; us being at a party together?"

"Just because we're under the same roof doesn't necessarily mean we're together. In any event, he'll be busy taking care of his guests and besides, the lights will be down low and we'll all be wearing costumes. Spies be damned."

He held up his empty wine glass. "Spies be damned."

"Do you have a costume?"

He shook his head. "No, I'm afraid I was ill prepared for this adventure."

"There's a costume store in town, right on the Main Street just north of the city center. You can't miss it... Can we watch the movie now? We were just getting to a good part where the witches raise the zombie from his grave."

"Sure, go ahead. I wouldn't want to miss that."

Pointing the remote, she clicked play. Five minutes later he said, "What are you going as?"

She paused the movie again. "What would you guess?"

He grinned, "A French maid with fishnet stockings and lots of cleavage."

Laughing she said, "Me with lots of cleavage? You obviously need glasses. No, guess again and be serious."

He thought it over for a few seconds. "Hmm, okay, I got it. I see you as a pirate, a real swashbuckling outfit, with a ruffled shirt, a red head scarf, a saber, and maybe an eye patch." He looked at her. "Definitely an eye patch."

"A pirate, huh? I kind of like that, playful yet a little dangerous. Do I get a pistol?"

"Sure."

"You don't see me as a witch with a black, pointed hat, and a broomstick?"

"Nah, too cliché."

She laughed. "Goodness, I wouldn't want to be cliché."

"What kind of costume do you think I should wear?"

She sat up a little and studied him carefully before saying, "Raggedy Andy. I see you as Raggedy Andy. Red curly hair, funny pants. You'd look great."

He was quiet as the color rose in his cheeks. He didn't know what to make of this. "You see me as a children's doll?"

"Sure. Raggedy Andy is adorable. You don't agree?"

"I'm not sure what to think, but I'm a little concerned that you're not taking me seriously."

"What do you mean?"

"Earlier in the park you scoffed at me when I jokingly suggested I could beat Brom up and now you want me to dress up like I'm going to be the grand marshal at the LGBT Halloween parade in Key West."

She started giggling uncontrollably and he added, "And now you're laughing at me."

"I'm sorry. I don't mean to laugh. It's just that you're so damn cute. I'm just teasing you about Raggedy Andy, and although I'm sure you can take of yourself, I really do think you should stay away from Brom. One way or another that sort of confrontation would not end well for anyone involved, and I wouldn't want you to get hurt for purely selfish reasons. You see, John, I have this feeling about you…"

She hesitated. He was mollified and said, "I'm listening."

Instead of saying anything, she snuggled in close and pulled his head down to her for a kiss. After a moment she said, "Do you see now?"

He kissed her again. "I'm starting to."

"Can we finish the movie?"

"Not until you answer the question of what costume you think I should wear."

She smiled. "All right, the truth is I would prefer that you came as Tarzan wearing nothing but a simple loin cloth. I could slather oil all over you so that every muscle and sinew glistened in the light. Then I would parade you around as my prisoner and every girl at the party would die of jealousy. How's that?"

He kissed her again. "Much better. Now you can turn the movie on or you can turn me on."

She hit the play button before things got out of hand and he took the hint. By the time the movie ended at 11:00 p.m., he was drowsy and having trouble keeping his eyes open. Jasmine was also feeling the effects of the wine and carb load and dozed lightly against his shoulder. Ichabod was curled up on the back of the couch behind them. Cesari's arm had fallen asleep resting around Jasmine but he was loathe to move it. He was very content exactly where he was and wanted it to last as long as possible, but he knew he'd have to leave soon. Tomorrow was Monday, his first day in the office and he needed to be on his game and on time. In addition, it would be very unseemly, if he crawled out of her apartment at 2:00 a.m.

He shook her gently and whispered, "Jasmine, it's getting late. I'd better get going back to my room at the inn."

Groggy, she said, "I don't want you to leave."

174

"I really should."

She stretched and yawned and reluctantly agreed. "I know. Tomorrow it begins; operation take down Brom. I'll walk you to the door."

He liked her attitude. "Just keep me posted as to what you want me to do. I'll take your cue."

"All right, I'll see you at the hospital tomorrow, but even there we'll have to be careful. He has spies everywhere. There are lots of people in this town who expected me to marry Brom and feel that I did him wrong."

"And they're holding grudges about it ten years later?"

"It's a small town."

"Great."

Chapter 18

Brom

Cesari left Jasmine's apartment and walked back to the inn, four very long blocks away. It was quite dark, and he was chilled by the cool, damp, autumn air as he strolled along the lonely sidewalk guided by glow of shimmering street lights. He was deep in thought about Jasmine and all that had transpired since his arrival in town. Last week, he was in the middle of Manhattan living it up and enjoying everything the world's most sophisticated city had to offer. In less than a few days he was getting ready to go bobbing for apples at a Halloween party in a small town with a girl who had a jealous ex-boyfriend. Truth was, he felt really lucky to have met Jasmine. She was nice and had a great sense of humor, and she liked him too. She was a little complicated, but weren't they all?

A sudden gust of wind made him shiver and he picked up his pace wanting to get to the warmth of his room and under the covers of his bed. Tomorrow was a big day for him; new office, new desk, new secretaries, maybe a couple of procedures in the OR and of course, more Jasmine. He was excited.

Reaching the driveway of the inn, he was about to cut across the front lawn to the entrance when he noticed a light in the distance coming from the rear of the building in the vicinity of the honey-house. Curious, he walked to the back of the inn and paused there, watching intently. There were several parked cars and pickup trucks in front of the honey-house, and one had its lights on facing down the driveway in his direction. He didn't observe anyone standing around and he assumed that whatever was going on was taking place inside. Did they leave their lights on purposefully or did they forget to turn them off? It was none his business. He was convinced that any friend of Brom's was no friend of his.

Still, it bothered him. What if this was simply a midnight tour of the honey-house? Then some unsuspecting guest might return to find a dead battery. Did that even make sense? Not really, but this was Halloween week and all bets were off on what made sense right now in this town. He was convinced that he needed to suspend his disbelief a little if he was going to get through the week. Ultimately, the good Samaritan in him won out and he trudged along the path to the collection of vehicles to let the owner know his light were on.

As he neared the building, he heard the rumbling voices of men inside, dull, low, chanting, almost as in prayer, but there was another sound too, frantic, harsher…frightened and unfamiliar. He couldn't quite place it. The hair on the back of his neck stood up and he became instantly alert. The truck with the lights on was a Chevy, old, beat up and covered in mud from off-road activity. Its owner must have been a hunter. There was scoped bolt action Springfield rifle leaning against the passenger seat and a box of .30-06 ammunition on the cushion. Cesari noted an NRA sticker on the rear bumper, but there was no one around.

Closer to the house, he noticed more light filtering out from the doorway and windows. He entered stealth mode as he crept past the Chevy. The strange sounds emanating from within and the sight of the gun told him this was most likely not a harmless midnight adventure by some community group.

The door to the honey-house was closed which didn't really matter because at this point, he had made up his mind to avoid whoever it was while he reconnoitered, so he stole around to the side finding an eye-level window. It was shuttered tight, but he could see through a narrow space between the two panels and was enthralled. He was looking into a large rectangular room that Jasmine hadn't shown him during their tour last night. It was off to the side from where all the honey making machinery was. There were several very old looking wood stalls and Cesari remembered that the building used to be the carriage house and stable for the mansion before it had been converted into a honey-house.

In the center of the room were a dozen black robed and hooded men standing in a circle surrounding a very naked Brom facing away and partially hidden from view by the group. They held lit candles and were speaking or reciting something in a tongue foreign to Cesari. Brom's back glistened from sweat and some type of exertion that was not readily apparent. The tattoo he had seen previously on Brom's back gleamed in the candle light. His hands were at his sides and his thick neck and back muscles tensed in mighty bundles. Veins bulged, and he seemed to grow larger with each passing second. He was a bull in a man costume and Cesari thought Jasmine was right about avoiding physical conflict with him. Brom soon joined in the chorus with the others and slowly raised his arms up over his head in a circular arching manner like a warrior. As he did, he turned around towards Cesari.

Shit!

Brom's arms, massive chest and face were covered in blood. In one hand he held a two-foot long double-edged battle axe, and in the other hand he held the freshly cut head of a twelve-point buck with its life force dripping down from its recently severed neck. All the men suddenly went quiet, staring at Brom and admiring his prowess. What the hell was going on here? Cesari was mesmerized and sickened by the scene. He decided it was time to leave. He had enough problems with Brom without being caught spying on him while he was holding an axe and pumped full of testosterone.

He retraced his steps back to the front of the honey-house only to realize that he was now trapped. There was a gorilla-sized guy in cammos smoking a cigarette and leaning against the Chevy pickup. Damn, he must have been a sentry. Maybe he had walked over to the trees to relieve his bladder or perhaps he was inside watching the ritual for a minute. It didn't matter because there was no way he could make it back to the path without being seen.

Looking around, the only feasible way back would be to snake around the beehives and then up along the hedgerow on the other side of the property. It would be quite a trip from his current location and, in the pitch-black darkness that now enveloped him, it would be fraught with potential difficulties such as tripping over unforeseen obstacles or knocking over beehives. Then there were assorted minor concerns such as groundhog holes, thorny vines, poison ivy, snakes, and other unfriendly pets of mother nature.

He took in a deep breath and let it out slowly. He wasn't as cold anymore. In fact, he was starting to sweat. His heart raced, and he felt his adrenalin rushing as he quietly headed toward the beehives. Once he was a good distance from the light of the pickup truck and the honey-house he was forced to slow down to a snail's pace. Each step tentative and measured, visibility being near zero. He walked like a blind man with hands outstretched searching for impediments. After ten minutes, he encountered the first of the beehives and heard the gentle humming coming from within as the bees did their best to keep warm. Another ten minutes and he arrived at the hedgerow lining that side of the property. He walked along it slowly, occasionally stumbling on a thick root, but he didn't fall or make noise. Eventually, he was close enough to the back of the inn that ambient light from inside made the going easier, but it had taken him almost thirty minutes to make it this far and now he had a new problem.

Noise from behind him made him freeze in place. He turned to see the men leaving the honey-house and getting into their vehicles. Multiple engines roared from big cars and trucks. Bright lights flicked on and started moving toward the house. He wasn't directly in their path, but their lights might discover him, and he didn't want to get caught like that. It would be difficult to explain why he was creeping along the hedgerow at midnight, so he dove to the ground and rolled under the bushes disappearing from sight. Wet and cold, and just yards from the inn's rear parking lot he waited for them to pass up the driveway and out to the street.

Most of them did, but two trucks didn't. They parked in the lot and four men piled out. Brom was among them, mostly cleaned up and now wearing jeans and a dark hoodie pulled over his head to hide any residual bloodstains from casual inspection, not that there was anybody around who would care. He must have cleaned off with the hose in the basement of the honey-house Cesari mused as he watched the group. The men leaned back against their vehicles, pulled out cigars and started to smoke and joke. They were in a good mood, and Cesari wondered where the buck was. He was probably not in a good mood. Being dead did that to you. Maybe he was in the back of one of the pickups.

They puffed and chatted in low voices and he couldn't quite make out what they were saying, but the gist of it sounded like they were praising Brom. Cesari was getting cold again lying there on the wet leaves and mud but resigned himself to his fate. He waited patiently, but Brom and his friends showed no inclination to disperse as one of them took a cooler out from the back of his cab and started passing around beers.

But of course. What else would you do on a brisk, fall night after cutting the head off a deer but smoke cigars and drink brews? Cesari was starting to wonder if he might as well try to take a nap when he felt a gentle tapping on his back. He rolled partially around toward the hedgerow and saw a pair of large yellow, inquisitive eyes.

He whispered, "Ichabod?"

Ichabod made no sound but kept pawing at him until Cesari finally realized that he was trying to tell him something. He turned quietly to face Ichabod more fully and saw that the cat was sitting in a natural opening of the hedgerow. Maybe one of the bushes had died some time ago and its neighbors had interlaced their branches overhead but left a significant space between them below. Ichabod pawed and even tugged at him. Cesari wondered if he was trying to get him to follow. He shook his head. Not possible. Cats were smart but not that smart. That would require a level of higher reasoning that only humans were capable of. He would have to understand that Cesari was trapped, first of all, and that he was hiding from some sort of threat. Could he know that? Then it would require that he had found a safe passage for him. No way.

But the space between the plants was definitely big enough for a man to squeeze through, and he didn't want to stay there all night. When it looked like he got the message, Ichabod withdrew to the other side of the hedgerow and Cesari could see his eyes waiting for him. Gingerly, Cesari squeezed and crawled silently eventually dragging himself through the tight spot and in due course found himself in somebody's flower bed, mulched and winterized.

Ichabod rubbed himself against Cesari's leg as he stood up. In a hushed voice, Cesari said, "Thanks, little buddy."

Scanning around, he determined that he was in the backyard of the private home next to the inn. All the lights were out in the house and he made his way around a covered in-ground swimming pool to the street with Ichabod by his side. Once on the sidewalk, underneath a light he asked, "What are you doing out by yourself, Ichabod?"

Ichabod meowed and took a few steps in the direction of Jasmine's apartment. He stopped and glanced back at Cesari. Cesari shook his head. "I like you too, Ichabod, but I can't come with you. Jasmine wouldn't approve. Now go on home."

Ichabod meowed disapprovingly and slowly started to walk away.

Damn, this cat was clever. It was like he understood everything he was saying. For a moment, Cesari was tempted to follow him to make sure he got in okay but decided against it. How did he get out was another question. On the other hand, he certainly seemed capable of taking care of himself.

Cesari glanced down at himself. He was grimy and wet, and it was late. He needed to get some sleep.

He went up to the front door of the inn and let himself in. No one was around, and he went directly to his room guided by the eerie orange night lights. A quick shower and he was in bed by 1:00 a.m., but he couldn't sleep. The image of Brom holding a bloodied medieval battle axe consumed his thoughts. What kind of a freak was he? He had never seen anything like that before. They must have brought the stag there after a hunting trip, but was it still alive when he decapitated it? Now that he thought about it, it may well have been. What else could have been that sound he had heard? But was it possible to transport a live buck like that? Did they trap it or shoot it with a tranquilizer dart? Dear God, he hoped that's not what they did. Cesari shook himself and hoped beyond hope that they had killed the deer in the field and brought it here for some type of bizarre ritual.

At 1:30 a.m. his phone rang. The caller ID said private caller.

He answered it promptly. "Hello."

There was no response and after a few seconds the line went dead.

Great.

Chapter 19

The Office

Cesari took a cab to the office on Genesee Street and walked through the front door at 8:30 a.m. wearing his suit and holding a cup of Dunkin' Donuts coffee. The suit, he mused, was getting quite a workout and he'd worn the same white shirt three out of the last four days. He was exhausted. The harassing phone calls came at hourly intervals all night and he couldn't turn his phone off because he needed to be available to the hospital. Each phone call was the same, a few seconds of nothing and then the call ended. He was seriously annoyed. He was sure it was Brom. He had given him his cellphone number when he registered at the inn and now he or his friends had it to torment him with at will. Nice play, Brom.

He knocked on the door to the office manager and was greeted by a forty-year old woman with short brown hair in a bob. Pleasant looking and professional, she checked out his ID badge and greeted him with a big smile and an outstretched hand. "Dr. Cesari, I'm Linda Lu Bennett, the office manager. Sal told me you were coming. It's a pleasure to meet you."

"Hi, Linda Lu. Yes, the feeling is mutual. I hope I'm not inconveniencing you. I know you weren't given much notice."

"It's no problem at all. Come with me. I'll show you to your office." He followed her down a corridor while she spoke, "Things are crazy around here but that's pretty much the way it is all the time. Obviously, we didn't have time to schedule you any patients, but we'll have that fixed in a day or two. Dr. Katz is in the OR this morning and he'll usually come back to the office at around 1:00 p.m. or sometime after. That's his routine, morning scopes and afternoon peeps. Due to lack of space, the three GI guys share an office. I hope you don't mind. The good news is that you have your own bathroom."

"Our own bathroom? What more could anyone ask for?"

She smiled and as they walked, she introduced him to several busy secretaries and nurses, showed him the break room and gave him a lightning lesson on how to use the coffee machine. They concluded the tour at the GI office. The door was closed and she knocked politely, glancing in his direction. Cesari thought she seemed uneasy.

"Have you met Dr. Kamil, yet?" she asked.

He shook his head. "No, I've only met Katz."

When no one answered, she opened the door and stuck her head in. "I thought he was in here, but he may have started seeing patients already."

The room was fairly large and empty. There were three metal, no frills desks; two had computers, paperwork, stethoscopes, candy bars, and other items that gave them a lived-in appearance. The door to the bathroom was closed.

She walked him to the middle desk and said, "This is yours. The hospital will issue you a new laptop this week. In the meanwhile, I can dig up an old one you can use for a while until you get your own."

"Thank you." He looked at the desk and the room and added. "This will be fine."

She asked, "You'll have to tell me how you want me to arrange your schedule. I called the OR already and told them you'll need block time. Dr. Pullman was the GI doctor who just left. He scoped on Mondays, Wednesdays and every other Friday. He saw patients on Tuesdays and Thursdays. The easiest thing for us is to simply slip you into his space on the schedule."

Cesari thought this was an easy way to score points so he said, "That will work for me. I have no preferences."

She smiled and Cesari thought, *Happy Staff, Happy Life* or something like that. They were in the middle of exchanging pleasantries like that when the bathroom door swung open and a man walked out. He was about thirty, average height and lean with dark skin and jet-black hair. He had a distinctly middle-eastern appearance to him.

Linda Lu turned to him. "Oh Dr. Kamil, I didn't..." Before she could finish her sentence, a young woman came out of the bathroom behind him. She was short, also dark-skinned with long hair and big almond-shaped brown eyes. She was decidedly frazzled and had that universal deer in the headlights look when people got caught doing something they shouldn't be doing.

Kamil stood there staring at Cesari blankly. Linda Lu was speechless, and the girl tried to conceal herself behind Kamil. Cesari wanted to say to her, *I can see you.* After a long awkward silence, Cesari extended his hand and said, "John Cesari, the new gastroenterologist."

Kamil looked at the outstretched hand with misgiving and slowly raised his own to grasp it. He said, "Khaled Kamil."

That was all. Nothing else. No how are you. No welcome to town or I'm looking forward to working with you. It was one of those, I don't know you and I don't want to, kind of moments. The handshake was polite and formal and Kamil quickly pulled away. Cesari sensed that he would wash his hand immediately after they parted company.

They continued to stand there uncomfortably while the young lady hid behind Kamil, barely visible. She made no effort to come forward or leave the room. Finally, Linda Lu said, "Lauren, this is Dr. Cesari. He's going to be working here."

Reluctantly, she stepped forward but didn't say anything or make eye contact with Cesari. Linda Lu added, "Lauren is Dr. Kamil's nurse."

Cesari offered his hand and instead of taking it, she looked at Kamil for guidance. He nodded, and she politely placed her hand in Cesari's and then withdrew it one second after making contact. She said, "Is nice meet you," in a thick accent and then stepped back behind Kamil.

Cesari chose to put them out of their misery and turned to Linda Lu. "Well, why don't we go to your office and go over my schedule?"

The awkward scene came mercifully to an end. As they entered Linda Lu's office, he closed the door behind them. She said, "I'm sorry. That was..."

"Different."

"Yes, very."

"Where are they from?"

"Egypt. They're both on a J-1 visa sponsored by SUNY Upstate. As you can tell, we have some cross-cultural issues we're working on. He's impossibly chauvinistic, in case you didn't notice."

"She didn't seem to mind."

"She doesn't know any better yet. We've been trying to teach her but she's suspicious of us."

"Am I allowed to talk to her?"

She shook her head. "I wouldn't. You and Dr. Katz share Patty. She's the RN you met on the way in. I would just leave the Lauren thing alone. Kamil's got a bad enough temper as it is."

"Fine. Look, I saw a patient in consult over the weekend that needs to be scoped today. What's the process?"

"Just give me the name. I'll pass it along to Katz and make sure it gets done."

He wrote down the name of the patient and his room number on a piece of paper. "He needs a colonoscopy and an upper endoscopy."

"I'll take care of it."

"When do you think you'll have patients scheduled for me?"

"Soon, I think. Dr. Pullman had a very large practice and we have a huge back log. He left us in quite a lurch. Today's Monday. I bet I'll be able to fill you up at least a morning by Thursday. That'll give me time to requisition your laptop. Are you familiar with the EMR?"

"I'm getting there. One of the nurses at the hospital started showing me last week. She was very good. I'm supposed to go there today for another session with her."

"Which nurse?"

"Her name was Jasmine. Do you know her?"

She let out a deep breath and got very serious. "Of course. Everybody does. She's…"

He waited but she didn't finish her thought so he prompted her, "She's what?"

"I shouldn't say anything but do yourself a favor and stay as far away from her as you can. In fact, there's another nurse who can teach you the EMR. Her name's Darlene. She's not as much fun to look at but she's very good. If you want, I'll call her right now and set up an appointment."

"That won't be necessary. I kind of liked Jasmine. Is there something you'd like to tell me about her?"

She was very concerned. "It's a small-town Doctor. People hear things. People talk."

"People also gossip, Linda Lu. So unless you have something to say…?"

"She's weird, Doctor. Something's not right with her. Some people think she's jinxed, maybe even cursed," she blurted out.

Cesari laughed, "Cursed? Did you hear what you just said?"

"I'm not joking. That's what people say, and I believe them. There's something wrong with that girl and everybody knows it, and that creepy black cat of hers is even worse."

"I've met Ichabod. He seemed okay to me. What's wrong with him?"

"Nothing's wrong with him except that he's older than any cat I've ever heard of. She doesn't think anyone pays attention to these things, but we do. Her parents adopted that cat for her when she was a baby. By my calculation he's more than thirty years old. You said you met him. Did he seem like he was thirty years old to you? Have you ever even heard of a cat living that long?"

He didn't know much about cats but that did seem like a very long time. He said, "Okay, so the cat's old. How close are you to Jasmine and her family?"

"Do I look like I want trouble? I don't go near any of them."

"Then it's possible they replaced the cat at some point with an identical one and you're just unaware of it."

"Oh Doctor, please…"

"I'm just saying, but you know Linda Lu, you made an outrageous accusation that Jasmine's cursed in some way. That's not a very nice thing to say about anyone. Would you care to elaborate or am I supposed to use my imagination?"

She made a face at him and rolled her eyes upward as if he was being unnecessarily difficult. This was a tough way to start off a relationship he thought and decided that they needed to move on. He said, "Okay, look. You made your point. You don't like Jasmine and you gave me fair warning. Thank you."

"You're welcome…and watch out for her parents too."

He was starting to get annoyed. "To be perfectly honest, I already met Jasmine's parents and they seemed like nice church-going people."

Linda Lu shot him a look of shock. She was having none of it. "You call that a church? What kind of church calls itself *The Order*?"

"*The Order*?" he repeated. "I didn't know that, but still, there a lot of churches with odd names."

"Please, there's something whacky about all of them. I think it's a cult."

"That's not fair. Do you have any proof that they've hurt anyone or kept anyone against their will?"

She was passionate but seemed to cool off a little. She folded her arms and shook her head. "No, not that I know of."

Cesari was worldly enough to know that rumors were the lifeblood of small towns. He said, "There you go. Look, I have to head over to the hospital. Thank you for taking care of that patient for me. I'll see you bright and early Thursday morning and if anything comes up sooner just give me a call." He jotted down his cellphone number for her and stood to leave.

She said, "Doctor…"

"I promise to be careful, Linda Lu."

Chapter 20

The Wazoo

It was a fifteen-minute walk from the office to the hospital and Cesari spent most of it thinking about Linda Lu and their conversation concerning Jasmine. It was unusual to say the least, but in retrospect the thing that struck him most odd was that she hadn't once mentioned Pullman's relationship with her. She must have known about it and given her rather strong feelings toward Jasmine, he was surprised she hadn't brought it up. It didn't matter, and he scrubbed it from his mind as he entered the front doors of the hospital.

Arriving at 10:00 a.m., he meandered over to Sal's office where he found him and Dicky in decidedly bad humor. Sal's office had a large window that looked out into the main vestibule of the hospital. It made him feel as if he always had his finger on the pulse of things. However, it was a double-edged sword in that anyone could see what was going on inside his private sanctum, and right now Cesari could see that he and Dicky were visibly upset about something. They were standing, waving their arms and pointing their fingers at each other. He knocked gently on the door and Sal waved him in.

"C'mon in, Cesari," Sal said. "This is as much your problem as it is ours."

Dicky sat down in one of two chairs in front of Sal's massive wood desk. Sal sat in a leather chair and motioned

Cesari to do the same. He reached under his desk and came out with a bottle of Johnnie Walker Black and three tumblers.

He said, "Dicky, close the blinds. I need a drink."

Dicky got up and Cesari watched Sal pour three fingers in each glass and pass them out. Dicky returned to his seat and he and Sal started drinking. Cesari didn't want to be rude but this was way too early, so he let his glass just sit on the coaster in front of him.

He asked, "What happened, guys?"

"Listen to him, Dicky. What happened guys, he says. I'll tell you what happened. New York State's about to give it to us in the wazoo, Cesari. That's what happened."

Dicky said soothingly, "Let's not think the worst until we have to, Sal. It may not be as bad as you think."

Cesari was confused and waited for an explanation. Sal's eye twitched rapidly reflecting his underlying agitation as he spoke, "The state geeks that were here Saturday. Remember them?"

Cesari nodded. "Of course."

"Well, they got good and soused Saturday, right? But they looked okay for the most part. Anyway, it's not my fault they can't handle their liquor. I mean we're all grown-ups. Am I right, Cesari? People have to take responsibility for their actions."

"What happened?" he asked.

Dicky explained. "You know how it is, Johnny. You've been there. We started early, and the party went right through dinner. I offered to get them a hotel room, but they wanted to get back to Albany."

Sal added, "Yeah, they wanted to get back to Albany. I tried to talk them out of it. Didn't I, Dicky?"

Dicky continued, "Yes you did, Sal. Yes, you did. I'm a witness." He turned to Cesari, "We didn't think it was such a great idea for them to drive anywhere, but they insisted. It's a little over two hours from here. They were tanked pretty good, especially the chick in charge."

Sal interjected. "You want to know what happened? I'll tell you. They DUI'd on the thruway. That's what happened."

Cesari raised his eye brows and let out a breath. He said, "That's not a good thing but it's not the end of the world. Lots of people DUI. You go to court, pay a fine, mandatory counseling, probation and if it never happens again, you're okay."

"Listen to him, Dicky. Atticus Finch right here in my office. Where'd you get your law degree, Cesari? It ain't that simple." He downed the rest of his scotch in one long gulp. "Dicky tell him. I just can't get the words out."

Dicky crossed his legs and rested his glass in his lap. "They resisted arrest with the trooper who pulled them over. The woman jumped on his back and started screaming rape. He's got scratch marks on his face. The other two tried to drive away and ran the car into a ditch. It's all documented on the officer's dash cam. They're all in a cell in Utica awaiting a court appearance later today."

"You've got to be kidding?" Cesari gasped. "How'd you find out?"

"The Department of Health called us this morning. Now that everybody's sober, they're trying to blame us like we did something wrong," Sal said.

Dicky added, "And it gets worse. Unbeknownst to us, the woman is the second cousin to our governor, and he already has the state's attorney general looking to see what laws we may have violated."

"What laws could you possibly have broken?"

"Bribery, conspiracy to obstruct an inspection, inappropriate sexual contact with a state official..." at that last Dicky cleared his throat and straightened his tie and Cesari thought he even blushed a little. "The bottom line is this is New York State. If they can't find a real crime, they'll make one up."

"Guess who else called this morning, Cesari. Tell him to guess, Dicky." Sal's facial tic was firing on all cylinders the more upset he got.

"Guess who else called, John."

"The attorney general?"

"Wrong!" Sal exclaimed. "The governor himself called and promised me a new rectum by the time this is all over. Can you believe that? Those were his exact words, a new rectum." Sal poured himself another scotch and continued, "The main review of the hospital which was supposed to come in six months, has now been moved up to start next week as punishment. I can't even imagine the amount of violations they're going to find and what that's going to cost us in fines. Instead of sending ten guys, he's going to send twenty and instead of spending three days, they're going to spend six. Are you getting the message, Cesari? They're looking for blood."

Dicky sipped his scotch. "This couldn't have come at a worse time with all the Halloween parties and the gala coming up."

Cesari said, "Definitely, not good."

"Doctor, you're not drinking your scotch?" Sal asked, concerned.

"I have to see a patient on the wards right after I leave here," he lied. "It wouldn't be good if I had alcohol on my breath…" He glanced at his watch. "… at 11:00 a.m."

"That's a good point. Dicky, you want to finish his or should I."

"I'll take it, Sal. Say, John, how was your weekend?"

"Not bad at all. I feel like I really know my way around already, and I met Linda Lu and the office staff before I came here. Linda Lu gave me a tour. She seemed very nice. All I need is my car back to be complete."

Sal winced at that. "Sorry, Dr. Cesari, but there's a bit of a problem with your car. My mechanic, Ralph, called me. Your transmission is shot, and your clutch is on the way out. They don't have replacements for cars like that lying around so I told him to go ahead and order the parts. It'll be a couple of days."

"Why didn't he call me?"

"He said you never gave him your number."

Cesari thought about it. When he had been towed he had simply left off that he would call Monday morning to see what the status of his car was. He said, "He's right. I didn't give him my number. I forgot. So what's he thinking, one or two days?"

"Something like that. If you need wheels for a day or two, I can loan you one of my vehicles."

"I hate to put you out like that. Maybe I can just find a car rental place?"

"Nonsense, Cesari, you're family now."

"Are you sure you don't mind?"

"Dicky tell him."

"He doesn't mind, John."

Cesari hesitated, then said, "Sure."

"Great, I'll drive you to my house later." He looked at the wall clock. "Shit, where does the time fly? Dicky and I have a finance committee meeting to attend, Cesari. It's been fun talking. Come and find me later."

"I will, but one more question before I leave. Can you tell me how to get to the costume store in town? I need to pick up an outfit for the gala."

Dicky smiled, "I'm glad to see you're getting in the spirit of things. How are you going to get there? If you can wait an hour, I can drive you."

"That won't be necessary. I'll either take a cab or walk. It's a beautiful day."

"And we don't get many of those this time of year. Well, it's easy and not that far. Certainly walkable. If you do walk, go straight out from the main entrance three blocks to Genesee Street and turn left. Then it's one, two…three lights. Look for Osborne Street. It's right after that. You can't miss it, and if a local cab driver doesn't know where it is he should be shot. You're going to love the place. They can put anyone in the mood for Halloween."

"I have to admit, the atmosphere around here is contagious."

Sal said, "Just don't get the devil costume. Half the town will be dressed as Beelzebub."

Dicky said, "And I'm Raggedy Andy."

Cesari suppressed a laugh. "Okay, no devil and no Rag-gedy Andy."

He thanked them and left the office to find Jasmine. This place was wild. Every day was a party it seemed. When he arrived at the nursing office, Jasmine was in a meeting that appeared to be in the process of breaking up. He waved to her through the door's window, and she acknowledged him with a nod but then turned away. There were several people in the room with her and he guessed that maybe she felt one of them wasn't to be trusted so he turned tail and walked up to the cafeteria on the second floor, texting her on the way.

After a couple of minutes, she texted him back confirm-ing his suspicions about having a Brom spy in her presence and that she was stuck with him for the next few hours. He'd survive although he was dying to tell her about seeing Brom in action last night with the battle-axe. He wondered if she knew anything about that. He was also curious about what kind of church she belonged to that a guy who decapitates deer is the pastor of, but these questions would have to wait.

Linda Lu had quite a bit to say about Jasmine, but he chalked that up to small town gossip possibly related to petty jealousies and grievances. He never took stuff between women too seriously anyway. Even in New York City, the back-biting was ferocious. Women would destroy each other over something as trivial as wearing the same color dress to a party, and they never let anything go. He recalled two OR nurses in Manhattan feuding over a misunderstanding about the on-call schedule. One of those, 'I thought it was your turn to work this weekend' kind of things. The conflict esca-lated and before long the entire OR nursing staff was in-volved taking sides. Ridiculous, unfounded complaints were filed with administration on behalf of both sides. Half the

OR refused to talk to the other half and it went on like that for months. It was ugly. Trying to perform a colonoscopy on a patient with two nurses who wouldn't talk to each other was nearly impossible. It only ended when administration, with the approval of the nursing union, stepped in and threatened both with termination. They were eventually transferred out of the OR to departments on polar ends of the hospital. As far as he could remember, they never reconciled. That's the way it was with women. They always fought to the death and he never understood why.

In the cafeteria, he grabbed a ham sandwich and ate on the move, deciding to walk to the costume store rather than take a cab. He left the hospital and walked to Genesee Street turning left like Dicky had instructed. It was a nice day out, sixty-five degrees and sunny. You really couldn't ask for better in this part of the country in late October. He was thankful it wasn't snowing already. His clothes and other belongings should be arriving this afternoon, and he hoped they'd be there early. In fact, he would check right after his trip to the costume store.

As he walked, he heard a powerful rumbling engine approaching and he turned to see a shiny new fire-engine red Corvette with the top down pulling up slowly beside him. The ZR1 was a sleek machine, powered by a 6.2-liter supercharged V8 engine with 755 horsepower and 715 pound-feet of torque. It could go from 0-60 in 2.8 seconds with a top speed of 212 mph, and Lola looked damn good in it. She was wearing a blonde wig today and large round sun-glasses. A tight top and long legs stretching out from beneath a short skirt made her quite a sight rumbling down the main drag.

She gave him a big smile, "Want a ride, Dr. Cesari?"

Who wouldn't, he thought and said, "I was going to the costume store."

"So was I, lambchop. So was I."

Chapter 21

Scaramouche

The costume store was no small affair occupying at least half a city block. Aptly named Halloween City, it was a three-story department store complete with escalators and a bank of elevators. It was devoted to and had a wide selection of all things Halloween from lawn ornaments to wall decorations to costumes to every candy ever made. There was a small café on the main floor selling pumpkin spice lattes, apple cider, and pastries. The two waitresses were dressed up as round jack-o-lanterns. Cesari doubted they liked that. Toward the back of the second floor was an X-rated adult section with specialty costumes, lingerie, and other forms of mature entertainment. The devil section on the main floor had no less than three dozen distinct Satan outfits to choose from. Many were traditional and cliché, whereas others were incredibly unique. The more serious ones were designed from strict interpretations of the Old Testament and depictions of his Evilness in medieval folklore. Some had long horns, some short. Others had pointy tails and ears. Some had fangs and grotesque masks. Most were red or some shade from that spectrum, but others were black. The materials varied as well from cotton to wool to satin.

In the basement were dozens of broomsticks, real cast iron cauldrons in all sizes, polished axes, swords, daggers, chainsaws and coffins. Row upon row of magical potions and the necessary ingredients one might need to make such potions lined one of the walls. There was even eye of newt and dried rat tails. Cesari was as impressed as he was overwhelmed by the myriad of choices.

After checking out costumes for himself for nearly forty-five minutes, he grew weary and frustrated, and sat on a bench watching Lola try on assorted outfits. After several tries, she settled on the good witch Glinda costume from the Wizard of Oz. She twirled around in front of him in a long pink dress, a staff with a silver star and a large crown. With three-inch heels, the five-inch-high crown gave her the appearance of being close to seven feet tall.

He said, "You look just like her if memory serves me right."

Beaming she said, "Glinda?"

He nodded. "Yes, you look great."

"Thank you. I think I'll go with this one. What about you? Have you seen anything that appeals to you?"

"Only you, Lola. Only you."

She liked that and smiled. "Seriously, you need to get a costume."

"I'm torn between good and evil."

"Honey, aren't we all?"

He laughed. "I don't want to wear something that's very uncomfortable. I want to be able to talk and dance and mingle without working up a sweat, but I don't want people to recognize me either."

"Let's take a look together. Maybe I can help?"

She took him by the hand and they walked up and down the aisles occasionally stopping to take a closer look at items that caught their eye. He put the kibosh on superhero stuff like Batman or Superman. It wasn't his style. Neither was anything that involved wearing tights or leotards like Peter Pan. Not that physically he couldn't handle it, but he would be too self-conscious wearing something like that. The last section and also the smallest was the historical costume aisle. Here you could dress up as Marie Antoinette, Genghis Khan or Abraham Lincoln. Nearly frustrated, Lola pulled a costume off the rack and studied it. It consisted of black, knee length breeches with accompanying white stockings, ruffled white shirt, red waist coat, tri-cornered black hat and removable half mask. Cesari was fascinated and stepped close.

He asked, "What's that?"

Lola looked at the tag with a brief description of the costume and the price. "It says this is Scaramouche, a recurring, mischievous character in European comedic plays since the seventeenth century. According to this, he was a bit of a scoundrel."

Cesari took the mask from her and tried it on. It fit over the top part of his face and would allow him to eat and drink comfortably. The mask was mostly white with a large hooked nose and red blush marks on the cheeks. Covering only half his face, he wouldn't get too hot and feel the need to take it off. He liked that and after examining the rest of the ensemble, found it intriguing. He'd need to get matching period shoes but was sure they had something here to accommodate him. He also liked the idea of carrying a sword. One didn't come with the costume, but in for a penny, in for a pound.

Lola was thrilled that she had helped him find something to his satisfaction. She said, "Try it on to make sure it fits. It says it's a large."

He went into a changing room and did just that. Looking at himself in the mirror, he laughed at the image. The clothes fit pretty well, a little loose in spots as was to be expected in an off the rack suit, but better than too tight. He would be fine. He stepped out of the changing room and Lola, still dressed as Glinda, sized him up.

She smacked her lips and purred at him. "Boy oh boy, if I weren't a married woman…"

"It floats your boat?"

"Like sipping a pina colada on a desert island with a warm summer breeze blowing up my skirt while watching men's beach volleyball it does."

He looked at her. "Then it's settled. I'm Scaramouche, the scoundrel. Let's find some shoes and a sword to go with it."

"Now you're talking."

They actually had a large shoe department and he picked out a pair of historically accurate shoes with a large shiny buckle. In another part of the store, he found a thin blade known as a rapier which came with a scabbard. The shoes were basically slip-on loafers made of leather and comfortable. The buckle was decorative. The rapier, the salesman explained, was prevalent in use in Europe at about the same time as the costume he chose and thus would be appropriate. It was a very thin, long sword with a sharpened tip made primarily for thrusting as opposed to slashing. It was a dueling weapon and the one he bought, although a replica, was authentically reproduced and therefore quite dangerous. All told he was out more than five hundred dollars. He shook his head trying to imagine how much money was spent on this holiday nationally.

Placing their packages in the small trunk of the Corvette, she drove him back to the inn. She pulled to a stop in front of the house and he thanked her for the ride and the help with his costume.

She said, "Anytime, Dr. Cesari. I hope to see more of you."

"You'll be seeing more of me in a couple of hours. Sal is going to loan me a car to drive around in. The transmission blew on mine and it's going to be in the shop for a couple of days."

"He must have meant the pickup truck. There aren't any other cars except for Bobby Jo's Mustang which she took back to law school on Saturday."

Cesari thought about that. "A pickup will be just fine. It's just for a couple of days until they fix my car."

"How were you planning on getting to the house?"

"Sal offered to drive me. I was going to go call him later after I unpack. I'll either go back to the hospital to meet him or he could pick me up here. To be honest, I might just take a cab. It's no big deal."

"Nonsense. What are you unpacking?"

"Hopefully, my luggage which was supposed to have been delivered here from New York today. I'm keeping my fingers crossed that it's waiting for me inside."

"That's all you have to do?"

"That's all."

"Then I'll come in and wait for you. I'll drive you back to the house. Why bother Sal? Even better, do you have dinner plans?" He shook his head and she continued, "That settles it. You're having dinner with Sal and me."

Without waiting for a response, she turned the engine off, popped the trunk and got out of the car. Cesari sighed but then smiled. She had just given him an idea. He caught up with her at the rear of the car, cleared his throat and said, "Um, Lola, do you think I could ask you a favor?"

She handed him his packages. "Of course, sugar. Don't be shy."

"Would you mind doing a little play acting with me when we go inside the inn. I'll explain later. Just kind of go with the flow."

She smiled. "I always go with the flow. Is there anything in particular I need to go with the flow with?"

"You'll see. It'll be self-explanatory."

As they walked through the front door with the purchases, Cesari spotted Brom and a member of his staff deep in conversation. He glanced at Lola and then nonchalantly took her hand and walked over to them. Lola understood and went along with it, smiling happily. This was the second time today they'd held hands.

Brom looked up at them as they approached, his gaze focused on their hands. He was curious, a little puzzled and not sure what to make of it. Cesari asked, "Brom, has my luggage arrived from New York?"

"Yes, it arrived an hour ago, Doctor. I had the suitcases placed in your room," he said pleasantly enough considering the circumstances, all the time studying Lola. Either he'd never seen a black person in his inn before or he'd never seen a woman that large and flamboyant before. It was probably a combination of both. In any event, Cesari had just introduced a new variable into the equation for Brom. The question was; what did it mean?

Cesari cleared the air for him on that score. "Thank you very much. Lola and I will be in my room unpacking. I would like very much for us to be left undisturbed for a couple of hours…" He let that hang out there for everyone's imagination to digest.

Brom stared at him for a moment and said, "I'll let the staff know."

"Great, and would it be possible for you to have someone bring us a bottle of your best pinot noir?"

"I'll see to it."

Cesari walked slowly up the staircase hand in hand with Lola knowing Brom was watching them. Once inside the room, Lola laughed. "Who was the Viking God? I thought he was going to throw me down and have his way with me."

She was smart and funny. Cesari liked that. He gave her the short version about Brom's interference in his life. "If he thinks I'm interested in someone else, he may just back off a little on me. I hope you don't mind me using you like that?"

"Oh please. You have no idea how badly I've been used. That was kind of fun. You're a bit of a pisser, aren't you? I wouldn't have thought that after our first meeting. So how far do you want to take it in terms of the real factor," she asked, smiling at him.

He put his hands up. "That was perfect."

She pretended to pout.

"Have a seat while I unpack and make yourself at home."

She sat down on the sofa and flicked on the TV as he hoisted one of two large suitcases onto the bed and opened it. He began to place things in a bureau and nearby closet. In a few minutes, there was a knock on the door and Lola went to answer it. Cesari waved her back. He unbuttoned his shirt and pulled it partially out of his pants, kicked his shoes off and mussed his hair up. Nice and disheveled, he opened the door just enough for Brom to see he was 'busy.'

Brom raised his eyebrows as he handed him the wine bottle. "Domaine Carneros, 2007. A great vintage."

In a distracted hurry, Cesari took the bottle. "I'll let you know. Thanks."

"There's a wine opener and glasses in the credenza in the living room."

"Perfect."

"Will there be anything else?"

"No, but I'll keep you posted."

Brom left and Cesari smiled. He knew Brom would come up himself and not send one of the staff. He was busting at the seams with curiosity. He opened the bottle and poured himself and Lola a couple of glasses. They sat back, clinked a toast to a successful mini-operation and drank the wine. It was very good. Lola had just given him some breathing room. Brom was probably pondering just what kind of a guy he really was. Hopefully, he would think he's a womanizer who doesn't dwell too long on missed or failed opportunities. Let him think that. He would have no pressing reason to keep Cesari under house arrest or strict observation if he thought he was chasing after other women. In fact, he would want to encourage it as much as possible. It just might work.

He said, "Lola, would you mind if I invited a friend over to dinner with you and Sal tonight?"

"You mean the girl Thor is trying to keep you from?"

"Yes."

"Of course, honey. I'm all about love. You got to get it wherever and whenever you can. What's her name?"

"Jasmine."

"What a pretty name, but at this point, I'm not going to have time to cook a real meal like I would prefer. We have some great restaurants here in Auburn. Why don't you tell your lady friend to meet us at Lasca's."

Cesari grimaced. "That might not be a good idea. Brom has a lot of friends in town. Someone might see us. We don't have to do anything special. Takeout or delivery would be fine."

"Takeout it is. I'll have Sal pick up dinner when he leaves the hospital and we'll make a night of it. I'll let him know I'm bringing you home with me."

"Great and I'll let Jasmine know."

Chapter 22

The Church

Sal pretended to be in good humor, but Cesari knew the stress he was under from the recent escalation of hostilities with the state. As a result, he had been drinking harder than usual both before he arrived with the food and after. Halfway through the meal he'd hardly eaten anything and appeared numb. Usually boisterous, he had grown quiet and morose and except for his glassy-eyed staring at Jasmine, was mostly unengaged.

Cesari had decided to keep Sal in the dark as to what was going on between him and Jasmine and Lola had agreed that was best. His personality was much too direct and lacking in nuance, but this was not the type of problem you solved by calling the two parties into a room to air out their differences. Sal was the kind of guy that if he caught wind of what was going on, he'd arrange an emergency board meeting with Brom on one end of the table and Cesari on the other.

By 9:00 p.m. Sal was well on his way to complete and total inebriation and possibly passing out. Slurring badly and losing coordination, Sal nearly hit himself in the eye with a forkful of pad thai. Mercifully, Lola recognized it was time to ferret Sal away. She handed Cesari the keys to the pickup in the garage and pushed, pulled and dragged Sal up to the bedroom.

As she did she turned and said, "I'll say goodnight now, Dr. Cesari. It was a pleasure meeting you, Jasmine."

They thanked her for a lovely evening and after she left, they sat in the kitchen looking at each other. Jasmine said, "This was a pretty clever idea."

"Thanks. I thought so, but you'll have to thank Lola. She's a real romantic deep down."

"I can see. I never met her before, but I don't get many invites to the boss's house."

He grinned. "We may be eating here a lot until this blows over."

She laughed. "I can think of worse things although I had no idea Sal was so…"

Cesari nodded. "Open-minded?"

"Yeah."

"You picked up on the subtleties here pretty quick. That's better than I did."

"Are you kidding?" She leaned close whispering, "I had heard through the grape-vine that she was black, but I had no idea she was a he. Did you see the size of those hands?"

"It gets better."

"How so?"

"Brom thinks she and I are…how do you say…?"

He winked at her and she laughed out loud. "How could that have happened?"

He filled her in on the little scene they had play-acted for Brom's benefit at the inn.

She grinned, "Wouldn't that be nice if he bought that one?"

"I'm keeping my fingers crossed... Anyway, about us?"

"What about us?"

His gaze caught hers and held it. "What are we going to do about us? We're going to need a plan."

She looked downcast. "I've been thinking about that all day, and as much as I enjoyed the subterfuge of tonight, we can't do this very often. Sooner or later, Brom or one of his guys is going to get suspicious and follow us here."

"Speaking of Brom..." He glanced over his shoulder at the kitchen door. "Let's go in the backyard or your car where we can talk more privately just in case..."

"Sure."

They went out the back door and found her car parked in the driveway. They got in and she turned the engine on for heat. The temperature had dropped into the upper forties. She settled back into her seat and said, "This is a very complicated and delicate situation with Brom."

He didn't see any point in wasting time and cut right to the heart of the matter. "What kind of church do you and your family belong to?"

She was taken aback by that. "What do you mean?"

"I mean I saw Brom cut the head off of a stag last night in the honey-house. He was with a bunch of his friends. It was pretty sickening. He doesn't strike me as the overly religious type."

She was horrified. "Did he see you?"

"No, I was lucky. Which brings us to another thing. How old is Ichabod?"

"Ichabod? What's he got to do with anything?" she asked, side-stepping the question.

"He miraculously found me hiding from Brom and led me to safety. Pretty smart cat, wouldn't you say? Smarter than most people if you ask me."

She didn't say anything, and he continued, "Someone at work told me the name of your church is The Order. Is it a Christian church? Because I never heard of a Christian church with that name. Look, I don't really care what you believe in but I would like to know what's going on."

She was annoyed at his tone which had unconsciously become accusatory. "And here I thought you went through all of this maneuvering tonight because you cared for me. If I had known you brought me here for an interrogation, I could have saved you the trouble. Yes, John, we're pagans and eat Christians and Jews and anybody else we can get our hands on, and Brom is the Grand Wizard. Would you please leave now? I'd like to go home."

Silence settled on them like a thick fog and they both stared straight ahead. He made no effort to leave her, and after a minute, said contritely, "I'm sorry. I didn't mean to come at you like that... Please forgive me."

She sensed his sincerity and turned to him. "I already have."

"Thank you."

A solitary tear rolled down one side of her face. "You saw Lola, right?"

Puzzled, he responded, "Yes, why?"

"Do you think can she help being who she is? Do you think her life has been easy? Do you think she has enjoyed all the hate and prejudice she must have experienced?"

He said, "I guess not."

"Just remember that, John. We can't help being who we are."

"I understand and I'm sorry I offended you. If you don't want to talk about it, I won't bring it up again and you were right the first time. I brought you here because I do care about you and I want to be with you. No more third degree, all right? I'm far from perfect myself. I know that."

She seemed better, let out a deep breath and was ready to move on. She said, "Let's go for a drive."

"I'm all yours."

"Are you?"

Putting the car in reverse, she started backing out of the driveway before he could answer. She added, "We can come back for the pickup later."

She drove in circles for twenty minutes, first east, then west, then north and then south. Quiet and frustrated, he just let her get it out of her system whatever it was that needed getting out. Every now and then, he would comment on the view like 'That's a nice looking building' or 'Would you look at the size of that tree' kind of comment. She wasn't buying it. Eventually, she pulled into the driveway of a steepled building several miles from her house in a secluded wooded area not too far from the lake.

She said, "This is my church."

It looked like any other New England style church he had ever seen. Set back far from the road, it was a small white clapboard building, with two large front doors and of course, a tall steeple. He had been raised Catholic, but he always enjoyed the Protestant design of this type based on its New England roots.

He sighed deeply. "I thought we were past this about the church. I said I was sorry for going there."

She parked in the rear of the building and cut the engine. "You might as well get to know me."

"There are other ways I could do that."

"What else did you hear about my church or me?" she asked clearly determined to clear the air.

"I'm sure you don't want to know."

"I'm sure I do and since you started it…"

Oh brother.

With resignation in his voice, he said, "Someone told me today you're cursed and that I should stay away from you. They didn't expand on what they meant by that and I told them they weren't being very nice."

She smiled but it was a sad smile not a happy one. "Thank you… Come with me."

"Where are we going?"

"I want to tell you a story."

"Okay," he said slowly.

They got out of the car and walked back to the front of the church. She opened the door and let them in. He glanced at the handle and noticed there was no lock mechanism.

"There's no lock?" he asked. "Isn't that unusual? What's to prevent theft or vandalism?"

"The church is more than a hundred years old and it hasn't happened yet, not even once. Why worry about it now?"

The lights went on, but he didn't see her flip a switch. He was tempted to ask her how she did that but felt he had asked enough questions along that line for one night.

She saw his curious look and said, "The lights are automatic, triggered when we entered the room and on a timer just as you suggested we do in the old part of the hospital. You see, John, there are logical explanations for most things if you just step back and look for them."

He nodded in agreement as he scanned the room. There were two rows of ten pews on each side of the central aisle. The pews weren't that big, and he wondered how many parishioners could fit in the church comfortably. There were stained glass windows adorning the sides of the church and a very large round one high up in the back wall behind the altar, but he didn't recognize any particular pattern or biblical scene in them. The altar was simple and looked like nothing more than a large wood table with two fat candles on either end sitting in brass holders. He walked up to it to get a better look. It was solid, made of oak, eight feet long by four feet wide. The four legs were thick and carved with strange designs he had never seen before.

Off to the side was an elevated pulpit where he imagined Brom would deliver his sermons all hot and bothered no doubt. What was missing from the room were signs of any organized religion that Cesari was familiar with. There were no crosses, statues of saints, stars of David, bibles, crescent moons, or Buddhas...nothing. Just an empty room set up to look like a typical church.

He said, "All right. We're here. I get it. It's a church like any other. You didn't have to bring me here to prove it. I believed you. So what's the story you wanted to tell me?"

She sat down in one of the pews and beckoned him to sit next to her which he did. She said, "Put your arm around me. It's chilly in here."

He put his arm around her and glanced around in all directions admiring the simple but inspiring architecture while he waited for her. Eventually, she said, "John…"

"I'm not going anywhere, Jasmine, and there's not much you could say that would shock me. In fact, some of the stories I could tell you about myself would undoubtedly make your skin crawl."

"You think so?"

"I know so."

"John, I really am cursed."

Chapter 23

The Order

"Cursed?" he said, mouthing the word slowly, carefully, not wishing to be dismissive or mocking.

She nodded, "Yes."

He held her just a little bit more tightly to reassure her that he had no intention of invalidating her feelings. He said, "You're going to have to explain that one a little better."

"You know my name, right?"

"Of course, it's Jasmine."

"My last name."

"Van Tassel."

"Have you ever heard that name before?"

He thought about it for a moment and shook his head. "No, not really. Should I?"

"Yes, you should. Do you remember the story of the Headless Horseman?"

"You mean *The Legend of Sleepy Hollow* by Washington Irving?"

"Yes."

"Of course. We all read it or had it read to us as children. What's that got to do with anything?"

"The girl in the story. Her name was Katrina Van Tassel."

"Fine, what's your point?"

"I'm her direct descendant as is my mother."

He shot her a look and said, "Jasmine, that's not possible. Katrina Van Tassel was a fictional character. A figment of Irving's vivid imagination probably fueled by one too many hot-buttered rums."

"No, John, she was real and so is the legend."

"The legend of the Headless Horseman was real?"

"Not was, is."

"Go on. I didn't mean to interrupt."

"During his travels in the eighteenth century Washington Irving met the real Katrina Van Tassel and she told him the story of the Horseman which he wrote down, only she left out key parts. Those parts were then handed down generation to generation in my family. What most people don't realize is that the Horseman wasn't just a vengeful Hessian mercenary who lost his head in battle and roamed the earth at night looking for it. He was headless all right but much more than that. He was a creature of unspeakable horror summoned forth from the abyss by black magic to do her bidding."

"Who's bidding?"

"Katrina Van Tassel's."

Cesari was incredulous that he was even having this conversation. "Jasmine, I don't know about this."

"Let me finish and then if you think I'm crazy and want to leave, we will."

"All right. Take your time but let me remind you again that I scare easily."

She smiled, "I remember. Anyway, Katrina Van Tassel was a powerful witch. The most powerful of her coven at the time."

"A witch?"

"You promised not to interrupt."

"I'm sorry."

"As I said, she was the most powerful witch of her coven. She made a pact with the devil in exchange for her powers and sealed it with a kiss. It is common lore that Katrina's children were fathered by Satan. Well, periodically in that day, there would be witch hunts which resulted in burnings, drownings and hangings of whole villages. Men, women and children, the witch-hunters didn't discriminate whom they murdered. Satan gave Katrina the ability to summon the Horseman to defend the coven using the most extreme measures whenever the hunters got too close for comfort.

There was a man, Abraham, who shared Katrina's passion for devil worship. He too was gifted in the black arts though not to her degree. They married, raised Satan's children together and for generations, they lead the coven. For their own protection, and to keep the bloodline strong, members of the coven frequently intermarried."

Cesari sat dumbfounded and slack-jawed. Eventually he said, "Incest? Eww, is this story going to get much creepier?"

"It's not as creepy or unusual as you might think, and remember, back then a family might have had ten or twelve children. Their cousins down the road might have had fourteen. There might not have been anyone to socialize with outside the family for hundreds of miles. Cousins marrying cousins was very common."

"Aren't there laws against that?"

"Does anyone say that to the Amish? Even today in one or two states, though frowned upon, it's not necessarily illegal."

"Still… All right, I'm listening."

"Well despite that, it was quite common for members of the coven to marry non-witches. Katrina noticed this and to ensure the continuity of her bloodline, she cast a spell decreeing that in alternating generations of the coven, members must intermarry and bear children."

"You can't be serious?"

"I am."

"And what happens if they don't want to marry someone from within the coven?"

"Bad things."

"Why every other generation?"

"Believe it or not, she understood the importance of having genetic diversity introduced into the community from time to time to minimize the adverse consequences of inbreeding."

He stood up and looked around. "So what's all this; a witches' meeting house?"

She nodded. "Yes, it is."

He was silent for a moment as he absorbed that. He then said, "Okay, just for the record, you're telling me that you believe you're descended from witches, real witches, as in real serious devil-worshipping witches?"

She replied in a whisper, "I am a witch, John, not just descended from one, and I am the last of the Katrina Van Tassel bloodline."

"And that's a big deal, I gather?"

"Huge."

"And Brom? What's that make him, a warlock?"

"We don't differentiate by gender. That's more of a Hollywood stereotype. We're all just witches. Brom is descended directly from Abraham Van Brunt. The same Brom in the story of *Sleepy Hollow* who married Katrina. Brom is the last of the Van Brunts."

"Brom is a nickname for Abraham?"

"Yes."

He thought about that. "If they married, and you're her descendant wouldn't your last name be Van Brunt, not Van Tassel?"

"Our tradition holds that the female offspring keep the mother's surname and males keep their father's. Anyway, I know I'm giving you a lot to think about, but I wasn't quite finished with my story… At some point, the witch hunts intensified, and a little over a hundred years ago, the coven escaped to this part of New York State. The community flourished for a time but has been in steady decline now for a number of years with many of the remaining members being quite old."

"Just how many of you are there?"

"An exact count would be hard to say because quite a few have married outside the coven and although they live nearby, they choose not to identify as witches anymore, but more than a hundred and less than a thousand would be a reasonable guess."

"A thousand?" he asked in amazement.

She nodded, "Brom and I are amongst the youngest in the coven with just a handful left in their teens and early twenties."

"Which is why he thinks it's his destiny to marry you."

She nodded. "It's also our family ancestry that drives him toward me. He feels that as the last remaining Van Brunt it is his duty to marry the last remaining Van Tassel, and I am starting to believe that no matter how hard I try to avoid it, he may be right. Every man I have ever been romantically inclined with outside the coven has either run off in fright or simply disappeared without a word, and I fear the worst."

He sat back down next to her. "What do you fear?"

"That whenever I fall in love with someone outside the coven, the Horseman comes for them. The Horseman sees them as a threat to the coven and it's his duty to neutralize that threat. It's the curse I was telling you about."

"Jasmine, you can't believe that."

"I do, John."

He stared at her with incredulity. He had heard about well-organized complex delusions but this one far exceeded anything he learned about in medical school. She had a well-scripted response to everything. She needed help, but first, he thought it prudent to let her get it all out.

"So what goes on here? Do you sit around summoning the devil? Sacrificing animals?"

"You're being facetious. No, we meditate mostly. Those awful days are behind us. We're mostly spiritual now, trying to live in peace with nature and our adopted communities. Despite the attempts at safe-guarding the lineage, centuries of breeding outside the coven have greatly diluted our powers. Any rituals or acts of conjuring these days are mostly for personal entertainment like that little show you saw Brom and the others put on last night in the honey-house. They're like frat boys who can't put the glory days behind them."

"They were just fooling around?"

She nodded. "I hope they didn't frighten you."

"So you don't have any real powers?"

"I'm pretty good at card tricks."

He smiled at that, rubbed his chin and said, "Yet you believe the Horseman is real and part of your life you just said."

"Just because *we* have no real power anymore doesn't mean there is no power. The evil power that brought the Horseman to life in the first place was tangible and still exists. We just don't wield it anymore. The last actual evidence of witchcraft by anyone in the coven was by Levi Blackburn."

"Levi Blackburn? The Night Nurse? The crazy guy who hung himself in the old hospital?"

She looked at him but didn't say anything. It took him a minute, but eventually he caught on. "He was a witch, a member of this coven?"

"He was desperate to increase his powers and to restore the coven to its previous glory."

"So he really was trying to summon the devil that night, but you downplayed that when I brought it up."

She gave him an exasperated look. "John, we'd just met. I wasn't sure how you'd react. I thought I owed it to you to let you know what happened there, but I didn't see the need to go overboard with information. Besides, most people don't believe in this stuff and I didn't want you to think I was nuts. Remember, how crazy that nurse Sandy sounded to you?" She let out a deep breath. "Anyway, I didn't think I'd be sitting here like this baring my soul to you."

Cesari was both alarmed and fascinated by Jasmine's disclosures. "Tell me more about Levi Blackburn. Did the devil actually come for him?"

"I don't know. No one does…maybe. Certainly that was his plan, but more than likely he got to meet the Horseman instead. We'll never know for sure."

"The Horseman? Why do you say that?"

"The Horseman's main function as I said was to protect the coven from threats. He would kill anyone, even a witch, who threatened the existence of the coven. There are rumors that he might have been summoned by other witches to stop Levi. At least that's what my parents told me. Not everyone, including my parents and myself, believe that going back to the old days of human sacrifice and playing footsie with Satan is a good thing and many think it's dangerous folly."

Cesari took that in and contemplated it for a moment, eventually saying, "Speaking of your parents. This threat of Brom exposing you would destroy them because this is the only life they know?"

"That's one thing, but it's more than that. The coven is their family, and for me to defy Katrina's will to marry an outsider and possibly leave the coven would effectively end our line. That would be a humiliation my parents could never survive. I'm an only child, John. They live and die by my successes and my failures and the older they get the worse that gets."

"Some other girl witch wouldn't suffice to save the coven?"

She shook her head and he understood saying, "I get it. It has to be you because you're the last Van Tassel... Well, you're thirty-one years old, Jasmine. If you're supposed to save the coven from extinction shouldn't you get cracking?" he asked, trying not to make it sound like a joke.

"I only need one or two children for that purpose so I have plenty of time, but there's something you should know about witches."

"What's that?"

"We have a very high tendency toward multiple gestations."

"Like twins?"

She pointed her thumb upward.

He said, "Triplets?"

She pointed upward again.

"Quadruplets?"

"Highest rate of quadruplets on the planet, and sextuplets are not that uncommon. No one knows this because we always give birth at home with other witches serving as midwives. With a little luck I could have eight, ten or even twelve children by the time I was thirty-five if I set my mind to it."

Cesari gasped. Not just at that imagery which was amazing in and to itself, but her ability to explain away obvious pitfalls in her fantasy was nothing short of phenomenal.

He asked very reasonably, "If that's the case, then how is it you're an only child. Shouldn't you have eight or ten siblings?"

"That's an astute observation, but the first thing you should know is that my father is not a witch. Mother was the generation who married outside the coven and that is why I am bound by the curse of the Horseman. Because he loved her so deeply, my father accepted her for who she is and embraced our way of life. The second thing is that when witches do marry outside the coven, our ability to conceive is limited and approaches that of non-witches with rare exception."

Cesari vaguely wondered if he was in any physical danger. He'd never been alone before with someone this psychotic, but he couldn't imagine her doing him any harm. She was slender and no more than one hundred and ten, maybe one hundred and fifteen pounds. He had at least a hundred pounds on her. Still, she could be armed. If he turned his back on her at the right moment...

He said, "Your parents told me they knew you were dating outside the coven. They didn't seem overly concerned."

"They love me and they want me to be happy and to marry for the right reasons just as they did. My decision not to marry Brom has been almost as difficult for them as it has been for me, but they will support me no matter what even if it means being cast out from the coven. At this point however, they don't seem to have anything to worry about."

"You mean because the Horseman will keep you in line?"

"Yes."

"What about the others? Did they know you sought romance outside the coven and if they did why would it be such a big deal if Brom were to denounce you now?"

"The short answer is they didn't know, at least not that I'm aware of. I've kept my affairs very quiet mostly for fear of antagonizing Brom. Of course, I couldn't keep such things from my parents. The real problem is that over the years Brom has grown into a man of great standing and influence in our community and although everyone knows of my importance to the coven it wouldn't stop them from turning against my parents at Brom's urging."

Cesari thought about that. "Okay, but what about you? Aren't you taking a bit of a chance? I mean, what if you had an accident and the coven found out?"

She found that amusing. "Witches don't have accidents, John. We have to want to get pregnant, and everything has to be in alignment."

Damn, this was incredible. He wished he had a tape recorder. "So why is Brom so bent out of shape about me? If the curse will bring you back to him, he's got nothing to worry about and in fact, if you can't fight it, why not just marry him and get it over with?"

She shook her head with frustration. "First of all, Brom is bent out of shape because you humiliated him at dinner and then again when he found out about us in the honey-house. That was my mistake I admit, but in his view, you have brought the fight to his turf. To your second question, I won't marry him because I don't love him. I may be a witch but I am also a woman with feelings and certain views on the subject. I've tried to convince myself to love him but I can't. Believe me, I didn't just wake up one day and think to myself how can I crush Brom, my parents, and my coven all at the same time?"

Cesari took in a deep breath and let it out. "I understand."

"Do you believe me?"

"The important thing is that I believe *you* believe you. A lot of this is going to take time to sink in. You don't hear stuff like this every day."

"Are you still going to be my friend?"

"Unless some guy missing his head shows up and orders me out of town. Then I might have a problem."

She tried to smile at his witticism but couldn't. "Then don't make me fall in love with you."

"You have to be in love for the Horseman to come out of hiding?"

"Yes."

"So we can have as much sex as we want as long as we don't fall in love? This may not turn out to be as bad as I first thought."

She smiled, "Sleeping with women and hoping they don't fall in love with you is a dangerous game to play."

He said, "I'll do my best to be a total asshole. It's worked for me in the past."

She laughed and agreed. "And it might work again."

"Tell me about the cat."

"What about him?"

"How old is he and why is he so smart?"

"I don't know how old he is. My parents adopted him when I was born, and he's been with us ever since. So even if he was a kitten when he came to us that would still make him at least thirty-one years old."

"That's pretty old."

"I agree, it's pretty old but not unheard of. I don't have an explanation."

"Fine, but isn't he kind of smart for a cat?"

"Women say the same thing about men all the time."

He chuckled, "Touché."

"Any more questions?"

"Just one; why call your church *The Order*?"

"*The Coven* would have been too much of a giveaway for witch hunters. Don't you think?"

"Touché again."

"*The Order* is short for *The Order of Nine Angels,* the real name of our coven. Lucifer was an angel after all, a fallen angel, but an angel nonetheless. He supposedly took eight lesser angels with him in his descent to hell."

"I read a little bit about *The Order of Nine Angels* when I looked up Levi's story. There are more than one chapter. Are you all related?"

"Possibly, as members moved away they were certainly free to start their own covens. We don't really communicate with the others. It wouldn't shock me if some just stole the name to capitalize on its past notoriety. We here in Auburn are the original descendants of Katrina Van Tassel. Of that I am certain." She yawned and suddenly looked tired. "It's getting late. We should go now."

"Are we going to drive or do you have a broomstick lying around?"

"That was unkind."

"I'm sorry."

"The broomstick's being repaired anyway. The last time I rode it I went through a stop sign and rear ended a Toyota."

They both started laughing.

Chapter 24

Dr. Greenberg

Buried under a soft down comforter, Cesari lay on the large bed staring at the ceiling thinking about Jasmine and trying to decide what to do. It was Tuesday morning 9:00 a.m. and he had no plans, patients or procedures scheduled. He did have wheels however. After their little heart to heart in the church Jasmine had dropped him off at Sal's to pick up the truck, a two-year-old white Ford F150. The cabin and flatbed were pristine and there were only ten thousand miles on it. It would serve its purpose just fine.

He sighed deeply and was very disturbed by what he had learned last night. The situation was even more complicated for him because of his personal feelings for her. He really liked her, but she needed some serious counseling. Jasmine was profoundly troubled, and possibly psychotic if she believed half the things she told him. He wondered how many other people in this town were aware of her eccentricity. Could she possibly keep all that a secret or were others caught up in the same delusion?

With all this obsession about Halloween, it wouldn't surprise him. He thought that some might find it very amusing to have a woman living here who really believed in all of it to the point of immersing herself fully in the fairytale. Maybe that's what happened? You grow up in a place where nearly every living soul is obsessed with witches, devils and ghosts. From your earliest days you're overexposed to the stories and legends. Maybe, just maybe her mind was susceptible to it all and she fell down the rabbit hole and simply couldn't climb back out again.

He wasn't a psychiatrist, but he did know one he could trust. Getting out of bed, he was suddenly energized to help this woman. As he showered the thought crossed his mind to just walk away. He barely knew her after all. Why get involved? Most people would think that he was already in too deep for comfort, but he shook his head smiling at himself in the bathroom mirror. Because the double XX chromosome was his fatal flaw, that was why. He lived for damsels in distress and he knew it.

He went downstairs, waved at Brom who was catering to guests in the breakfast room, and left the inn. The F150 handled well and he found a Starbucks in the center of town. After purchasing a large black French roast, he settled into an oversized leather chair in a lonely part of the store to make a few phone calls in private. First, he called his office manager, Linda Lu, to make sure she didn't need him for anything and then he called the hospital switchboard to make sure they knew how to reach him and finally he called the emergency room. In medicine, it never hurt to reinforce the lines of communication because in general, communication or lack thereof was the weakest link in the delivery of care.

After that, he settled in and dialed an old friend in New York, Mark Greenberg, a psychiatrist living in Manhattan. He was older than Cesari by about fifteen years and had been a mentor and a friend, guiding him through some difficult times when he was a young man. They had been close once, but they hadn't spoken in over a year. No particular reason for that. Just life ebbing and flowing in different directions for different people. Mark in addition to having a very busy clinical practice on the upper west side was very active in the Jewish community there and taught a course called *Understanding the Religious Mind* at Yeshiva University. He was one of the smartest people Cesari knew both from an educational point of view and also from an insightful, common-sense perspective.

"Hello, Mark."

"Cesari, long time. How've you been?" he said affably with a marked New York accent.

"Good, Mark. Things are good. I just started a new job in upstate again, a town called Auburn. It's about thirty minutes from Syracuse."

"Never heard of it. Why on earth would you willingly move back to hell on earth? Didn't you learn your lesson the last time?"

Cesari laughed. The familiarity in Mark's voice felt like they had just talked yesterday and everyday let alone a full year ago. He said, "You know me. I'm a glutton for punishment."

"Apparently… So what's up? If this was just to catch up, you wouldn't have called in the middle of office hours unless you think I hit the lottery and am now living on a Caribbean Island with servants fanning me with palm branches."

"No, it's not just to catch up although we should do that the next time I come down to New York. Nice imagination you got there by the way. The servants with palm branches will give me something to think about when it starts snowing. No, I'm calling because a couple of days ago I met a girl…"

Mark laughed, interrupting him. "You met a girl? What else is new? You're always meeting girls, Cesari. That's your biggest problem. You can never stay away from them."

"Keep your yarmulke on, okay?"

"Fine."

"May I finish?"

"Sure, go ahead."

"As I was saying, I met this girl. She's very nice, but I'm concerned about her mental health. She seems to be a bit…off."

"Off? You've never been one to mince your words, Cesari. Say what you mean."

"I think she may be delusional but in a serious complex sort of way. She doesn't think she's Catherine the Great or anything like that."

"All right. I have a few minutes. Tell me more." Mark asked, interested.

"It might take more than a few minutes."

"Hold on. Let me see what my schedule looks like." After a minute or two, he returned to the call and said, "You got twenty minutes. Don't be too wordy. Get right to the point."

It took Cesari seven and a half minutes to condense the story Jasmine had told him. When he finished, Mark whistled into the phone. "Jesus Christ, Cesari. You got a live one there for sure, but before we rush to judgement, I need to know a few things. First, are you completely sure she's not pulling your leg just for the fun of it? Maybe she's got a bet going with somebody at the hospital that she can jerk your chain? You know, one of those welcome the new guy to town kind of things?"

Cesari hadn't even considered that and hesitated for a second before saying, "I really don't think so."

"Fine, I'll accept that on face value because I've known you a long time and I know you would never be taken in by a pretty face. I'm assuming she's pretty. Am I right?"

Cesari smiled at the amount of sarcasm coming at him across the phone. "Yes, she's attractive."

"Then there's second; maybe she is psychotic and has a long history of mental illness. How well do you know her? Obviously not too well. You said you just met a few days ago. Did you ask her if she's seeing a psychiatrist now or in the past?"

"No, I…uhm…didn't think to ask."

"You didn't think to ask? A girl tells you a story like that and you didn't think to ask? Didn't you learn anything in medical school? Are you sleeping with her? Because I suggest you don't if you know what's good for you and if you really want to help her."

"I do want to help her, and I haven't slept with her."

"I know you, Cesari. You mean you haven't slept with her *yet*. Don't do it. If she's mentally unstable you're just going to make things worse for both of you as in, you might push her over the edge and you might lose your medical license if it comes out that you knew she was nuts and did it anyway."

"Understood. What do you think about her cat?"

"So she's got a smart cat. Big deal. I have a parrot that tells me I look good in blue, and a goldfish that I swear gets an erection when I smile at him. Look, I got to go, but I'll call you at noon. Hopefully, things will slow down around here. Meanwhile, try to get me some real information like, is she on medications, does she use drugs, drop acid? That kind of stuff. Does she carry any psychiatric diagnoses such as schizophrenia, and most of all with a potentially psychotic patient, does she fantasize about hurting anyone, herself included?"

"I'm on it.

Mark hung up and Cesari stared into space. He felt stupid. Of course he hadn't thought about those things. He was as usual too busy thinking about what she would be like in bed. He had a lot of ground to cover if he was going to find out that information for him by noon. He thought about what Mark had said about Jasmine scamming him as a joke or maybe a Halloween prank, but didn't think that was possible. Too many people would have to be in on it, her parents, Brom, and Linda Lu for starters. Not a chance anyway. He wasn't that gullible…he hoped.

He drove to the hospital, went directly to the physician's lounge and booted up the computer. Might as well start here, he thought, and searched Jasmine's name on the internet. Up came a few hits but nothing special. She had won a talent show when she was a teenager and the local papers had covered it. She graduated high school with high honors and went directly to nursing school. She joined the staff at Auburn Memorial ten years ago and won employee of the year five years ago. That was it. Nothing dramatic. No run-ins with the law. No scandalous episodes like being arrested for murder or hospitalized for attempted suicide, not that those things always made the papers. Still, nothing screamed out at him.

He left Google and logged into the medical records system. Now he was doing something that could really get him in trouble, but he had no choice if he wanted to help her. Peeking into someone's medical records who wasn't a patient of his was a big-time violation of healthcare privacy laws. Doing so to a woman he was in a personal relationship with was that much more egregious and could potentially bring down the wrath of the system on him including employment termination and suspension of his medical license. He hesitated momentarily and then typed Jasmine Van Tassel into the query box.

He held his breath as her file came up and he began to read. He read and read and re-read. He checked the name again and demographics to be sure it was the right Jasmine Van Tassel not that there were many people running around with that name. An old picture of her in the electronic record appeared just in case he tried to kid himself about whose record this was.

When he was done, he slumped back in his chair, his stomach churning. He was depressed and didn't want to believe what he'd read. It was pretty bad. He wiped beads of sweat from his brow and closed her record. What to do? He didn't know. According to the chart, she hadn't been to a physician in years, but all that really meant was that she hadn't been to a physician here in Auburn for years. She could have transferred her care elsewhere. Syracuse wasn't that far. Maybe that was it. Alternatively, she may have thrown her physicians overboard and decided to wing it on her own. People with mental illness did that all the time when they became frustrated with their care or impatient with results. Sometimes the disease itself told them it was time to move on.

A noise from behind alerted him to the fact that he wasn't alone anymore. It was Funkelman. Geez, just what he didn't need. The guy was a walking, talking, headache causing machine. He said, "Hi, Herb."

"Yeah, I figured you say that."

He was in a mood. Cesari tried to ease the tension and said affably, "Why don't you have a seat, Herb?"

"I think I will, but I don't need your permission. I was replacing hips when you were still in high school, Cesari."

"Are you still upset about the other day, Herb?"

"Who me? Not a chance... Of course I'm upset about the other day. I've been trying to get this PAC off the ground for a whole year and you waltz in and blow it apart for me."

"How did I blow it apart?"

"Those two physicians you met over the weekend, Max Jensen and Sally Webster, have been working the phone lines overtime telling everybody there's a new sheriff in town and his name's Cesari that's how. They've got everybody worked up that you're their salvation. They're all gung ho about the PAC now that's for damn sure but I've been voted out and you've been voted in if you want it."

"But I don't want it...whatever that means."

"What it means is that whoever we select to represent us goes to D.C. to lobby on our behalf with the congressman from this district. You'd also represent us with the other New York State PACs and potentially could be selected to represent the entire state. It's all on our dime from dues collected from PAC members and others who wish to contribute to the cause."

Cesari was frustrated. He had much more important things on his mind right now and politics was never his strong suit. He'd more than likely throw some obnoxious, self-serving congressman out the window of his own office. Besides, he was hired to be a gastroenterologist not a sleazy lobbyist.

He said, "Well tell everyone that I'm truly flattered, but I don't know the first thing about lobbying and I should add that I don't think I have the right temperament either."

"You're preaching to the choir, Cesari. You shouldn't be the one to snag all the glory. This was my baby from the get-go. I'm the one who should be wining and dining the politicians. I was born for it, but the people have spoken if you know what I mean."

"I'm not sure you have the right temperament either to be perfectly honest, Herb. I've only been here a short time and I've already met a number of people who think you should treat them better. I even met one nice young lady who said you made her cry."

He looked up at that. "What? Who said that?"

"It doesn't matter who, but you should pay a little more attention to how you speak to people, especially women. Now, if you don't mind, I have somewhere to go."

"Just like that. You dump a load on me and then you walk away? You're really not going to tell me who's talking smack about me?"

Cesari was starting to believe that Herb might possibly be the most annoying person he had ever met. He stood to leave, stared directly at him and lowered his voice so that there was just a hint of menace in it. "Just like that, but I'll tell you this. If it happens again, I'll make sure to come directly to you because I don't like it when guys make girls cry."

"Is that a threat?"

Chapter 25

Ups and Downs

As he walked down the corridor, Cesari thought he was perhaps a little bit short with Funkelman and regretted his tone with the senior physician. He made a mental note to take it down a notch with the guy. He wouldn't apologize but maybe buy him a cup of coffee as a peace offering the next time he saw him. On the way to Dicky's office, he passed the medical ward where he had seen Mr. Cortese in consultation over the weekend. Curious as to the outcome of his colonoscopy, he stopped at the nursing station and logged into his chart.

He scanned through the procedure report which was complete with color pictures. Not good. Santiago had a large mass in the colon. Biopsy results were pending but Cesari had seen enough of these things to know that this was cancer. Santiago was seen by a surgeon last night and was scheduled for a CT scan today. Surgery to remove the mass was already planned for tomorrow. Too bad, Cesari thought, but maybe they'd caught the tumor in time. You could never tell with these things. It all depended on whether the cancer had penetrated through the wall of the colon and that wasn't always dependent on size. Of course, if even one malignant cell had slipped through and implanted itself at a distant site such as the liver then that would change everything including the treatment plan and prognosis.

Cesari found him in his room and knocked politely before entering. He was sitting in bed propped up by a pillow reading his book, *The Old Man and The Sea.* Cesari greeted him, "Good morning, Mr. Cortese. How are you today?"

He put his book down. "Well, I was wondering if I'd see you again."

"Here I am."

"Have a seat. I'm glad you came by. I wanted to thank you. They found a pretty big tumor in my colon, about the size of a grapefruit, but you probably knew that. The surgeon came in last night and has me on the schedule to remove it tomorrow. He seemed very optimistic that I won't have to wear one of those bags. He also said they won't know for sure until the biopsies come back later today, but that it's probably cancer."

Cesari nodded, "I'm sorry."

"Don't be. If I hadn't liked you I wouldn't have agreed to the colonoscopy. On a lighter note, that Dr. Patel guy has really stepped up his game because of you. He's been coming in two and three times a day and really talking to me like a fellow human being. He told me that you said something to him. Thanks."

"You're welcome… You seem to be taking the news well."

"What choice do I have? Let's just hope this CT scan turns out all right. It's been explained to me that everything sort of hinges on the result. Is that right?"

"To some degree, yes. The tumor is large enough that it will have to be removed no matter what because it could potentially cause a bowel obstruction. The CT scan will help determine if the tumor has spread beyond the bowel. If it has then you may need some serious chemotherapy."

He nodded his head with resignation. "Life has its ups and life has its downs. I'm ready."

"That's about as positive an attitude as anyone could have under the circumstances. That'll help you a lot in the days ahead. How is your family taking it?"

He looked down. "My wife's upset as you can imagine. I came in here a week ago thinking I had a cold and now I have colon cancer. We haven't told my daughter yet. She's flying in tonight from Miami. She knows I'm sick and need an operation but doesn't really know why. We were waiting for her to get here before we told her the details."

"Well, I wish you the best of luck, Santiago. If there's anything I can do for you, don't hesitate to ask."

"Thanks, Doc, but you've already done plenty. I'm starting to like that Patel guy and the doctor who did my colonoscopy was terrific. Thanks again."

"You're welcome. I've got to run now, but I'll swing by after your surgery tomorrow."

Cesari shook his hand and left the room. Five minutes later he found Dicky in his office holding a small microphone in one hand and staring down his binocular microscope. Cesari let himself in and quietly took a seat waiting for him to finish what he was doing. What he was doing was analyzing Mr. Cortese's biopsy result and dictating a report for the chart.

When he was done, he greeted Cesari. "Good morning, John."

"Morning, Dicky. That was Santiago Cortese you just dictated?"

"Yes, do you know him?"

Cesari nodded, "I saw him over the weekend. Katz did his colonoscopy."

"It looks like poorly differentiated adenocarcinoma. Has he had a CT scan yet for staging?"

"Today he will. Surgery tomorrow. The tumor's pretty big. Nearly obstructing from the pictures I saw."

"That's too bad."

"Life has its ups, and life has its downs," Cesari said slowly, repeating Santiago's philosophical code.

"It's true. So what can I do for you or is this a social visit because I'm a little behind." He pointed to a stack of pathology slides waiting for him to review.

"I'll be quick… I was just wondering how well you knew that nurse Jasmine, the one you introduced me to last Friday to teach me the EMR."

"Jasmine? I've known her since the day she started here, seven or eight years ago… maybe ten years ago now that I think about it. Why? Are you interested and doing a little background check?" he winked at Cesari.

"Something like that. I heard she was pretty close to that GI guy, Pullman."

"Really? I hadn't heard anything about that, but Pullman was a very private guy who kept to himself most of the time so that doesn't surprise me. Well, if they were an item, it's been about three months since he left, so she may be ready to saddle up again. Either way, I wouldn't let that slow you down. A fine Italian stallion like you might be just what the doctor ordered for her."

Cesari smiled but pressed him further. "Thanks, but seriously, how well do you *really* know her?"

Dicky sat back in his chair. "I'm not sure what you're getting at, John. I don't have a personal relationship with her. I just know that she's an excellent nurse and a great employee with an impeccable record. Is there something specific you had in mind?"

Cesari chose his words carefully. He didn't want to start or spread rumors. "Well, I wouldn't want to begin a relationship with someone who might not be emotionally and... mentally up to it."

Well said, Cesari. He was proud of how he had artfully worked the word 'mentally' into the conversation, but Dicky didn't go for the bait. If he knew some deep, dark secret about Jasmine, he wasn't letting on about it, at least not today.

He said, "You could always come right out and ask her but in lieu of that my advice would be to take it slow. Don't rush in and smother her. Give her breathing room. Go to a movie, have dinner, get a drink and just let nature take its course. No commitments. You're a big boy and I wouldn't dream of telling you what to do, but young people today rush too fast into physical relationships before they're ready and it always ends up with someone getting hurt."

"Solid advice. I'll keep it light."

"I hope I was helpful."

"You were. I'll let you get back to your work."

"Anytime."

Cesari started to leave and then turned back to him. "Say, Dicky, do you know the guy who owns the Dulles House? His name is Brom."

Dicky grinned. "Brom Bones? The Bromster? Yes, of course. He's on the board of the hospital. Helluva guy and helluva businessman. He took that rundown old house of his that was about to be condemned and turned it into a thriving inn and apiary. He's singlehandedly put this town on the map with Michelin, TripAdvisor and Wine Spectator. There's even some talk about GQ coming to feature him as upstate New York's most eligible bachelor." As an afterthought he added, "And man, he can really take a punch."

"Take a punch?"

"Close the door."

Cesari did that and Dicky lowered his voice. "There's an underground fight club in town. It meets once or twice a month. It's a riot if you're interested. I can get you in. Brom's undefeated now for two years in a row."

"Underground? Meaning…?"

"Illegal, but the cops know about it. They don't care. Some of them even participate. It's boys will be boys kind of stuff. The hospital provides EMT and ambulance services."

"Seriously, the hospital officially supports this?"

"Not officially of course, but we can't just let guys beat their brains out without at least giving them some minimal access to care. So we make sure there's an ambulance within a short distance of the fights and encourage off duty EMT's to attend. We throw cash bonuses their way as a reward for their civic mindedness."

Jasmine had told him about the fight club but Cesari didn't imagine the entire town was in on it. He thought it might have been some brawling between Brom and a few of the locals behind the honey-house or maybe inside where he had seen them gather.

"Is it safe to say there's some gambling involved?" he asked out of curiosity.

Dicky laughed. "Oh yeah. You can pick up some nice coin at these things as long as Brom isn't fighting. He ruins the odds, but thank goodness he doesn't go to every one. Hold on." He flipped through a small black appointment book on his desk. "There's one tonight at the pavilion. Want to go?"

"The pavilion?"

"Emerson Pavilion down by the lake."

"Where the Halloween Gala is going to be?"

"One and the same. We throw rubber mats down so no one breaks anything falling on the hardwood floors. Are you in?"

"Let me think about it. All right? I'll let you know."

Dicky looked at his watch. "You won't be able to get in without a sponsor so give me a call or text by mid-afternoon. I'll need to let my wife know what I'm doing and get some cash to lay down bets."

"I'll let you know by three. Is that good enough?"

"Perfect."

Chapter 26

Keep it in your pants

Cesari waited patiently in the cab of the Ford F150 for Mark Greenberg to call him. It was almost 12:30 p.m. and he was parked on the street outside Angelo's pizzeria nibbling on the crust of what had been an amazing slice of pepperoni pizza. He was frustrated at recent events and needed to blow off steam. Going to fight club with Dicky might be just the thing he needed to come down from his emotional high. Watching grown men brutally pummel each other for sport was oddly relaxing. He hadn't spoken to Sal today and suspected he was nursing a hangover judging by the way he looked at dinner last night. He'd drop in on him later to thank him for his and Lola's hospitality.

Jasmine hadn't texted him yet today and he hadn't reached out to her. She was probably giving him some room to digest the things she had told him. If he were in her shoes, he'd be very concerned about ever hearing from him again. He wondered how many guys would disappear into the woodwork after hearing that story. Most, he thought. Then he thought about her boyfriends that had run out on her. Was that the reason why? Did she tell them the same thing and simply scare them off and in her mind attribute it to the Headless Horseman? Possibly, but Pullman literally ran away in the middle of the night. That's not the same thing as just not calling someone again. Did the other guys do the same thing; pack up and vanish without saying goodbye? If they had, that really would be very strange.

He wiped his face with a paper napkin and was trying to decide whether to keep waiting there in front of Angelo's or go somewhere else when his phone rang.

"Cesari."

"Mark, thanks for getting back to me. I know how busy you are."

"No problem. What did you find out?"

"I went through her medical record and she was seen by a psychiatrist right here in Auburn eight years ago. He diagnosed her with Major Depressive disorder and…"

"And…?"

"He thought she was psychotic, possibly schizophrenic."

"Bingo!"

"He was unwilling to commit to that diagnosis however. Apparently, she had just gone through a very traumatic personal relationship where the guy literally left her at the altar. The experience shattered her emotionally and she was very depressed. During therapy she revealed to him that she believed she was a witch."

Mark let out a long deep breath into the receiver. "I'm sorry, Cesari. I was secretly hoping she was just pulling your leg with the witch stuff but go on. What did he treat her with?"

"The usual anti-depressants and neuroleptics; Prozac, Zoloft, Abilify, Risperdal etc. Lots of counseling, but it only lasted for six months before she either dropped out or went to a different shrink."

"Or got better," Mark interjected. "That happens sometimes, and I resent deeply your use of the term, shrink."

"Sorry... The notes don't reflect that she showed any improvement or resolution of her problem. They just end. The last entry says that she was still fully committed to her delusion of being a witch and that although she was fully functioning and didn't appear to represent a danger to herself or anyone around her that could potentially change at any time. He was worried about her, and even contemplated admitting her for electroshock therapy."

"What happened?"

"It doesn't say. She was scheduled for a follow up appointment in eight weeks for reassessment but never made it. There's nothing after that."

"What about her medications? Did he continue writing or calling in prescriptions for her?"

"Not that I could tell."

"If she was that crazy, she might have switched her care to another psychiatrist for her meds."

"Well, if she switched her care I'll have no way of finding out who or where she switched to without asking her directly."

"I wouldn't do that just yet. We've learned a lot. Good job."

"Yeah, but what does all this mean and how can I help her?"

"For one, it means she needs to be under the care of a psychiatrist if she isn't already. It also means that you need to be supportive without being judgmental or selfish."

"Selfish?"

"Keep it in your pants."

"Got it, but how am I supposed to behave around her? It's already getting a little weird."

"Whatever you do, don't let on that you know she has mental illness. You don't want to get confrontational with a psychotic patient. Nothing good can come of it. If she offers it up that's a different story. Just keep doing what you've been doing but with your clothes on."

"Should I try talking to her psychiatrist? He might still be around."

"Only if you want to lose your medical license. If someone came to me out of the blue and told me they had been spying into the records of one of my patients, I would be obligated to report them to the state for disciplinary action. I'm cutting you slack because you're my friend and I pretty much told you to commit the crime, so we'll keep it between us. In addition, you don't know why she stopped seeing him. It could've been something minor like his overuse of cheap after-shave to something serious and traumatic like inappropriate behavior so I would definitely not touch that hot potato. He's out of the loop because she wanted him out of the loop and that's all that matters. Besides, there's nothing he could do anyway. You can't just grab a patient off the street and force them into therapy. They have to come to you voluntarily."

"But I feel so helpless."

Mark's tone became much more sympathetic. "John, I do this for a living, remember? Every family member, friend and distant relative feels just like you do, and I tell them all what I'm going to tell you. You didn't make her sick and you're not going to make her well by forcing yourself on her. Like it or not, the decision's hers if she wants help."

"I understand. So just play along no matter how nuts it seems?"

"Within reason, yes. I'm not suggesting you perform ritualistic sacrifices with her but if she wants to tell you tall tales and stare at the moon while she reminisces about the good old days of bubbling cauldrons and sorcery then let her. She's not hurting anyone and as she comes to trust you she might possibly confide in you the truth. That is, if she understands it. She may not."

"But if she's been to a shr...psychiatrist she must know she has a problem?"

"Not necessarily. She may have rejected her doctor's diagnosis. Sometimes the problem is so deep-seated that it's nearly impossible to peel through the layers of deception that a patient like this might cover themselves with."

"Why do they do that?"

"Frequently, complex delusions like Jasmine's are a way for the patient to protect themselves from some awful reality or trauma they may have suffered. The delusion keeps them safe from the truth and the more severe the trauma the harder they cling to their alternate reality."

"How do you get to the bottom of it then?"

"Most of the time we don't. We just treat the symptoms and hope they don't hurt themselves or anyone else. Once in a great while, we get lucky with extensive counseling and occasionally regressive hypnosis works."

"Seriously? Hypnotism?"

"I said once in a great while, didn't I? Not everyone believes in it. In fact, most psychiatrists don't but I've seen it work and have even dabbled in it myself with positive results so I keep a healthily open mind."

"That's interesting."

"And potentially harmful. You never know what's going to happen when you take the lid off someone's subconscious. That's why very few guys even attempt it."

"Is regressive hypnosis some sort of subspecialty of psychiatry?"

"No, it's more or less a carnival act that almost anyone can perform. The psychiatric part is knowing who would benefit from it, what to look for when you do it, and most of all when to stop. Remember, that old joke from medical school; the operation was complete success, but the patient died. It's the same thing with hypnosis. You dig into somebody's brain, you find out what's wrong and, in the process you scramble things around so bad they never recover."

"How good are you at it?"

"I've used it on and off for twenty-five years and have been to every conference and academic discussion ever held on the subject from New York to Moscow. Hell, I've even sought out every charlatan hypnotist in the tri-state area just to see what they had to offer, but most of it's smoke and mirrors."

"So I shouldn't try it on her as a lark?"

"Jesus Christ, Cesari. Don't even joke like that, but I do see one bright spot here. You said that some guy dumped her a month or two before you got to town, right?"

"It was three months before I arrived but yeah. He didn't actually have the courage to break up with her in person. He left town without saying goodbye."

"Ouch, what a lousy thing to do."

"Yeah, I know."

"Well, that other guy left her at the altar eight years ago when she went to the shrink. See my point?"

Cesari chuckled quietly at Mark's use of the word shrink. "Yes, I do."

"I'm wondering if her delusion of being a witch is some sort of conversion reaction which she uses to protect herself from her feelings of rejection and abandonment. Maybe she wraps herself up in her delusion so that as a 'cursed witch' she can't have a normal relationship with a guy. Therefore it's through no fault of her own that they leave her. It's a pretty convenient excuse and probably gives her comfort."

"Wow, that would be very sad if that were the case, but you don't know her. It's hard for me to believe that she could possibly be the problem in these relationships. She's beautiful, intelligent, and has a great personality. She can even cook."

"Sounds like you've been busy pouring it on and maybe aren't seeing all the warts and blemishes. Put on the brakes, all right? There are some things Cesari charm can't fix."

"I'll do my best, but you know me."

"I do and that's why I'm worried. Don't be impulsive and remember, now that you've dug into her history and know she's not well, you have an obligation to be professional at all times. She's your patient until further notice whether she is aware of it or not. Don't forget that."

"I won't. All right, Mark. Thank you for your help. I'll keep you posted. If you're ever up this way give me a buzz. It's a beautiful part of the country."

"Where are you exactly again?"

"About a half hour south and west of Syracuse."

"Is that anywhere near the Turning Stone casino?"

"It's about an hour from here give or take."

"You're kidding? Sarah and I are going there this week-end to catch a show, roll the dice, that kind of stuff. I heard it's great."

"I've never been there but I heard the same thing. Do you gamble?"

"Like a drunken sailor on leave in Bangkok."

"Really? I had no idea… How is Sarah by the way?"

"Hates me but what else is new?"

"I'm quite sure she doesn't hate you, Mark."

"Trust me. As a trained psychiatrist that is my official diagnosis. Why else would she stay married to me for thirty years if only to exact her revenge?"

Cesari laughed. He'd forgotten how funny Mark could be. "That's a good point you make."

"I'm glad we agree."

"When are you coming up?"

"Thursday and leaving Sunday morning."

"This might be a touchy subject, but are you are allowed to gamble on the Shabbat?"

"What are you; some sort of undercover rabbi?"

That was the second time in a week he'd been called that. "Forget I said anything. Well, as long as you're that close we should get together… Hey, you know what? There's a big Halloween party going on in this town Saturday night. It's sponsored by the hospital and apparently it's huge with thousands of guests, a band, open bar, food. From what everybody tells me it's supposed to be the party to end all parties. You and Sarah could be my guests."

"You're inviting Sarah and me to some sort of Pagan-Christian gathering on the Sabbath? I always knew you were an insensitive anti-Semite, but this takes the cake. Are you kidding?" Before Cesari could apologize he added, "But since there's an open bar, I'll ask Sarah. It sounds like it might be fun. No promises, okay?"

"Okay."

Chapter 27

Fuggedabout it

Cesari found the Auburn Public Library without too much difficulty and parked on the street outside. It was an old three-story building with great nineteenth century architectural lines. Wrought iron gates and gothic bronze lions guarding the front steps, along with tall spires and windows gave the place a distinct almost haunted mansion feel. The leaf strewn front lawn needed some kid to rake it up, and the brick steps leading up to the front doors needed pointing. Other than that, it appeared to be in great shape.

There was a metal placard just inside the main entrance giving a brief summary of the history of the library. Its official name was the Case Memorial-Seymour Library and was a registered historic site. It was built in 1898 and designed by architects Carrère and Hastings in the Beaux-Arts style, whatever that meant. It was a square, three bay building constructed of Flemish bond brick and limestone topped by a gabled roof and opened in 1903. Cesari was impressed and entered the carpeted, very quiet lobby.

At the main desk, he politely asked for help from an elderly woman who clearly took a lot of pride in her job. She scanned through her computer, wrote down the information he needed, and pointed in the direction he needed to go. He thanked her and disappeared into the rows of book cases. In minutes he came across the library's only copy of *The Legend of Sleepy Hollow*. It was published in 1820 as part of a collection of thirty-four essays and other short stories by Washington Irving entitled *The Sketch Book of Geoffrey Crayon*. Next to this on the shelf was a companion piece called, *A Guide to Understanding Washington Irving* published thirty years ago.

Cesari placed the books under his arm and went to another part of the library. Walking down the aisle he scanned the rows of books continuously until arriving at his destination, *Witches: Facts and Fiction*. He grabbed that book and returned to the front desk.

The old woman greeted him again. Her name was Martha. She had white hair, wrinkled skin and scrawny arms. She looked at him over her reading glasses as he placed the books down on the counter in front of her.

"I'd like to take these out," he said.

She smiled. "Of course, may I see your library card?"

"I don't have one. I'm a new doctor in town and was hoping I could use my driver's license until I got an official library card," he explained.

Given her age group's respect for physicians he thought that was a good touch for him to title drop like that. It was like telling a cop you were a marine or telling a marine you were a member of the NRA or telling a judge you were a lawyer… Scratch that last one. You never told anyone you were a lawyer.

She said pleasantly, "I'm sorry, but I can't let you borrow books using a driver's license. We have a lovely reading room and you can spend as much time as you want in there until closing at 5:30 p.m. that is. As you can plainly see, you have the entire library to yourself."

Cesari was disappointed. The 'I'm a doctor thing' usually worked with old people. He had expected a wink and a nod and to already be halfway home with the books. He glanced around. She was right. It was early afternoon and he was the only one in the library, so he smiled and said, "Sure thing. Where is the reading room?"

"Just beyond the central hallway and off to the left. You probably walked past it as you were browsing."

He thanked her and went to the reading room which he found to be very cozy. It was maybe twenty-five feet square with one long table in the center and several large comfortable chairs scattered around. He sat at the table on a cushioned chair and started reading *The Legend of Sleepy Hollow*. By today's standards the writing was tedious and long winded, but the story itself was short, intriguing and fun. Around 1790 Ichabod Crane was a school teacher from Connecticut looking for work in the small New York hamlet of Sleepy Hollow, now Tarrytown in Westchester County. With pronounced physical features, his comical image practically leapt off the pages. He was tall and lanky with huge ears, a gigantic nose and a spindly neck which made his head resemble a weather-cock. Irving didn't hold back anything.

Katrina Van Tassel was the eighteen-year-old daughter of the wealthiest man in town, Baltus Van Tassel and Abraham 'Brom Bones' Van Brunt was the town tough-guy who had his eyes set on Katrina. The interesting thing about the story in Cesari's opinion was that none of the characters were particularly likeable, not even Ichabod who ostensibly should have at least earned some sympathy points for being the victimized outsider. At any rate, Ichabod wanted to marry Katrina to gain her father's fortune, practical but not exactly endearing, and of course Brom had no intention of letting that happen. Ichabod was eventually driven out of Sleepy Hollow by the Headless Horseman, never to be seen again and Katrina went on to marry Brom. There was a strong implication that Brom actually played the role of the Horseman seizing upon Ichabod's naturally superstitious nature to scare him off but that part of the story is left open-ended for the reader to decide.

What Cesari didn't particularly like about the tale was that there was also the suggestion that Katrina may have used Ichabod simply to make Brom jealous in order to spur him down the aisle toward wedded bliss. There you have it. In a nutshell, *The Legend of Sleepy Hollow* was the story of an opportunistic schoolmaster, a local bully and a manipulative wench. It was very difficult to care about what happened to any of them.

He closed that book and opened up the guide to Washington Irving, zooming in on the sections referencing his writing of *The Legend of Sleepy Hollow*. He read for an hour and then sat back. Cesari was fascinated. Although Irving wrote the story while living in England, the characters were based upon real life people he had met in New York including Katrina Van Tassel with whose family he had stayed with for a while. So Katrina was real and a contemporary of Washington Irving just as Jasmine had told him. He hadn't really believed her until now.

He continued reading. At that time in history, the countryside was rife with stories of witches, ghosts and headless spirits wandering aimlessly and frequently with evil intent. Digging further into the period, Cesari read that after the

Battle of White Plains in 1776, during the Revolutionary War, the countryside south of the Bronx River was abandoned by the Continental Army and occupied by the British. North of that, was a thirty-mile stretch of no-man's land, vulnerable to outlaws, raiders, and vigilantes leading to the fortified American position in Peekskill. Bands of marauding loyalist rangers, British light infantry, and Hessian Jägers, renowned sharpshooters and horsemen, roamed this land terrorizing patriots and noncombatants alike. The legend of the Headless Horseman, was probably based on the discovery of a Jäger's headless corpse, decapitated by a cannon ball, found in Sleepy Hollow after a violent skirmish, and later buried by the Van Tassel family, in an unmarked grave in an old Dutch burial ground near their property.

At 4:15 p.m., Cesari's phone buzzed with a text message from Jasmine asking him if he was okay. Almost immediately, another text from Dicky came through about the fight club. He answered quickly saying yes to both. The phone rang almost immediately. It was Jasmine.

"Hi, John."

"Good afternoon."

There was an awkward silence as they both carefully screened their words. She asked, "Are you all right?"

"Of course. Why wouldn't I be?"

"Because I told you a lot of things about myself that are...unusual to say the least."

"Don't be silly. I hear stuff like that from girls every day. Almost every woman I've ever gone out with has been just like you."

"You've dated witches?"

"Witches, bitches... You say tomato, I say tom-ah-to. You see?'"

She laughed. "Yes, I see..." Another long pause. "So everything's okay? Nothing's changed?"

"If you mean between us, no. Nothing's changed."

He heard her breathe a sigh of relief into the phone. "Am I going to see you later?"

"What did you have in mind? I don't want to go to Sal's house again. Two nights in a row wouldn't be right and Brom probably has someone watching your house. The inn is out of the question and I assume that almost any public place would be risky given Brom's large network of friends."

She thought about that for a minute and said, "Where are you now?"

"The Auburn Public Library."

"The library? Why are you there?"

"I'm a big fan of libraries. They're very interesting places."

"Meet me at the church and park around back and out of sight from the road like we did last night. Do you remember how to get there?"

"Yes, it's right down the lake from your parent's home. I'll find it."

"Wait until it's good and dark. Let's say at least 6:30 p.m. I'll bring food for us."

"We're going to eat in the church?"

"No we're going to eat in my car."

"Okay, I'll be there." As he was speaking another text from Dicky came confirming fight club and telling him exactly where and when to meet. 10:00 p.m. in the parking lot of the Emerson Pavilion.

She said, "Great. What do you want to eat?"

"What are my choices?"

"I was thinking of picking up sushi. Would that be okay?"

"Doesn't sound much like witch food."

"Are you going to obsess about that?"

"No, sushi will be fine. Can you ask them if they make a chicken-parm sushi?"

She giggled, "I will."

Upon reflection he said, "Are you sure the church is the smartest place to meet? As pastor wouldn't Brom possibly drop by to say a few prayers or sweep the floors or something? I thought about that last night too."

"The church hires professional cleaners and they come once a week usually on Monday mornings. Brom only shows up for services on the weekend. Trust me I know the goings on over there like the back of my hand. I grew up practically living there. We could even go inside if you want but it'll be warmer in the car."

She was good and had an answer for every contingency. He wondered if Brom was even following her. Did he really threaten her parents? He thought about that. Her parents were the ones who said he threatened them, and Brom was at the house and he really did seem angry. So that part must be true. Did Brom know she was mentally ill and still want to marry her? Maybe he was crazy too? Maybe everyone in this town was mentally ill? Maybe there was something in the water?

Good questions.

But he had another problem that was developing, and he wasn't sure how to deal with it. Mark had told him to continue to act normally with Jasmine and to avoid intimacy which he agreed was sage advice, but perhaps not practical. Not practical because the only way they could spend time together would be if they were completely alone and away from Brom's prying eyes. The more time they spent alone, the closer they would grow. She was an adult woman and sooner or later would entertain adult thoughts. He could only sidestep that for so long without raising her suspicions. Going slow might endear him to her at first, but sooner or later she would want more from him than just talk.

He didn't pretend to be an expert on women but he knew enough that once a woman decided she wanted a guy there was very little he could do to prevent it. In Mother Nature's infinite wisdom, only women had been given the evolutionary advantageous adaptation of sexual emergency brakes. A man, alone with a woman who wanted to do the nasty, had no chance. He needed to think of a reasonable explanation to tell her if and when the time came.

The curse was interesting though because that was potentially a way of keeping her at arm's length. He could use that against her if she got frisky. He could remind her that it wouldn't be a good idea because it might bring the wrath of the Horseman down upon him. She would laugh and remind him that sex had nothing to do with it, and that as long as she didn't fall in love they would be fine.

He in turn would remind her that women, with rare exception, tended to fall in love with men they were intimate with. It was an inexplicable fact of nature. She might accept that. After all, she was the one who brought it up last night when she said that sleeping with women and hoping they didn't fall in love with you was a dangerous game to play. That could work. A little circuitous perhaps but certainly in line with her logic. There was only one thing to be concerned about. People felt differently when they were in the heat of the moment and frequently threw caution to the wind.

He let out a deep breath. There was an old saying that came to mind. The best made battle plans meant nothing after the first shot was fired. The same was true for men and women.

Once the kissing and hugging started…fuggedabout it.

Chapter 28

Sushi

He arrived at the back of the church at the designated time. Jasmine was already parked with her engine running and lights off. They were completely hidden from the view of the street. He cut his engine and got out of the truck. It was mostly dark out and getting cold again. He was thankful he had worn a sweater, a wool thing, green and thick and Irish. He liked Irish men's apparel. The clothes were different, functional, stylish, manly, and comfortable all at the same time. Plus, he hoped some of the proceeds went to fund the IRA in their quest for complete Irish independence and unification. He was probably kidding himself about that, but you never knew. Deep down, Cesari was a raging anti-establishment subversive son-of-a-bitch.

As he opened the passenger side door and sat down, Jasmine greeted him warmly with a big smile. "Hi."

"Hi back," he returned, rubbing his hands together for warmth. "What's with this weather? It was sixty degrees just a few hours ago."

She turned up the fans to high. "That's upstate. Thirty degree temperature swings sometimes. Don't be shocked if you wake up to six inches of snow on the ground in the morning and then see people wearing shorts in the afternoon... I'm glad you came. I wasn't sure if you would."

"Why wouldn't I?" he said in an offhanded manner to allay her concerns. "I told you nothing's changed."

"I know…"

Moving past that subject quickly he glanced at the grocery bag she was holding. "What do you have to eat? I'm kind of hungry."

She reached into a Wegman's grocery bag and came out with a large round plastic container loaded with several types of sushi. There were California rolls with avocado, fried tofu pouches filled with rice and salmon, tuna sashimi, and some type of spicy prawn concoction accompanied by dipping sauces. It was a veritable smorgasbord of deliciousness and remarkably good for grocery store sushi, but Wegmans wasn't like other grocery stores. They were the Rolls-Royce of supermarkets; the champagne of beers, the John Cesari of gastroenterologists. They hired professional sushi chefs right from Japan, flew them to the states, put them front and center in all their stores to practice their trade and for all the world to see. Wegman's was the real deal.

They ate quietly for a few moments and he asked, "How was work today?"

"The usual grind, but more stressful with Brom's people watching me all the time."

"How do you know they're watching you?"

She looked at him. "They're not very subtle about it, John. They stare at me all day, even when I go to the bathroom."

"Okay, but who are they exactly?"

"Half the people that work in the hospital grew up in this town and know Brom and me on some level."

He nodded. In psychiatric terms, this was known as an organized delusion. Well thought out and so far with no obvious holes that he could exploit to try to bring her down to reality not that it was his job to do so, but it couldn't hurt to try.

He replied, "What would happen if they saw us together? I mean in the short run? I know that ultimately they would call Brom but how would they react in the more immediate here and now?"

She thought about it. "Probably they wouldn't let on that anything was wrong. They would most likely just slip away to alert Brom privately when it was convenient. They wouldn't get confrontational if that's what you mean."

"Yes, that's what I meant. So I wouldn't be able to pick these people out of a crowd? They would just pretend everything was normal."

"Exactly. How's dinner?"

"Amazing."

"Healthy too."

"That's what matters." He glanced in her direction and saw she was watching him. "Do I have food on my face?"

She said, "You're asking a lot of questions."

"I'm just trying to understand how things work so I don't slip up and get us both in trouble."

She said, "Hmm," and then she covered the sushi plate tightly and moved it from the center console to the dashboard.

"Hmm, what? Is dinner over?"

"Hmm no, but it's time to pay me for your share."

He stared at her for a second and saw that she was serious, so he reached clumsily into his pocket for cash saying, "What do I owe you?"

She laughed watching him and he froze in place. "What's so funny?"

"You are," she said as she unbuckled her seat belt. She crawled out of her seat onto her knees, leaned over and wrapped her arms around his neck, planting a long, gentle kiss on his lips.

He said, "I wish I could have been funny like that in high school."

"Aww, did no one pay you any attention back then?"

"It was the loneliest six years of my life."

She liked that. "You really are funny."

"It's a survival technique."

She was inches from his face, gazing into his eyes. "How so?"

"Studies have shown that when women are laughing, they're much less likely to try to kill you."

"You're kind of paranoid when it comes to women, aren't you?"

"Experience makes the best school."

She inched closer until the tips of their noses touched and he could feel her breath. She was flushed, and her eyes glazed, sending him a message that she meant business as she pressed her lips against his again. This was no ordinary kiss. This was what biologists called *the kiss*. There were all sorts of kisses. There were the kind that signaled friendship or hello between strangers, like in Europe. There were motherly kisses, and in mob movies there was the kiss of death. Husbands and wives kissed each other goodnight and goodbye, but this was not like any of those. This was the kind of kiss where somebody was reaching out from deep inside themselves, yearning and desiring and telling, no demanding you to respond in kind or all hell was going to break loose.

Nerve endings fired all at once creating chaos internally and his heart rate quickened. He felt hormones surging from top to bottom as a result of the stimulus. Good that everything was in working order but not good at the same time.

He cleared his throat and whispered. "I'm glad we cleared that up."

"Why don't you put your seat all the way back," she suggested as she climbed completely out of her own and onto him. No easy feat in a Honda Accord, but she made it look easy. It always amazed him how much more flexible women were than men.

She knelt awkwardly on his lap waiting for him to recline back, but he made no motion to do so. He said, "Do you think this is wise? I mean...here, in the back of the church?"

"I've been thinking about that," she whispered into his ear. "I mean since we're already doing the time, why not just do the crime?"

He put his arms on her shoulders and gently pushed her back a little. "Aren't you forgetting one teeny tiny little thing?"

She looked at him puzzled. "Such as?"

"Such as the Headless Horseman and what he might do to me."

"But I'm not in love with you."

"You mean not yet. That could change if we keep going down this path."

Thinking it over, a look of dismay gradually spread over her face and she said, "You're right. I'm sorry. I don't know what came over me. I'm being selfish."

With feigned indignation, he added, "No kidding? I can't begin to tell you how much I really don't want to be dragged off to hell by a two-hundred-year-old dead guy."

"Of course. I don't blame you. That makes sense."

Pouring it on he said, "Of course it does. Look, I like you and all that and we can be friends, but until we resolve this curse thing we have to keep it between the navigational buoys, okay?" It was refreshing, and to some degree enlightening, to be on the other side of this kind of reprimand for a change.

Surprised at his tone, and a little ashamed, she hesitated and then quietly moved back to her seat. There ensued an uncomfortable silence which ended only when he said, "Could you pass me the sushi?"

She glanced at him with her eyes wide open as if to say, *How could you possibly be thinking of food at a time like this?*

Handing him the container, she said, "I'm a little embarrassed right now. Maybe we should talk about it."

"Why are you embarrassed?" he asked knowing exactly why but for her sake pretending not to.

"John, I just threw myself at you, and you…you rejected me."

"I don't see it that way at all. I would never reject you. Think of it as taking a rain check. Look, you have feelings for me and I have the same feelings for you."

"You do?" she said, suddenly feeling a bit better.

"Of course I do. I've been pretty clear about that from the start. You're very attractive and if things were different, we'd already be making babies... maybe for the second or third time." She smiled, and he finished that thought. "But as things stand, if you and I make love, I might not live long enough to brag about it to my friends. At least that's the message I got from you last night? Am I right?"

She nodded, "It's a distinct possibility."

"Ergo, you stay on your side of the car and I'll stay on my side."

"You're very disciplined. I was weak there for a minute."

He grinned. "Don't worry. I'll be strong for both of us."

Cesari felt he handled the situation well. She'd caught him off guard but at least now the ground rules had been established. He said, "Any new thoughts on what we should do about Brom?"

She shook her head. "No, almost anything I say is surely going to trigger him."

"How about if I say something to him?"

"You? What could you possibly say to him? You're the reason he's angry."

"Not really."

"What do you mean?"

"He's angry because of you. Not me. You're supposed to marry him and have many children..."

"Witchlings, actually. That's what we call them." she explained.

"Witchlings?"

"Yes, that's the proper name."

"Fine, but that's why he's so mad. I didn't do anything. Not really. I just kissed a girl who invited me to."

She looked down dolefully. "I guess, but what could you possibly say to him to make it better?"

"I could tell him that I'm really not interested in anything but being your friend and his too if he wants."

"Good luck with that," she said rolling her eyes. "And besides, wouldn't you be lying?"

"He doesn't need to know that. I'd be softening the blow and letting him adjust to things more gradually. I'll buy him a drink and talk to him. I'll explain to him that it wasn't my intention to hurt his feelings and that I'm very sorry."

She got annoyed. "You're going to tell him you're sorry you kissed me?"

"Of course I'm not going to tell him that, only that I didn't mean to offend him. I have absolutely no regrets about us."

"I should hope not, but it won't change him just so you should know. I advise against it."

"Well, I think it's worth a try... What was that?"

Something caught his eye in the side-view mirror and he turned around in his seat to look backward, but it was too dark, and he saw nothing. She turned to join him, saying, "What did you see?"

"I don't know. It was more like a fast-moving shadow, but I don't see anything now."

"Could it have a been a bear?" she asked. "We have a lot of them around here and they're very bold. They eat out of garbage cans and destroy bird feeders all the time. They usually come out around this time."

"I didn't know that. Are they fast moving? Whatever I saw was moving like all get out."

"I guess they could move pretty quickly if they wanted to, but I'm not a bear expert."

"Turn the car around with the lights on. I'd rather not get out if there's a bear waiting for me."

She put the car into gear and turned it around slowly with the bright lights on. There was nothing there but the back of the church, a couple of trash containers and the empty parking lot.

He said, "I guess it was nothing."

Chapter 29

Fight Club

They finished their meal, talked and listened to music until almost 10:00 p.m. He was in no rush to leave and wanted to convey the clear message that he cared about her. From time to time he gently tried to reveal inconsistencies in her story, but she had all her bases covered and never faltered. He was in the end impressed that except for the witch stuff she was extremely normal. In fact, she was what people would call a keeper. If she wasn't cuckoo, he could easily see himself in a long-term relationship with her.

Jasmine in turn was in good humor despite her concerns about Brom and her parents. She enjoyed his companionship and was quite the chatterbox once she got going. Now that everything was out in the open, and he had accepted her for who she was, she seemed very much at ease. There was a certain amount of physical tension in the air between them and he was glad the Horseman was lurking in the background as a defacto chaperone. His presence real or not made it easy to maintain the status quo.

She was a bit melancholy when he kissed her goodbye, but after nearly four straight hours he was confident that she knew he wasn't going to abandon or judge her. He didn't tell her he was going to fight club however. He suspected she would disapprove and try to talk him out of it.

When he reached the Emerson Pavilion, he found Dicky parked in a Chevy Blazer. It was black, shiny, and new with over-sized tires, a high-riding suspension and a rear hitch suggesting off road use or the urban pretention of such purpose. There were about a hundred vehicles of various makes and models parked in orderly rows. An ambulance sat near the main entrance of the event center along with an Auburn police cruiser. Small groups of men walked slowly toward the door some smoking cigarettes and cigars, some drinking beer. The pavilion was part of the Emerson State Park complex and overlooked the lake. Owasco Lake was one of the smaller of the Finger Lakes, but it was larger than a swimming pool and that was all Cesari cared about. He could swim…barely, and had no interest in water sports or activities. The park was across the lake from where Jasmine's church was and he glanced across the water at the lights on the other side wondering where exactly.

Dicky got out of his car and they shook hands. "Hey, Johnny. Glad you could make it."

"Wouldn't miss this for the world, Dicky."

"You bring any cash?"

"I have a couple of hundred on me, but I wasn't planning on betting. I figured to just hang back and check things out since it's my first time."

Dicky nodded. "Probably best that way. Well, I have ten grand on me if you want to borrow any."

"Thanks, but like I said, I'll probably sit this one out."

The event center was basically a large room, two hundred feet long and just as wide. There was a dais at one end for performers and a bar at the other which Cesari noted was in full swing. There were easily more than two hundred, probably closer to three hundred, people milling about, most crowded toward the center of the room which had been set up with a makeshift boxing ring.

Interlocking rubber mats marked off a twenty-foot square, and poles with red velvet cords stretched from corner to corner to mark the boundaries both for the combatants and for the audience. He counted about twenty women in the group. A small card table at the side of the ring had two guys sitting at it smoking cigars, taking bets and laughing. EMT guys were chugging long necks next to them. There was a stretcher and oxygen tank against the wall.

"There are three to five matches on any given night, John. With twenty minute breaks in between fights to get a drink and to clean the sweat and blood off the floor," Dicky explained. "Do you want a drink?"

"Nah, I'm good."

"You're probably right. It always surprises me how one drink turns into ten, and you can only come to work with a hangover so many times before it starts to catch up with you... Follow me. I'll show you how to place a bet."

They went up to the end of the line at the table and patiently waited their turn. It only took five minutes to reach a weasely looking pot-bellied guy sitting in front of an open metal box filled to overflowing with cash. He tapped the ash from his cigar into a styrofoam cup and said, "Hi, Dicky. What'll it be?"

"What do we have tonight, Dom? I didn't get a chance to see the scorecard."

"Only three bouts tonight, Dicky. A couple of sad sacks for the first two, but the last one features a bruiser from Syracuse. An ex-nose tackle for the Orangemen, Troy Bennigan, he didn't get drafted and's been bumming around for the last couple of years doing this and doing that. Still in great shape though. I scouted him out at the YMCA the other day. He was in the squat cage doing deep knee bends with four-hundred pounds and not even working up a sweat...a real beast. Remember him?"

"I do remember him. He was a great player. A behemoth if I recall correctly. He could block out the sun."

"Oh yeah, six feet one inch tall and at least two-hundred and seventy-five pounds, maybe more. I'm just guessing."

"That's a good guess. His neck alone must weigh fifty or sixty pounds if memory serves me right."

"That's him."

"Who's he going against?"

"You mean who would be insane enough to get in a ring with him? That's just it. We're not revealing that until all the bets are in because no one would bet against Bennigan. What we're doing instead is guaranteeing if his opponent can last just one full minute then it's a ten to one return. We're calling the guy Man X."

"That's all, just one minute?" Dicky asked incredulously. He glanced at Cesari and then back at Dom. "I'll take it. Here's a grand on Man X."

Dom wrote the bet down in his notebook, took Dicky's money and handed him a receipt. They wandered off together to get a spot close to the ring. The room had filled up and there was closer to five hundred people present now. Cesari and Dicky stood ringside three men back from the velvet rope. Dicky was delighted at his wager.

He said, "Like taking candy from a baby."

"Are you sure? From the description of Bennigan, a minute sounds like a long time."

"A minute can be a long time if you're getting pummeled but to actually finish a guy off with a knockout or a tap-out, a minute's nothing. I could last a minute in there just by running around the perimeter. Hell, I could probably last a minute if he had me on the ground and was gouging my eyes out."

"I'm glad you're optimistic, but my sense of it is they wouldn't give odds like that if they thought they were going to lose. What kind of rules are there anyway?"

"Rules?" Dicky laughed. "Johnny, this is fight club. There are no rules except one. You'd better fight. If the crowd thinks you're not trying your best or God forbid they think you're throwing the match, then you'll get a beating for real. I've seen it happen. About a year ago some punk tried to throw a fight. He went down for the count with a phantom punch. They dragged him out of here and pistol-whipped him in the parking lot. He's lucky one of the EMTs intervened or they might have killed him."

"An EMT saved him? What about the cops?"

He grinned. "It was the Auburn chief of police who was pistol-whipping him. He lost five grand on that fight and he's got kids in school."

Cesari stared at him. "Okay, I get it. People are passionate here, but no rules? How long are the rounds, three minutes?"

"These are bare knuckled old-fashioned brawls. There are no timed rounds. You get in the ring and when the bell rings you fight until either you or the other guy can't fight any more."

A bell clanged from the table and a guy in black pants and white shirt stepped into the ring with a scantily clad twenty-year-old brunette with long hair and high heels. She paraded around the ring holding a large poster that read, *Round 1*. Cesari thought that was strange since all the fights were technically only one rounders. The guy in black pants introduced himself as the referee for the night. These guys thought they were in Vegas.

Dicky nudged Cesari, "The ref is Kevin Barnes a big attorney in town if you ever need one."

"What about the girl? What if I ever need her?" Cesari quipped.

Dicky laughed, "Now you're thinking like a native Auburnian."

The referee introduced the first two fighters. They were middle-weights in the one-hundred and sixty to one-hundred and seventy pound range, average height and build and in their early twenties, wearing boxing trunks. They were barefoot, bare-knuckled and didn't use mouth guards. This could get ugly fast, Cesari thought, and it did.

Using no particular strategy or technique, they charged each other from their corners and started slugging, kicking and gouging, sometimes upright and sometimes rolling around on the mat. Occasionally separating to regain their breath, they would resume their primitive struggle for dominance with even fiercer determination. It was tough to watch as the blood started to flow from facial lacerations on both of the men. After fifteen minutes of pure mayhem one of the guys landed a vicious roundhouse to the side of the other man's head and he went down like a brick tossed out of a window.

The victor danced around the ring with his arms up in the air and a broad bloody smile across his face as EMTs attended to his vanquished rival. Smelling salts and oxygen revived him and he was able to walk off to the approval of the crowd. It was a bloody, unpleasant spectacle and it got worse.

Cesari changed his mind about having a drink and bought him and Dicky a couple of Buds during the break. Twenty minutes later, the brunette came back wearing even less than before and holding a sign that said, *Round 2*. The next bout was a couple of light heavy weights, in the two-hundred-pound range. One had a buzz-cut and the other a mohawk and beard. Both were covered in very aggressive tattoos. Both were hard and brawny with six-pack abs, and veins popping out of their biceps. The ref announced their names and stepped out of the ring.

Again the bell rang but unlike the first fight, they walked toward each other a little more cautiously and deliberately. They began with a few jabs and counter jabs. A quick kick here and a robust flurry of fists in response. One guy got a little too close and paid for it with an eye-popping uppercut which sent him reeling backward. The other guy closed in without hesitation to finish him but was met with a knee to the groin. He doubled over to the floor and as he did, managed to grab his foe's ankle yanking his leg out from under him. He landed on his back slamming his skull against the floor. Cesari winced as the guy's head bounced up and then back down again on the rubber mat. If it hadn't been for the cushion of the mat his brains might have been all over the place. He stopped moving and the crowd let out a thunderous roar. The other guy clutched his groin and couldn't even stand up to take a victory lap.

EMTs converged on both of them. The guy with the probably swollen testicles eventually limped off with assistance and the other one was carted off on a stretcher out to the ambulance in desperate need of a head CT. Cesari saw his eyes flutter open momentarily as they carried him past. At least he was still alive.

He said, "Jesus, Dicky. This is dangerous."

Dicky laughed. "It's fight club, baby. Wait until the heavyweights come out."

The second break between fights was a little bit longer than the first due to the necessary medical evaluation by the EMTs but by 11:30 p.m. the referee was back introducing the fighters for the last match. The big ex-Syracuse football player was in his corner loosening up. He wasn't that tall, but he was enormous and heavily muscled, thick in the chest, neck and thighs. The ref said he was two hundred and ninety-five pounds and an inch over six feet. He was even bigger than Dom had told Dicky earlier. He tore off a sweatshirt and pants and jumped in place to warm up. He took a few practice swings at the air. His face was huge and beefy, and his nose was bent to the left from a previous break. He wasn't cut up like the last guys. His muscles were like gigantic rolling waves beneath a thick hide. Cesari thought he looked a little like an African water buffalo.

They waited patiently for a minute and suddenly a roar erupted from the crowd as his opponent appeared wading and pushing his way through to the ring. He wore a black hooded robe and Cesari had difficulty seeing his face. He shadow boxed and stretched and finally, when he was ready, he took the robe off and threw it to a guy in his corner.

It was Brom!

The ref didn't have to introduce him but did so anyway. Six feet even and two hundred and thirty pounds. He was only ten pounds heavier than Cesari but made of solid, perfectly sculpted muscle without an ounce of fat on him. Layer upon layer of hardened chiseled sinew, he was the reincarnation of a Nordic god. However magnificently carved and proportioned as he was, he still yielded no less than sixty-five pounds to the gargantuan in the opposite corner. In street-fighting terms that was the equivalent of bringing a knife to a gunfight.

If Brom was concerned, he didn't show it. He flexed for the crowd and some cheered, but others groaned knowing they had inadvertently bet against him. Cesari wasn't sure. He acknowledged that Brom should be able to last at least a minute if he stayed out of reach but a well-placed punch from someone sixty-five pounds heavier could really ruin your day. He knew that for a fact because it had happened to him.

Brom glanced around and Cesari instinctively lowered his head. He didn't even know why, but he preferred not to be seen by his nemesis. Was that what he was now, his nemesis? He looked up again. Brom stood in his corner making and unmaking his fists and cracking his neck waiting for the bell to ring. His face was impassive, and his icy blue eyes stared straight ahead in a business-like fashion. Whereas the other guy paced and snorted like a bull at a rodeo, impatient to get started. He didn't have to wait long.

The bell rang, and the former linemen charged forward, his plan easy to see. He was going to use his weight advantage to simply tackle Brom and once on top of him simply pummel him until he could no longer see straight. Not a bad plan given his significant size advantage and previous expertise in the art of open field tackling.

Brom, however, was a warrior. His long blonde hair and drooping mustache gave him a fierce appearance and if the football player thought he was going to intimidate him, he had made a tactical miscalculation. The ex-nose tackle's wild charge up the center of the ring resembled an all-out blitz on the last play of the game. Normally the smaller player would attempt an evasive maneuver because the law of conservation of energy was one of the cardinal principles of Newtonian physics. M1V1 must equal M2V2. Mass times velocity equals mass times velocity.

If an object with a certain mass was traveling at a certain speed, it had a certain amount of energy. If it struck another object with a certain amount of mass traveling at a certain speed with a certain amount of energy there would be an energy transfer until the equation zeroed out. The object with the greater amount of energy would transfer that energy differential to the object with less energy. So if a two-thousand-pound car traveling at sixty miles an hour hit a two-hundred-pound man standing still on a sidewalk. The energy of the car's mass times its velocity is imparted to the man and he goes flying through the air.

M1V1 had to equal M2V2.

In this case, if Brom didn't get out of the way quickly, the resulting energy transfer as the bigger man slammed into him would either cause massive internal injury and shock or possibly catapult him out of the ring. In either case, Brom's brain would rattle inside his skull, membranes would stretch and tear. His heart might even develop some type of irregularity from the impact, but none of that happened.

None of that happened because Brom did the unexpected. He didn't try to evade the big man or duck or flee from the ring in a cowardly retreat. Instead, realizing his foe's intention, Brom decided to meet him head on and charged back at him as if they were two mountain goats about to butt heads in a battle for control of the herd.

Cesari held his breath, waiting for the potentially fatal collision as the football player lowered his head with the intention of ramming Brom. Five feet from impact, Brom stopped abruptly, put his feet together and jumped straight up like an Olympic gymnast flipping and twirling way in the air, clearing the bull-rushing man's head by inches, but that was all he needed. The ex-lineman's momentum was too great to stop on a dime and he continued on for a few more steps. Brom landed on his feet behind him and sprang onto his back like a panther, wrapping one arm around his exposed neck and securing it in place by grabbing his wrist with other hand. He then wrapped his legs around the man's midsection locking his ankles together.

The man had been caught completely off guard and off balance. With a mighty heave, Brom jerked backward and both he and the guy fell to the floor. Brom tightened his grip and grimaced as his entire body contracted. His prisoner gagged and turned red in the face as he clawed at Brom for his freedom and oxygen. Completely in control, Brom shrugged him off and with every second tightened his hold further like a python. His sinews strained and bulged from the exertion. The man's larynx was in danger of being crushed long before he lost consciousness and Cesari reflexively stepped forward concerned for the man's life.

The football player also realized the danger he was in and frantically tapped out. The referee ran into the ring with others and pulled him free, declaring Brom the winner as his conquered opponent gasped and wheezed for air attended to by the medics. The crowd went wild with deafening refrains of Brom! Brom! Brom! It wasn't lost on Cesari that it only took forty-five seconds for Brom to nearly kill a guy much bigger than himself. While he digested that, Brom strode defiantly around the ring beating on his chest. Suddenly, he stopped where Dicky and Cesari were standing. Not quite hidden in the crowd, Cesari tried to make himself small.

But to no avail.

Brom raised his arm, his face in a snarl, pointed at him and roared, "You!"

The men standing in front of him melted away giving Brom a clear line of sight. He shouted even louder as the room went quiet. "You! I want you!"

Cesari turned to Dicky for help. "I think we should we leave."

Dicky was confused. "What's going on?"

"It's a long story."

"Okay, but I need to collect my money first. Jesus, that was the easiest ten grand I ever made."

They made their way to the bookie sitting at the table ignoring Brom's taunting which eventually gave way to laughter and then cheers and then chants of Brom! Brom! Brom! again.

Dicky handed Dom his receipt for the bet. Dom looked at it and then looked at Dicky. "What's this?" he asked.

"It's my receipt. I placed a grand on Man X and he won."

Dom smiled wryly. "You trying to be funny, Dicky? You placed a grand on Man X to last one full minute and he didn't last one full minute. He only lasted forty-five seconds. Now hit the road. I have business to conduct."

Dicky was silent and a little dumbfounded trying to comprehend that. The color began to rise in his cheeks and smoke billowed out of his ears.

He grabbed Dom's shoulder and said, "What kind of bullshit is this? You owe me ten G plus one and I want it now."

Dom gave Dicky's hand a nasty glance and Cesari sensed trouble.

Too late.

Two large guys with slicked back hair appeared from behind Dom and walked toward Dicky with ominous looks on their faces. Both had one hand hidden from view. That was never good in Cesari's experience. One said, "How goes it, boss?" His voice was deep, rumbling, and raspy.

Dicky took his arm off Dom who looked up and smiled. "These two gentlemen were just asking where the door was, Petey. Would you show them the way out?"

Livid now and ready to blow, Dicky could barely control himself. Cesari touched his arm gently. "C'mon, Dicky. Thanks guys. We can find our own way out."

Dicky turned to follow Cesari, took one step and without warning turned back, lunging at Dom. Stunned, the bodyguards didn't react in time. Dicky landed one, two and three blows on the unsuspecting bookie before he even considered defending himself. Alarmed, Cesari watched in disbelief as the goons brought their hidden hands into view holding blackjacks. The decision taken out of his hands, Cesari hurled himself into the nearest bodyguard who, caught off-guard, tripped backward, toppling onto his partner. Both of them hit the ground hard with Cesari on top flailing away at the awkwardly positioned men. He alternately punched one in the face and then the other, their heads not being too far from each other, while Dicky continued to pound Dom senseless.

The bodyguards, surprised and momentarily on the defensive, began to gather their wits. Cesari saw that soon they would push him off and then he would be the one getting thumped. In the background he vaguely noticed the crowd of men had shifted from the fight ring to surround them. Cheering erupted anew, and he heard bets being laid down. Undeterred by this new distraction, he reached down to grab a blackjack that one of the thugs had dropped when he tackled them. It was leather, weighted with lead at one end and heavy, weighing close to pound, a truly formidable weapon. He whipped it back and forth ferociously, landing multiple blows on their faces. One, two, three and he was just getting started when whistles started blowing and the cops from outside came in to break up the riot. He felt a pain in the back of his head and then everything went black.

The last thing he thought about was Jasmine.

Chapter 30

The Aftermath

He heard the rhythmic beeping of the heart monitor long before he woke up. Nauseated and confused, he had a throbbing low-grade headache. Suddenly he sat up, leaned over the side of the stretcher and wretched sushi, beer and green foul-smelling stuff onto the floor. A stout, middle-aged nurse came rushing into the room and tried to position a plastic emesis basin by his mouth, but she was way too late. He had made a mess, but once he was done, he was done and sat there catching his breath. She handed him a towel to wipe his face as she called for a janitor to clean up.

"Where am I?" he gagged and noticed that he had an IV in one arm with fluid running in and a blood pressure cuff on the other. He was still in his street clothes, but his shirt was unbuttoned to the waist and someone had rolled his sleeves up. His Irish sweater lay folded on a chair.

"The emergency room, Doctor. How do you feel?"

He squinted at her as he wiped his face. He said, "I'll be okay... I remember you. You're the nurse who gave me coffee and a blanket when I was here on call over the weekend."

"My name is Marsha and yes, that was me. Seems like you couldn't get enough of us."

"What happened?" he asked glancing at his watch. It was 1:00 a.m.

"You don't remember?"

It was coming back as his head cleared. "I got dragged into a fight."

"Maybe you got dragged in or maybe you started it. There seems to be some confusion on that point. Anyway, the EMTs who brought you said you took a chair to the back of the head. You've been in and out for about half an hour to forty-five minutes. You've already had a negative head CT."

"I did? Jesus..." he whispered and rubbed the back of his skull searching for a lump. There was a sore spot but no swelling.

"Jesus has got nothing to do with it so don't blame him. You men get out of control sometimes and that's all there is to it. As if that fight club wasn't bad enough. You all have to get into a brawl afterward like it was the World Cup Finals or something. What happened, your fighter lose?"

He looked around. "No, I didn't place a bet. You know about fight club?"

A porter walked into the room with a mop and bucket and started cleaning up. She answered him, "Everybody knows about fight club. I've even gone to a few. How many people were there last night?"

"I'm not sure. It seemed like a big crowd, maybe five hundred."

"Oh, a small turnout and still a fight broke out? I don't think I'll ever understand men. Killing each other over other men killing each other."

As they talked, Dicky and an emergency room doctor walked in. Dicky smiled. "Hey John, you're up. Hi Marsha. What happened in here?" he asked watching the janitor work. He was almost done and was now spraying disinfectant on the floor.

Marsha said, "Hi, Dicky. Dr. Cesari threw up before I could get to him. It wasn't too bad, but he looks okay now."

Dicky looked sympathetic and asked, "You doing okay, pal? You really saved my ass."

Cesari nodded. He was now fully awake and focused. "I'll be fine. The nausea's passed. Marsha, can you take the IV out and maybe give me a glass of water?"

She glanced at the ER doctor for approval. He nodded and extending his hand said, "Hi, I'm Rudolfo Molinari but everyone just calls me Rudy."

They shook hands briefly. "Hi Rudy. I guess you know who I am."

"I do. You are the famous John Cesari, GI doctor during the day and UFC fighter at night. Dicky and I have been chatting about you for the last twenty minutes waiting for you to fully wake up, and I must say that I am impressed."

Cesari said, "Well don't be. It looks like I lost."

Dicky smiled. "He's being modest, Rudy. He was like Leonidas and the Spartans."

Marsha took his IV out and excused herself from the room. The janitor soon followed. Cesari swung his legs over the side of the stretcher and said, "What's next?"

Rudy said, "What's next is I do a quick neurological exam to make sure you're intact."

He listened quickly to Cesari's heart, lungs and abdomen; checked his reflexes and motor strength; looked into his pupils and oriented him to person, place and time. For the final test he had him stand up and walk back and forth across the room. It took about fifteen minutes to satisfy his sense of due diligence.

Cesari asked, "Can I leave now?"

"I don't see why not, the CT scan was negative, and your vitals have been rock stable. You otherwise seem totally fine from a neurological perspective. You will probably have a nasty headache tomorrow if you don't already. I'm not happy that you vomited but I'm not totally surprised, and it's only been the one time. I'll give you a couple of days' worth of antiemetics. Normally we would keep someone like you overnight for observation but you're relatively young and appear very healthy, so you should be okay. Dicky has promised to keep an eye on you and that's good enough for me. Concussions can be tricky things so keep an eye out for symptoms, worsening headache, confusion, more vomiting, that kind of thing. Well, I'll be on my way then."

Cesari thanked him and he left the room to save others. As Cesari buttoned his shirt and donned his sweater, he was relieved that he wasn't the slightest bit unsteady and even the headache seemed to be fading fast. Marsha returned with a large glass of water for him. He thanked her and chugged it down in one long gulp. Feeling refreshed, he walked out of the ER with Dicky to the parking lot. He asked, "Where's Sal's pickup?"

Dicky replied, "It's still at the pavilion. We'll get it tomorrow."

They got into Dicky's Blazer and started driving. Cesari said, "Is there going to be any fallout?"

"I wouldn't worry about it."

"It's too late for that."

"Okay, let's see. You beat up two of the most connected guys in town with their own blackjack. One's got a broken cheek bone and the other a black eye. Both of their faces are swollen and purple and their pride's been hurt. Because of their incompetence, Dom fired them on the spot as his bodyguards. They both want you dead, but I don't think we should dwell on the negatives. I still like you."

Cesari grinned. Just another day in his life. "How are your knuckles?" he asked Dicky noticing that both of his hands were bruised.

"Compared to Dom's face, they're fine."

"How is he? You didn't look like you were holding anything back."

"I wasn't. He was in another room in the ER just now having his broken nose splinted by ENT. That worthless piece of shit."

Cesari drew in a deep breath. "Is it always like that? Fight club I mean?"

"No... it can be worse, but let's not talk about that. I'm going to take you to my place for the night, so I can watch you."

"I'm fine Dicky just take me back to the inn. There's plenty of people there that can call 911 if there's a problem, but really I feel great. In fact, I'm hungry. I wouldn't mind going to a drive through."

Dicky was silent trying to decide. Eventually he said, "Are you sure you're okay? You really should be with someone, and I wouldn't load up on grease right now."

"Fine about the grease and think about it, even in your house we're not going to sleep in the same room so one way or the other if I need help I'm going to have to knock on someone's door. I can do that just as easily at the inn and I'll have my toiletries and clothes there when I wake up. It'll be fine."

Dicky let out a breath. "All right... I guess. Are you sure you feel all right? I mean it's no big deal. We have plenty of room."

"I'm all right, Dicky. I swear. I appreciate your concern."

"All right, I'll drop you off at the inn."

"I'm curious. What's going to happen with you and Dom? He did rip you off. That was worse than a carnival trick he played on you."

"I'll take care of that little weasel. Don't worry about that. He'll either pay me what he owes me, or he'll never work the fights again. There are a half-dozen other bookies in this town that would love that concession."

Cesari hesitated and asked, "Is there a chance anyone might press charges? We did assault people."

Dicky laughed. "I suppose there's always a chance, but I doubt it. A bookie getting beat up after he welshed on a bet at an illegal fight club with illegal gambling, protected illegally by the police, isn't exactly something that's going to get much sympathy from anyone. For the record, in case you didn't know it, those blackjacks they were carrying are also illegal. No, I don't think anyone's going to complain."

"You have a pretty good right cross by the way."

He pulled the Blazer to a stop in front of the inn. "Me? You were unbelievable. What a move that was taking those two guys down before they could ambush me. I'm in your debt. Really, I am. If it wasn't for you, I'd be the one with a purple swollen face right now instead of those animals."

"You owe me one."

"You got it… anytime."

Cesari thought about it. "How about dinner tomorrow night?"

Dicky was a little surprised. When people said anytime, they usually didn't mean tomorrow night, but he shrugged politely and replied, "Sure, why not? I'll pick a restaurant."

"How about your house? I haven't been there yet. It'll be more casual and I don't want to put your wife out. Pizza and wine would be perfect."

"My house will be fine but asking my wife not to put out would be futile so just let her do her thing. It'll probably be a four or five course meal. If you want to be casual we'd be better off going to a restaurant."

Cesari thought it over. He was going to ask if he could bring Jasmine, but he wanted to be able to talk to her alone and a five-course meal would potentially keep them all trapped at the dinner table for hours.

"Can I be perfectly honest?"

"You saved my life tonight, so I'll hazard a guess and say yes."

"There's a girl I'd like to bring."

"So bring her."

"It's a little complicated. There's a guy in town she was in a serious relationship with and he's never gotten over their breakup. She and I aren't an item or dating or anything like that but if he sees us together he most likely will get triggered. For that reason, she'd prefer that we don't be seen in public. What I was really hoping was that I could meet her at your house, so we could talk and relax without worrying about who's watching."

Dicky nodded, comprehension slowly creeping in. "You'd like to be alone with her?"

"You do owe me one..."

"Yes, I do... Hmm... Okay, I'll tell you what. I'll take my wife out to dinner and you can use my house. I'll text you my address and will leave the door open. You can have it from 7:00 p.m. until 11:00 p.m. That sound good?"

"It sounds great."

"Dare I ask who this girl and her ex-boyfriend are?"

Cesari hesitated. The less people who knew what was going on the better, but Dicky was now involved and had certain rights."

"The guy is Brom."

Dicky raised his eyebrows and shook his head. "Shit, that's not good. So that's why he challenged you back at the pavilion?"

"Yes, and I'd kind of like to keep this between us, if you don't mind? He's already kind of wound up about me."

"And the girl?"

"Jasmine."

"The nurse at the hospital? Is that why you were asking about the both of them this morning?"

Cesari nodded. "Yes, we're just friends at the moment but she feels very intimidated by him. He's sort of a larger than life character and he's made it clear he doesn't appreciate me hanging around her."

"Well, that's too bad. That's not exactly the guy I'd want coming after me. That's funny. I thought he was over her, but I guess not."

"You know about them?"

"Of course. Everybody does. It's a small town. Their breakup practically made headline news around here, but it was so long ago you'd think he'd be past it by now. How'd he find out you're interested in Jasmine? You just got here."

"It's complicated, but thanks for the use of your house."

Cesari got out of the car, watched him drive off, and went inside. The inn was quiet, the lights turned low and no one was around. The bar was empty and the fire cold. He helped himself to a scotch and sat on the sofa in the gloom reviewing the night's activities. Damn, that was one wild scene and Dicky... Jesus, the guy went wild. He hadn't seen that one coming, but the main take away was that Brom was definitely not someone he was going to have a drink with and talk things out. Jasmine was right to scoff at that idea. He clearly operated on a much more primitive level than most guys Cesari knew. Even worse from a tactical point of view was that Brom was a savage and well-schooled street-fighter. He kicked a much larger man's ass in less than a minute. That didn't bode well at all for Cesari's chances if it ever came to it.

He finished his scotch, yawned and went to his room. The alcohol had finished off his headache and revived his spirits. It was after 2:00 a.m. and he was ready to hit the sheets. He undressed and lay down, but the room was very warm. Someone had turned the heat up for him. He lay there for a couple of minutes not wanting to get up to turn it down but soon realized that he wasn't going to be able to sleep like that. Resigned, he got out of bed, found the thermostat and saw that it was set to a comfortable sixty-six degrees but was reading seventy-six degrees in the room.

Great. There was something wrong with the thermostat, so he went to open the window. That should cool things off. He parted the drapes and lifted the window about a foot and brisk night air flooded in as warm air rushed out. The outline of the honey-house could be seen in the moonlight.

Something caught his attention and he looked hard. There was a shape next to the honey-house; a large, dark figure, not moving, not really doing anything and certainly not trying to hide. He couldn't tell if it was looking in his direction or just frozen in place as a precaution. Maybe it was a bear as Jasmine had suggested. It certainly was big enough. In fact, it was huge. He didn't know much about bears and wasn't sure how big they grew, but Jasmine had said there were lots of them around here and not very shy. Bears liked honey didn't they and there was plenty back there. There you go. Then again, maybe it was just a large bush. It was too dark and too far away to be sure. He blinked, stretched and glanced up at the moon. When he looked back down the shape was gone.

Definitely a bear.

Chapter 31

She's mine...

He woke up shivering at 6:00 a.m. and wrapped the down comforter around himself tightly. It didn't help that the wind had picked up in anticipation of another rainy day and was whistling through his window. Sunrise wasn't for another hour and the room was dark except for ambient moonlight filtering in past the whipping curtains. He let out a deep frustrated breath and rose. The thermostat was still set for sixty-six degrees, but now the room temperature was down to fifty degrees.

He was only living in Auburn a week and already hated it. He growled to himself as he stomped over to close the window. Suddenly, he sensed a presence in the room and turned to see a pair of yellow eyes staring at him.

Shit!

He jumped back in surprise and fright, stumbling on the carpet and falling on his butt. Scrambling quickly to the nightstand he turned on the lamp and saw Ichabod sitting on the back of the sofa, quietly watching him, his tail waving slowly back and forth. Cesari's heart thumped hard in his chest as he caught his breath.

"Damn it, Ichabod, how did you get in here?"

The cat didn't respond and Cesari looked out the open window and down at the parking lot. They were three stories up and except for ivy covering the side of the house, he didn't see any ledges for a foot hold. Cats were audacious and nimble climbers but was that possible?

He walked over to the feline, bent down and looked at him right in his yellow eyes. "What is it that you want from me, Ichabod?"

No reaction.

Cesari let out a breath, rubbed his temple and thought he'd try something else. "Did Jasmine send you?"

No reaction.

Frustrated, he stood to full height and said, "Stupid cat."

Ichabod suddenly arched his back, snarled, bared his fangs and let out a ferocious hissing sound. Cesari quickly retreated, put his hands up defensively and apologized, "I'm sorry. Take it easy. I was just trying to see if you were paying attention."

This was just wonderful, he thought. It's the middle of the night and I'm trying to reason with a cat that should be arrested for trespassing. Mollified, Ichabod settled down but didn't move from his perch atop the couch.

Cesari said, "Would you mind if I went back to sleep?"

No reaction so he closed the window, threw on a sweatshirt and wrapped himself up in the comforter. Trying to sleep when you've just had a major scare was more easily said than done and he lay there, still quite cold, staring at the ceiling. He felt a ruffling at the foot of the bed and looked down. Ichabod had joined him and was curling up.

"Getting a little presumptuous, aren't you pal?"

No reaction.

Jesus, this cat was trying to bug him. How did he even know which room he was in? "I know what you're trying to do, Ichabod... Oh yeah, I'm onto you and it isn't going to work. You're not magical or whatever and Jasmine isn't a witch. Just because you can climb doesn't mean anything. All cats can do that. Got it? Now go to sleep."

Ichabod meowed softly and closed his eyes. So did Cesari, and two hours later, he woke to rain pelting the window and side of the house. He was relieved that he didn't have a headache or any ill effects from last night's blow to the head. The back of his scalp was sore but there was still no lump. He stretched and stood up. The room felt much better and he checked the thermostat again. It was now exactly sixty-six degrees which is what the thermostat was set for. Good. The situation wasn't totally hopeless. He scanned around for Ichabod but didn't see him.

"Ichabod," he called out, once, twice and three times and then waited a minute. "Fine, you want to hide go ahead. I really don't care."

But he did care. This cat was an enigma that needed deciphering. He walked toward the living room and noticed the carpet was wet. At first, he thought Ichabod had relieved himself and thoughts of dragging him by the scruff of his neck to the nearest Chinese restaurant crossed his mind but then he felt a breeze. The window was open a few inches and rain was splattering in. Cesari stared at the sill and thought about when he had closed it a couple of hours ago. It had been very dark then, but he distinctly remembered closing it all the way...or maybe not. He had been pretty tired. He closed it all the way now for sure, practically slamming it shut. Did Ichabod leave through that space? Cats were amazing the way they could wiggle and worm their way into small openings he knew, but to do that in the rain and then to climb down a wall of wet ivy would be no less than amazing. Climbing up was one thing but down…

He searched the rest of the room briefly, under the bed, chairs sofa and in the closet just to make sure. Satisfied Ichabod was gone, he went to clean up. When he came out of the bathroom, he saw a text from Linda Lu telling him he had patients scheduled in the office starting in fifteen minutes. He hustled his clothes on, grabbed a coffee to go from the inn's kitchen and went to the rear of the home completely forgetting that Sal's pickup was still parked at the Emerson Pavilion. He ran back into the inn to escape the cold, driving rain and called Linda Lu.

"Hi, Doctor," she said cheerily.

"Linda Lu, I don't have a car and it's pouring."

"Where are you?"

"I'm staying at the Dulles Inn on South Street."

"I'll come right over to get you. Have you eaten yet?"

"You don't have to do that. I just wanted you to know I'm going to be a little late because I'll have to call a cab, and no, I haven't eaten."

"It's no big deal. I pick up Katz all the time when he's late which is all the time. Usually, I have to wake him up and pour coffee down his throat to get him kick-started."

Cesari stared at his phone as if he couldn't believe what he was hearing. Slowly, he said, "Okay, as long as it's not a problem."

"Not at all. Your first patient is late anyway. I'll be there in ten minutes. Look for a red Camry."

"Okay, I'll be waiting at the front door. I'll come right out."

He hung up, finished his coffee and tossed the paper cup into the trash. As he walked through the house to the front foyer, he accidentally crossed paths with Brom who looked none the worse for last night's excitement. But then why would he? The other guy never laid a finger on him.

He said, "Good morning, Brom."

Brom looked at him suspiciously. "I suppose, if you like the rain. Did you sleep well?" he asked flatly without a smile, more out of obligation as the innkeeper than someone who truly cared. It was the kind of thing fellow travelers said to each other to pass the time and Brom said it with even less sincerity than that.

"Like a baby," Cesari said, trying to be upbeat and friendly.

"Does that mean you cried and wet yourself or that you simply sucked your thumb all night?"

Spoken without the slightest bit of humorous intent, it caused Cesari to raise his eyebrows a little. That was quick. From neutral to hostile in less than three seconds. A warmth crept up his face as he absorbed the insult, but he remained calm, not wishing to escalate things. This was not the time nor the place he told himself, so he ignored the obvious provocation and smiled. "Nothing like that at all. What I meant is that my room is so marvelously furnished and the bed so very comfortable, I had a great night's rest. I would recommend your inn to anyone who is travelling through the area."

Brom's features registered surprise and he bowed ever so slightly acknowledging the compliment. He clearly had expected some type of nasty or even angry retort, but none was forthcoming. Cesari wondered if he might have caused him to feel a twinge of remorse.

Brom said, "I try my best."

Cesari continued with the charm offensive. "That was a great fight last night, Brom. You were incredible. I was really impressed."

Again he seemed taken aback by Cesari's niceties and Cesari thought he might try using sugar more often. Pleased, Brom explained, "It wasn't that big a deal. All the big guys do what he did, rush headfirst trying to make the big tackle or knockout punch. They never see it coming... Frankly, you didn't do too badly yourself," he grudgingly admitted. "A little crude and rough around the edges but you got the job done."

"Thanks. Too bad somebody whacked me from behind with a chair."

Brom made a wry smile. "That was me."

Cesari looked at him. "Really?"

He nodded.

"Should I ask why?" he said and immediately regretted it.

"You already know why."

"Brom, there's no need..."

"Wrong. There is very much a need." Brom took his big muscular index finger and poked it hard into Cesari's chest pushing him back a step. His eyes seemed to glow hot as he hissed, "She's mine…and no one, and I mean no one, is going to take her from me."

He poked Cesari in the chest one last time and then walked away. Cesari sighed. So much for trying to be pleasant with the guy and so much for the subterfuge he had tried with Lola. Brom apparently wasn't nearly as gullible as he had hoped. He went to the front door and waited for Linda Lu who showed up five minutes later in her red Camry. She pulled to a stop and rolled down her window. The rain was coming down in sheets as he ran quickly to the car and got in.

As he buckled up he said, "Thank you Linda Lu. I really appreciate this. Remind me to pick up an umbrella this afternoon."

She said, "I will, and I apologize for not telling you about this morning's patients. I meant to call you yesterday, but I got tied up in meetings."

"All's well that ends well. Besides, I should have called you, so we're even with the misfire. Put it out of your mind."

"Thank you."

Something smelled good and he noticed a McDonald's bag and large coffee in the cup holder. "Hmm, is that what I think it is?"

She smiled. "Sausage, egg, and cheese McMuffin and a large black coffee. There are creamers and sugar in the bag."

"Black is fine, thank you. You didn't have to do that, Linda Lu. You're going to spoil me."

"Nonsense. It's my pleasure."

"Well thank you again for the ride and for breakfast. Can I at least pay you for the meal?"

"Absolutely not."

"All right but lunch is on me then."

She laughed, "Have it your way."

"As long the first patient is late, do you think you could drive me to the Emerson Pavilion? I left my vehicle there last night."

She gave him a disapproving look. "Oh Doctor, please don't tell me you went to fight club?"

He glanced back at her and wondered if there was anybody in this town who didn't know about fight club. "I'm afraid I did. Dicky invited me, and I went out of curiosity. Not a smart move I gather from your expression?"

She tsk-tsked him and said, "Not at all, and I urge you to resist the temptation to get in the ring."

"Get in the ring? Why would I do that?"

"Because you're a man and God ran out of brains the day he made all of you."

Good point.

"Don't worry about that. I have no desire to ever get in the ring. I have nothing to prove to anyone."

"Good."

"Do you know where there's a hardware store or Home Depot type place? I need some tools."

"There's a Lowe's on Grant Avenue just outside of town, but we have some tools in the office like a measuring tape, a screwdriver and a level for minor things like hanging pictures. What did you have in mind?"

"Something bigger."

"Like…?"

"Like a crowbar."

Chapter 32

Just Do It

Cesari didn't have the opportunity to buy Linda Lu lunch because a smarmy salesman hawking a new type of stool softener brought food in for the office at noon. A tray full of different kinds of wraps, chips and soda and the only thing he wanted in return was the full attention of the new GI guy. So Cesari grabbed a chicken Caesar wrap and invited him to his office for some privacy.

"Thanks for lunch, Brian."

Brian Klepper was tall and athletic, in his early thirties. He wore an expensive suit, gold tie pin and matching cuff links. He was clean-shaven with neatly combed brown hair and Cesari noticed a diamond and onyx pinky ring. He surmised that Brian fancied himself on the fast track up the corporate ladder.

"You're welcome, Dr. Cesari. So Linda Lu tells me you're new in town?"

"This is my first week."

"Great. Have you heard about the new laxative from GoNow pharmaceuticals?"

He handed Cesari a small sample bottle to examine. Cesari read the name of the new drug out loud. It was spelled DOIT. He said, "*Doyt,*" as in adroit.

"That's Do-it, Doctor, as in 'Just Do It.'"

"I see. Very clever. How's it work?"

"It blocks the sodium channels in the mucosal lining of the colon. This allows water to accumulate in the large intestine softening the stool but not so much that the patient has diarrhea. It's a once-a-day pill and most patients respond within the first twenty-four to forty-eight hours. The stage three trials show there are almost no side effects except for occasional, mild cramping in two to four percent of patients. When compared to the other name brands on the market, DOIT has better long-term compliance and satisfaction."

Cesari took a bite of his sandwich as the rep droned on. He was used to the sales pitches and figured he owed it to the guy to at least hear him out as a way of thanking him for the meal, but he wasn't really paying attention. It was always the same thing; some well-dressed, attractive young man or woman force fed pharmaceutical propaganda about whatever drug it was they were marketing, trying to overwhelm the already overwhelmed physician with a combination of pseudo-science, charm, good looks, food and small bribes.

When he finished his spiel, Cesari politely thanked him and promised to consider trying the medication if the appropriate clinical situation arose. In his turn, Brian promised to return next week with more samples, patient education materials and of course, lunch.

"Are you married, Dr. Cesari?"

"Only to my work, Brian. Why do you ask?"

He smiled and winked in a conspiratorial manner. "I don't know if you're aware of this, but Syracuse has quite the nightlife if you're interested. It's the kind of city where men can be men if you get my drift."

"So I've heard." He remembered Dicky telling him about the gentlemen's club they had visited his first night. He had no recollection of it because he was drunk out of his mind but took it on face value that he had been there.

"Well, if you'd like to take advantage of the amenities there sometime let me know. I have an entertainment budget for our best prescribers. I can have a limo pick you up and drop you off right here in Auburn."

There it was. A bribe of debauchery wrapped in deli-meats and a silk suit and all he had to do was overprescribe a medication he knew nothing about to his patients whether they needed it or not.

"I'll keep that mind and thanks for lunch."

After Brian left, Cesari contemplated what to do with his afternoon. Linda Lu could only fill up his morning with patients on such short notice, so he was free the rest of the day. He thought about Jasmine and her parents. It bothered him that Balthazar and Hannah didn't seem to care about her mental health as much as they did about their own standing in their church. They seemed like nice enough people and he didn't want to judge them harshly, but it was Cesari's considered opinion that Brom's harassment of Jasmine and her family could potentially exacerbate her condition perhaps sending her even more deeply into a delusional state. He wasn't thrilled about getting in the middle of their family dynamics, but he now felt an obligation to do something.

The question was how to discuss it with them gently. They were old and sometimes when people reached a certain age they often tended to focus on their own issues. For good reason too, declining health, doctor's appointments, home-owner responsibilities, even the routine tasks of grocery shopping can become a confusing and exhausting ordeal for the elderly. He had no doubt they loved Jasmine but not being health professionals they may not realize fully the extent of her problem. Did they even know? They must. Well, one way or another he was going to find out.

First things first, he would stop at Lowe's and pick up a crowbar. He didn't like Brom's mounting ill-will toward him and the fact that he didn't even try to hide it was a bad sign. Last night and this morning were enough of a message for Cesari to take some minimal precautionary measures. It seemed to him that Brom was working himself up and he didn't want to be unprepared. Cesari wasn't a small guy by any means and he was quite capable of taking care of himself but after watching Brom manhandle that ape in the ring he thought it prudent to have an equalizer around. And very few things equalized like a six-pound steel crowbar.

As he was leaving the office, he ran into Linda Lu. "I scheduled you three colonoscopies tomorrow in the OR, Doctor. You're in Endo Room 1 starting at 7:00 a.m. You know where it is?"

"Yes, thank you. I've been there and met the nurses already."

"Are you going to be on time or do you want me to give you a wakeup call?"

"I should be fine, thanks."

"Have it your way, but if you don't show up I'll be knocking on your door."

He smiled. "Great."

As he walked away, he had this image of her dragging Katz out of bed and nursing him to consciousness with hot coffee like she described earlier. How did she do that if Katz was married? Maybe she was just speaking metaphorically like, *if it wasn't for me this place would fall apart.* He put it out of his mind once he hit the sidewalk outside.

It took less than thirty minutes to make his purchase at Lowe's and drive over to Jasmine's home where he found Balthazar on the front lawn raking up wet leaves. He was working up quite a sweat. Cesari got out of the truck and looked around. Although the leaves were dropping faster each day, they were still only halfway there, and he guessed Balthazar would be out here again next week. He caught the old man's attention with a wave and Balthazar took a much-needed break, resting against his rake.

"Dr. Cesari, what brings you to the Van Tassel estate?"

Cesari grinned. "I was driving to the inn to pick up my stethoscope. I forgot it in my room this morning and I saw you out here. I thought I'd stop and say hello. Don't you have anybody to help you rake the leaves? It looks like hard work."

"Nonsense, it's good for me to be outside and get my blood circulating once in a while. Well, how nice of you to stop, Doctor, and I do have to admit your timing is perfect. Believe it or not, I was in need of a momentary respite. Do you have time to join me for a cup of coffee? I put on a pot just before I came out here and Hannah made the most unbelievable apple pie last evening."

"Apple pie? Well the day I turn down apple pie will be the day they have to pry my dessert fork from my cold, dead hand."

Balthazar laughed. "A man after my own heart if there ever was one. Come with me."

As they walked toward the house Cesari asked, "How's Hannah?"

"A little under the weather today, I'm afraid. She's taking a nap in her room."

"I'm sorry to hear that. Nothing serious I hope?"

"No, nothing like that. She's been having trouble sleeping because of all that's been going on. She'll be fine. She's from solid stock."

They went inside and Cesari sat on the sofa as Balthazar went into the kitchen to get them coffee. He called out, "Milk and sugar, Doctor?"

"Black, please."

While he waited Ichabod came out from underneath a chair and jumped onto the sofa next to him. Cesari put his hand out tentatively and when the cat didn't change its demeanor or attempt to pull away he gently stroked his head which elicited a contented purring sound.

"How are you today, Ichabod?"

In response the cat rubbed his head along Cesari's thigh. Cesari said, "That good, huh? You sure get around."

"Vanilla ice cream with your pie, Doctor?"

"No, thank you."

Balthazar returned holding a tray with two massive pieces of apple pie and two cups of steaming coffee. He set the tray down on the coffee table in front of Cesari. "Help yourself, Doctor... Is Ichabod bothering you?" he asked.

"Not at all. We're getting along just fine. He seems to like me."

"Well, that's good because he's generally not very friendly."

Cesari was surprised to hear that. "Really?"

"Oh yes. He's usually very territorial and extremely protective of Jasmine, but I agree, he seems to have taken to you."

Cesari took a bite of pie, put the fork down and sipped his coffee with one hand all the while petting Ichabod with the other. "Well, I'm glad for that. At least somebody around here likes me."

Balthazar cleared his throat. "Ah yes, Brom."

"Yes, Brom. By the way, this pie is fabulous."

"Thank you. Hannah will be delighted to hear you liked it."

"Well, I do like it. Maybe I should have asked. Is it okay for me to visit you like this? I wouldn't want to cause you and Hannah any further trouble."

"Nonsense, of course you can visit us. Brom doesn't want you seeing Jasmine. It's okay for you to see us. What kind of life would it be if two old people couldn't entertain guests of our choosing?"

Cesari nodded and said, "I'm sorry I brought all this controversy to your home."

"You didn't do anything wrong, Doctor. That would be a gross exaggeration of events. The saga of Brom and Jasmine has been ongoing for quite a few years now. You are just the latest installment, and in fact I shoulder the responsibility more than anyone for the current crisis. I shouldn't have invited you to dinner with us that night. That was a grievous error on my part, but Brom had been in such good spirits lately, I took that as a sign he had finally moved on."

Curious, Cesari asked, "What about that GI guy, Dave Pullman, Jasmine was dating, the one who skipped out in the middle of the night a few months ago? Brom couldn't have been in a good mood about that."

"I'm not sure Brom even knew about him. Jasmine has been extremely secretive with her romances because of Brom. The fact that she took you to the honey-house was an extraordinarily reckless thing for her to do. She knew the potential risks. Clearly she's as taken with you as Ichabod." He paused for a moment searching his memory and continued, "Now that I think about it, Brom's recent upbeat demeanor does seem to have started around the time Dr. Pullman left town but that would have to be simply a coincidence. To my knowledge they never met nor did Brom ever let on that he knew about Jasmine's relationship with him."

"Tell me about Jasmine. I haven't talked to her much lately," he lied. "How is she taking all of this?"

"She's seething, naturally. Brom's obsessive pursuit of her over these many years has taken its toll as you can imagine, but overall I think she's handling it as well as possible."

"I hope so. That kind of stress could lead to all sorts of health issues for anyone... like depression or anxiety. I hope that doesn't happen to her. She seems strong, but I've only known her for a week. If she had any underlying emotional issues they could potentially flare up at a time like this."

Cesari let that float out there and he studied Balthazar's chubby face carefully but detected nothing that even vaguely suggested cognizance of what he was getting at. Balthazar shrugged and swallowed a mouthful of pie. "Yes, I see what you mean, but thankfully you needn't be concerned about Jasmine on that score. She's a rock and always has been. Trust me on that. Completely unflappable that one."

He looked at Cesari directly and without blinking, spoke sincerely with unwavering confidence and without hesitation. He had just given the man the opportunity to unload all his fears and concerns about his daughter's well-being and he didn't do it which in Cesari's experience would have been unlikely. So he didn't do it because he was either unaware of Jasmine's psychiatric history or he was the best liar Cesari had encountered in a long time. Balthazar did not strike him as a deceptive man which led Cesari to conclude that he had no knowledge of Jasmine's visits to the town shrink.

Was that possible? Could a parent be so blinded by their love for their own child that they would be unable to pick up on the fact that he or she was mentally ill? The answer was easy, it happened all the time. He sighed, drank some more coffee and said, "Glad to hear it and I suspected as much. I just wanted to make sure."

"Thank you for caring, Doctor."

"I do care."

They finished their pie and conversed like that for another thirty minutes with Cesari asking gentle but craftily loaded questions hoping to get some glimmer into the real Jasmine. Did she have trouble in school? No, she was a straight A student. No drugs. A great daughter. No parents could ever hope for better. The hospital loved her too. Promotion after promotion. Raises, bonuses, recognition awards.

317

On and on, it went. She was like Mary Poppins, perfect in every way.

Finally, Cesari said, "Well, I guess I'll be on my way. I still have to go to the inn to pick up my stethoscope and then get back to work. Thank you for the coffee and pie. Please tell Hannah I said it was delicious and I'm sorry I missed her."

"Of course and you're very welcome. This was a lovely visit. Come, I'll walk you to the door, Doctor, and thank you for stopping by."

He had a lot on his mind when he left the old man. This created a whole new problem for him to deal with. How could he help Jasmine if her parents didn't know she was sick? That news might irreparably break them, and certainly wasn't his right to tell them. So wrapped up in thought, he hadn't noticed Ichabod follow him outside, and as he opened the driver's side door, the cat jumped into the cab and scooted over to the passenger seat.

Cesari looked at him sternly. "Ichabod, c'mon. You can't come with me."

No response other than to stare back in defiance and whip his tail back and forth. Cesari watched him. They were gradually starting to understand each other's facial expressions. He slowly reached his hand toward Ichabod who slowly bared his fangs in response. Cesari pulled his hand away and Ichabod curled up on the seat. Clearly he intended on coming with him, but why?

He didn't like the idea of kidnapping or borrowing someone else's pet without their approval, but this feline was different. That was for sure. It's like he was trying to talk to him, but where did he think they were going? Cesari had told

Balthazar he was going to the inn, but in actuality he was returning to the hospital. Did Ichabod really understand him? This was a good opportunity to test his intelligence. On the other hand, maybe he just liked him and wanted to hang. Nothing wrong with that.

He studied Ichabod for a minute who appeared to be doing the same to him. Settling into his seat he closed the door and turned the ignition. Suddenly, he snapped his fingers and said out load as if to himself, "Doggone it. I just remembered I can't go back to the inn. I forgot I had an important meeting at the hospital. Oh well. Buckle up, Ichabod. We're going for a ride."

Ichabod jumped up and hissed his disapproval, tapping Cesari's arm with his paw. Cesari smiled at him and thought, *Okay, now for part two of the cat aptitude exam.*

"You would prefer we go to the inn, big guy?"

Ichabod purred gently and sat back down, suddenly calm again.

"Well, I'll be damned."

Chapter 33

The Mead's on Me

He didn't know why Ichabod wanted to go to the inn and he didn't one hundred percent believe that he did. What was starting to bother Cesari was the budding notion that Ichabod didn't just understand him in a rudimentary, intuitive kind of way but that he actually comprehended English and was attempting to communicate with him as an intellectual equal. Cesari shook his head. No, it just wasn't possible. He pulled the pickup into a spot in the rear of the house and they both got out.

He looked down at the cat. "What now?"

Ichabod started walking toward the honey-house. Cesari said, "Whoa, boy. I'm not going there. I'm already in enough trouble. What if Brom is watching from the house?"

The cat stopped in his tracks as if thinking about it. Then he reversed course and took off toward the front of the inn. Cesari followed him thoroughly amused. On the sidewalk they went to the neighbor's yard, the one through which Ichabod had helped him make his escape from Brom and his friends the other night. Ichabod walked along the side of the dense foliage of the tall hedgerow with Cesari in close pursuit glancing in all directions, hoping no one was home. The hedgerow was tall approaching eight feet in height and easily blocked him from view of the inn on the other side, even from a third floor window. But a person would have to be almost blind not to see them from the house in whose yard he was in. He tried to think of plausible explanations should the police suddenly arrive but no reasonable ones came to mind.

He moved quickly to get out of sight of the road watching the house windows carefully for signs of life. They made it to the swimming pool in the back yard and Cesari saw the narrow tunnel between the shrubs he had crawled through. Ichabod kept marching further back. The hedgerow eventually gave way to a thicket of trees and brush. He wasn't sure how far they had traveled but he estimated well over a hundred yards which would put them well past the honey-house.

The woods opened up and Ichabod veered to his right to follow the tree line, gradually tracing a course to the rear of the honey-house. Cesari could see a school complex in the distance with a football field, a field house and a massive parking lot across a busy road. He didn't see any homes or other signs of urban development and wondered how much of the property he was now standing on was owned by the county and possibly reserved for the school's future developmental needs.

They once again plunged back into the thicket only this time when they emerged, the back of the honey-house could be plainly seen some twenty-five yards in the distance. He said, "You're smart, Ichabod. I'll give you that, but what are you trying to show me?"

In response he trotted forward so Cesari took his cue and kept up. They were hidden from view of the inn and had arrived unseen, the bee hives off to the right and more woods to the left. The back of the building wasn't as well kept as the front and weeds, rusted farm tools, and abandoned beehives dotted the ground. There was no entry into the honey-house from where they were so if it was Ichabod's intention to go in for a quick sugar high he was out of luck. Apparently not. He went up to a patch of earth just a few yards from the rear wall and started pawing at it.

Now that was interesting. Cesari approached and watched him intently wondering what he was up to. The patch of earth was about three feet wide and circular. It was distinguished from the rest of the area by the lack of weeds and grass. It hadn't been freshly dug up but maybe within the last month or two. Cesari scanned around for a tool and found an old metal post; six feet long and pointed at one end; the kind used for staking tomatoes or grape vines.

He chopped at the patch of dirt and using the end as a shovel scooped out bits of earth and tossed them to the side. About a foot in he became frustrated by the slow progress, got his knees and used his hands to burrow deeper like a mole or ground hog. The ground was soft from all the rain and relatively easy to work with. Two feet down, he felt something man-made. It was a metal object. He reached into the hole, grasped it and pulled it out. It was the buckle of a man's belt, the leather strap partially detached but still there.

Cesari stared at it in dismay, his heart suddenly racing at the implication. What did this mean? He looked back into the hole and alternately used the metal tomato stake to poke and loosen the earth and then switched to scooping it out with his hands. In that fashion he was able to go another six inches down, but the opening was getting narrower the deeper he went which was natural. He took a minute to catch his breath and knelt there. Ichabod sat across the opening of the hole watching him patiently.

He nodded at the cat. "You saw something. Didn't you?"

No response.

Cesari redoubled his efforts and widened the field of inspection rather than just continuing to go straight down and a few minutes later was rewarded by finding fabric. He gently dug around so as not to damage it and realized that he'd found a dress shirt. It was tattered and torn and probably light blue at one point. It was a Brooks Brothers brand, neck size seventeen and thirty-eight-inch sleeve; a tall guy. He dug and dug and dug for another half hour, eventually finding a pair of black trousers, and a pair of enormous Edmond-Allen size fourteen triple E wing tip shoes, but no wallet or ID.

He lay back on the wet ground exhausted, sweating profusely, not sure what to do next. He had dug a hole nearly three feet deep with little more than his hands and a stick, and although he was concerned about what he found, he was also greatly relieved that he hadn't uncovered any body parts. It wasn't necessarily a crime scene yet. Without a corpse, there could literally be a dozen explanations for burying one's clothes. Still, where there was smoke, there was usually fire. Another way of looking at this however was that he was vandalizing someone's property. If these were Brom's clothes or some guest of the inn who forgot them in his room and this was how Brom chose to get rid of them then that was his right.

Cesari was a mess, wet and covered with dirt even on his face where he had wiped perspiration from his brow. When he gathered himself, he decided to put everything back in the hole. He knew where he could find them again if necessary and he had no place to store them. He collected his findings and was about to toss them down into the crater when something glinted at him in the waning late afternoon sunlight.

He knelt down again and stretched his arm down to the bottom and fished around until he came out with a wrist watch. It was a Mickey Mouse watch, old fashioned and classic with a leather strap. Round with Mickey in the center, his arms served as the hour and minute hands. It was battery operated and was still keeping time, the second hand slowly moving around. He looked at his own watch. It was only off by a few minutes. Not bad for a no more than fifty-dollar watch. Making a mental note to tell Disney they made good stuff, he wiped the grime off it and placed it in his pocket. Then he threw the rest of the apparel back in the hole and filled it in with soil.

He stepped back and looked at his work. Unfortunately, it definitely appeared freshly dug up now. Not good. He eyed the discarded bee hives against the back of the honey-house and took several of them, haphazardly arranging them over the recently dug up spot. That would work.

He looked at Ichabod. "Good job but it's time to go."

He meowed at him, and Cesari who was starting to understand his tones and inflections better than he wanted to, interpreted that as a *not yet*. "Is there more?" he asked hoping that he never had to explain this to a therapist.

Ichabod walked to the corner of the honey-house and peered around it like a soldier might, scouting enemy territory. Then he lay on his belly and crawled forward a few steps and waited for him.

This cat was killing him. "Do you really expect me to crawl on my belly after I just spent two hours digging a hole with my bare hands?" he whispered.

Apparently that was exactly what he expected. Cesari rolled his eyes. He was trying to reason with a cat again. Ichabod watched and waited patiently until Cesari finally conceded with a big sigh and got on his belly. They crawled along the side of the honey-house to the front door. It was close to 5:00 p.m. and the sun was setting fast, but they could still be seen from the house if someone was paying attention. Ichabod obviously wanted to go inside so Cesari fished for the spare key under the ceramic turtle that Jasmine had shown him. He found it and reached up to unlock the door without standing. Opening it just enough to squeeze through, they both entered the main operations room. Once inside, he stood up and used his phone's flash light app to look around. Everything was as he last remembered it. He also searched for cameras but didn't see any. That was odd. All the fuss was because he and Jasmine had supposedly been caught on camera entering the honey-house.

Ichabod made a bee line for the basement staircase and Cesari went with him. For whatever it was worth, he had developed confidence that his four-legged friend had something interesting to show him. He crept slowly down the old staircase and at the bottom considered switching the overhead lights on but thought better of it. Ichabod had beat him down the steps and was waiting for him by the large storage vat in the center of the room.

"What is it, Ichabod?"

No response.

Cesari looked around in more detail than he had that first time. Smitten by Jasmine's presence he might not have examined the room too carefully, but he did so now. It was a large rectangle with field-stone and mortar walls on three sides and brick on the fourth side with a roughhewn timber beams bracing the pine floorboards above. It was at least two hundred years old and Cesari suspected the mortar between the stones had long since disintegrated which allowed water to run in when it rained, making the floor wet and the air moist and cold. Even though he wore a sweater it was damp from laying on the ground and he was starting to feel a chill.

He went over to the jars used for storing honey and examined them row by row and then he saw it. Behind one of the smaller jars on a shelf was small video camera pointed at the center of the room, but it wasn't on. Why was that? It was hardwired but he didn't see any outlets down here. The honey vat and the incandescent light bulbs along the ceiling needed electricity, but it appeared Brom had simply dropped wires through the floor boards from upstairs rather than try to wrestle with the stone walls. So where was the electricity to the camera coming from?

He followed the wire from the back of the camera upward. It was discretely nestled against the stone wall until it reached a wood beam on the ceiling. From that point it was connected to a long dark extension cord which was held in place to the beam with a series of staples as it traveled across the room eventually plugging into a socket built into the side of the light bulb fixture. Cesari understood now. The electricity in the room was controlled by the switch at the bottom of the staircase. When the lights turned on the camera turned on. Not very sophisticated but Brom was concerned about kids and spray paint not national security. Besides, who was Cesari to criticize? He had gotten caught.

Other than that, the room was unchanged and offered up no surprises. He said, "Sorry Ichabod. No secret treasure room, buddy."

Ichabod meowed but didn't move.

Cesari's phone buzzed. It was a text from Jasmine. He hadn't spoken to her all afternoon. He texted her back that he would call her in a few minutes. She replied okay.

"Time to go, Ichabod."

He turned toward the staircase, but Ichabod didn't move. Cesari said, "I'm sorry, pal. Now be good. I did everything you wanted all afternoon but the party's over. I'm going whether you come with me or not. Besides, I'm freezing."

Cesari went up the stairs and at the top a dark blur that was Ichabod rushed by him to the front door. Cesari opened it a crack, peeked out and with alarm said, "Oh no."

It was quite dark outside now and he was in no danger of being seen from the house but there were trucks pulling up the path with their lights on heading straight for the honey-house. He quickly closed the door and retreated back down the stairs with Ichabod, running through scenarios in his mind. One, they may not come into the honey-house. Two, if they came into the honey-house they may not come down to the basement. Three, if they came into the honey-house and down the stairs, he would...? He didn't have an answer for that one.

He searched the room quickly for a place to hide. The vat was large and took up a big space in the center of the basement, and he thought about hiding behind it, but that would be problematic once the lights came on. Next to the honey jars were the large metal drums used for transporting honey to the wine makers. They were very large, and he thought that he could easily crouch behind them away from view, but they were also in direct line of sight of the camera. Not good.

He went up to one of the drums and lifted the lid. He was instantly overwhelmed with the odor of honey and…something else. Looking in he was confident he would fit.

He heard the door open upstairs and then footsteps and voices. Ichabod scampered off to a far corner. With his black coat, if he kept his yellow eyes shut, he'd be nearly invisible even with the light on. Cesari tilted the drum and lifted one leg in. He set the drum upright again and lifted the other leg in. Grabbing the cover, he crouched down and placed the lid gently over him just as he heard footsteps coming down the staircase. He kept the top open a crack wanting to see what they were up to.

The light went on illuminating the room and he saw too large men struggling with something heavy as they came off the bottom steps, grunting and cursing as they toiled. They wore cammos and muddied boots and then he saw the large buck. The smell of death filled the room. They flung the carcass down on the floor and Brom came down the stairs to join them.

"Open the lid and let's get started," he ordered.

The two men circled the honey-vat methodically undoing the metal clasps as Brom pulled a large Bowie style hunting knife from its sheath and began to masterfully cut the buck's head off. Not slowed down in the slightest by the neck bones, he sliced through ligaments and tendons as deftly as a surgeon, maybe even more so. Blood oozed onto the floor and suddenly Cesari realized what that peculiar scent was he had noticed.

The pipe leading into the vat from the honey extractor above was easily removed and swung to the side. The two men lifted the cover off the vat and placed it on the floor leaning against the wall. Then they picked the headless buck up, placed him in the vat and watched as he slowly sank to the bottom. Then they replaced the cover and pipe.

Brom grabbed the head by the antlers and said, "Good job boys. Clean the place up with the hose and I'll meet you inside for dinner. The mead's on me."

The men laughed and Cesari thought he was going to throw up.

Chapter 34

Dear John

After the men left, Cesari waited a solid half hour before coming out of his hiding space reeking of honey and moist soil. He found Ichabod sitting patiently by the foot of the stairs. Once they were safely outside the honey-house, they parted company with Ichabod scampering away to wherever and Cesari going directly to the inn. He was a sight to behold but thankfully Brom was occupied in the kitchen and no one else was around when he entered the house and bounded quickly up the stairs to his room for a hot shower.

He toweled himself, put on a robe and lay on the bed, examining the Mickey Mouse watch he'd dug up wondering who it belonged to and what had happened to him. The watch had cleaned up pretty well and appealed to him. He might even wear it someday although he would need to come up with a socially acceptable scenario of how he came across it. Back in the Bronx, most people would find the real story amusing, but probably not elsewhere in the country.

He called Jasmine and she picked up half-way through the first ring as if she had been holding the phone waiting. She said, "Hi, John. How was your day?"

"Swamped. They really went after the new guy hard today. Apparently, the gloves are off. That's why I haven't called until now."

"Of course. I understand. So do we have a plan for to-night? Unless you're too tired that is?"

"I feel great. There's nothing like rolling up your sleeves and getting dirty. I have a safe place for us to go tonight. Dicky leant me the use of his house for a couple of hours. He's going out with his wife and won't return until 11:00 p.m. He says it's all ours until then and not to break anything. It's on Burtis Point down the other side of the lake past the pavilion."

"I know where that is. It's a nice area. Should I meet you there?"

"Meeting me there is probably the safest option, but if you park in the back of the church I could just pick you up and we could drive there together. I mean no one is going to use the church tonight, right?"

She contemplated that for a moment. "That would work, and if someone were to be there, I'll call you and you could just keep driving, but no one will be there. I'm confident of that."

"I'll pick you up in half an hour."

"Bye."

Exactly thirty minutes later, she was sitting next to him in the truck at the rear of the church. She had really dolled up and looked like she was ready to go clubbing in Manhattan; designer jeans, new shoes, gold earrings, makeup, hair blown out, black leather jacket and a red scarf. She smelled nice too. He felt bad…a little. He wore blue jeans neither old or new but lived in and scuffed up walking shoes that he'd owned forever, an ordinary shirt, sweater and a windbreaker. He was freshly cleaned and scented however. Surely that must count for something.

331

It did because she said, "You smell nice."

"Thank you. I was just thinking the same thing about you."

She smiled. "Thank you."

The house was about ten miles down the other side of the lake and they arrived there shortly after 7:00 p.m. Dicky's Blazer wasn't in the driveway and the door was already opened for them. They were in a secluded neighborhood with expensive, oversized homes on half-acre lots with access to the lake. Dicky had a small dock but no boat in sight. It was probably in winter storage. The home was nicely decorated with granite counters in the kitchen, warm earthy colors and wall coverings, an enclosed porch with a hot tub and a fully stocked bar and wine rack. What more could you want?

Cesari opened the restaurant-grade double-doored steel refrigerator and rummaged around eventually finding some olives and cheese. Dicky had told him to help himself and that's exactly what he planned on doing.

"This was nice of Dicky to let us use his house," Jasmine said.

"Yes, it was, but he owed me one so we're kind of even now. Wine or cocktails?"

"Wine please."

There was an open bottle of chardonnay in the refrigerator, so he poured them both a glass and they went into the living room to eat and talk. The sofa was a large sectional with deep soft cushions and they sank in with their glasses in their hands, careful not to spill any wine.

"Dad told me you stopped in today."

"Yes, I forgot my stethoscope at the inn and was driving by after lunch to pick it up. I saw him on the front lawn raking leaves and he looked like he could use a break."

"He said you spent the better part of an hour having coffee and pie and chatting."

"Your father is a very hospitable and down-to-earth guy. He's very easy to talk to and your mom makes a great pie. The time just flew by."

"But you told me you were so busy today. How'd you find the time?"

Cesari took a breath and let it out. Lying was always like this. One lie always led to another and another and another. "I didn't want to lay blame on your father, but one of the many reasons I was swamped was because I spent so much time with him this afternoon. He was in such a talkative mood, I felt bad cutting him off although I desperately wanted to at times." He chuckled, "It crossed my mind that maybe he was trying to avoid having to finish up his lawn work. He really had quite a project going on out there. It seemed a bit much for a guy his age. He really should hire someone."

She nodded. "I've told him the same thing or at least wait for me to help, but he can be pretty stubborn. Anyway, that was nice of you to stop. He appreciated it."

"You do lawn work?"

She made a face. "Of course I do. Everybody does. Don't you?"

"I grew up in the city. I never had a lawn to work on."

"You've never raked leaves into a pile and then jumped in?" she asked with a look of disbelief on her face.

He shook his head. "I'm afraid not."

"Saturday morning I want you to come and help me finish raking up the lawn. The back is even worse than the front. It's a lot of work but it can be fun."

"Aren't you forgetting about Brom? He might see us or one of his friends might."

She sighed, "Yes, I am. Too bad. That would have been fun. So you don't think he fell for your routine with Lola?"

"I'm sure it's bouncing around in the back of his head, but I wouldn't want to risk everything on it." He didn't think there was anything to be gained by telling her how antagonistic Brom had been to him.

"That makes sense. You're very level-headed."

"It's a good thing I'm here to lend some balance to your exuberant personality."

She agreed and they sipped their wine and ate some smoked Gouda. After a while he said, "Remember the meal we had at Brom's restaurant last Saturday?"

"How could I forget? Our world has been upside down ever since."

"I mean the actual meal itself. Do you remember it?"

"Of course. It was Brom's specialty, the slow roasted loin of venison."

"Yeah, that was it. I was thinking about it, but so much happened that night that I never got to ask. The meat was so flavorful and tender. Do you know how he prepares it?"

She smiled. "This is going to sound ridiculous, but he told me once that he marinates the venison overnight in honey. I don't know if you noticed but it had a sweet flavor."

Cesari nodded. "I noticed."

The venison was flavored with honey, and the honey was flavored with the venison. That was why the mead had a peculiar, very different taste than anything he'd ever experienced. Well you couldn't get more gross than that.

"What are you thinking about, John? I seem to have lost you," she said, noting his distant expression as he was briefly lost in thought.

He said, "Nothing at all. Just enjoying the moment and wondering what new surprises tomorrow may bring."

He noticed that whenever she reached for an olive or a piece of cheese she inched that much closer as she settled back into the cushion so that now they were practically on top of each other. Apparently, she wasn't as scared of the Headless Horseman as much as he was of the New York State Office of Professional Misconduct. He reached for a piece of cheese and slid an inch or two away from her. This went on like that for the next twenty minutes as they wound their way around the sofa until eventually he reached the arm rest and had nowhere to go.

She let out a laugh. "Ha, you're trapped now."

He chuckled under his breath. "We're getting our exercise. That's for sure; up down, up down."

"I haven't had this much fun in a long time. It's almost like being on a Disney ride."

"You've been to Disney?"

"Yes, one time to Disney World, the one in Florida. Dave Pullman was a big Disney guy. We went there last spring."

Cesari flinched and suddenly got serious. "What do you mean by he was a big Disney guy?"

She noticed the change in his face and said, "I didn't mean to dampen the mood by bringing his name up."

"No, no, it's okay. Just tell me what you meant by that."

"He used to go all the time when he was a kid. His family had a timeshare there. We stayed in their condo when we went. He loved all things Disney. When we were there in April we bought each other matching wrist watches. His had Mickey on the face and mine had Minnie."

Cesari was at a loss for words. This was horrible news to say the least, and he didn't even know where to begin with it. She saw the blood drain from his face and misinterpreted his expression

"John, I'm sorry for mentioning Dave. I know it's impolite to talk about ex-boyfriends and girlfriends when you're with someone else."

"No, it's fine but as long as you brought it up. Could you tell me a little bit about what happened between you two? I'm curious."

"Really?"

"Really."

"Are you sure you want to talk about my ex-boyfriend?"

"I'm sure."

She looked at him for a long second and said, "Well, we met at the hospital of course. He asked me out and we hit it off. We dated for close to eight months before he... you know the rest."

"Were you getting serious?"

"I don't want to be overly dramatic about it, but we were getting along pretty well."

"Did Brom know about you and Dave?"

She shook her head. "I'm pretty sure he didn't. I jumped through hoops to keep him away from the inn and my apartment. I explained the Brom situation to Dave and he was very cooperative. He kept it pretty quiet at the hospital too. I don't even think Katz or any of the nurses knew about us."

"But can you be sure that one of Brom's spies didn't rat you out?"

She shrugged. "No, but Brom had no reason to be suspicious about Dave the way he is about you and his friends couldn't always be on high alert."

"Maybe," he said with a fair amount of skepticism.

"Well, as far as I know their paths never crossed and if he did know, he didn't let on, and that would have been very unlike Brom. As you have already found out, he's a very direct person. Why do you ask?"

"I've been curious and since you brought it up... Did you tell Dave you were a witch and that the Horseman might be a slight impediment to your friendship?"

She shook her head. "No, we never reached that point. Dave and I had a quiet, mature relationship. He was super busy at work and we only saw each other once a week with an occasional lunch in the hospital. As I said, we were very discrete. We never kissed or held hands in public."

"I don't mean to be critical but he doesn't sound like he was much fun," he commented.

"The point I'm trying to make is that Dave didn't come crashing into my life the way you did. I felt compelled to tell you about myself sooner rather than later because of Brom. I didn't feel the need to bring it up with Dave. We never experienced anything that could even remotely be considered a crisis, and it wasn't until he left that I started to put two and two together about the Horseman. Don't misunderstand me, eventually I would have told him everything, but you'll have to forgive me for going slow. Try to imagine the kind of strain that news would put on a relationship."

"Oh I get it all right… One more question, if you don't mind?"

"Fire away."

"Was Dave a tall guy?"

"Oh yeah. Six-five, with gigantic feet, but he was thin and gangly, almost no muscle, not like you. Why do you ask?"

"Humor me… And you think the Horseman got to him?"

She smirked. "That's two questions, but yes, that's what I think. I know it sounds crazy, but I can't explain it any other way."

"Well, I can. How about maybe he won the lottery and decided to cruise the world or maybe his ex-wife finally tracked him down for child support and he skipped out before the marshals found him? I mean anything but being scared off by a dead guy whose only motivation is to ruin your love life."

She laughed. "You obviously didn't know Dave. He was very cerebral and reserved. He loved it here in Auburn and he loved his work. We were together the night before it happened. He seemed totally content with life. He never would have left unless something shook him to the core, and an ex-wife… that's hysterical. I can't prove what happened that night since I wasn't there, but to me it all fits now."

"So you loved him?"

She seemed taken aback by the question. "I guess in a way, yes."

"I ask because you told me the Horseman's only a concern if you're in love with the guy."

"I hadn't thought about it because the idea that the Horseman had driven him off only came to me after he'd gone. Dave didn't make my heart race or anything, but I guess I must have been in love with him if the Horseman came for him."

"Is it possible the Horseman knows what's in your heart better than you do?"

She smiled. "I can't answer that, but anything's possible."

"Did Dave try to contact you after he left? You know, to try to explain himself."

"A few days later I received a letter from him saying he was sorry, and it had to be this way. It was very short and terse. There was no return address. I tried calling him over and over, but he turned his cellphone off. I was glad that no bodily harm had come to him, but I cried for days. As the tears were drying on my pillow, I remembered the curse of the Horseman I had learned about as a child. I don't know why it came to me just then. It's a subject that hasn't been talked about in the coven for years."

Cesari was pensive for a minute. "Can I see the letter?"

"No, I threw it out like I did with the others. I'm sorry. Why do want to see it?"

"Just curious… What others?"

"The other 'Dear John' letters." She looked away suddenly ashamed. "John, do we have to talk about this? It's embarrassing."

"I'm sorry, but it might be therapeutic to let it out with someone who cares and isn't judgmental."

She looked at him for a while and said, "Thank you for saying that."

He looked at her sympathetically, "You're welcome."

"Promise not to laugh."

"I promise."

"Including Dave, I've dated just three men since I broke it off with Brom ten years ago. I'm not exactly a social butterfly." She glanced at him half expecting him to break his promise and start laughing. He didn't. She went on, "All three men vanished from my life without warning and without a trace. All three sent me 'Dear John' letters rather than face me. I've come to expect it as normal behavior from the men I date."

He was silent. What could he possibly say to make her feel better? She continued, "The first one hurt the most and still does. I…"

She choked up and her eyes turned red. He reached out to hold her hand. "That's all right. You don't have…"

She took in a deep breath, let it out and seemed better. "No, it's all right… I guess. Well, after I broke it off with Brom, it was about a year before I dated anyone. Then Chad came along and swept me off my feet."

"Chad?"

"Chad Billingsworth. He was an investment banker from Syracuse who worked at Morgan Stanley. The hospital uses them to manage the employee benefits program. That's how we met. He was at the hospital for a business meeting with Sal. I won't bore you with the details, but it was a whirlwind romance and we were to be married on Halloween."

"Did Brom or anyone else in the coven know?"

"Only my parents. It was going to be controversial and we knew there would be fallout. We didn't want anybody harassing us until after the wedding. In any event, Chad and I arranged to be married at a nondenominational church in a neighboring town. It was to be a small ceremony with just a few friends from work. It felt more like an elopement than a planned affair. I was going to make an announcement to the coven after the fact and then when it was too late, let the Brom chips fall where they may. Long story short, Chad stood me up on our wedding day… I was crushed. No, I was devastated. I could barely eat or sleep. He just vanished without a trace. Never showed up to work and never called a living soul, not his friends, his family or work…just gone like the wind."

"I'm sorry about that, Jasmine, but I'm a little confused. Did your parents approve of the marriage?"

"Yes and no. They wanted me to be happy and since Chad made me happy they were at peace with it even though it was going to cause complete upheaval in their lives. Father in particular was sympathetic to me because he wasn't born a witch, but unlike him Chad wasn't willing to join the coven and embrace our ways. Even if he was, I don't think I would have agreed to let him because of Brom. The plan was to move after the wedding and take my parents with us, so they wouldn't have to deal with the coven."

"So Chad knew you were a witch and was okay with it?"

"Yes, of course. I wouldn't marry someone without being completely honest with them, and he handled it very well. He was not a religious person in the traditional sense although in some ways he was very spiritual and one of the most open-minded men I have ever known."

Cesari nodded. "Where were you going to move to?"

"Far, far away. We had our hearts set on Malta in the Mediterranean."

"No kidding?"

"No kidding. Chad had already signed a year-long lease for a two-bedroom townhouse with a view of the sea. Although it's such a small island almost every where you turned you could see water."

"So what happened when he didn't show up at the wedding?"

"Everything happened. First there was the worrying; did he get lost, was he in a car accident, did he fall ill? Then there was the sobbing, the lack of sleep, the poor appetite. Then the police were called and the painful questions about his fidelity followed. How well did I really know him and things like that. There wasn't much they could do because there were absolutely no signs of foul play. He didn't pack a bag or leave a note and never used his credit cards. He left a hundred thousand dollars in his bank account and thousands more in his investment portfolio. He left all his belongings behind including his BMW. They investigated as best they could, but the trail went cold almost as they started."

"Did Brom or anyone in the coven find out? I mean with the police nosing around."

"No, because they didn't nose around in Auburn. They spent most of their time in Syracuse where he lived and worked and where he was last seen at a pub with friends the night before the wedding. Of course they questioned me and my parents but no one else from here. As far as missing persons cases go, his was fairly mundane. It didn't even make the papers. The police were sympathetic to me, but I could read it in their eyes that they believed he ran off on me."

Cesari let out a deep breath. "I'm so sorry, Jasmine. That must have hurt immensely."

"You don't know the half of it. To say that I was a basket case would be the understatement of the century. I even went for counseling. I wasn't just broken-hearted but also worried sick that something bad had happened to him. I couldn't believe that he just abandoned me like that. A month later, the 'Dear John' letter showed up. Can you believe that, a month later he sends me a typewritten letter? How cold was that? It took me months to snap out of my depression."

She took a breath and with some hesitancy continued, "The second 'Dear John' letter came a few years after that episode. We weren't nearly as close, so it didn't hurt nearly as much when he left. I barely even looked at that 'Dear John' letter. In between these romances, there was Brom always standing there waiting for me, but I just couldn't do it. I didn't feel it. Then Dave came along and there you have it. It took a long time for me to accept that it was the curse of Katrina and the Horseman who was responsible but there's simply too much of a pattern for me to ignore."

"And yet you still plan on dating outside the coven despite the risks?"

"I'm a woman, John, and I need to be with someone I care about. I desire to hold and to be held; to love and to be loved."

"There's no one in the coven besides Brom that could potentially fulfill your needs?"

"There's no one that would dare stand up to Brom, and deep down I know that I will eventually find someone and love him hard enough that it will break the spell."

"That would be nice."

Chapter 35

The Norsemen

On his way to work the next morning Cesari called the mechanic to get an update on his Porsche and was regretfully informed that the parts would most likely not arrive until late Friday afternoon and therefore his car would not be ready for pick up until Monday afternoon at the earliest. The guy was apologetic, but it was what it was. Cesari was only mildly annoyed, Sal's pickup was a decent ride and had a pretty good sound system with satellite radio.

He reached the OR on time, gowned up and began his day. With only three colonoscopies scheduled, he finished in an hour and a half, then consulted on two patients in the ICU and stopped in to say hello to Santiago who was post-op from his colectomy. Mr. Cortese had done well but was in no shape for a chat because he was still in a lot of pain and had all sorts of tubes coming out of him. According to the chart, the pre-op CT scan was negative and the surgeon was confident he had removed the entire tumor. He hadn't seen any obvious metastases although several lymph nodes were removed as a routine and were still under review. Overall, the surgeon's note was very optimistic for a cure and Cesari was pleased.

By 11:00 a.m. Cesari was free and drove back to the library to finish reading about witches. He was thinking that the more he knew about them the easier it would be to discuss the subject with Jasmine and thought that she might appreciate his taking an above and beyond kind of interest in her life.

He was deeply disturbed by finding Dave Pullman's belongings in a hole in the ground behind the honey-house but at the same time confused because people had heard from Dave after he ran off, including Katz who received a phone call and Jasmine who received a 'Dear John' letter. He wasn't sure if anyone had been able to reach the guy after that however. He wasn't even sure if anyone besides Jasmine had even tried. He parked in front of the library again and went in, nodded at the old lady in charge and said, "Good morning, Letitia."

She remembered him, "Good morning, Doctor. Back so soon?"

"Yes, I didn't quite finish my research."

"Why didn't you just take the books with you?"

He was confused. "I don't have a library card and you told me I couldn't borrow books without one."

"Yes, but I could have issued you a temporary card. It only takes a minute."

He stared at her. She could easily have told him that the last time but didn't. Interpersonal communication was becoming a lost skill just as building pyramids had. He said, "I'll do that today if I don't finish…"

He rattled off a list of books he required and a minute later, she gave him a piece of paper with catalogue numbers and the location of the books he desired. He thanked her and went to gather the items. A few minutes later he was back in the reading room turning pages. After reading for a solid hour he became convinced that witchcraft is and always has been total nonsense. It was at best a way for primitive and uneducated societies to explain calamitous events by scapegoating individuals and groups. It was at worst, a cynical path for some to resolve personal disputes, jealousies and grievances with their neighbors. Historically, almost every culture throughout the world has experienced accusations of witchcraft. What struck Cesari the most was that while gradually disappearing in the western world or morphing into a more benign type of movement known as white witchcraft, it was still strikingly present in certain parts of Africa and Asia, and not to just a small degree.

Around seven hundred and fifty people were killed as witches in India between 2003 and 2008, most by hanging. Hundreds of women were mistreated every year because of accusations of witchcraft, and activists believed that only a fraction of these cases were ever reported.

Jesus! That was unbelievable.

In Nigeria over the last ten years, fifteen thousand children were accused of witchcraft and one thousand of them murdered, but the worst was the Congo where, as of 2006, twenty-five to fifty thousand children had been accused of witchcraft and thrown out of their homes. These children had been subjected to often-violent abuse during exorcisms. In Ghana, women were often accused of witchcraft and attacked by neighbors. Because of this, witch camps were established where women suspected of being witches could flee for safety. The witch camps in Ghana are thought to house a total of around 1000 women.

In 2008, a mob in Kenya burnt eleven people to death for witchcraft. As recent as 2011 and 2014, two individuals were beheaded in Saudi Arabia for witchcraft. Then there were the penis snatchers. It was believed in parts of the third world that witches could cast spells to shrink, shrivel or remove a man's penis. This belief has led to riots and vigilante justice.

Witchcraft in the modern U.S. for the most part has evolved to a different, less threatening situation where the practice thereof is more and more being seen as aiding the empowerment of young women. We, like most of Europe, have put our burning at the stake days behind us. While not completely embracing them, most people didn't fear witches anymore and some were even coming to admire them. This phenomenon has been fueled by the media's positive portrayal of female witch protagonists in theater and literature. Current witchcraft practices and ideals are often aligned with liberal principles such as the Green movement, and particularly with feminism by providing young women with means for control of their own lives. A 2002 study suggested that modern witchcraft actually represents the second wave of feminism.

Cesari put the book down and thought about it. Witchcraft varied from region to region and culture to culture, but nowhere did he read anything that even remotely suggested there was any real evidence to substantiate the notion that witches had any supernatural or magical powers. No matter how you sliced it, it was all superstition. The more uneducated the society, the more likely they were to react violently toward accusations of witchcraft. That was the main difference in regard to the various reactions throughout the world. Interestingly, not all witchcraft involved devil worship, but Jasmine's coven did. According to her they were the original Order of Nine Angels. He wondered why she had woven that part into her delusion.

That was a shrink question. He was just a gastroenterologist, but then it came to him like a baseball bat to the forehead. Brom had an odd tattoo across his back in old English, *ONA*. He had seen it in the honey-house and then again at fight club. Brom made no effort to hide it. *ONA*, O-N-A, The Order of Nine Angels. The Night Nurse, Levi Blackburn, was also a card-carrying member of that murderous satanic cult. He was trying to summon Lucifer the night he murdered everyone in the old psychiatric hospital. Jasmine said he was a member of her coven too.

Something wasn't making any sense. If she was making all of it up. If her delusion of being a witch was simply a highly organized and detailed fantasy brought up from the depths of her imagination, then why would Brom have a tattoo like that or could the tattoo have some other significance? O-N-A. What could that mean? The Order of Nine Assholes? He smiled. He liked that but probably not. Everyone in town must have seen the tattoo if Brom went to fight club regularly. He'd ask Dicky later if he had an opinion on the subject.

He spent the next hour reading about hypnosis and eventually concluded that it too was a crock; nothing more than a parlor trick despite what Mark had said about it occasionally being useful. The next book was about modern psychiatry. He turned to the chapter about psychotic disorders, specifically schizophrenia, and read with great interest. A mental disorder characterized by abnormal behavior and a decreased ability to understand reality, the symptoms could be controlled but few were cured. There were no objective tests and the diagnosis was usually made by the behavioral observations and interviews of a trained psychiatrist. The mainstay of treatment was antipsychotic medication, along with counselling, job training and social rehabilitation.

There were about twenty-five million cases world-wide and most were diagnosed in their teens or early adulthood. On average, people with this disorder died at a much younger age than those without for a variety of reasons including poor diet, smoking, higher rates of suicide and risky behavior including drug use. Delusions and hallucinations were common as was cognitive impairment. About thirty to fifty percent of people with schizophrenia failed to accept that they have an illness or comply with their recommended treatment. Both genetic and environmental factors played a significant role in the development of this illness. Childhood trauma, death of a parent, being bullied or abused and social isolation seemed to increase the risk of psychosis.

Hmm.

He closed the book and sat there deep in thought. Jasmine fulfilled some of the criteria for schizophrenia but not all. That's why her psychiatrist at Auburn was reluctant to label her as such. She certainly was delusional but clearly did not demonstrate even the slightest cognitive or social impairment. She was intelligent and high functioning, able to hold down a good job, and impressed all those who knew her with her winning personality. She took good care of herself and her parents and except for her assertion of being a witch had no other difficulties with reality. She was all there and then some.

Cesari concluded that he couldn't label her as schizophrenic either. So what was she? Some sort of unique as yet unclassified delusional disorder? A new diagnosis waiting to be identified? Maybe they would write papers about her or text books. Would they mention his name in medical schools as the physician who stumbled across her? He would be some sort of foot note in the history of psychiatry. Pinheads at Harvard who obsessed over minutia and obscure facts would drop his name at study hall to impress the other pinheads.

His phone buzzed. It was Dicky.

"Hey, Dicky, I'm glad you called. I wanted to thank you for the use of your home last night."

"No problem. How'd it go with Jasmine?"

"She says thank you too. I owe you some wine and cheese. We raided your refrigerator."

"Don't worry about it. Say, how's your head?"

"No headache. I feel great in that regard."

"Are you in the hospital, John?"

"No, I'm at the public library."

"The library? Why?"

"I like libraries. They're very interesting places, lots of books and comfortable chairs. Why'd you ask if I was in the hospital?"

"Sal and I are going out for a drink at the whiskey bar to discuss battle plans for when the state comes next week and thought you'd like to join us. I would've driven you but you can always meet us there. You're not that far away."

"Me? I'm not sure I'd be of much help."

"Don't sell yourself short. You've got a good head on your shoulders. People are already talking about you in a good way."

"Are they?"

"They are. I had lunch with a couple of the staff today and they mentioned to me that they were hoping you'd be the medical representative for the PAC they're forming. That's a high honor."

"Why would they bring it up with you? You're administration."

"We'd have to give you the time off if you were going to D.C. I told them yes of course as long as it's not excessive. We could spare you for a week or so. I might even come with you. The titty bars are incredible in that town."

Cesari cleared his throat. "Well, that's something to consider, but I'd have to think long and hard about it. I'm sorry to change subjects but can I ask you something about Brom?"

"He didn't catch you with Jasmine last night, did he?"

"No, at least not that I think. It was something I saw at fight club. I meant to ask you about it but then I got hit on the head. Brom had a strange tattoo across his back. You must've noticed it."

"ONA in old English. Of, course. It's the symbol of a motorcycle club that he started about ten years ago called the Norsemen. The O is for Odin, the most powerful of the Nordic gods. The N is for Norsemen naturally, who were his ancestors and the A is for Asgard, the mythical world where Odin lived."

Cesari was silent for a moment, feeling totally ridiculous. He said, "Of course, how could I not have known?"

Dicky laughed. "It's not Hells Angels but it'll do. There were fifty members at one point but that was a while ago. They used to go buzzing up and down the main drag on their Harleys, drinking, pissing and raising hell. Brom was a real rowdy in his younger days. As he got busy with the inn and the apiary he gradually got away from the club. I don't think

I've seen the Norsemen riding in formation for over a year maybe longer."

"Thanks."

Dicky said goodbye and Cesari returned to his studies. He picked up the last book he had selected to review, a thick reference text. The kind of book tenured academics spent their entire lives writing and no one read.

Seismologic Events in the Northeastern U.S.

Chapter 36

Poor Aunt Ginny

Cesari was depressed as he drove home from the library. No matter how he looked at the problem, it always led to Jasmine being mentally ill. As silly as it seemed, he was sort of hoping that maybe Brom really was a Satanist and that the tattoo on his back was undeniable proof. Bad as that might be, it would have at least given Jasmine's story some legs, but the tattoo was nothing more than evidence Brom was a local yokel with a penchant for leather jackets and loud V-shaped engines. He was just an old-fashioned bully boy.

Then he thought about that GI guy, Pullman. He had no doubt those were his clothes and watch he'd found buried three feet underground, but without a body what did that mean? Were they things that he'd left behind, and Jasmine in a fit of jilted rage had buried or had Brom bury them for her? It seemed unlikely she would do that. He doubted she would have ever confided her clandestine romance to Brom under any circumstances and if she had, he had no doubt she would have told him so. She didn't seem the vindictive type anyway. In fact, she seemed the type to package up his belongings and mail them to him after she had them dry-cleaned. There didn't seem to be a woman-scorned bone in her body.

So if he ruled out being scared off by the Headless Horseman why would Pullman leave town in a huff like that? The Horseman was convenient logic for Jasmine but not for him. Certainly Pullman might have changed his mind about his feelings for Jasmine and simply wanted to avoid having to break up with her in person. A bit extreme to leave like that yes, but he'd heard of guys doing way worse. A friend of his in medical school got cold feet and texted his fiancé on Christmas Eve that he didn't want to see her anymore. She received the text at her house where she was waiting for him with her entire family for a celebratory party. The wedding was a month away, tickets to Hawaii had been purchased. He added in the message that she shouldn't try to reach him because he was going to block her number.

It was bad. She went to his apartment with her father and two brothers, but he had already packed and taken off. The next day they went through the guest list contacting his friends. They came to Cesari's place looking for the guy and ransacked his apartment like CSI Brooklyn. Satisfied he wasn't hiding there, they eventually left, but not before one of her brothers waved a baseball bat in Cesari's face making him promise to pass the message along to his absent friend when he saw him. But Cesari never saw the guy again and a year later heard through the grapevine that he had resurfaced in a different city trying to get into law school. Not every guy was good at commitment. The idea of it did something to some men that couldn't easily be explained.

Still, this business with Pullman didn't feel right… He didn't like any of it. He'd been around the block a few times and as the saying went, he smelled a rat. Clothes buried in the ground in the secluded section of an estate meant only one thing to this Bronx boy. But why would anyone want to kill a gastroenterologist he mused. We were so damned nice.

As he pulled onto the block where the inn was located, he glanced at the time and suddenly made a U-turn. It was only 4:00 p.m. and he decided to go to the office and speak with Katz about it some more.

Ten minutes later, he pulled to a stop in front of the office building and walked in waving at Brooke, the receptionist, a twenty-something year old cutie pie with big eyes and bangs. "Is Katz around?" he asked.

"He's in his office, but I wouldn't bother him. He's an hour behind schedule as it is, and I want to get out of here on time."

Smiling disarmingly, he said, "I won't keep him long. I promise."

He walked up to the office where he shared space with Katz and Dr. Kamil, the other GI guy. The door was closed and Cesari knocked politely just in case he was in a private consultation with someone. There was no answer, so he tried again. Again, there was no response, so he let himself in. No one was around but the bathroom door was closed so he took a seat and patiently waited. After five minutes, he started to wonder if Brooke had been mistaken and that maybe Katz had gone to an exam room to see his next patient.

He went over to the bathroom door and knocked. After a moment's hesitation Katz said, "Occupied."

Cesari didn't say anything and went back to his chair, picked up a medical magazine from Katz's desk and flipped through the pages. After five more minutes, he was starting to feel silly waiting for a grown man to come out of the bathroom. Maybe the guy didn't take in enough fiber and had run into unexpected difficulties? There was no telling how long he might be in there. He sighed and decided to go make himself a cup of coffee in the breakroom and wait there.

He put the journal down, got up and left, closing the door. As he took a few steps toward the break room, he changed his mind about leaving the journal behind and returned to retrieve it. This time he entered without knocking and saw Katz a bit breathless, walking toward his desk adjusting his yarmulke.

Katz saw him too and froze. Before Cesari say anything, Linda Lu appeared from the bathroom several paces behind him. Her hair was disheveled, and she was too busy straightening her rumpled skirt to notice him at first.

Cesari said, "Hi guys."

Katz was still speechless and continued to stare at him. Linda Lu looked up abruptly as if a gun had just been discharged. She blushed, turned her face away and scurried past him like a mouse trying to avoid detection. Katz and Cesari stood there for a long moment and eventually Cesari said, as if nothing at all unusual had transpired, "Can I talk to you about Dave Pullman, Henry?"

He stammered briefly and then recovered, "Of course. Have a seat." They sat next to each other and Katz seemed relieved that Cesari wasn't going to pursue the obvious. "What would you like to know?" he asked.

"Well, you told me that he left town suddenly after he received some type of fright. Could you expand on that?"

He thought about it for a minute. "No, not really. What I told you is all I know. When he phoned he was almost hysterical and didn't get into specifics other than it was something

that happened in the old hospital where the on-call room is...
Why do you care what happened to Pullman?"

Cesari nodded. "I'm just curious is all. I've been hearing
different opinions about that night, and since I've been told
those are my sleeping accommodations too when I'm on call
I thought I'd look into it... Have you ever slept in the on-call
room?"

"Why would I do that? I have a beautiful home in town a
half-mile from here."

Cesari couldn't help himself and added, "Plus a wife and
six starving children."

The color rose in his cheeks and Katz said, "Look, maybe
I should explain..."

Cesari raised his hands, "Please don't. First of all I don't
care and second of all... I don't care. Just tell me what you
know about Pullman. Did he have family? Did anyone ever
try to find out where he went?"

He shook his head. "He was single. He told me he came
from upper Michigan somewhere and had a sister in Texas. I
don't know her name. That was his bio as far as I know. He
was only here about a year and a half and we weren't that
close. You know how it is. I did my thing and he did his. We
were cordial enough but didn't pry into each other's lives.
No one went looking for him that I know of. Why would
they? It's not like he was a missing person or anything. He
did call to resign... sort of. If he wanted to quit a good job in
the middle of the night, then I guess that was his right."

"And that left more colonoscopies for you."

Katz felt the barb. "It wasn't like that at all. I kind of
liked him."

"But it was better for you if there was one less guy to share the pie with."

He shrugged. "That doesn't make me a bad person, Cesari."

"No, but it's not exactly a mitzvah either." He didn't say anything so Cesari continued, "Look, I'll let you get back to work. I know you're behind schedule. Thanks for your time, Henry."

"I'm not a bad person," he said again.

"I never said you were."

"But you're thinking it."

"What I think doesn't matter Henry, but what God thinks…now that's a different story."

Cesari left the office and drove back to the inn, parking the pickup in the rear next to a shiny new black CT6-V, Cadillac's high-performance model sedan with a 550 horse-power V-8 engine and twenty-inch alloy wheels. He'd read somewhere that it cost close to one hundred thousand dollars fully loaded. It looked like it had just rolled off the assembly line. He walked close and peered through the lightly tinted windows. He could practically smell the new leather. This was one nice car.

He went inside the inn and as he walked past the bar area he heard loud garrulous voices using vulgar language as they snorted and guffawed. Cesari was surprised because the inn was usually pretty quiet as most upscale establishments tended to be. In general, places that cost as much as this one did per night generally attracted a more refined clientele. Curious, he stepped into the lounge and shook his head in disbelief.

His friend Vito from New York was sitting in a chair facing away from the door and toward twin gorillas in silk suits holding wine glasses with amber liquid in them resting on their protruding bellies. They were identical in every way with beefy faces, round squinty eyes, short curly hair and thick necks bulging out of tight white collars. Cesari felt bad for their mother. He could smell their cheap over-powering cologne from where he stood. They were listening to something profound Vito was telling them.

No one noticed him standing there, not even the bartender, Timothy, because he was also raptly listening to Vito who said, "And then I told her. Hey honey, what were you expecting, a freaking elephant? Bada boom. You know what I mean boys?"

Whatever the joke was, everyone thought it was hysterical. The fat guys slapped their thighs and Timothy nearly fell over laughing. Cesari stepped close and cleared his throat.

Vito was a large man unto his own right; three inches over six feet and a heavily muscled two hundred and sixty pounds. His greatest weapon was his fierce, large head with jet black wavy hair and sharp chiseled features. His prominent nose and distinctive cold gray eyes made him unforgettable in a dangerous way. He was the kind of guy you didn't want looking at you too carefully. He was impeccably dressed as always, and today sported a two-piece dark navy Armani suit and a crisp white shirt with diamond cufflinks and red tie.

Cesari said, "Nice shoes, Vito. Calf-skin?" he asked admiring the high-quality finish.

"Not bad, Cesari. They're Berluti, all the way from Paris. Two grand a pair and a steal at that. So how are you, pal?"

Cesari shook his hand and noticed a diamond encrusted Rolex. "Surprised to see you."

"I guess I should have called. After we talked last week, I couldn't stop thinking about that casino you told me about and decided to come and spend the weekend. I got the last available room here, but my boys are staying at the Hilton Garden across town. Right after dinner, I figured we'd hit the craps table, get a couple of drinks and catch up. I assume it's not too far from here."

Cesari said, "I don't know how to break this to you chum, but the casino isn't in Auburn. It's at least an hour east of here. I'm pretty sure I mentioned that to you. You passed it on the way up."

"You're kidding?"

Cesari shook his head. "I'm afraid not."

Vito scratched his chin, narrowed his eyes and glared at his men. "How stupid can you guys be? I give you simple instructions to get me to the casino and you screw it up massively. Get out of my sight before I lose my temper."

One of the fat guys squirmed and clearly wanted to say something. Vito encouraged him. "Spit it out, Lou."

"But you drove the whole way, boss, remember? You wanted to test out the new caddie. You even plugged the address into the GPS."

Vito was quiet for a moment and Cesari worried about what was going to happen next. Then Vito said in a low tone, his voice deep and edgy. "Are you saying it was my fault, Lou?"

Both of the men's eyes went wide and Timothy discretely retreated back behind the bar to find a safe space. The other guy chimed in, "No, of course not, boss. He would never say that."

"Shut up Lou, and let your brother speak for himself." Vito turned his gaze back to the other guy. "So what are you saying, Lou?"

They were both named Lou?

The first Lou glanced quickly at his brother and then back at Vito, cleared his throat and said, "We messed up big time, boss. There's no other way of looking at it. Sorry."

"That's exactly my point. Now scram. You're giving me indigestion."

The fat guys wiggled and squirmed their way to the edge of their seats, placed their glasses on the coffee table, groaned their way upright and waddled off. One of the Lous stopped abruptly and turned back.

Vito growled. "What?"

Sheepishly, the big guy said, "You have the car keys, boss."

"Get out of here right now before I forget I'm a civilized human being. A little walking ain't going to kill you. Cesari, you're a doctor. Is walking a couple of miles going to kill them?"

Cesari said, "He's right. Walking isn't going to kill you."

They both turned and practically ran out of the room. Cesari sat down in their place on the sofa. Vito finished his wine with a look of disgust on his face. He called out to Timothy. "Hey Tim, how about another glass of mead? It's going to be a long night." He looked at Cesari. "You want one too? This is great stuff. I've never tasted anything like it."

"I'm good, thanks… So they're both named Lou?"

"Sick joke, huh? They're my Aunt Ginny's kids, may she rest in peace. She loved Louis Prima, the jazz singer. Couldn't get enough of him. Only one of the twins is actually named Lou. The other is Prima but being identical no one could tell them apart growing up and everyone long since forgot which one is which. Even the kids aren't sure anymore. They're orphans now. Poor Aunt Ginny and Uncle Mimmo died in an accidental car explosion a couple of months back."

"An accidental car explosion?" Cesari asked as Tim set another glass of mead in front of Vito.

"Thanks, Tim."

"My pleasure, Mr. Gianelli."

"Yes, the explosion wasn't an accident of course. The accidental part was that Aunt Ginny and Uncle Mimmo weren't supposed to be in the car, but what are you going to do? These things happen and now I'm stuck with these two mopes. As you can see, they're not exactly the sharpest tools in the box. They barely made it through high school despite cheating in almost every class."

"They look pretty young."

"Twenty to be exact."

"They're your team for the weekend? I mean that's it? Not exactly pros. What if something happens?"

"What's going to happen? I'm just here to blow a few grand at the casino, Cesari. I don't need a whole lot of help for that. As long as they can drive and find me smokes, we'll be okay. Besides, take it easy on me. They're the nephews of my favorite aunt, may she rest in peace. I have sort of an obligation to take care of them until they're fully grown."

"Fully grown? They're over three hundred pounds now. What's fully grown in your family?"

"You know what I mean. Until they can take of themselves."

"Why is this your problem?"

"It just is, all right? So stop asking questions."

They were quiet for a minute as Vito enjoyed his venison flavored mead and Cesari studied him. He'd known Vito since the first grade and they'd been very close over the years, so he knew there was something important he was holding back, but what?

Then it dawned on him and he shook his head in disgust. "You're such a prick, Vito."

He looked at Cesari with surprise on his face. "What are you talking about?"

"That was your bomb that accidentally blew up Aunt Ginny and Uncle Mimmo, wasn't it?"

Vito instinctively glanced over his shoulder to see who was listening. Tim had gone to another room. Vito whispered, "Keep it down, will you? I said it was an accident, didn't I?"

"You're unbelievable."

"Well, we're not having this conversation, understand? And don't bring it up in front of the Lous. They still cry themselves to sleep every night over it. They have no idea who did it, and they're never going to find out. That's why I have to keep them close."

"And what happens if they do find out?"

He shrugged. "Like I said. That's why I have to keep them close."

Cesari rolled his eyes. "Your own nephews?"

"I never liked Aunt Ginny anyway. Now enough with the unpleasant conversation." He looked at his watch. "Let's go eat."

"Fine, let me make a call first."

He took his cellphone out and moved to a private corner of the room to call Jasmine. She said, "Hi."

"Hi back. Still at work?"

"Just got in a few minutes ago. What's the plan for tonight?"

"That's just it. I don't have one and a friend of mine from New York showed up unexpectedly. He wants to have dinner with me. Do you mind?"

"Of course not. Have fun. We've been spending too much time together anyway."

He smiled. "You don't really mean that, do you?"

She laughed. "Not a chance. What I meant was that you don't have to ask me for permission. We're not even dating... Are we?"

He contemplated that. "Interesting question. It certainly feels like we are."

"It does, doesn't it?"

"Yes, it does. I'll tell you what. I'll give you a call when we've finished. Maybe we can meet for an hour somewhere like behind the church or even better down at the pavilion."

"That would be great."

He hung up and went over to Vito who finished his mead and stood up. "Ready to go?"

Cesari put his open palm out.

Vito said, "What?"

"I want to drive the caddie."

Chapter 37

Lasca's

Lasca's was a casual, modestly priced restaurant located on Rte. 5 just outside of Auburn heading toward Syracuse. The interior was large and bustling and clearly a local favorite with a definite family atmosphere. The eatery's claim to fame were its over-sized portions of everything guaranteed to provide you with at least two meals to take home. They sat at a table for two and were in the middle of their thirty-six-ounce prime rib entrees with baked potato and grilled asparagus. An attractive waitress had just uncorked a second bottle of Chianti for them. Cesari finished up the story of his trials and tribulations since arriving in town exactly one week ago and left nothing out. Vito whistled as he sat back to take a breather from his meal.

He said, "Man, Cesari you've had a heck of a week. Where do you go from here with this girl, Jasmine?"

"That's just it. I don't know. She clearly needs help and even more clearly doesn't know it. I've done some reading about this kind of problem. Many patients are in total denial and there's nothing anyone can do about it. Her family also appears completely unaware she's not well and then making everything that much worse there's this insanely jealous ex-boyfriend who wants my head on a platter."

"Hey, wait a minute. You saw them throw a dead deer into the honey? The same honey they use to make the mead?"

Cesari nodded. "Yes."

"And I drank that swill?"

"You have to admit, it tasted pretty good."

He made a disgusted look. "I can't believe this."

The waitress walked by and Vito signaled her. She came over and he said, "The food's great sweetheart, and we're not done, but me and my friend here need to take a cigarette break. Just leave everything where it is. We'll be back in five minutes, all right?"

She gave him a knowing nod. The one smoker to another kind of nod and said, "Certainly. I'll bring out plate covers to help keep your meals warm."

"Thank you."

She left and Cesari asked, "You're going out for a cigarette in the middle of dinner?"

"No, *we're* going out together. It would be rude for you to keep eating without me. Besides, we need to talk where no one can hear us."

Cesari took a deep breath and let it out. He was pretty stuffed already. Maybe it wasn't such a bad idea. "Fine, let's go."

They walked out to the parking lot and leaned against a cement planter box. It was fifty degrees without wind which was downright balmy compared to the last few nights. Vito lit a Camel and puffed away. Cesari watched him wondering how many more years he could go on smoking two packs a day before it finally caught up with him. Maybe it would never catch up with him. Some guys were lucky like that. They were all alone.

Vito said, "All right, let's go over this. You think this Brom guy offed your doctor friend, so he could have Jasmine all to himself?"

"I didn't say that he killed him. I don't know exactly what happened to Pullman and he wasn't my friend. I never even met him."

"Fine, but you implied he killed him, and it kind of fits. He's jealous, possessive, prone to anger and you found Pullman's clothes buried in the back yard. How much more evidence do you want?"

"A body would be nice."

"In a court of law maybe but not in the court of Vito. He did the deed all right."

Cesari nodded. "I know. It does kind of fit. The problem is that Pullman wrote a 'Dear John' letter to Jasmine which arrived two days after he left and he called one of the other doctors to tell him he was leaving."

"Did you see the letter?"

"No, she tossed it."

"The letter could have been a forgery, but the phone call's harder to explain unless…"

"Unless what?"

"Unless he was coerced into making the call." Vito spoke from experience and let that sink in for a minute before adding, "Forcing someone who's scared, to make a phone call, isn't that hard a thing to do if you're dangling their freedom and safety in front of them."

Cesari thought that sounded plausible and agreed. "It's possible sure, but why go through the trouble? Why not just make him disappear? No 'Dear John' letter, no phone call at all."

Vito took a long slow drag from the Camel and blew it out of the side of his mouth as he considered that. After a while he said, "If the guy simply disappeared then it would be a potential missing person's thing, with police and possibly FBI involved. Jasmine would worry and never give up hope of finding him. If he dumps her and runs that's a different ballgame. She'd cry, curse, burn his pictures and then move on."

Cesari snapped his fingers coming to a sudden realization. "You're right because that's exactly what happened eight years ago when she got left at the altar. The police were involved but eventually gave up. Jasmine was devastated. The experience threw her into a deep depression and that's when she started seeing a psychiatrist. A 'Dear John' letter eventually did show up a month later, but the emotional damage was already done. She also told me the letter was typewritten which sounded strange."

Vito was quiet for minute thinking it over. "Before you weren't sure if Brom iced Pullman. Now you're implying that he killed all three of her boyfriends."

Cesari nodded. "The more I think about it, the harder it is to believe their disappearances aren't related. The patterns are so similar; she dates a guy for a while and when she gets too close, they vanish into thin air followed by a 'Dear John' letter."

"It's not looking good for Pullman if that's the case."

"Or any of those guys. She told me that Brom didn't know about Pullman or her other romances, but I find that difficult to believe."

Vito said, "It's not logical. This is a small town and you said he knows everybody. How clever could they have been?"

"I agree. It just doesn't seem possible. She has to be mistaken on that point. It doesn't make sense otherwise. More than likely, Brom chose not to let on that he knew about her boyfriends. It may have helped him save face in the coven or maybe it provided him with a wider latitude to deal with them."

"The wider latitude part makes more sense. Jasmine and her guys would have let their guard down over time. It would only be natural, and if Brom acted like a jealous resentful suitor then suspicion would understandably fall on him when something happened."

Cesari added, "So he plays it cool, biding his time for the right opportunity. My guess is he's been stalking her for years. He's felt that she was his property since they were kids. He made that clear to me and I've only been here a week. This makes a lot of sense."

Vito puffed on the cigarette and nodded. "Yeah, I agree. So far so good."

"Okay, so for the sake of argument, let's assume Brom killed all three of her boyfriends starting with her fiancé eight years ago. The first one is an absolute disaster and the guy turns into a missing person's case. Law enforcement gets called and the thing becomes a mess. Jasmine is emotionally broken and winds up in a shrink's office. Brom realizes he's made a massive miscalculation and a month later creates a phony 'Dear John' letter to try to mitigate the fallout with the cops but mostly to reassure Jasmine that he's not dead, just a jerk. It's clumsy but it's the best Brom can do under the circumstances and since there's no body, it works.

He learns from his mistake and makes the subsequent boyfriends write her 'Dear John' letters before he does whatever it is he does to them. She receives the letters within a day or two after they've gone so it doesn't become a legal matter and she doesn't worry. It hurts her yes, but isn't nearly as traumatic as not knowing what happened to them, and this way she has nothing to cling to. She doesn't stand around hoping they'll return with flowers and a heartfelt apology."

"And Brom just hangs around waiting for her to realize he's the only man for her," Vito added.

"That's right. He also learns to not let her relationships get as far as the altar. That was a mistake too. You have to nip these things in the bud before they get to that point."

"And she creates the Horseman in her mind as a way to rationalize their leaving because she's basically nuts."

Cesari got annoyed. "Take it easy with the judgement, all right?"

"Fine, but here's a question for you. Was Jasmine always mentally ill or is it because of what we suspect Brom's been doing to her all these years?"

"I don't know, but I intend on finding out. You with me?"

Vito threw his cigarette butt onto the pavement and squashed it underneath his very expensive French shoe, saying, "Of course."

"That's a very unattractive habit."

"Really? I didn't notice."

Cesari shook his head in frustration and said, "It would still be nice to have a body before I accuse the town's leading citizen of being a serial murderer."

"A body would be nice or some proof that Pullman never actually left town… You said that he sent a moving company to pick up his stuff. They should have an address. If he really left town voluntarily, they'll know where he went."

"That's a good point. I should have thought of that." Cesari looked at his watch. "C'mon, it's not that late. Let's go to his apartment building and see if we can find out anything from his landlord. Go pay for our meals and I'll pull the car around."

"You can't be serious? I have half a prime rib dinner sitting in there on a plate."

"Have them box it up."

"For crying out loud, Cesari."

Despite Vito's protestations, Cesari was already walking away fishing for the car key in his pocket. He pulled the big Caddie around to the entrance and called Linda Lu while he waited for his unhappy friend to pay the bill.

"Yes, Doctor?"

"Hi Linda Lu, I'm sorry to bother you after hours like this."

"It's no problem. What can I do for you?"

"Do you happen to know where Dave Pullman lived?"

"Dr. Pullman? Of course. He lived in Logan Park Lofts. It's an apartment building on Logan Street in Auburn. You can't miss it. It's a renovated piano factory. I think the address is number 11 Logan Street. Why do you want to know?"

Vito got in the car with a bag full of food and the opened bottle of chianti as they were speaking. "Somebody mentioned that his apartment might still be available, so I thought I might go take a look at it."

"Oh, he had a beautiful apartment. You'll love it."

"Thanks."

"Doctor…"

"Yes, Linda?"

"About this afternoon…"

"Linda, please don't. It's none of my business and I really don't want to be involved."

"Have a good night."

"You too and thanks once again."

He hung up and Vito asked, "Who was that?"

"My office manager. I called to get directions to Pullman's apartment. Would you mind plugging the address into the GPS and spare me the learning curve? It's number 11 Logan Street, Auburn."

Fifteen minutes later they pulled to a stop in front of a square, brick, five-story building that was undeniably a factory of some sort years ago. Two monstrous chimneys rose from either side of the building into the night sky. As far as residential buildings went, it was most uninviting with a wrought iron fence wrapping around it and a security guard sitting in a booth at the front gate. They parked on the street and walked up to him. He was an older guy and unarmed.

Cesari asked, "Hi, I know it's a little late, but we'd like to speak to the landlord or the super?"

"Yeah, well so would I. It's freezing out here and they both promised me a heater."

"I'm sorry about that. Any chance we might speak to one of them?"

"The landlord doesn't live around here but I'll call the super. What's it about?"

"It's about Dr. Pullman. The doctor who left town suddenly."

The guy's eyes went wide. "Oh he'll definitely want to talk to you then. He's still pissed off about that."

Cesari and Vito glanced at each other and the guard made a quick call. A few moments later he buzzed the gate open saying, "He's in apartment 1A. It's the first one on the right past the main entrance. His name is Milford, but everyone just calls him Milf."

"Milf?"

"You got a problem with that?"

"No."

They entered the old building and Milf was waiting for them with his door half-open. He was a balding middle-aged guy with thick eye glasses and two days' worth of salt and pepper stubble wearing a terry cloth robe and slippers. A TV was turned up high inside and a small dog yapped at them between his legs.

He kicked the dog back into the room said, "Shut up Princess or no treats tonight." Then he sized up his visitors. "You guys know Pullman?"

Cesari replied, "Not personally. I'm Dr. Cesari and this is Mr. Gianelli, a friend of mine. I'm new in town and needed to reach Dr. Pullman to ask him some questions about his patients but it seems nobody knows where he went and he may have changed his phone number. I was hoping you could help me with that."

"How can I help with that?"

"Well, I've been told that a moving company was sent to pick up his possessions and bring them to his new residence. If you don't know where they went I was hoping you could tell me the name of the moving company so I could contact them directly."

"His possessions? They're on the side of the road some-where in the desert outside of Phoenix. He gave us the ad-dress to a Tex-Mex restaurant in a strip mall out there. They never heard of any Dr. Pullman and he wouldn't answer his phone. They even went to one or two local hospitals asking for him. They tried to do the right thing until they finally came to the conclusion their chain had been yanked. Proba-bly thinks he was being funny having some moving company haul his crap twenty-three hundred miles as a prank. They were justifiably angry and tossed his stuff out to save money on fuel coming back. If I knew where he was I'd go find him myself and tear him a new one."

Cesari glanced at Vito and said, "He gave a phony ad-dress to the moving company?"

"I already told you it wasn't a phony address. It was the address to a place where he wasn't."

"Isn't that the same thing?"

"No, it's not. If he had given us a completely made-up address the moving company would have known that when they programmed their GPS. He's a clever little shit, that's for sure. He gave me the address, and I gave it to the moving company, so now they're pissed at me. We had a whole big to-do about it. They felt I should at least split the moving expenses with them; gas, tolls, meals and the like. I told them it wasn't my fault and that I was simply asked to do one of my tenants a favor by calling them."

Puzzled, Vito asked, "They didn't want anything up front like a credit card?"

"That's another reason they're pissed. They usually do want a down payment for such a long haul, but I vouched for the guy that he was a doctor and he'd be good for it. I don't think my reputation's going to recover from that hit."

"Did you tell anyone about this?" Cesari asked.

"Like who?"

"Like the police."

"Why would I do that?"

"Didn't it occur to you that something might have happened to Dr. Pullman?"

"I hope something did happen to the sumbitch. Now is there anything else I can help you with? I was in the middle of watching the game and Princess needs a doggie treat."

"No, thank you. You were very helpful."

They walked back to the Caddie and Vito sighed as they got in. Cesari read his mind. "I guess that settles that."

"It sure does."

"The only question is what did Brom do with the body?"

"No, Cesari, there are two questions that need to be answered. That's just one of them. The other is why did Brom go ape-shit over you so fast. You hadn't even been to first base with Jasmine and he immediately went to DEFCON 1. The other guys he gave a chance for things to peter out on their own, and then he acted decisively once he realized the relationships were going in the wrong direction, but with you he worked himself into a lather before you even got started. Plus, he wasn't even subtle about his approach. He went right for the jugular. Why?"

Cesari thought about that and said, "I don't know."

"Well, you better start thinking about it before the moving guys show up for your stuff."

"Thanks."

Chapter 38

Publius Ovidius Naso

"I don't want to go back to the inn. This isn't fair. You get to park somewhere with a pretty girl and I have to go back to my room? I thought we were going to hit the town tonight," Vito whined. After they left Pullman's apartment Cesari had called Jasmine and arranged to meet her at the Pavilion.

"Be reasonable, will you? I'm trying to help this girl and no one's forcing you to go to your room. When we get back to the inn, I'll switch vehicles and take the pickup. Then you can go wherever you want."

"By myself? Thanks for nothing," he said peevishly.

Cesari said nothing as his friend became pensive. Finally Vito growled, "Where can I get a drink in this town?"

"Probably plenty of places but what's wrong with the bar at the inn? You seemed to be having a grand time when I found you there earlier and the drinks are on the house."

"Are you serious? You expect me to drink there knowing about the deer-flavored mead? Not a chance. There are too many bad memories now, and another thing…I know you got there after the first glass, but you could have stopped me with the second."

379

"Okay, you need to stop it, all right? I drank a whole bottle of mead with dinner and I'm still here… I didn't want to make a big thing of it in front of the bartender…just get a scotch or something."

"Hey what's that?" He pointed to a bar with bright overhead lights and crowds of people hanging outside smoking and holding drinks. Music drifted in from his open window.

Cesari said, "That's A.T. Walley & Co. It's a whiskey bar."

"Stop the car. I'm getting out."

"You're getting out?"

"Yes, now stop the car."

Cesari pulled to the curb and Vito exited the vehicle. "How are you going to get back to the inn?"

"I'll figure it out."

Cesari watched him disappear into the crowd and then drove off to meet Jasmine. He arrived before her and was the only car in the large parking lot. While he waited, he played with the radio until he found a mellow jazz station that floated his boat. Minutes later, she pulled up next to the Caddie and waved. She was beaming as she got in the car and sat next to him. It was 10:00 p.m.

He smiled at her and she smiled back. He said, "Hi."

She said, "Hi."

"How was dinner with your friend?" she asked.

"It was okay, but I would have preferred being with you. We ate at Lasca's. The portions were huge. I still have most of it in a bag on the floor of the back seat."

She glanced backward. "I thought something smelled good. What did you have?"

"The prime rib, and I also have most of a recently opened bottle of Chianti too if you're interested, but no wine glasses. We'll have to just pass it back and forth like winos."

"Sure, why not?"

"Really?"

"Yeah."

He reached into the back seat and grabbed the bottle of wine out of the bag with the food, yanked the cork out, and handed the bottle to her. She said, "Thanks," and took a swig.

She passed him the bottle and he took a swallow. Then they both laughed. She said, "So who's this friend? Did he come to Auburn specifically to visit you?"

"His name is Vito and we grew up together in the Bronx. No, he didn't come all this way to visit me. He was on his way to Turning Stone Casino and missed his exit."

"Seriously?"

"Unfortunately, I am. I spoke to him last week about the casino and all he heard was Auburn and the Dulles House. He'll be leaving tomorrow, and I'll make sure to program the correct directions for him this time. I might even do it for him tonight if I can figure out how to use the GPS in this car."

She laughed. "This is his car? It's very nice and smells brand new."

"It is brand new."

She felt the luxurious leather seat and studied the intricate electronic dash board. "I bet this is pretty expensive."

"You'd win that bet... So how was your day?"

She shrugged. "Same as yesterday, always glancing over my shoulder to see who's watching, but I do look forward very much to these clandestine meetings with you. It's funny how much you want something the minute you're told you can't have it."

"We are ever striving after what is forbidden, and coveting what is denied us."

"That's very profound. Did you just make that up?"

"Hardly. It's a quote from Publius Ovidius Naso known as Ovid to us English-speaking peasants. He was a famous Roman poet who lived during the reign of Augustus, the first emperor of Rome. I learned about him in high school Latin class."

"He was a very wise man."

"Not wise enough. He ticked off the emperor and was banished from Rome to live in exile the last ten years of his life in a place called Tomis on the Black Sea."

"Am I to assume Tomis wasn't the place you wanted to be?"

"Hardly, and it still isn't, but back then it was on the edge of the civilized world. It would have been like being banished from Manhattan and ordered to live in…well, it would have been like being ordered to live in Auburn the rest of my life and never allowed to wander outside the city limits. Could you imagine that?"

He made a pretend chill as if horrified by that thought. She laughed and grabbed the wine bottle. "That was rude. Auburn's a nice place."

Grinning, he watched her drink the wine. "I apologize… Are you going to save some for me?"

"Yes, but you better not say anything mean about Auburn again. I like this town."

"I see… Well, in the interest of self-preservation I'd like to change the subject. Are you ready for tomorrow night's costume party at the inn?"

She sighed. "As ready as I'll ever be, I guess. I'm so mad at Brom I don't even want to go, but I know I must control myself for my parent's sake."

"You're in a tough spot, but I think you're wise for playing it cool. So who usually gets invited to this thing?"

"Mostly church members, the inn's guests, certain notables in the community. It's not that big an affair. There will only be a couple of hundred people or so."

"Not that big an affair? Two hundred people is bigger than most weddings."

"It's all relative, I guess. Halloween parties around here are big deals. Almost every self-respecting home has one."

"What about your costume? You haven't told me what you're going as."

"And you haven't told me what you're going as."

"I wanted to surprise you."

"And I wanted to surprise you."

"I surrender."

"Smart," she said with a big smile. "So what's your costume?"

"I'm going as Scaramouche, a seventeenth century clown. According to the short history that came with the costume, he was a recurring character in comedic plays for a hundred years."

She liked that and repeated softly, "Scaramouche, the clown."

"Have you heard of him?"

"I read a book many years ago by that title. It was written in 1921 by Rafael Sabatini and was set in revolutionary France. My recollection is that the role of Scaramouche was generally one of a buffoon and a coward. Is that you?"

"I prefer scheming rogue to cowardly buffoon but I guess you're close enough. Okay, so I told you what I'm going as. It's your turn."

"Guess…"

She was having fun, so he went with it. "I told you I saw you as a pirate."

"Yes, you did, but I didn't see me as one. Besides someone in my house already claimed pirate so guess again."

He nodded. "Okay, a superhero then, like Wonder Woman or Super Girl or maybe something not quite as goodie two-shoe, like Cat Woman."

"Not bad. I do like Cat Woman but no, not Cat Woman."

"Are you going to help me out here?"

"Think powerful… a powerful woman."

"I thought all women were powerful."

"Ooh, you're a real charmer, aren't you?"

"I've been told that once or twice. Okay, so a powerful woman."

"The most powerful of all women," she corrected.

"The most powerful of all women," he repeated and then snapped his fingers. "I got it. You're going as my mother."

She started laughing and playfully pushed him. "You're being silly. Fine, I'll tell you. Get this... I decided to go as... Katrina Van Tassel, the matriarch of my coven and the most powerful witch ever."

Cesari gasped and was speechless, his mind racing. This wasn't healthy and now she was going to wear her delusion on her sleeve for all the world to see. He said, "Are you sure that's wise, Jasmine? I mean isn't that a little disrespectful of her memory?"

She gave him a puzzled look. "Not at all. It's a great tribute to her. Personally, I'd be honored if one day people dressed up as me on the most special of all days."

"What does this costume consist of?"

"That will have to be a surprise, okay? It's going to take all day to prepare so I won't see you before the party. I took tomorrow off because I have so much to do."

He nodded glumly, not liking this at all. The little that he knew about psychiatry told him that it probably wasn't a good idea for someone to so thoroughly immerse themselves in their psychosis like this.

He let out a deep breath. "All day?"

"I have a hair appointment, manicure, pedicure, shopping for shoes... I have to help my mom get dressed too. Yeah, all day or most of it."

"I understand. It starts at 8:00 p.m., right?"

"Yes, and we'll have to be extra careful there because it will be wall to wall Brom's spies."

He nodded. "I'll bet. Speaking of the devil, do you know what Brom will be? I'd like to be able to keep an eye out for him."

"We haven't talked, but I have no doubt he'll dress up in the same costume he always does."

"What does he usually go as?"

"Satan of course. He's obsessed with his lord and master."

"That figures…and you're not as obsessed?"

"No, I'm not. He has no hold over me and I have no fear of him. Katrina's bloodline runs too strong in me."

Great.

Chapter 39

Sleepwalking

Cesari and Jasmine parted company at midnight and he drove back to the inn deep in thought. He was worried that the further Jasmine delved into her fantasy world, the harder it might be to bring her out. He needed to talk to his friend Mark and called him despite the hour.

"Cesari, what are you doing up so late?"

There was a cacophony of noise in the background and he could just barely hear him. He said, "Where are you, Mark?"

"I'm at Turning Stone where I told you I would be."

"The casino?"

"Is there another Turning Stone in upstate New York? What is it, Cesari? I'm at the craps table, the dice are hot, I'm up several grand and the pit boss is starting to give me the evil eye."

"Oh yeah, I forgot you were coming up today. You can call me in the morning. I need to talk to you about my friend."

"The crazy girl? Has something happened?"

The noise in the background quieted down considerably and he guessed Mark had stepped away from the action. He replied, "Yes and no. Look, I don't want to ruin your karma. We can talk in the morning."

"It's too late. Apparently, you can't talk on your cellphone when you're the shooter. The pit boss just gave the dice to someone else and made me cash out. This is ridiculous. He's just trying to cool off the table. What kind of crackers work at this place, Cesari?"

"I'm sorry about that. I'll bring it up with the gaming commission. Try not to get thrown out of the place, all right? They can do whatever they want to people they don't like, and the people they like the least are the ones who win. Keep that in mind. Well, as long as you got a moment..." He then brought him up to speed regarding Jasmine's plans to dress up as Katrina Van Tassel for the Halloween party.

"Definitely not good, Cesari. She's clearly in a critical stage of her illness and her subconscious is struggling with who she really is; Jasmine the human girl or Jasmine the witch. Seems to me Jasmine the witch may be winning. One of two things can happen. One, people will laugh at her or two, people will encourage her. Either is not good for her mental well-being. Can you talk her out of it?"

"Not a chance. I tried."

Mark sighed deeply into the phone. "Look, Sarah said she wanted to come to your Halloween party Saturday night. I'll talk it over with her about coming to tomorrow night's party instead or maybe even both. You arrange for me to meet with Jasmine. Something natural and casual, all right? Don't be heavy-handed with her. She's not some ferocious frying pan throwing guinea girl from the Bronx you're used to. She's fragile so handle her like a delicate flower and I'll see what I can do. If I have to, I'll begin therapy right there at the party. Is there a costume store in that town?"

"There's a big store right on the main drag as you enter the city limits. You can't miss it. It takes up almost an entire city block."

"What are you going as?"

"Scaramouche, an eighteenth-century Italian clown."

"How appropriate, a twenty-first century Italian clown dressing up as an eighteenth-century Italian clown."

Cesari laughed. When Mark was on a roll, he was on a roll. "I'll be wearing a red cape, tri-cornered hat and a colorful half-mask. I even have a sword."

"Now there's an image I won't easily forget. Text me directions to the party, okay? Will I need some sort of secret Wiccan password to get in?"

"Yes, if you see a really big guy who looks angry tell him he's not nearly as ugly as his mother. He'll let you right in and buy you a drink."

Mark snorted. "Funny as always, Cesari. I'll see you then."

"Thanks, Mark. I really appreciate this."

"Fuggedaboutit. Isn't that what your people say? Fuggedaboutit."

Cesari stared into the phone's receiver for a second, wondering how much his friend had been drinking. "Yeah, that's exactly how we talk. It's from an ancient dialect spoken only on the small island of wop off the coast of Sicily."

Mark guffawed into the phone. "Good comeback, Cesari. You still got it, baby."

Cesari chuckled. "Thanks. I'm looking forward to seeing you and Sarah tomorrow. Call me when you arrive. Is Sarah gambling too?"

"I'm not sure. I lost track of her about an hour ago. She might be getting a massage."

"A massage? At this hour?"

"I didn't say it was legal one, Cesari. I saw her flirting with a waiter before and I'm assuming the worst. You have no idea what she's like after a few martinis."

"Go find your wife. I'll see you tomorrow."

"Bye."

Cesari hung up, smiling as he pulled into the parking lot of the inn. The guy was too funny. As he got out of the Caddie, he noticed a shiny red Corvette in one of the spaces. He went inside and heard soft lounge music and quiet voices drifting from the bar area. He glanced at his watch. It was late.

He peeked around the edge of the entranceway and saw the fire blazing and Vito sitting on the sofa very close to Lola. They were sipping Manhattans and gazing into each other's eyes. There was no one tending bar but there was a bottle of bourbon on the counter and he surmised Vito had helped himself. Lola's legs were crossed, and her skirt hiked way up.

Cesari thought about what to do but decided to do nothing and discretely continued on his way to his room. Vito was a big boy and should know better than to mess with another man's wife, so it wasn't Cesari's problem although, it would make for great story telling with mutual friends in Manhattan. That was the important thing. Under normal circumstance, he might have wondered how they had met, but tonight he was too distracted.

Upstairs, the orange floor lighting seemed eerier than usual, and as Halloween approached, he was starting to feel an energy that he hadn't earlier in the week. He wondered what that meant as he unlocked his door. This town, Jasmine, Brom…they were starting to get to him.

He flipped on the overhead light and saw Ichabod curled up on his bed. The cat stretched and yawned. The window was open again. Cesari walked over to it and closed it tight before turning to Ichabod saying, "Let's see you get out of here tonight."

In response, Ichabod closed his eyes and went to sleep. Cesari undressed and got under the covers trying not to disturb his feline companion. Soon he was asleep as well. At precisely 3:30 a.m., Cesari felt hot breath on his face and opened his eyes.

He looked at Ichabod and said, "Let me guess. You'd like to go home?"

Ichabod meowed, jumped off the bed, went to the window sill, hopped up and looked out. Cesari yawned and thought about ignoring him. Serves him right, he thought, but compassion got the better of him…and practicality. What if he had to go outside because there was no litter box in the room? He grunted, got out of bed and walked over to the window.

Looking out, he saw the same dark shadowy figure again hanging out by the honey-house. It was just standing there not doing anything. He glanced at Ichabod. "It's just a bear, big guy. Don't lose sleep over it."

Ichabod bared his fangs and hissed.

Cesari looked at him again, puzzled. He couldn't recall if cats got like this. He knew dogs did because of a protective instinct they had for the pack. He said reassuringly, "There's nothing we can do about it so let's just go to sleep, all right? He'll be gone in a few minutes."

He gazed out the window again and saw that the figure had come closer to the inn. Away from the honey-house he could see that it was much larger than he thought but it was still too dark to make out details. It just looked like a big black shadow slightly darker than the gloom around it. He didn't like that it was brazen enough to approach the house, but maybe it was coming for the garbage cans.

Ichabod hissed again only this time more urgently, his tone gradually morphing into a throaty growl. Cesari ran his hand over the cat's head trying to soothe him. "It's all right, pal. I don't like that thing either but we're safe in here."

When he looked back down, he saw the shadow moving quickly down the path in their direction. Just then, a cloud blocked the little moonlight there was and he completely lost sight of it. For some reason his heart skipped a beat and he felt the hairs on the nape of his neck stand up. Ichabod was very agitated now and meowed incessantly circling Cesari's legs.

Suddenly, the cat bolted toward the door and scratched at it. Cesari was concerned but not frightened. He was getting used to the weird goings on around here, but this was different. Ichabod was upset about something, but what? They were three stories up.

He watched Ichabod urgently scratch at the door. What was he trying to tell him? He looked back out the window as the cloud cover moved on and...

Holy shit!

The thing was at the side of the inn and starting to climb up the ivy. Ichabod ran over to him and gently bit his ankle to get his attention and then raced back to the door. This time Cesari understood and ran after him, his heart pounding and breathless. They burst into the hallway and ran down the corridor and down the stairs. At the front door he hesitated. He was in his underwear and it was fifty degrees out, maybe colder by now. Where was he going? Should he alert Brom or the other guests? Would they believe him or call an ambulance to have him carted off to psychiatry for his own protection? He didn't even know what he was running from and was suddenly starting to feel ridiculous.

The front door opened and Ichabod ran out. It was Vito and he stood there staring at him. He said, "Cesari, what the hell is going on? You're in your skivvies."

He didn't have a good explanation and stood there silently, still catching his breath. Vito finally said, "Are you sleepwalking? Why are you shaking? Did you have a nightmare?"

Cesari thought sleepwalking was as good an explanation as any and feigned confusion, "Where am I? How'd I get here?"

Vito let out a breath and closed the door behind him. He grabbed Cesari's arm and said, "Come with me. You need a drink."

He led Cesari back to the bar and sat him in a chair. He then went over to the large sliding door and closed it. He poured them both two fingers of bourbon and handed Cesari one of the glasses. He chugged it down in one gulp, the warm liquid calming him down immediately.

Feeling extremely foolish now that the fright had passed, he said, "What happened?'

Vito replied, "You're asking me? You were sleepwalking, I think. Have you ever done that before?"

"Not that I recall. Did I do anything embarrassing?"

"You were about to go outside in your underwear in forty-degree weather. That would have been pretty embarrassing getting picked by the cops like that. It's a good thing I found you when I did. There's a bear running around the neighborhood. It's been all over the news. I was just listening to it on the local radio on the way back to the inn."

"There is? Where are you coming from anyway?"

"I met a babe at the that whiskey bar. Her name's Lola. Smoking hot, Cesari. She had just gotten into a major argument with her douchebag husband. He was there too but he totally blew her off and left her all alone and crying her eyes out. I felt bad so I went over to say hi. You know, to see if there was anything I could do to…"

"Console her?" Cesari finished the sentence for him.

"Yeah, something like that. We came here for a while, had a couple of drinks and talked. Man, I was tempted to tap that tonight but it's never a good idea when they're in the middle of a fight like that. They always regret it the next morning so I drove her home. Besides, she was so drunk who knows how she would interpret events. She's the one who told me about the bear sightings, so I tuned in to the local news on the drive back."

"How'd you drive her home?"

"She drove us from the bar to here in her Vette, and I drove her home in that. She was in no shape to get behind the wheel of a car anyway. I saw you brought the Caddie back but I didn't feel like going up to my room for the spare key. Maybe you can follow me to her place tomorrow to return her car?"

"Of course. Well, good for you, Vito. I'm proud of you for showing restraint like that."

"Well, don't pat me on the back too much. We did mess around in her driveway a little bit before she went into her house. She wanted to thank me for being so nice."

"Was there any exchange of bodily fluids?"

"In a Corvette? No, that would be nearly impossible the way they're designed."

"Then I'm proud of you."

"Yeah, well, I ain't exactly throwing that fish back in the sea just yet. She invited me to a Halloween party tomorrow night right here at the inn and if she's still into it then you may not see me for the next couple of days."

"You're not going to the casino tomorrow?"

"Not now. If you had seen her, you'd understand. There's no way I'm going to pass up this opportunity. Well look, we'd better both hit the hay."

"You're right. I'm exhausted. You go first to make sure there's no one around to see me like this."

Vito opened the door, looked both ways and waved to Cesari the coast was clear. Vito's room was two doors down from his and they bid each other good night. Cesari went to his room, but he hesitated in front of the door before he turned the knob, uncertain of what he might find. The room was just as he had left it except for one minor detail.

The window was open.

Chapter 40

Scarface

Cesari slept fitfully, waking up every fifteen minutes or so to stare at the window praying each time that it was still closed tight. Finally exhaustion overwhelmed him and just as the sun was coming up, he fell into a deep slumber and stayed that way until 10:00 a.m. when a loud banging on his door roused him. With great reluctance he rose to answer it.

Vito stood there all perky and cheery like a man who didn't have a care in the world. Because he didn't. Your more primitive types only concerned themselves with the basics; food, shelter, and the fulfillment of certain physical needs.

Vito pushed the door open and walked past him. "Cesari, you look like shit. C'mon get dressed. We'll grab breakfast and return Lola's car."

Cesari's brain hadn't quite come around. He murmured something that sounded like fine and then staggered into the bathroom to shower. When he came out again, he felt like a new man. His confidence was returning and he felt a renewed determination not to succumb to the power of suggestion or superstition. He told himself that had to have been a bear last night and it was definitely not climbing the wall to his window.

They were too late for breakfast at the inn and decided to go out. In the parking lot, Cesari noticed a metal dumpster that had been pushed up alongside the house. It hadn't been there the day before and Cesari rationalized that the bear must have gotten on top of it giving him the impression it was climbing upward. He breathed a sigh of relief at having found a logical explanation for his fears. They drove the pickup to the same run-down diner Jasmine had taken Cesari to a week ago, which now seemed like years in the past. They sat and ordered piles of eggs on top of piles of corned beef hash with bottomless mugs of coffee. Vito was in heaven.

"I could get used to this town, Cesari. Look at the portions they serve everywhere you go. Did you save the prime rib from last night by the way? I might want it for a snack later."

"Sorry, Vito. I forgot to bring it in. It's still in the back of the Caddie."

"No worries. It's probably still good. It got pretty chilly last night. I'll bring it into the inn's kitchen when we go back to pick up the Corvette."

"You can have mine too. I don't eat things that have been sitting out all night."

"Fine with me… I'll need a costume tonight. Where can I get a good one? I want to impress Lola."

"There's a store not too far from here. After we drop the Corvette off, I'll drive you there. I don't have anything scheduled today at the hospital so I can hang with you, but Vito, aren't you moving a little fast with Lola? After all, she is married."

"Oh please…if you had seen the way this guy treated her at the bar you'd know he doesn't love her. He was yelling at her almost as if she had no right to be there. It sounded like he was with his friends and didn't expect her to show up. I don't blame her one bit for wanting attention. It's a good thing I came along when I did. A dame like that won't last long on the market or in her case, the black market…if you get my drift?"

Cesari suddenly felt a pang of guilt and thought that he should at least try to intervene. He said, "I don't get your drift."

"She's African, colored or whatever it is these days."

Cesari shook his head. "You mean she's black?"

"As the night my friend…as the night."

"Oh no, Vito. I can't believe it. I know this Lola. If it's the Lola I'm thinking of, she's my boss's wife. You saw the husband, right? Was he a big white guy, middle-aged with a facial tic?"

"That's him. His eye was twitching like crazy last night."

"You can't go near her buddy. You'll get me fired."

Vito raised his eyebrows as he sipped his coffee, a look of disappointment starting to settle upon his face. "Are you sure you know her? I'd hate to let this one get away. I was dreaming about her last night."

"Tall girl. Forty-six chest. They live on the lake, right? A big house with lots of windows? There was probably a Jaguar in the driveway when you dropped her off last night?"

Vito nodded. "That's her."

"You stepped in it this time, Vito. I know them well enough that they fight like that all the time. It turns them on. They probably went at it like sexaholics at a nymphomaniac's convention the minute you pulled out of the driveway. You really need to stay away. The whole situation is bad."

"Bullshit. I know a real fight when I see one, and I talked to her for two hours last night. She's genuinely unhappy."

"Vito, I need this job."

"Well, I'll keep that under consideration, but I'm not sure you have anything to worry about. I have no intention of sending him a postcard with a picture of me and Lola on it. Furthermore, even if he were to find out about me and her, he doesn't know you and I are friends and I'll make sure it stays that way. The bottom line is this Cesari, if this babe wants a home-made cannoli then she's going to get it and that's all there is to it."

Cesari was silent for a minute and then laughed as he signaled the waitress for the bill. He had tried his best and now his conscience was clear. "What's so funny?" Vito demanded.

"Nothing… I hope you and Lola hit it off, but don't say I didn't warn you, and if I get canned, I'm coming to live with you."

"Relax, Cesari. Nothing like that's going to happen. Now let's blow. I need a costume and it's almost noon."

They went back to the inn, picked up the Corvette and drove to Sal's house. Lola wasn't home so Vito left the car in the driveway with the key tucked away behind the visor. Fifteen minutes after that they walked into the costume store and Vito started browsing.

Two hours later Cesari was napping sitting upright on a bench while Vito tried on numerous outfits. Eventually he woke, yawned, found his friend and tapped his watch. He said, "C'mon, Vito, only girls take this long to shop for clothes. No one's going to care what you wear."

"I want to look just right."

"For whom?"

"For Lola. I have a feeling about tonight."

It was after 3:00 p.m. when he came out of the dressing room, modeled in front of a full-length mirror and finally appeared satisfied. He wore an Al Capone suit; a black double-breasted model with pin stripes and wide lapels, black patent leather dress shoes with satin button-down spats, and a matching broad-rimmed fedora with a white band around it which he wore cocked to one side just the way old Scarface himself used to wear it.

"What do you think, Cesari?"

"A gangster?" he asked drolly.

"Not just any gangster. The most famous one of all."

"You look very dapper. Can we go now?"

"Let me see if they sell carnations to pin to the lapel. I think red will look better than white. What do you think?"

"Vito, they're not going to sell flowers here."

They did sell flowers there and Vito bought a red carnation along with the rest of the ensemble. By the time they finished it was almost four and too early to get dressed for an eight o'clock party. So they went to the whiskey bar, ordered a round of Dickel's neat, and reclined back into soft leather chairs with their tumblers.

"I've been thinking about your problem, Cesari."

"I have so many. Which one?"

"The big one, Brom."

"Go on."

He sipped his liquor. "The thing that bothered me the most as I mentioned to you last night is why Brom took such

a disliking to you right out of the gate. It seemed dispropor-
tionate. I mean yeah, you kissed his girl, but so what? She's
kissed other guys. In fact she almost married one, right? It
didn't make any sense that he went off the cliff like that over
something so minor."

"Yeah, but Jasmine thinks he lost his head because I did
it on his home turf and it came on the heels of me showing
him up at dinner that same night."

"Maybe, and I agree it had something to do with you
being your usual abrasive self, but I think it was more than
that. I think he went ballistic not so much because you kissed
Jasmine on his home turf as much as where on his home turf
you kissed her."

"You mean the honey-house?"

"Exactly, I think it was the location that triggered him
not the kiss itself although I'm sure that bugged him too. I
think he was trying to cause you and Jasmine so much grief
you never went back there again."

"But I did."

"And look what you found."

"You think he went nuts because he doesn't want
anyone finding out he's marinating his venison in the honey
vat?"

"What else did you find there?"

"Pullman's clothes."

"You're getting warm."

"Help me out here, Vito."

Vito let out a deep frustrated breath. "Cesari, are we worried about a missing deer or a missing doctor?"

Cesari was quiet for moment as he let that sink in. He said, "You can't be serious?"

"You tell me… Your guy Pullman is missing and you find his clothes buried in a hole behind the honey-house. Then you see Brom tossing dead animals into the honey vat. It's a pretty big container from the way you described it, right? Well, you don't have to be a genius to put two and two together."

"No, you don't, but it's a long stretch from putting a dead deer into the honey vat to putting a dead human in there."

"Is it? You know how hard it is to get rid of a corpse these days? Nearly impossible anymore with helicopters, DNA, satellites, blacklights, constant camera surveillance. A guy has to learn to be creative."

He had a point. Gone were the days of just dragging a guy off into the woods and digging a shallow grave. Even the slightest contact with the cadaver would leave a trace of DNA evidence.

"Fine, but why not just padlock the honey-house and keep everyone out?"

"Good question. Maybe he didn't want to raise suspicions about what might be going on in there? You know, for a hundred years it was no big deal and now all of a sudden, he's worried about security. People might have raised their eyebrows about that. Maybe that's why the only camera in the building is facing the honey vat?"

That was also a valid point. Cesari said, "Now that you mention it, you're right. Jasmine's father told me Brom said the camera was installed because of vandalism, but that wouldn't make any sense to have only one camera in the basement if that was your concern."

"I'm right? Of course I'm right. In fact, I'd like to know just when Brom started marinating deer in there in the first place. I wonder if it coincided with Jasmine's boyfriends disappearing. Maybe carving up deer and putting them in the vat was a perfect cover story if anybody ever saw blood stains or noticed a funny smell coming from the honey-house? A pretty sickening cover story, I agree, but one that might sell if it ever came to it."

"You think there might be more than one ex-boyfriend in there?"

"You described it as being a very big container."

"It was big, at least twenty-five feet long by ten feet wide and six feet deep."

"If I can get three and a half guys into the trunk of my Caddie then you could get a lot more into that easy."

"Three and a half guys?"

"Don't ask."

They sat there staring at each other for a long time before Cesari said, "We need to look inside the honey vat, don't we?"

Vito swirled his whiskey glass around and then finished it off in one gulp. "Well, I don't see how we can possibly put the issue to rest until we do especially now that we know about the moving company."

"Brom is a pretty dangerous guy. We'd have to be very careful."

Vito snorted, "More dangerous than me?"

"Maybe not but I still wouldn't trifle with him and all you have for backup are a couple of kids who eat too much lasagna."

403

"Who needs backup? We can handle this on our own. Look, Brom's going to be tied up tonight with all those guests at the inn's Halloween party. It'll be the perfect time for us to snoop around."

"Fair enough, but we should wait until the party's in full swing before we sneak off. Jasmine and I really can't spend time together anyway because there will be too many of Brom's friends watching so this could work. I've seen how they take the lid off the honey vat. It's not that complicated. Just remember not to turn the light on down there. It'll trigger the video camera."

"Understood. I have a flashlight in the Caddie."

"One question; why are you suddenly so interested in helping me with all this?"

"Brom sucker punched me with that venison-tainted mead, and quite frankly, I'm a little pissed off about it. If I find out that I've been drinking human-flavored mead, then he and I are going to have words for sure."

Cesari's stomach turned at the thought.

Chapter 41

Katrina Van Tassel

At 8:30 p.m. Cesari was performing the final touches on his ensemble. The costume fit well for the most part and he thought he looked sharp. The buckled shoes and knee-length stockings seemed a little silly at first but after he donned the waist coat and tri-cornered hat he conceded to himself that he was having fun. The multi-colored half mask fit over the upper part of his face, resting on his nose and was held in place by arms that wrapped over his ears like eye glasses. Satisfied that he was sufficiently disguised, he strapped on the sword and scabbard that came with the outfit. Last but not least was a dark maroon velour cape that he flung around his shoulders and clasped around his neck securely by a brass chain.

Studying himself in a full-length mirror he took out the rapier and thrust it at his image. He laughed at himself and said, "Damn, Cesari, you clean up good."

He walked past Vito's room without knocking and went down to the party by himself. Better they just be two guests of the inn rather than best buds. The restaurant and bar had large sliding doors which had been pulled back to make one large ballroom when merged with the central receiving area between them. The fireplaces in both rooms were roaring, music played overhead and by 9:00 p.m. the crowd had swelled to well over Jasmine's estimate of two hundred guests. Probably twice that he thought.

Decorated with carved pumpkins, broomsticks, ghouls and other ghostly figures, there was no shortage of campy Halloween imagery. In the center of the room was a large, three-foot-high by four-foot-wide cauldron with plumes of white smoke billowing out of it which he presumed was manufactured by dry ice. Cesari walked up to it and touched the side carefully. It was cold and made of cast iron. Inside he saw small blocks of dry ice sublimating into their gaseous state. The cauldron was thick-walled and probably extremely heavy. He wondered if Brom got it from the Halloween store or had it specially made.

The bar was packed and waitstaff walked around with shrimp cocktail and other hors d'oeuvres. The guests were animated in lively and oftentimes lavish costumes. There were warlocks, goblins, Roman emperors, pharaohs, zombies, vampires, princesses and devils. He counted no less than a dozen satans and the night was young. He spotted Vito chatting up one of the many witches in the room. This one was blonde with black heels and a pointed hat. Cesari guessed she was plan B if Lola disappointed him. Vito was a perfect Al Capone, holding a Manhattan in one hand and a pistol gripped AR-15 with an extended magazine in the other.

Cesari tapped him on the shoulder and Vito turned to him, grinning ear to ear. Vito said to the girl, "Abigail, give me a minute, will you, honey?"

She smiled, "I'll be waiting, Al."

"Cesari, what are you supposed to be, George Washington?"

Cesari was annoyed. "Never mind. Is that real?" he asked nodding at the assault rifle.

"Of course it's real. I'm supposed to be a gangster."

"Is it loaded?"

"Naturally, fifty NATO 5.56 rounds in the magazine. It's not chambered though and the safety's on."

"Oh, I feel better now... Are you out of your effin' mind bringing that in here?"

Vito was offended, "Relax, will you? So far I'm getting nothing but compliments. People think it's a prop."

"I don't care. That thing is highly illegal and there might be cops, maybe even lots of them here. Sooner or later somebody's going to realize it's not just a decoration to match your outfit and besides, they used Tommy guns back in Al Capone's days not AR-15s so will you please put that somewhere safe where no one can see it?"

"Jesus, will you calm down. I'll put it back in the Caddie's trunk, all right? Now get a drink and simmer down. I'll be right back."

Cesari let out a deep breath as he watched him walk away and then turned to the bar nearly tripping over Abigail. She said, "You didn't have to be so hard on him."

"Sure I did."

She laughed and then did something extremely odd. She leaned close to him and sniffed. He said, "Is everything all right?"

"You're Jasmine's friend, aren't you?"

Caught off guard, he didn't say anything. How could she have known that? Even if she had seen him around the inn or the hospital, he was wearing a costume and a mask. A commotion behind him captured his attention as Lola arrived to much approbation. She looked great as Glenda the good witch. Tall and elegant, resplendent in a golden blonde wig and carrying a gigantic wand with a star at the end, she rapidly became the central attraction as people gathered round to greet her, but Sal was nowhere in sight. Cesari knew he didn't like to be seen with her in public, but this was one of those social obligations that, as a major player in town, he couldn't afford to miss. Cesari suspected he'd show up later hiding behind a mask of some sort. He turned back to Abigail to ask how she knew he was friends with Jasmine, but she was gone.

He put it behind him and ordered a scotch and soda which he sipped as he scanned the room searching for Jasmine. Given the amount of effort the guests put into their costumes and the amount of alcohol that was being consumed he was starting to feel better about Jasmine not being made to feel ridiculous. Almost everyone here seemed to be getting into character, so it would seem natural that she would as well.

Vito returned sans weaponry and holding an empty Manhattan glass. He placed it on the bar counter and ordered another one. He said, "Are you happy now?"

"I'm getting there and take it easy with the Manhattans. We have work to do."

"One more. I'll be fine. So when do you want to get this show on the road?"

"It's still much too early." He glanced at his watch. "Not before 11:00 p.m., all right? I'd like the party to be in full swing with most people either drunk or well on their way and the dance floor hopping. Brom should be at his busiest at that point."

"Sounds about right, although from the way this crowd is throwing down cocktails that point may come a lot sooner than you think."

He was right about that. Someone had turned the music up a notch and the central area around the cauldron had already cleared out for dancing and howling at the moon. Cesari said, "We'll stick with 11:00 p.m. just to be safe. Your girl Lola made quite an entrance. Did you see?"

"I saw. Man, she looks great, and she came alone. I thought I'd give her a few minutes to mingle before I go over, so it won't seem too obvious just in case her husband is lurking somewhere. Did you see your girlfriend yet?"

"No, and I'm a little disappointed. Hey…there she is."

His gaze had drifted toward the top of the staircase where he saw Jasmine with Ichabod by her side. He nudged Vito to look. She wore a floor length black velvet dress which hugged her at the waist and had simple white cuffs and collar. Her strawberry blonde hair was done up beautifully and barely concealed by a matching white bonnet resting delicately on top with its strings dangling down around her neck. Her hazel eyes twinkled in the light and she radiated confidence as she took in the room. She was gorgeous, and the outfit was exquisite in its simplicity and humility. She looked like an eighteenth-century country maid of Calvinist stock and virtue.

She saw him and smiled as she began her slow measured descent down the steps with Ichabod close behind. After the first step, the music stopped. After the second step, the dancers stopped dancing. After the third step, everyone stopped talking, and by the fourth step, a slow movement took place as everyone was drawn to the bottom of the steps to await her advance.

Vito whispered, "What's going on here, Cesari?"

"And just how would I know?" Cesari whispered back.

Jasmine reached the bottom of the stairs, curtsied for the crowd and the music suddenly came on again as normalcy returned to the room. Cesari and Vito glanced at each other and watched Jasmine greet guest after guest as if she knew each and every person in the room intimately. Gradually, she made a long circle and arrived at the bar where she stood in front of him.

"Hi John. What do you think?" she asked twirling around in front of him.

"I think you're the most beautiful Katrina Van Tassel I've ever seen."

She smiled. "Thank you, and this must be your friend Vito."

Vito offered her his hand, "That's me and you must be Jasmine. Johnny here has told me a lot about you."

"Oh Johnny has, has he?"

"Only good things I assure you. Well, I'll leave you two to talk, I feel a tango coming on and need to find a partner."

She looked at him. "There's a beautiful woman on the other side of the room in desperate need of companionship. You might want to start there. She's dressed as Glenda, the good witch from the Wizard of Oz."

For maybe the first time in his life Vito was at a loss for words, mumbled something that sounded like thank you and walked away.

Cesari said, "How did you know that?"

"That he was interested in Glenda? I saw him staring at her in the parking lot when she arrived. He was putting something in the trunk of his car. I was helping mom out of my car when I noticed him pining away at her from a distance. I like your costume. It's so you."

"Thanks. What were you doing upstairs?"

"My parents and I parked in the back but came in through the side of the house. They had decided to make a night of it and reserved a room on the third floor. Brom has a small elevator by that entrance. It's easier for my father than climbing stairs. We threw our coats down, freshened up and here we are."

Jumping on to the bar's countertop, Ichabod tapped Cesari with his paw. Cesari turned to him and said, "What do we have here?"

Ichabod wore a black eye patch over his right eye, a red neckerchief and a gold clip-on hoop earring on the left. Cesari hadn't noticed at first because he was so mesmerized by Jasmine when she made her arrival. Jasmine came close to Cesari and whispered, "He thinks he's a pirate. Play along."

"He's the one who claimed pirate in your house?" he asked.

She nodded, and he turned back to the cat and said, "I thought pirates were supposed to be scary? He looks cute."

Ichabod hissed, and Jasmine chastised him. "Ichabod be nice. You know John is just joking." Then she turned to Cesari and giving him an admonishing look said, "Do you have to provoke him like that?"

"I'm sorry, Ichabod. Let's start over." Cesari cleared his throat, lowered his voice and did the best pirate imitation he could. "Hey there matey, looks like stormy weather we be havin'. Time to cuddle up with a warm bottle of rum and a sturdy pirate wench I be thinkin'."

Jasmine laughed and Ichabod loved it meowing appreciatively. "Would you like a drink?" he asked Jasmine.

"A glass of chardonnay would be nice."

He put the order in and said, "That was quite an entrance."

"How so?"

He hesitated as he looked at her. "You didn't notice anything different just a moment ago when you came down the stairs?"

She shook her head. "Such as?"

"Such as the whole room stopped what they were doing to greet you."

"Oh that," she laughed. "They were just being polite."

"Polite?"

She nodded and he didn't know what else to say on that subject so he asked, "Where are your parents?"

"They came down the elevator and are mingling somewhere around here. They're Santa and Mrs. Claus."

Cesari grinned. "Cute. Whose idea was that?"

"Mine, of course. I thought we might as well use Dad's size to his advantage."

"Good thinking. I hope he didn't mind."

"Not at all. He has a great sense of humor and it's a refreshing change from dressing up as the world's largest pumpkin every year."

"I'll bet... I don't mean to spoil the moment, but maybe we shouldn't hang around each other too long? Remember Brom...?"

He didn't want Brom or his people paying special attention to him tonight. She said, "How could I forget, but he's in the kitchen. I'll know when he comes out."

"Yeah, but what about his spies in the room?" She looked at him hard trying to read his mind. It was almost as if she were thinking, *if I'm not worried then you shouldn't be either.* He said, "I'm not trying to cut our time short, but you said we should be extra careful here and I agree."

Satisfied she said, "Yes, of course. I'll go mingle. We'll catch up in a bit."

She walked away, and he looked at Ichabod who remained on the counter, his tail waving slowly back and forth.

"I'm missing something, aren't I, Ichabod?"

The cat just looked at him.

Chapter 42

The Honey Vat

By 10:30 p.m. the place was rocking like no Halloween party Cesari had ever been to. The lights were turned down low and half the guests were dancing to now nearly deafening music. The other half were drinking mead and other spirits right out of the bottles. Countless people were staggering, laughing or in some cases, undressing. Jasmine's mom, Hannah, had tuckered out early and Jasmine had helped her to her room. It was a little sooner than he had planned but Cesari seized the opportunity to leave and signaled Vito who was hitting on Abigail the witch again. Sal had shown up in a policeman's uniform, his appearance only marginally disguised behind reflective aviator sunglasses. Apparently he was trying hard to make amends with Lola and they were slow dancing in a corner dashing Vito's amorous designs.

Cesari left first. Outside he took his mask off and shoved it into his coat pocket. He sucked in the cool night air and had advanced about half way up the path to the honey-house when Vito caught up to him. He held a large flashlight, but they didn't want to use it while they could still be seen from the inn, so they walked the rest of the way in the dark, occasionally stumbling and cursing the night.

As they neared the entrance Cesari said, "Turn your cellphone off. It'd be best if we made as little noise as possible while we're in there."

While Vito did that, Cesari found the key under the ceramic turtle and unlocked the door. Inside, Vito turned on the flashlight and they went down to the basement quickly. Vito scanned around and said, "Wow, the smell of honey is pretty strong down here."

"That's because there's no ventilation."

Vito searched the ancient stone walls with the light as if to confirm that for himself. "Will you look at this place. It looks like something right out of horror flick."

Cesari let that go and pointed at the large metal storage container in the center of the room. "That's the honey vat. Let's not waste any time."

Walking around the container he undid the metal clasps one at a time and then gently lifted the drain pipe coming down from upstairs just as he remembered seeing Brom's men do it. He swung it out of the way and then, with Vito on one end and he on the other, they wiggled the cover off the honey vat. They placed it on the floor leaning against a wall. The smell of honey in the room increased instantly to almost suffocating intensity.

They climbed the steps to the small platform outside the vat and peered inside, observing a sea of dark amber liquid, but nothing floating near the surface. Vito said, "What do you think?"

"I think one of us is going to have to stick his hand in there and fish around."

"Not me brother."

"You have longer arms."

"I ain't doing it."

Cesari said, "Give me the flashlight."

Vito handed it to him. "What are you going to do?"

"Find a stick. Now wait here."

He searched the basement from side to side and eventually found a long metal pole with a sharp hook at one end. It looked like something that you might find on a deep-sea fishing boat, and he surmised that Brom must use it to grab the deer from the bottom. What a mess that must make he mused. They probably brought a tarp in here and laid the thing on it dripping with honey. He handed Vito the pole and shone the light into the vat.

Vito said, "What's this thing?"

"They probably don't want to reach in there with their arms either. Give it a whirl."

Vito plunged the hooked end into the river of honey and fished around until he hit something. They looked at each other. Cesari said, "Pull it up."

Vito swished the hooked end around until it attached to something and then slowly pulled the object to the surface. He grunted and strained. "Damn, it's heavy."

"It's the honey weighing it down. You can do it."

Slowly but surely it came into view and both of them gasped at the sight. It was a human being with a thick layer of honey oozing down off of it into the vat. Vito had pierced the upper back and had managed to bring the corpse's head and shoulders into view. Cesari studied it with the flashlight.

He said, "Who on earth is this?"

416

Vito didn't respond. He was too busy trying to keep the body afloat. It was a woman, an older woman, not ancient just old, maybe seventy or thereabouts. She had shoulder length hair and bloated cheeks and was extremely well-preserved without any signs of decay which made Cesari wonder if she was a recent arrival.

Vito was horrified. "Get a good look because I can't hold her up here forever, Cesari. She's a load and a half."

Cesari ignored him as he continued to study the woman's features. She was wearing a dress which was all matted down and discolored from the honey. There was a hearing aid in one ear and a diamond earring in the other. It was quite a unique bauble and it struck him that he had seen something like that before, but he couldn't think of where. He reached out and removed the piece of jewelry to study it better. He fully expected part of the ear to tear off with it but it didn't. The flesh still had a fair amount of resiliency.

Suddenly, without warning, Vito let out a breath and let the body slide back into the vat. He huffed and puffed. "I'm sorry, I just couldn't hold it any longer."

Cesari stared at the honey-covered earring wondering why it felt so familiar. He said, "It's all right. Take a breather. I'll give it a shot in a minute."

He went over to the hose against the wall and rinsed off the earring. It was a dangly thing made of three gold strands of varying length each with a round diamond at the end. The largest of the three diamonds had to be at least a karat. It was a very nice piece. The woman had clearly been well-off.

He showed it to Vito who asked, "Is it safe to assume that body isn't your doctor friend?"

"No, it wasn't and now we have another mystery."

"Great. Well whatever Brom is up to, it's clearly not for the money. Who would toss away a piece of jewelry like that?"

"I agree. I bet the other earring is at the bottom of the vat."

It was Cesari's turn and he grabbed the pole as Vito held the flashlight. It was still hooked into the corpse and he dragged the body to the far end of the container before wiggling the hook free. He then dredged the hooked end along the bottom of the vat all the way up one side and then back again. A third of the way back he bumped into another object and jabbed it with the hook. Once he had a good grip, he began to bring the pole out. Just like Vito, by the time he broke the surface, he was sweating and sucking wind. This time it was an old man, bald with a little hair at the temples and large mutton chop side burns. He was a big guy in life and wore a suit and tie. This was macabre to say the least and made Cesari uneasy.

"Vito, search his pockets."

"I'm not touching it."

Cesari let out a deep breath and said, "Fine, then you hold the pole while I search him."

Vito grabbed the pole and Cesari took his cape and waistcoat off and rolled his sleeves up. Then he gingerly put his hands into the cold honey to reach into the man's jacket pockets, coming out with a honey-drenched handkerchief which was probably white at one point but was now golden.

"Yuk," Cesari said observing honey drip off his arm.

"Like I said before, hurry. He's even heavier than the other one."

Cesari plunged his arm back into the liquid to search the trouser pockets but couldn't quite reach them. "Lift him up just a little higher, Vito."

Vito hoisted upward another couple of inches and Cesari rummaged through the clothing and found nothing. Vito let the corpse slide back to the bottom. Both men were deeply disturbed. It was one thing to have suspected and another to have confirmed this kind of atrocity, but who were these people? This wasn't what they had expected and clearly had nothing to do with the disappearance of Dr. Pullman.

For good measure, Cesari dredged the bottom of the vat again just to make sure they hadn't missed another body, but they hadn't. There were no other human or deer cadavers marinating in the sweet liquid.

Cesari rinsed his arm off with the hose and cleansed the handkerchief as best he could before ringing it out. In silence, they placed the cover to the vat back into place, fastened it and positioned the drain pipe the way it had been. Cesari put the handkerchief and earring in his pocket and put his coat and cape back on.

He looked at his watch. "Not a bad night's work. It's almost midnight. Let's get back to the party."

"Are you kidding me? What are we going to do about those two?" he nodded at the honey vat. "Shouldn't we call the police?"

"We will just not now, all right? I need to sort out what's going on first and I'd rather not do it while Jasmine is nearby. This will definitely be traumatic for her and might even further add to her mental problems. She might somehow rationalize that her Headless Horseman was responsible for this. Besides, there's no rush, these corpses aren't going anywhere."

"Why'd they look so fresh? You think they just got dumped in there?"

"I don't know much about the preservative effects of honey, but I do know that without oxygen and moisture, being submerged in honey could potentially be a great way to mummify a person. Hell, even bacteria don't grow in honey. It's the one food source you could leave lying around at room temperature for a hundred years and won't spoil."

"Really?"

"Really. Now let's go."

They went up the stairs and turned the flashlight off as they carefully opened the door to outside. Music and light from the house reached them, but they were alone and stepped into the night. Cesari locked the door and returned the key to its hiding spot. As they started to walk back to the house, they heard a grunting sound off to the right somewhere in the dark. They froze in place and glanced around. It was a gurgling, sloppy sound that Cesari found both unfamiliar and equally uncomfortable. He looked at Vito who was inches away and barely breathing. Cesari had the flashlight and turned it on and then off, a brief burst to identify the source of the noise but not long enough to attract attention from anyone in the house.

About twenty-five yards away, a large black bear had toppled over one of the beehives and was wreaking havoc with its contents. The bear stopped what it was doing momentarily, startled by the sudden flash of light but soon the racket continued as he resumed his mayhem. Cesari couldn't make out what the bees' reaction was but didn't think they'd survive long in this weather outside the hive. Although startled by the size and proximity of the animal, Cesari was somewhat relieved that there actually was a large bear roaming around to explain the shadowy apparitions he'd seen. The mind could play funny tricks on a person he mused.

Vito was not nearly as fascinated as Cesari by the sight and said with alarm, "Jesus, Cesari. Look at the size of that thing. Let's get out of here before he thinks we're on the menu."

"I'm on board with that."

They trudged quickly back to the house in silence and entered through the rear door walking through the kitchen to the party. As they arrived the music died, and all went very quiet. The lights flicked off completely and the room went pitch-black, the only sound that could be heard was the anxious breathing of four hundred people. Then just as suddenly, candles lit simultaneously throughout the hall. The cauldron glowed brightly from some hidden light source within which gave the smoke from the dry ice a creepy feel. A low murmur of approval filtered through the room. Cesari looked at a nearby wall sconce and saw that it was a real candle. He counted more than three dozen around the room and hadn't seen anyone actually light them. How did they do that? He turned to ask Vito what he thought about that but he had melted into the crowd to look for Abigail.

A minute later at the stroke of midnight, Jasmine appeared at the top of the stairs again, holding a candelabra with five lit candles. Just as she did hours earlier, she walked graciously down to the main floor and stood in front of the cauldron as everyone waited anxiously. Someone took the candelabra from her and she addressed the room dramatically. Her eyes gleamed, and her features were animated.

"Listen friends and brethren alike

To a tale oft told two centuries old

Of witches, spirits and the like

Who on Hallows Eve become so bold.

T'was a small country hamlet sleepy

A maid did summon the prince of evil

Into whose grasp she fell so deeply

And did awaken unholy powers primeval.

Katrina Van Tassel, the mother of us all

Satan's consort and the source of our line

All your deeds and memories we do always recall

Your children so many grapes on the vine.

To honor you we do pay tribute

By spell and progeny to continue

That which you have begun

For all eternity or until we are none!"

She raised both arms to the crowd and shouted out with glee, "Happy Halloween everyone!"

The crowd cheered with an earsplitting roar and clapped thunderous approval at the incantation and Cesari realized that it was indeed officially Halloween. The music came back on as the waitstaff wheeled out carts laden with open bottles of mead and the revelry resumed in earnest. It dawned on Cesari that this party was just getting started.

A hushed voice close to him said, "Hey Scaramouche, is it safe to assume that was Jasmine?"

Cesari immediately recognized the New York accent and attitude. He turned and saw Mark Greenberg. Five feet six inches short and thin, wearing a black fedora, dark sport coat, white shirt and tie. He had a neatly trimmed white beard, thick black framed glasses and held an overcoat folded over one arm.

Cesari smiled, "You look like Freud, Mark. When did you grow the beard?"

"Obviously since the last time you saw me and is that a yes to the girl?"

"Yeah, that's her in all her witchly glory. What do you think?"

"Well, if that wasn't just an act for the crowd then I think we have our work cut out for us. That's for sure. I'm sorry I'm so late. I tried to get here sooner, but Sarah and I were out till three in the morning and well... we're not exactly spring chickens. I can't even remember the last time I woke up at noon; probably not since college."

"No worries, Mark. I'm glad you could make it. Where's Sarah?"

"I booked a room at the Hilton Garden Inn. I didn't see any point in trying to drive back to Turning Stone tonight. She's there now, probably sleeping. She was exhausted today. By the time we rolled out of bed and our hangovers cleared, it was late afternoon. We were dragging bad, so we just hung around the casino and ate dinner at one of their restaurants. We arrived here late of course; too late to pick up a costume, but I'll remedy that tomorrow. I was pretty tired myself and almost bailed on you tonight but now that I've seen what's going on I'm glad I made the effort. I have a feeling there's more than one person here who needs counseling."

"What time exactly did you get here?"

"We checked into our room at 9:00 p.m., and I arrived here at around 10:30 p.m. maybe a few minutes later. I had a beer and looked all over for you. I thought maybe I was at the wrong party and was getting ready to leave when the young lady began casting her spell and then suddenly, there you were. You should try answering your phone sometime."

Cesari had turned his phone to silent when he'd gone to the honey-house to avoid unnecessary noise. He said, "I'm sorry about that. I had my phone off. You must be pretty exhausted yourself."

"No kidding... What's that smell?"

"What do you mean?"

He got close to Cesari. "You smell like honey."

"Oh that. It's a new after shave... Well look, if you're too tired to drive back to the hotel later you can stay with me. I have a suite here on the third floor with a full-sized sofa. You can have the bed."

"That won't be necessary. I'm a big boy and the hotel is only a mile or two from here. Besides, Sarah will kill me if I'm not there when she wakes up."

"Well I'm definitely not in favor of domestic violence, but just in case here..." He reached into his pocket and came out with the key to his room. He handed it to Mark and said, "I'm in room 308. Don't use the mini-bar and don't forget to give me the key back if you decide not to take advantage of my offer."

Mark laughed. "Thanks, but how are you going to get in the room if I leave and forget anyway."

"I'll have the innkeeper or one of the staff let me in. They all know me."

"Fine… Well since it's late would you mind introducing me to my patient? I'd like to at least break the ice with her tonight and maybe a little more if she's in the mood."

"Follow me."

"And knock off the Freud jokes. You have no idea how tiring that gets."

"I'm sorry. It must have been a Freudian slip."

Chapter 43

The Van Brunts

They found Jasmine deep in conversation with two devils, neither of whom was Brom. Jasmine smiled when she saw Cesari and excused herself from the group.

He said, "Jasmine, I'd like you to meet a friend of mine. This is Mark Greenberg, a colleague from downstate. Mark is up for the weekend to tour the local wineries and I invited him to the Halloween parties. Mark, meet Jasmine."

Mark extended his hand. "The pleasure is all mine."

She took his hand. "Mine as well. You have a lot of friends visiting this weekend, John."

"I'm a popular guy," he offered with a swagger.

"Are you a doctor as well, Mark?" she asked politely.

"Yes, a psychiatrist."

She glanced at Cesari. "How interesting."

"I practice in Manhattan and as you can see from my gnarled and shriveled appearance, plan to retire soon."

She grinned. "Nonsense, you don't look old at all, and I love your costume by the way."

Mark said, "Excuse me?"

"You look like Sigmund Freud. Isn't that who you're supposed to be?"

Cesari chuckled, remembering Mark's warning about the Freud jokes. He said, "I told you that's who you look like, Mark. Get this, Jasmine… The guy at the costume store told him this was a Carl Jung outfit, but that's patently absurd to anyone who knows anything about the history of psychiatry. I mean they were contemporaries, but Jung was much younger and had a mustache not a beard. Everyone knows that. Isn't that right, Mark? I'd demand my money back."

"Silly of me," Mark said good naturedly going along with the gag. "The man at the costume store must have pulled a fast one on me. I paid good money for this outfit."

Jasmine smiled. "You're not a very good liar."

Mark said, "And why do you say that?"

"Because you're not wearing a costume at all, are you? I was jesting about that, and when I said you're not a very good liar I was referring to John."

Mark laughed and shook his head. "No, I'm not wearing a costume. Sadly, this is how I actually look, but I am impressed at your powers of perception. How could you be sure?"

"About John lying or about you not wearing a costume?"

"Both."

"Well, John is an easy read. I've only known him a short time, but I've already noticed that whenever he's about to tell an untruth or something misleading, he seems to preface it with a joke, almost like a magician using misdirection as he pulls a coin out from behind your ear."

"And me?"

"The whole premise of the deception was that you had a false beard given to you by the costume store and while some costumes and makeup kits can be quite realistic, they can't simulate the fact that for some reason you didn't shave today and have at least one day's stubble above and below your beard line. If you were putting on a false beard just for the party you would have made sure to be clean-shaven. Hence the beard is real."

"That's amazing."

"I've always been good at discerning the truth. It's a gift I was born with."

Mark said, "I think I'm going to like you, Jasmine."

"Well, I resent what you just said about me. I happen to be an excellent liar," Cesari complained.

She stepped close to him and looked into his eyes. After studying him for a few seconds, she said very seriously, "No, you're not. You have too much goodness in you. Whatever you were once, you are no longer that person and probably never really were."

Cesari was silent and Mark raised his eyebrows saying, "I thought I was the psychiatrist here."

Before anyone could respond further, Vito came up to them interrupting the conversation. He pulled Cesari to the side and whispered in his ear, "We have to talk."

"I'm a little busy, Al," Cesari said under his breath, annoyed at the intrusion.

Vito was insistent. "We have to talk…now."

Cesari turned to Mark and Jasmine. "Please excuse me. I left the lights to my car on."

Jasmine cocked her head and smirked as if to say, *"Really?"*

Mark said, "Take your time. I'd like to get to know Jasmine."

Cesari followed Vito from the central hall to the restaurant area. They stopped a few feet in front of the massive fireplace there. Cesari glared at him. "I'm waiting," he said impatiently.

"Look."

"At what?"

"The picture over the fireplace. I was talking to Abigail when I noticed it."

Cesari looked upward at the large gold-framed painting and after a few seconds his mouth opened as he saw what Vito was talking about. It was a portrait of a husband and wife in older age. He was large and bald with mutton chop sideburns. She was plump with gray shoulder length hair and wore beautiful diamond earrings. The same earring he had recovered from the honey-vat. Cesari stepped closer ignoring the heat of the fire. He was stunned by the revelation and just wanted to make sure he wasn't mistaken. He wasn't. That was why the earring seemed familiar to him. He had seen it a week ago when he dined here with Jasmine and her parents. There was a small brass placard at the bottom of the portrait that read, *Hendrick and Anika Van Brunt*.

Vito pulled him away from the flame. "Do you see what I mean? They're his parents, aren't they?"

Cesari nodded and despite the cacophony and crowd, he felt all alone lost in thought. He said, "Man, this is even worse than I could have imagined."

Vito agreed. "What kind of a sick bastard would do that to his own parents?"

"Jasmine said they've been missing for ten years."

"Well, now we know why, but they looked like they've only been gone a day."

"It's the honey. It preserved them."

"This really pisses me off, Cesari."

"Simmer down, all right? This isn't your first rodeo."

He let out a deep breath and nodded.

"Enjoying the portrait of my parents, gentlemen?" asked a new voice from behind them.

They both turned in unison to face Brom who had come up behind them. He was dressed as Lucifer, but not the benign, harmless version people had become used to with pointed tail and pitchfork. He was the grotesque, worst kind of nightmare version with massive horns and cloved feet footwear. His makeup must have taken hours to put on and he was bare chested albeit with red makeup covering every inch of his skin. His six pack and massive pecs rippled with every movement. He had done his best to appear hideously powerful and in that regard was highly successful.

Cesari said, "Yes, it's lovely."

Vito had met him at check-in and said, "Hi, Brom."

He nodded. "Mr. Gianelli."

A strange look came over Vito's face and his features darkened. Cesari knew that look and knew that a storm was brewing. It was the look he had when he was about to unload a full clip on some unfortunate who had crossed him. He said, "The artist who painted this was a genius, Brom."

"Thank you."

"They look so alive."

Brom said, "Unfortunately, they were taken from me ten years ago, but yes, the artist captured them in a rare moment of rhapsody."

Vito had turned fully to face Brom. "How sad. I'll bet they were really sweet people…sweet like honey."

Brom was quiet for a moment as he tried to interpret that and then said, "Yes, they were the salt of the earth and good parents."

Cesari didn't like where this was heading and coughed to distract them. he said, "Well, I think we'll be heading back to the bar. I could use a drink. It was nice talking to you, Brom. Great party."

Cesari grabbed Vito's arm to tug him away. Brom said, "Mr. Gianelli looks as if he'd like to stay and chat some more."

"Sometimes Mr. Gianelli doesn't know when he needs a drink."

Vito stared at Brom for a few seconds but eventually relented, letting Cesari pull him away. At the bar, they ordered whiskey shots and Cesari was tempted to slap his friend.

Instead he simply chided him, "Nice job. Nothing like giving away the element of surprise to your enemy. What were you thinking back there?"

"I got angry, all right?" he stated defiantly before tossing down his shot, slamming the glass down and signaling Timothy the bartender for another one.

"Did I mention that he almost killed a guy a lot bigger than you with his bare hands?"

"Yes, you did. Are you going to drink your shot?"

"Yes, I am." Cesari picked up the glass and chugged down the whiskey. "Another one for me too, Tim...and just why are you so angry? You've never killed anyone?"

"Killing your own parents is way out of line."

"You killed your Aunt Ginny and Uncle Mimmo, remember?"

"They weren't my parents and I told you it was an accident and thanks for comparing me to Brom."

As the second round of shots was placed down, Cesari said, "You calming down?"

"Yeah, a little... I'm sorry."

Cesari thought it over. "It's okay. He probably just thinks you're drunk and being a little goofy... It's not like you accused him of drowning his parents in honey."

They laughed and Cesari added, "For what it's worth it's not as if he liked me before tonight, but if I were you, I'd keep the Lous around just in case he thinks it over and decides he doesn't like your attitude. Don't underestimate Brom, all right?"

"The Lous? What are they gonna do? They're seven hundred pounds of useless blubber."

"Just watch yourself is all I'm saying. That was stupid to provoke him like that. People who murder other people tend to be paranoid. You should know that better than anyone."

"I know... Do you think he caught on to what I was getting at?" he asked sheepishly and suddenly remorseful.

"Why would he do that? You were so subtle," Cesari said sarcastically. "Okay, forget about it. Can I leave you alone or are you going to get in more trouble? I'd like to go find Jasmine."

"I'm fine."

"I see Abigail over there by the cauldron all by herself. She's practically begging for someone to come over and ask her to dance."

Vito turned. "And here I come."

With a big smile on his face, he left Cesari at the bar. Cesari watched him, and with the music playing overhead was reminded of that famous line from the tragedy *The Mourning Bride* by William Congreve, "Music has charms to soothe a savage breast."

Cesari muttered under his breath, "What a chooch."

Chapter 44

Reverse Hypnosis

Cesari phoned them both twice to no avail and searched high and low but couldn't find Jasmine or Mark. He could only think of one reason why that might be. Mark had managed to convince her to go somewhere private where they could talk on a more substantial level without interruption. Hence, their phones were turned off. Mark was very skilled at getting people to open up to him, but could he have worked his magic on such short notice at a party like this? If he had, Cesari's hat was really off to him. That had to be some sort of Nobel prize-winning effort.

Waiting in the bar, he nursed the same scotch and soda until 2:00 a.m. He made small talk with various guests who approached and then eventually moved on. He lost track of Sal and Lola and assumed they had left. The party was starting to clear out and even Vito had disappeared with Abigail. Brom hadn't started the cleanup up yet but was busy saying good night to people and helping others stumble to their cars. By 2:30 a.m. there were maybe fifty hard-core partiers left and even they seemed to be running out of steam. Cesari was tired and decided that Jasmine was in good hands wherever she was. Ultimately, he concluded that his staying up all night wasn't going to help anyone, so he went to his room. Ichabod was on the stairs and Cesari stopped to pet him goodnight. He was still wearing his pirate's eye patch.

He said, "You really look good, Ichabod. Very scary."

In response Ichabod purred softly and rubbed his head against Cesari's leg. He smiled at the cat and continued on. As he reached the door and fumbled for the key in his pocket, he realized he'd forgotten that he'd given it to Mark. He was frustrated and was about to go back downstairs to find one of the staff to let him in when he instinctively tested the handle. Relieved to find the door unlocked, he entered. The room was dark, but he made out a figure on the bed and smiled. Mark was sound asleep with his clothes on. Too funny. He hoped he had at least called his wife or she'd worry. Moving to the bureau to get a sweatshirt to sleep in, he heard a sound coming from the living room. He turned toward it and saw a pair of yellow eyes.

This startled him. He had just passed Ichabod on the steps. So who was this? He didn't want to wake Mark by turning on a light so he reached into his pocket for his phone. In his haste, he dropped the device and it bounced quietly on the rug. He bent quickly to retrieve it, and as he rose, the eyes were gone. A woman giggled softly.

He found the app light on the phone, turned it on and went into the living room. Jasmine was sitting on the sofa watching him and smiling. He scanned the rest of the room but didn't see the cat. The window was closed and there was no one else there. He shook his head, sat next to her and turned off the phone light.

"Was Ichabod just here?" he asked.

It was dark but he was close enough to her to be able to just make out her features. She shook her head. "No, why?"

He said, "It doesn't matter. May I ask what happened here?"

"Mark and I were having a delightful conversation downstairs in the ballroom. He's really a very charming and intelligent man. Anyway, I could tell he wanted to ask me some delicate questions but felt inhibited with so many people around, so I suggested we go somewhere private where he would feel more at ease. Since he had a key to your room... Well, here we are."

"*You* suggested to go someplace private?"

"Yes, he obviously wanted to, but I guess asking a young woman he'd just met to go someplace alone with him was a bit..."

"Inappropriate," he said filling in the gap.

"Yes, that was my sense of it, so I took the initiative. I hope that's okay."

"It'll have to be, but that doesn't explain why he's sleeping on my bed and you're sitting in the dark."

"Oh that. He tried to hypnotize me and wound up putting himself to sleep. I thought I should wait until you arrived to explain."

"You're kidding?"

"Not at all. He's been sound asleep for over an hour now. I would have woken him up, but he was so exhausted I thought it might be a good idea to let him rest."

"I mean you're kidding that he tried to hypnotize you and put himself to sleep? How did that happen?"

"He didn't seem to believe I was a witch and..."

"You told him you were a witch?"

"Yes, of course. He's a friend of yours and a trained psychiatrist. It didn't feel right not telling him the truth, and since he wasn't being judgmental…"

"Okay, what happened then?" he asked slowly mouthing the words.

"He was polite but clearly doubted me and thought that I might think I was a witch because of something that had happened to me long ago as a child that I couldn't remember. He mentioned the use of hypnosis as an aid to dive into a person's past to see what made them tick."

"I told him that it wouldn't be possible unless I fully submitted, and I didn't think I ever would because I know there is nothing wrong with me. He didn't believe that I couldn't be hypnotized, so I challenged him to try."

"You challenged him to try?"

"Yes, I said give it your best shot, Doc."

Cesari could see her grinning. He said, "And this is what happened?"

"I just reversed all the hypnotic suggestions back at him. It wasn't very hard. I've been waiting for you ever since."

"Why didn't you just call me or answer your phone when I called you?"

"I apologize for that. I left my phone in my parents' room, and I didn't come looking for you because I didn't want to leave him here alone. I was concerned that he might be frightened if he woke accidentally. Besides, surprising you was infinitely more fun."

Cesari nodded. "I'll bet… I have to admit I'm a little flabbergasted you let him have a go at you like that."

"Why? I could tell Mark has a sincere heart and meant only to help me, but you should know that. After all, he came at your request."

"He told you that too?"

"Since he was already hypnotized, I figured I'd ask him a few general questions. It only seemed fair."

"So how did you do all that reversing of stuff back at him?"

"John, I'm a witch," she answered matter-of-factly.

Cesari didn't know what to say and she reached out to touch his hand. He said softly, "Jasmine, please don't be mad at me for asking him here."

"Do I look angry?"

He leaned closer to see her better. She was still smiling and put her arms around his neck, pulling him in. She pressed her lips against his and they kissed.

When they were done, she whispered, "What's it going to take to convince you that I am who I say I am?"

"Jasmine, I want to believe you. I really do…"

"But…?"

"But there's no such thing as witches."

She hesitated for a moment and said, "Hmm, if I turn your friend Mark into a toad would you believe me then?"

He looked at her and then toward the bed and nodded seriously. "That would pretty much do it."

She laughed. "I'm just kidding. I can't do that. I don't think witches ever could. That was more of a Hollywood thing."

"What can you do?"

"I can make children, four or even six at a time. At least that's what the elders have told me."

He grinned. "I remember you saying that… Jasmine, as long as we're having a heart to heart can I ask you a question about Brom?"

"Of course."

"I was down in the restaurant area and was looking at the large portrait of his parents hanging over the fireplace. They seemed like such nice people."

"They were very nice people and like second parents to me. What is it you would like to know?"

"It kind of bothers me that no one knows what happened to them. I like closure. That's just my nature. I was wondering if the state department or law enforcement got involved?"

"I don't know about the state department. Brom notified everyone he thought he should, and I do know the police did come by. There were all sorts of legal issues Brom had to deal with including his inheritance and the transfer of the property to his name. It took more than a full year for him to work it all out."

"Did he get along with his parents?"

Jasmine gave him a curious look. "For the most part…I guess."

"But there were some issues?"

"Aren't there always with parents? But I guess with Brom it was a tad more serious than most."

"In what way?"

"Well, as I mentioned to you the coven has long since avoided the dark side of witchcraft. I won't say that we've completely turned our back on Satan, but we have sort of let our relationship with him wither on the vine so to speak. The Night Nurse Levi Blackburn was trying to re-establish that relationship the night he was found dead in the psychiatric hospital. When he was younger Brom was of the same mindset. He started practicing black magic in secret and this caused a fair amount of conflict with his parents when they found out. They were adamantly against it."

"Black magic you say?"

"Yes, he wished to commune with the Devil to restore the power of the coven."

Cesari thought about that. "How upset were his parents about this behavior?"

"Very upset. I came over one day not too long before their trip to South America and they were having a major argument about it. They almost cancelled their trip for fear of leaving him home alone."

"Did Brom ever abandon his dream of conjuring up the devil?"

"I think so although we haven't talked about it much since then. Remember, it was around that time when I rejected his proposal of marriage. I wouldn't have expected him to confide in me things of that nature… Did I help satisfy your curiosity or stoke it even further?"

He smiled. "As always, for every one question you answer you raise ten more, but enough about Brom. It's late and Halloween day is almost upon us. We all need to get some well-deserved rest."

She made no move to leave at that hint, and in fact sat back into the sofa in an even more relaxed posture. "Yes, Halloween day and night to come. You are probably unaware but this is sort of a tough time for us witches."

"Really, and why is that?" He asked, finding it a great curiosity that she didn't seem to mind or be offended by his skepticism. She was probably used to it.

"Well…Halloween night is when Katrina Van Tassel made her pact with the devil. Because of its significance our biorhythms have come to revolve around this night."

"Meaning…?"

"We generally do it like rabbits hopped up on Viagra for a twenty-four-hour period starting two hours ago," she blurted out with a giggle.

"You go into heat?" He was incredulous at this new revelation.

"Such a primitive expression."

"But accurate?"

"Yes."

"And this happens every Halloween?"

"From the stroke of midnight to the stroke of midnight."

"Are you telling me all those women I saw at the party tonight are in…?"

"No, but a lot of them will use tonight as an excuse for excessive behavior. The truth is I'm the only witch effected in that way on Halloween."

"Just you and why is that?"

She let out a deep breath. "I should have told you this before, but I'm sort of special."

He smiled. "You did allude to that but even if you hadn't I would have guessed."

"Thanks but I'm really special. As I mentioned to you the other day, Mother and I are the last of the direct descendants of Katrina. Her blood runs strongest in me, much stronger than anyone else in the coven."

"I remember you telling me that. So what does it mean?"

"It means that I'm… Well my official title is Grand Mistress."

"You have a title?"

"I have many titles. Grand Mistress is short for Grand Mistress of Witches, but I have also been called The Devil's Consort, Queen of Satan's Children, Witch of Witches and many more."

"I get it, and this special position in the coven means what?"

"That I'm the only one effected physically by…"

"Mother Nature?" he offered. She nodded, and he added, "You're like the queen bee. Your job is to procreate and ensure the survival of the hive and everyone else are just bit actors in supporting roles."

"Not quite that dramatic. The others can bear offspring but I'm the only one that *has* to for the sake of the coven."

"So you're programmed for certain needs on certain days like Halloween to ensure you take care of business."

"I'm glad you understand."

"I'm trying, and what happens if you don't have access to a suitable partner to tend to your needs during these difficult times?"

"A lot of howling and screeching," she laughed. "It can be pretty bad."

"And…"

"And what?"

"Have you found a suitable partner?"

She gently squeezed his hand. "I think so."

He said, "But the Horseman might not agree."

"That's the beauty of it. Tonight won't be an issue for him. You would be in no danger."

"Why is that?"

"The Horseman's only concern is with whom I fall in love and potentially bear offspring with. That's the real threat to the coven. As long as that's not on the table, he will have no interest in you."

"And that's not on the table?"

"Not for the next twenty-two hours or so."

"Because this is one of those... uncontrollable things that has nothing to do with love or making little witches?"

"Exactly."

He was impressed at the way she could spin things anyway she saw fit. Two nights ago the Horseman was the reason not to get physical but just like that he was no longer a problem. He said, "Jasmine, may I be totally honest?"

She nodded in the dark. "I would expect nothing less."

"Some of what I'm going to say may hurt and I want to apologize in advance."

"Go on."

He took his time and began slowly. "Jasmine, I'm very worried about you. I think you have..."

He hesitated clearly uncomfortable with what was about to come out of his mouth. She helped him. "John, please speak your mind. I told you it's okay."

"Jasmine, I don't know how far you and Mark got in your discussion, but I brought him here to talk to you because I think you have some type of mental illness and are trapped in a delusion you have constructed to protect yourself from some stark reality. Inside this world you have created, you are powerful and in control of events and this gives you confidence and security. I don't know why this has happened to you. I asked Mark to come here because he has many years of experience in psychoanalysis and I thought he could help you. Why he is snoring right now I don't understand other than he is in his sixties and partied too hard last night. But I emphatically do not believe that you reverse hypnotized him using your witch powers."

He paused to take a breath and then went on. "What I do know is that I can't sleep with you. It would be wrong for me to do so for multiple reasons but mostly because I am a physician and aware of your illness. I couldn't possibly take advantage of you in the condition you're in and it could possibly make things worse for you."

She let him finish and said softly, "Thank you for being direct."

There followed another long empty silence as each gathered their thoughts. He finally said, "I'm sorry."

"There's nothing I can do to change your mind?"

"It's not about changing my mind. It's about doing what's right for you as a person, as a woman and as someone who isn't well. I took an oath to protect people like you and to do no harm. Please don't misunderstand me. You're beautiful and sexy and I want you very much, but it would be terribly wrong, and I couldn't live with myself knowing what I do.

Even this story tonight about going into heat every Halloween. Don't you see how outlandish that sounds?"

"You care about me, John?"

"I do care about you. Very much so. We haven't known each other long but you've touched me deep inside and I want to help you. I've become a big Jasmine fan." He held her hand and added, "Friends?"

She said, "Yes, of course... I should go now. It's late and you're probably very tired."

"I am, and we have to do this all over again tomorrow night at the pavilion."

They both stood and faced each other. She placed her arms around his waist and he held her close. She said, "Tell Mark that I'm sorry I reverse hypnotized him and if he wants another crack at me tomorrow, I'll let him do whatever he needs to. I hope he won't be insulted by what happened?"

He smiled. Hearing that made him very happy. He was glad she was keeping an open mind to therapy. "He won't be. I'll tell him what you said. I think it's the right thing to do."

"But I want you to be there... No, I need for you to be there. I want you to understand me."

"I'll be there. I promise."

She looked at him. "Can you kiss me before I go or is that against the Hippocratic Oath."

He leaned down and kissed her gently. She stared at him for a while, then pulled away and walked toward the door. As she reached it, she stopped and turned around. "If you want Mark to wake up just snap your fingers and say three, two, one Jasmine. Otherwise he'll be out until 9:00 a.m. That's what I set his internal clock to. If you do wake him and want him to fall back to sleep again just clap your hands twice quickly. It will only work once like that and he won't remember anything."

Cesari was still nodding his head in disbelief as the door closed behind her. He went over to the side of the bed and watched Mark's rhythmic breathing. He considered not doing anything but he was curious.

He whispered, "Mark, wake up."

He didn't respond so Cesari repeated it louder, but nothing happened. Mark just kept breathing; in and out, in and out, unlabored and very relaxed. Cesari didn't like the way he was getting sucked into this experiment, but she'd gotten his attention. He reached over to the night table and turned the lamp on. Mark didn't flinch, so he shook him fairly vigorously, "C'mon buddy. Time to get up. Rise and shine."

Not even the slightest eye flutter in response. Okay, he thought, she might have drugged him, but he shook his head unable to believe that. Well the way he saw it, he had two choices. He could go to sleep and set the alarm to just before 9:00 a.m. and see what happens or he could do what she said and snap his fingers with the catch-phrase. If he did that and it worked was that proof she was a witch? Not necessarily, maybe for some reason she was just better at hypnosis than Mark. Did they teach that in witch high school? He'd have to look it up. Maybe that was a required class for them like trigonometry or biology.

He leaned close to Mark's ear and snapped his fingers. "Three, two, one Cesari."

Nothing happened, and he sighed loudly in frustration. He almost didn't want to know but couldn't help himself now, so he snapped his fingers again. "Three, two, one Jasmine."

Mark's eyes popped open, instantly awake. He said, "Okay, Jasmine on the count of three you will…" He looked around confused and sat up. "Cesari, what are you doing here. Where's…?"

Cesari clapped his hands twice quickly and Mark fell back down onto the pillow asleep again. Cesari walked over to the window mumbling to himself as he looked out toward the honey-house.

"This is total bullshit."

Chapter 45

Stop Being Selfish

"Tell me again what happened?" Mark asked incredulously for the third time over coffee at the run-down diner that had officially become Cesari's go-to breakfast place. It was 10:00 a.m. the next day and they had driven there in separate cars.

"When I came to the room you were in a deep hypnotic sleep on my bed and Jasmine was on the sofa waiting for me."

"Bullshit, Cesari. I've been practicing psychiatry for nearly thirty-five years. There's no way some psychotic girl hypnotized or *reverse hypnotized* me without my knowing it."

"Isn't that how hypnosis always works; the subject never realizes it's happening?" Cesari asked meekly.

"She must have drugged me."

Cesari shook his head. "I don't think so. You woke right up with the catch-phrase and then went right back to sleep with the signal she instructed."

He sipped his coffee. "I can't believe it. Not only have I never heard of anything like this happening, I've never even read about anything like this in the thousands of obscure journals on hypnosis that I subscribe to."

"I guess there's a first time for everything."

"And then she proceeded to ply you with the Grand High Witch stuff?"

"Her official title in the coven is Grand Mistress of Witches, but her friends just call her Grand Mistress."

"Jesus."

"Oh yeah, she went at me pretty hard last night, Mark. Too bad you missed it. She has a well thought out explanation for every aspect of her dream world. It's absolutely phenomenal. Finally, I just blurted out that I believe she's mentally ill."

Mark raised his eyebrows and whistled. "How'd she take that?"

"Actually, quite well I thought."

"She didn't get angry or launch into a massive denial."

"Not in the slightest. She accepted my opinion and in fact agreed to meet with you again today if you were up to it?"

"If I were up to it? What did she mean by that?"

"Truthfully?"

"Of course."

"I think she's afraid she might have hurt your feelings because she's a better hypnotist than you are."

Mark was ticked off, but in a good way. He always liked a challenge. "That did it. The gloves are off now. When does Broom Hilda want to dance?"

"Now, now…let's not take this personally. It's up to you but it will have to be early afternoon because there's another Halloween party tonight that she wants to go to. This is the big one I told you about."

"Fine, set it up for 1:00 p.m. if her Grand Witchness is available."

"Where?"

"Wherever she'll be most comfortable. Tell her I'll bring Sarah this time. She's a trained psychiatric nurse. They might relate to each other."

"I'll ask her and get back to you. I don't think you should use my room again. Brom might get nosy. How'd you wind up there last night anyway?" Cesari knew already what Jasmine had told him but was curious as to Mark's impression of what had happened.

"It was Jasmine's suggestion. You left with your big friend and we were making small talk. I was worming my way into her confidence. Given the late hour, I figured I had to work fast. She saw right through me and said that she knew why I had come to the party and that if I wanted to talk to her alone we could go to your room since I had the key. I was surprised but figured okay, if she doesn't mind. You could have told me you gave her a head's up about me by the way."

"She told you that I told her why you were coming?"

"Not exactly in those words now that I think about it. She said she knew why I was there, not that you told her why. I guess that means she could have heard from someone else."

"Someone else like who?"

"I don't know. Maybe you talk in your sleep. It doesn't matter. She understood that you were having a tough time accepting her as a witch and thought it perfectly reasonable to have a friend like me check her out."

"But how did she know you had my room key? I didn't tell her I gave it to you."

"Well, maybe she heard us talking or a friend of hers heard us talking and reported back to her or maybe she saw you give it to me. We weren't that far from her at the time."

"You don't find that strange?"

"No stranger than waking up in your room fully clothed and not remembering how it happened."

"She wants me to be there for the second session."

"Not a chance. I forbid it. You're the biggest trigger in her life right now and I want you to stay as far from her as possible."

"That might be difficult, we work together."

"Get with the program Cesari. I'm not talking about next week. I mean until midnight tonight when her impulse to gain carnal knowledge of you supposedly ends. That's what you told me right? Midnight to midnight?"

"Yes, that's what she said."

"She's defined the rules, so we'll play by them for now. It's the path of least resistance."

"I don't understand these rules. Why even have any?"

"Not sure. Possibly, it gives her a window whereby she can act any way she wants without consequence. If she's a repressed personality type that would be important. It also allows her to chase after you and at the same time nullifies her own bogeyman, the Headless Horseman. It's a beautiful construct. You've been fighting her off using the Horseman as an excuse and now she comes right back with this. You've got to love how the psychotic mind works, but we can't let her impose her conditions on us. If you let her get her way, then you'll be feeding into her delusion and strengthening it. There is no Horseman, she's not in heat and she's not a witch but she has to come to accept these realities of her own volition."

"Great. So I'm not coming to the party tonight?"

"Will you stop being selfish?"

"I'm not. I'm just asking."

"No, you're not. As the day and evening drags on and midnight approaches, she's going to work herself into a frenzy over you. I think she made that pretty clear. So not only are you not going to the party, you're going to disappear like they do at a Sicilian wedding when the FBI show up. You make one phone call to set up our meeting, give her some harmless excuse why you can't be there, and then turn your phone off and melt into the wood work until tomorrow morning. And Cesari, when I say melt, I mean really melt. Don't even go back to your room where she could easily find you."

"Oh brother. I have to lie to her after that scene we had at the party about lying?"

"It's a white lie, Cesari, in order to help her. Think of it as a mitzvah."

"It's still a lie, Mark, and maybe she's a nutcase, but I have feelings for that nutcase."

"Cesari, I've known you for what, twenty years? You don't have feelings you have urges, just suppress them."

"Fine, I'll think of something. By the way, was Sarah okay when you called her this morning?"

He laughed. "She didn't even know I was missing. I woke her up. Now she's mad as hell I wasn't there. Cesari, if I had to give you one piece of fatherly advice."

"I know. I know. Don't get married."

"I can't believe it…you've been listening all these years."

"Yeah, I've been listening. Look, I better go. I need to think of a reasonable cover story to tell Jasmine and I don't have a lot of time to think of it," he said grumpily.

"C'mon, how hard can that be?"

"You don't understand, Mark. She's going to be upset if she doesn't see me. We've been pretty close this week. I'm surprised she hasn't called already."

"All right, then go think of a plan. I'll be waiting to hear from you."

"I'll call as soon I know something. You okay with finding your way back to the Hilton?"

"I'm a big boy. I'll figure it out."

Cesari signaled the waitress for the bill but Mark waved him off. He thanked him, left the diner, and drove back to the Dulles House to pack an overnight bag. He had a lot on his mind not least of all was the distasteful prospect of having to disappoint Jasmine. Arriving back at the inn just before 11:00 a.m., he glanced at the honey-house and shook his head as he walked to his room. He was going to have to deal with that real soon. He laid down on his bed and stared at the ceiling when the perfect excuse came to him. He called Jasmine who answered quickly.

"Hi, John," she said as upbeat as always.

"Good morning, Jasmine. How are you today?"

"Tired and you?"

"The same… Say, Jasmine, did you really mean it last night about meeting with Mark again today? I just had coffee with him and he's open to it."

"Certainly, if you think it's wise."

"He's a pretty smart guy. I think it's for the best. If it's okay with you he'd like to bring his wife Sarah with him this time. She's an R.N. like you. You'll like her."

"That's fine. Where and when. We'll have to do it early."

"How about 1:00 p.m."

"That's fine. How about my apartment. I'll give him one hour all right? I have too much to do to get myself and my parents ready for the gala."

"I think that will be plenty of time. I'll give him your address."

"Won't you be coming?"

"I intended to, but Katz phoned me this morning. He was supposed to be on call today but he's sick and asked me if I could cover for him. He sounded awful. I'm on my way to the ER as we speak to evaluate a GI bleed. I'm sorry."

"Oh that stinks. I really wanted you here for support, but I guess it will be all right. I trust Mark. He's really very nice. What about the party tonight? Do you think you'll make it?"

"I'm planning on it but you can never be sure with these things. You know how it is."

"I do… Did you run into Brom this morning?"

"No, why do you ask?" She was quiet for a minute and he said, "What happened?"

"He was cleaning up after the party and saw me come out of your room last night. We exchanged words. I told him mother wasn't feeling well and I was just asking you for advice."

"Did he buy it?"

"Hardly."

"I'm sorry."

She let out a deep breath. "It's not your fault."

"What's he going to do?"

"I can't be sure. He was pretty angry. Anyway, please call me later when you're free, all right?"

"I will."

"And John…?" She hesitated and then said, "Are you all right?"

"Yes, of course… Are you all right?"

"I'm hanging in there. The hormones are driving me crazy. I feel like filling up the bathtub with ice water and submerging myself in it."

"I've felt like that every day since the age of fourteen."

She laughed. "And how do you deal with it?"

"I fill up the bathtub with ice water and submerge myself in it."

"You are so bad."

Chapter 46

Tommy Boy

Vito wasn't in his room when Cesari left the inn, so he called him as he drove to the hospital.

"Where are you, Vito?" he asked hearing noise in the background.

"In town somewhere, having a late breakfast with Abigail. She's in the ladies room right now. We can talk but make it quick."

"Abigail, the girl from last night?"

"Yeah, we hit it off pretty well if you know what I mean. She brought me to some gourmet pancake house with French press coffee and house-made sausages. It's pretty good."

"Well, congratulations... Look, I just thought I'd give you an update. I'm going to lay low until tomorrow morning. It's a little complicated but Jasmine is entering therapy today with a psychiatrist friend of mine. He heard the story and thinks she may be a little obsessed with me and that it might be best if I weren't around to distract her at least for a short while. He was the little guy with the beard I was talking with when you came to get me last night. His name is Mark Greenberg."

Cesari didn't feel the need to spell out all the details. Vito said, "The guy dressed as Freud? He really was a psychiatrist? Talk about looking the part."

"Yeah."

"So what are you going to do?"

"Basically, avoid her calls and stay away from the inn so she can't come looking for me. I told her I'm on call and potentially will be unavailable. She's a nurse and understands the drill. What I didn't tell her is that I won't be going to the party tonight. Mark feels that would be unwise."

"Seriously? You're going to miss the gala? That's a shame. After last night's warmup soiree I can't wait for tonight. Me and Abigail are going together. Get this, she's going to ditch the witch look and we're going as Bonnie and Clyde. I'm just going to wear the same clothes and she's going to try to find a matching outfit. She told me tonight is going to be off the hook. I'm in such a good mood I even told the Lous they could come too."

"That was nice of you. Maybe you won't have to kill them after all."

Silence on the other end. After a moment, Cesari followed up with, "Vito, are you still there?"

"Yeah, I'm still here," he replied lowering his voice, his tone changing. "What's wrong with you, Cesari? You should know better than to say stuff like that on the phone."

"Sorry."

"Fine, and the verdict hasn't come in yet on the Lous so don't you or I get too attached to them."

"I promise not to."

"So how long are you going to be under the radar?"

"Until tomorrow morning. I'm going to sleep at the hospital. They have an on-call room I can use. There something about Halloween that's triggering Jasmine and since I seem to be the focal point Mark wants me to stay out of sight until it passes."

"I don't know too much about shrink stuff but it kind of makes sense. Well, as long as you won't be using your room tonight would you mind if I put one of the Lous in it."

"Why?"

"I was thinking about what you said last night about Brom. It couldn't hurt to have someone watching my back."

"Sure, go ahead. I don't care."

"They're pretty useless though except as an early warning system. If you hear them screaming, you'll know something's up."

"You might as well put them to good use. Housekeeping should let him in the room. They're pretty relaxed, I've noticed. If not, send him over to the hospital to pick up the key from me. Okay, got to go. I'm pulling into the hospital garage. Have fun with Abigail."

He hung up, parked the truck and was about to get out when he hesitated, reached down to the floor in front of the passenger seat and picked up the crowbar. He placed it in the duffle bag and entered the hospital. Walking to the on-call room, he ran into Sal who was bursting with energy. He hadn't had a chance to talk to him at the party last night and Cesari felt bad about it.

"Cesari," Sal greeted him with a scowl, his eye twitching frantically. "I can't talk now, but great party last night. I saw you there, but I was a little tied up or I would have come over to hang."

"That's okay. So where's the fire?" he asked noting the man's excitement.

"Those asswipes from the state decided to call in their chip today. They're beginning their inspection in an hour. Can you believe this? On freakin' Halloween? They got no class. I've got them holed up in the boardroom right now with Dicky while the hospital lawyers are seeking an emergency injunction to stop them."

"An emergency injunction? Is that possible?"

He grinned. "Of course not, but they don't know that. The people the state picks for these jobs are political hacks and throwaways. Most of them are useless relatives of the governor who couldn't land a job flipping burgers at minimum wage. Suddenly they're bringing home six figures for doing nothing more than wearing dress shoes and a tie. Look, we're here. I got to run. Would you like to join us? I'm going to tear them some new orifices if you'd like to learn how it's done. Baiting bureaucrats is one life's rare delights. Sometimes I feel so lucky that God granted me this skill."

"Thanks, and I appreciate the opportunity, but I was on my way to consult on a patient in the emergency room. Any other day, and I would have loved to ride along."

"Okay, maybe next time."

"Definitely."

Sal stepped into the boardroom and Cesari continued on his way to the on-call room. He entered the old psychiatric hospital and went up to the third floor. As he stepped out of the elevator he hesitated, remembering the fright he had experienced the last time he had been up there. But all looked calm at the moment, so he entered the room, unzipped the duffle bag and placed the crowbar on the desk, hoping he wasn't going to have to use it. Then he threw the duffle bag on the floor. Since he was stuck there all day, he figured he might as well be nice to whoever it was that was really on call, so he picked up the landline and dialed the switchboard.

"Hello, this is Dr. Cesari."

"Happy Halloween, Dr. Cesari. What can I do for you?"

"Well, I just wanted you to know that if the ER or the medical wards need a gastroenterology consultation, I'll be available from now until tomorrow morning. I'm not officially on call but I'll be around, so you don't have to bother anyone else."

"That's so nice of you, Doctor. I'm sure they will be happy to hear that. Will you be staying in the on-call room all night? I see you're calling from there."

"Yes, I'll be here all night."

He hung up and went to lie on the bed. Exhausted from last night's festivities with nowhere to go and nothing to do, he did what any red-blooded American male would. He fell asleep.

Two hours later he woke even sleepier than before to the sound of his phone buzzing on the night table. It was after 3:00 p.m. Groggy and confused he looked at it. It was Jasmine, so he let it go to voicemail. He felt bad doing that but if a trained psychiatrist felt it was necessary then that's what he would do. She called twice more and then texted him no less than four times asking him if everything was okay. She made no mention in either voice message or text of her encounter with Mark.

He dialed Mark, but the call went to voicemail. He wasn't concerned and figured he'd get back to him soon enough. Knowing his friend he was probably making detailed notes of the session with commentary and thoughts for research and further lines of inquiry. He shook off the sleepies and went to the bathroom to splash cold water on his face.

It wasn't dinner time, but he was hungry and hadn't eaten since breakfast with Mark, so he decided to go to the cafeteria. He was disappointed when he got there. Long past lunch and too early for dinner there was next to nothing to eat except yogurt and ice cream sandwiches. The place was deserted. It was Saturday and Halloween in a Halloween obsessed town. Everybody was probably hungover or getting ready for the gala at the pavilion, and he was going to miss it. He looked at all the decorations on the walls, the ceiling and the tables. There were bowls of candy next to the condiment counter by the unmanned check-out register and he grabbed a handful of chocolate kisses. As he unwrapped one, he made up his mind to leave the hospital and grab a burger somewhere.

He calculated that the risk of running into Jasmine in town would be minimal. It was late afternoon and she would be in full swing getting both her and her parents ready for the party. He had to give them credit. For people as old as they were, they weren't giving up without a fight. Two late-night parties in a row was taxing for him and he was half their age.

As he walked to the garage and found the truck, he thought about Brom. This was a big problem and would undoubtedly rock this city when it came out. If he called the police anonymously would they brush it off as a crank call? Given Brom's prominence in the community that was certainly a possibility. Cesari had nothing but the greatest respect for law enforcement in general but he had already witnessed firsthand the local police shirk their responsibilities at fight club. They didn't just look the other way, they were active participants in the law breaking and cover up activities. It wasn't much of a stretch that they may treat accusations against Brom with great disinclination.

What happened between Brom and his parents was a separate situation and one that Jasmine had shed quite a bit of light on. He was practicing devil worship and black magic and that was a source of much friction in the Van Brunt family. Enough to provoke Brom to murder? Why not? People who worshipped Satan weren't necessarily inclined to worry about the Ten Commandments. The parts about honoring thy father and thy mother and thou shalt not kill were probably considered optional.

Dealing with Brom would have to wait for a while, however, and might depend on how Jasmine's therapy with Mark went. He certainly wouldn't want to stress her out right now with news of Brom's villainy. She was already on edge from her recent confrontation with him. He wondered if her parents knew about any of this and if it would be worth discussing it with them. He shelved that idea as he drove down Main Street. He would only involve them as a last resort. The Brom dilemma needed careful management. He would not act rashly and take the risk of misfiring to the detriment of Jasmine and her family.

There was a bar and grill just outside the city limits heading toward Syracuse called Berlucchi's. It had the outward appearance of a roadhouse honky tonk if there was such a thing in upstate New York. At this hour, it seemed pretty quiet. Happy hour hadn't even started yet. There were a few cars, trucks, and Harleys parked out front but judging from the size of the building he guessed the place would be packed later tonight with some blues rock band tearing the house down.

He found a parking spot right in front of the entrance and went in. There was a typical layout with a large central bar surrounded on all sides by multiple wood tables and booths. Maybe about a dozen people were there having beers, late lunches, or early dinners. Musical equipment was neatly organized at one end too early for anyone to be doing sound checks and last-minute tuning of guitars.

A big guy with a white apron behind the bar was drying off glasses from a dishwasher and organizing himself for the coming onslaught of unruly, thirsty guests that would flood the place in just a few hours. Cesari stepped up to the bar and took a seat on a stool catching the guys attention.

He was even bigger up close, maybe fifty, full head of hair and ruddy cheeks. From the size of the guy's biceps bulging through his shirt, Cesari guessed that he doubled as a bouncer. "What're you having?" he asked in a low rumbling baritone.

"Anything on tap. You can surprise me. Can I eat at the bar?"

"You can do whatever you want so long as you pay your bill and don't break anything. Give me a sec and I'll get you a menu."

Before he could leave Cesari asked, "Berlucchi's sort of an odd name for a honky tonk, isn't it?"

"Is it?"

"You don't see many roadhouses with Italian names, I mean."

"I didn't know that. Well somebody should have told that to my father when he opened it forty years ago, but now that you've brought it to my attention, I'll move quickly to have it changed."

Cesari laughed. He liked the guy's sense of humor. "You don't have to do that. It's a fine name. So you're the owner?"

He dried his hand with the towel and then extended it to Cesari. "Scott Berlucchi."

Cesari took it and replied, "John Cesari. I'm a new physician in town."

"A new doctor? Well welcome to town Doctor, and since we're all in agreement that the name stays, I'll get you your beer and a menu."

As he walked away, Cesari glanced around the room for a more thorough inspection. One table with three people caught his attention and he groaned. Herb Funkelman stood and waved enthusiastically for him to join his group. Caught between a rock and a hard place, Cesari signaled Scott the new seating arrangement, then sighed and went over.

He said, "Hi, Herb."

"Yeah, I bet. Look no hard feelings from the other day all right? Have a seat. We were just getting ready to order. You remember Sally Webster, she's the rehab doctor you met last weekend, and this is Tommy McShane your friendly neighborhood congressman. His friends call him Tommy Boy. Tommy Boy this is Dr. John Cesari. He's the guy Sally and I were just telling you about. Tommy Boy's up for re-election in a week and would love your vote, Cesari."

Tommy Boy was classic. Fat, soft and middle-aged, with a pink face he was halfway through the largest martini Cesari had ever seen. He wore a flag pin on the lapel of his dark navy suit. They shook hands. "A pleasure to meet you… Tommy Boy."

"Likewise, Doctor."

Cesari sat down reluctantly and turned to Sally. "Hi, Sally. How's it going?"

She smiled and whispered out of the side of her mouth, "I've never had a pulled groin muscle, but I always imagined it would be like this."

"That painful, huh?"

"I was toying with the idea of excusing myself to the bathroom and climbing out the window to escape."

"Give it a few minutes and I'll join you."

Chapter 47

Uncharted Water

Within an hour six more physicians had joined them. Happy hour had begun in earnest and the bar filled up with patrons looking for cheap drinks, lively music and finger food. Cesari ordered a dozen Buffalo wings extra hot with extra blue cheese to go with the Yuengling Scott had poured him in a cold frosty mug.

Herb ran the event as if he were chairman of the armed services committee. He did everything but pound a gavel. Apparently his dream of a PAC going to Washington was coming to fruition thanks to the largesse of Tommy Boy who sat on the congressional subcommittee for health care improvement in upstate New York whatever that meant. As long as he retained his seat in congress, we were golden. Which brought us to the crux of the matter from Tommy Boy's point of view. Namely, if the physicians wanted his support for the PAC to be recognized officially, they would have to pony up a hundred-thousand-dollar donation to his campaign for re-election. He was planning to blitz local radio and TV every hour on the hour up until poll closings on election day next week and needed every red cent he could muster. Every physician at the table except for Cesari had agreed to donate ten thousand dollars. They were twenty thousand dollars short.

Sally was made chairman of the PAC since Herb was so unpopular. Herb was made the behind the scenes power broker which suited him just fine as the second prize and Cesari had been elected in absentia to represent them in D.C. even before the meeting began based on Sally's relentless campaigning on his behalf. Cesari and Tommy Boy hit it off for the most part. The guy was a big Syracuse basketball fan and actually came up from the nation's capital on a regular basis to see the games. He was originally from Camillus, a suburb of Syracuse, and was easy to talk to as well as more knowledgeable about healthcare than would have been Cesari's first guess. For a self-serving, baby-kissing, palm-greasing, double-talking politician, Cesari decided that deep down he was probably an all right guy.

In the middle of his meal, his face covered with hot sauce and hands dripping with grease and blue cheese, Cesari's phone rang. He wiped himself clean as best as he could with a paper napkin and walked away from the table to answer it in private.

"Hi Mark."

"Hey Cesari. Am I interrupting anything?"

He walked all the way to the front door. "Are you kidding? Tell me what happened."

"Okay… First of all, I'm sorry it took me so long to call you. I know you've been on pins and needles. I should have at least texted you. Anyway, I've been on the horn with various colleagues for their opinions… Cesari, we are in unchartered waters. This is worse than Columbus trying to cross the Atlantic without a map."

"Thanks for the drama, Mark. Why don't you take a step back and give it to me blow by blow and don't leave anything out, all right?"

"Okay, fine. We arrived at her house a few minutes early. Going there was golden by the way. Probably saved me weeks in trying to evaluate her."

"Why is that?"

"Most psychotic or delusional patients can't take care of themselves. It's just part of the disorder. Sometimes it's obvious when they come to the office and sometimes it's not. Sometimes they have family and friends who will be embarrassed for them and clean them up before they come in. Seeing how she really lives is a tremendous bonus for a psychiatrist. Her house is pristine; clean, neat and nicely decorated. She's a wonderful hostess, made us tea and served us cookies. That shows empathy and the recognition of social rules and norms of etiquette. These things go against the diagnosis of schizophrenia but doesn't completely rule it out."

"Okay, well that sounds good, right?"

"Very good and she was very cooperative. A model patient if you ask me. She didn't deny anything. Nor did she try to hide or circumvent any of the things you told me she said. Just like last night, she was one hundred percent honest about who she believes she is; a direct descendant of Katrina Van Tassel a witch of unheralded power who sometime in the late eighteenth century slept with the devil."

"Okay, and then what?"

"Then she allowed me to perform regressive hypnosis on her. Cesari it was the most unbelievable thing. She responded beautifully. I took her back to early adulthood, the teenage years, childhood. The idea is to see if we can identify any subconscious trauma as a root cause for her break with reality."

"Did you find anything?"

"Nothing. Her parents are wonderful people. No one abused her either physically or emotionally. She was a model student in school and everyone loved her. She didn't like Brom too much but that was more of a personality thing. He never did anything mean to her."

"That's kind of what she told me. He just wasn't the one for her. What else?"

"Here's where it gets complicated. This idea that she is a witch has been with her for her entire life. There is no point in her memory that she ever was not a witch."

"You're kidding?"

"No, I'm not. I went all the way back to pre-school. This girl was born believing she's a witch."

"Is that on par with other psychotics?"

"What do you think?"

"Probably not."

"Good guess. Which is why I've been trying to reach colleagues for the last four hours. I've never heard of this and it gets worse…"

"How much worse?"

"A lot… As the session progressed, she continued to travel back in time. Early adulthood, the teen years, child-hood, pre-school, which was great. She spoke with clarity. There was no confusion or uncertainty and then all of a sud-den, she's talking about the womb and floating around in amniotic fluid. Then she went beyond that."

"Beyond the womb?"

"Cesari, I'm telling you the truth when I say there is no one like her in the annals of modern psychiatry. Her case is going to fill a textbook all by itself. I can't even begin to understand how her brain is wired. She kept going back and back is if she had discovered a wormhole or some equivalent."

"Where'd she end up?"

"The late 1700's with Katrina Van Tassel in Sleepy Hollow, New York. The night she claims Katrina made her pact with Satan. She gives alarming historical detail and descriptions of people, furniture, dress, farm equipment and the Revolutionary War itself. She can even tell you who the New York representatives were to the Constitutional Convention in Philadelphia. For God's sake, Cesari. How many people know things like that?"

"Not many would be my guess."

"Well none would be mine except a PhD in American history perhaps."

"What's all this mean?"

"It means I don't think I can help her. I've never encountered anyone who was born delusional. She's out of my league. Several of my peers were also baffled. There's a guy in Dartmouth I reached out to, but he wasn't available. He wrote a book on childhood psychosis and the uses of regressive hypnosis. I'm not sure this falls into that category but it's the best I could do. I would recommend an antipsychotic right now but I'm not sure it would help and if she develops a side effect, things could get complicated. Overall, my recommendation is to stay the course. She doesn't seem to be any threat to herself or anyone else so there's no real pressing need to intervene, but boy oh boy is she a live one."

"Where do I fit in?"

"She likes you obviously and that's good, but you need to stay away from her at least for tonight. She is obsessed with the idea that somehow Halloween sends her into estrus and that her need for sexual gratification will progressively increase until the stroke of midnight. She expressed her desire for you in terms that made Sarah and I blush, and we don't blush easily."

"It I'm not around, won't she just find someone else?"

"I don't believe she will. This is about you specifically. This is her manipulation of her own delusion to reach a predetermined end. In other words, she cares for you, but she's also afraid that if she commits to you physically and emotionally you might hurt her and abandon her like the others, so she tells you about the Horseman to ready herself for your betrayal. But she didn't expect you to push her away because of that. It probably never happened before so now she has a problem of her own making, namely the Horseman. So she creates this great story about being able to make love to you all she wants on Halloween and how the Horseman won't care. It's truly amazing. In psychiatry we have an expression for people like this."

"What's that?"

"She's crazy nuts."

"Thanks."

"I'm just telling it like it is Cesari, and you need to be careful. After all the abandonment she's experienced, I don't think she could handle another one. She's grown quite attached to you in a very short period of time, and frequently these kinds of intense relationships can be the most painful when they sour."

"What else did she say about me?"

"Some of it was babbling and some of it was wishful thinking. During the session she mentioned that her assessment of your virility was that you could potentially...let me check my notes. I don't want to speak out of turn." He fumbled through the pages of a notepad for a few seconds. "Here it is. She said that you give off an unprecedented aura of masculinity. She believes that if she were to conceive with you on Halloween night, she could possibly have a record, get this, a record brood of twelve witchlings. Those were the words she used...brood and witchlings. I'm telling you, Cesari, she is a treasure trove for psychiatry. She's the mother lode, baby. She's the holy grail of psychoanalysis."

"Twelve witchlings? That's what she said?"

"All at once. Can you believe that? This is just amazing."

"Mark, how was she when she came out of hypnosis?"

"She was fine, like nothing happened. I told her everything including my belief that she is delusional and needs lots of help and that I didn't feel I was up to the task. She accepted that very maturely and agreed to further discussions."

"Further discussions? What's that mean?"

"That means as soon as I find the appropriate referral center, I'm going to ask her to take a trip for consultation. There's not going to be anyone around here who can help her. My guess is she'll either wind up at Dartmouth with that guy I mentioned or in Boston or New York. I already told Sarah we're not leaving until we have a clear path to resolution with her so get used to me being around."

"Did you tell Jasmine that?"

"No, one step at a time. Besides, when she woke up she was too happy for me to play the heavy."

"Happy?"

"About the party tonight and about being with you. She's really looking forward to it. I didn't say anything about it not being a good idea for her to see you. I don't want her thinking that we're conspiring behind her back which we are. Has she tried to reach you?"

"Only five or six times. All right, Mark. Thanks for your help. If anything unusual happens tonight give me a buzz."

"Will do."

Cesari hung up and went back to the table. Glancing at his watch, he realized he had been on the phone for more than thirty minutes. The gathering was breaking up and Herb was paying the bill.

Tommy Boy extended his hand and said, "I'm looking forward to working with you Dr. Cesari and thank you for your campaign contribution."

Cesari raised his eyebrows. Herb added, "We'll talk about it later."

Tommy Boy walked out the door along with the other physicians leaving him alone with Sally and Herb. Cesari said, "What did I miss?"

"Absolutely nothing thanks to me," Herb said. "You are a full member of our PAC and the designated representative to D.C. You can float me a check next week for the twenty grand. I reassured Tommy Boy you were good for it so he's going to start greasing the wheels in his subcommittee."

"Twenty grand? I didn't agree to any of this and I'm not giving anybody twenty grand."

Herb was very frustrated. "What's with you, Cesari? This is an effin' big honor. You march into town like Wyatt Earp and now you're crapping all over our dreams. Sally, would you talk to him? I'm at the end of my rope. I'm not even sure what language he's speaking anymore."

He threw his hands up and stormed away. Cesari sat down with Sally. He said, "I can't do this Sally, and I feel like I'm being railroaded."

She was sympathetic and said, "You are being railroaded, but that's just the way these things are occasionally. Sometimes the cream rises to the top naturally and sometimes it has to be coaxed into doing so. You'd be perfect for this. You just have to give yourself a chance, and you'd be doing a lot of good. If it's the money, I'll talk to Herb. I'm sure the rest of us could increase our contributions to cover you."

"It's not the money. It's the fact that I don't believe in the cause. I just met Tommy Boy a couple of hours ago and now I'm helping him get re-elected? I don't even know him. I mean he seems okay, but what if he's a rat?"

She smiled. "He is a rat. They all are. It's the nature of the beast but he's better than most. I grew up with him in Camillus. We went to grammar school and high school together. He's a good man as far as politician's go and I'm friends with his wife. I can vouch for him."

He liked her assessment of the situation and softened up to a whimper. "But what if I'm not any good at lobbying?"

His weakness brought out her nurturing. "All we're asking is that you try. We need a voice because right now no one is listening."

"Why do I have to pay twenty thousand and everyone else only ten."

"That was Herb's idea. He was still mad at you for usurping his role."

Cesari laughed, "Well, look. I'll promise to think about it, but I'm not contributing twenty thousand dollars. If I agree to do this, I'll give ten like everyone else. Herb can make up the shortfall. He's an orthopedic surgeon. He makes more than everyone else who was here combined."

"That sounds fair."

Chapter 48

The Horseman

At 7:30 p.m. Cesari's phone buzzed. He was watching TV in the doctor's lounge and sipping bad coffee from a machine.

"Vito, shouldn't you be primping for the gala?"

"I think I messed up, Cesari."

"How so?"

"I ran into Brom on the way out the door to pick up Abigail for the gala. He was all dressed up as the devil like last night and he was royally pissed off. He said he's been looking for you all day and that he had a bone to pick with you."

"That's no surprise. He's been pissed off at me almost since the day I arrived, but last night he saw something he shouldn't have and I guess it set him off even more."

"What did he see?"

"Jasmine coming out my room at three in the morning."

"Whoa…"

"It's not like that. We were just talking but you can understand how it might be misinterpreted."

"I'll say."

"So how'd you mess up."

Silence.

"Vito…?"

"He was being such a jerk I couldn't help saying something."

"Like what?"

"He said that you're a coward and that there's no point in hiding because sooner or later you're going to have to face him like a man. That kind of annoyed me so I said, 'Why don't you tell him yourself if you're so tough. He's in the on-call room at the hospital where he'll probably be all night and if you got the balls, I'm sure he'd love to hear from you.'"

"You didn't?"

"I did. I spoke in haste. I'm sorry."

Cesari sighed. "What did he say to that?"

"He made this evil grin and said, 'That's good to know,' and then walked away. What did he mean by that?"

"I don't know… All right, don't lose sleep over it. He's not going to do anything tonight. There's too much going on and besides, if I'm here that means Jasmine's up for grabs. I'm sure he'll focus on that."

"You're probably right but I shouldn't have pin-pointed your location for him."

"No, you shouldn't have but what's done is done. I'm really not worried and you shouldn't be either. What I think he's trying to do is goad me into the ring with him at fight club. Then he can clobber me in front of the whole town. Anyway, thanks for the head's up."

"I feel like I ought to do something like maybe send the other Lou over there just in case."

"Vito, please don't. There's no place for him to sleep. All the other rooms on this floor are unfurnished."

"I can tell him to bring a pillow and a blanket. He can sleep outside your room on the floor. I'd feel better now that I gave you away."

"What's he going to do for me? You said yourself he and his brother are next to useless."

"He can stop a bullet if you stand behind him. That's my plan."

"Thanks, but really unnecessary."

"I'll have him call you when he gets there."

"Fine."

Cesari left the lounge to lie down in his room and watch some TV. Jasmine called twice and sent another text asking him if he was going to make it to the gala. It made him feel terrible but he didn't respond and settled in to watch the local news. He unconsciously eyed the crowbar on the desk. An hour later, Lou arrived with a pillow and blanket tucked under one massive arm and a large Snickers bar dangling out of his mouth.

"Uncle Vito says I should guard you with my life," he mumbled.

"Your Uncle Vito is a wise man. Unfortunately, your job is to sleep on the floor here blocking my door. The light switch for the hallway is on the wall."

Lou looked around and peeked into the room behind Cesari. "This stinks. Why does my brother Lou get a nice king-sized bed and I get the floor?"

Cesari studied his basketball shaped fat face with piglet eyes deeply recessed inside layers of adipose. His black hair was moussed and shiny in tight little curls and his triple chin was almost ready to sprout a fourth.

Cesari said, "You call your brother, Lou? What's he call you?"

"Lou, of course."

"Isn't that a little confusing?"

"Not as confusing as trying to understand what I'm doing here right now. Why would anyone want to hurt a doctor anyway?"

"Have you ever seen a bill from a colonoscopy?"

He shook his head no. Cesari was tired and a little short-tempered. "Lou, you're here to act as an early warning system. If somebody comes for me in the middle of the night the plan is for them to trip over you and hopefully make enough noise that I can make my getaway."

"And what happens to me?"

"That's the thing, Lou. I just don't know."

Cesari closed and locked the door leaving the Lou to think it over as he went back to watching TV. Fifteen minutes later there was a knock at the door. Cesari opened it and Lou said, "I have to go to the bathroom."

"Did you check down the corridor or in any of the rooms? This used to be a hospital. There's probably half a dozen or more bathrooms on this floor, some of them may even work."

"Isn't there one in your room?"

"There definitely is."

Cesari closed and locked the door again thinking that maybe Vito was right about terminating the Lous. It would be a mercy killing at the worst. He glanced at his watch and decided he might as well get ready for bed, watch the tube and hopefully get a good night's rest. He threw his clothes on the floor, opened the window a smidgeon for some air and snuggled under the sheets with the remote control in his hand. After flipping through multiple channels he finally settled on some show about the conservation efforts underway for the endangered Himalayan Snow Leopard. With the lights off and the narrator's voice droning in the background he was soon asleep.

He wasn't sure how long he was out when he sensed a presence in the room…in his bed. He opened his eyes and in the dark, made out Jasmine lying next to him under covers. She reached over and wrapped her arms around him pressing her naked flesh against his. He wondered how she found him.

As if reading his mind, she smiled, "I called the switchboard and they told me where you were."

"Am I dreaming?"

She shook her head.

"How did you get in the room? There's a baby whale lying on the floor outside the door."

When she didn't say anything, he looked around and saw the door was closed but the window was wide open. The night air was chilly, and he held her even tighter for warmth. "Did you use a ladder or just fly in?" he asked.

"Shh, the time for talking is over."

She kissed him ardently. Tongues met and swirled around as hearts pounded and breathing became more rapid. Their eyes locked and their hands explored sensual zones for the first time, learning what pleased the other. Almost at the point of no return he said, "Jasmine, are you sure you want to do this?"

Gazing at him and barely able to speak she whispered hoarsely, "I have no choice. It's unbearable what I feel. I counted twelve."

"Twelve what?"

Instead of explaining, she pushed him back, climbed on top and suddenly he didn't care. Her hair fell down around their faces and they became one as backs arched and toes curled. Overwhelmed by desire, they let their passions consume them, time and again and again and then repeat until he thought he might not survive the encounter. Eventually exhausted, she rolled off him and he closed his eyes, panting, unable to speak and exhilarated beyond anything he had ever experienced.

She said, "Once more and then I have to go make sure my parents are all right."

In a complete and utterly helpless fog, he whispered, "I don't think I can do it once more."

"Sure you can."

Afterward, he lay there in a trance, half unconscious and with almost no awareness of his surroundings. His eyes fluttered shut and he thought he heard her speak softly into his ear, "I promise to come back."

"I'll be waiting," he replied or simply thought in his mind. He wasn't sure.

When he finally opened his eyes again, she was gone. He turned on the light and searched for her, but she was nowhere to be seen, not under the covers or under the bed or in the bathroom. The door was deadbolted securely from the inside. The clock said it was almost midnight. He scratched his head and yawned. Just not possible he thought. He concluded that he must have been dreaming. Wishful thinking on his part. Then he felt a blast of cold air from the wide-open window.

He went over to it, closed it tight and looked out. The room overlooked the back of the new hospital and directly below his window were the backup generators enclosed by a chain link fence. He was three stories up. Conceivable with a ladder but why come through the window at all? Why not just come up the elevator like she had done many times before? It didn't make any sense. It had to have been a dream. He wished he could have dreams like that every night.

There was a knock at the door and he went to answer it thinking that maybe he had woken Lou, but when he opened it, Lou wasn't there. His sheet and pillow were but no Lou so who had knocked? Had the slug deserted his post? Cesari heard an odd, slow, rhythmic sound coming from the far end of the corridor but couldn't see anything in the gloom. He reached out and turned on the hallway lights. They flickered briefly and went on.

Shit!

At the end of the hallway, the Lou was hanging by his neck from the same pipe the Night Nurse had been exactly fifty years ago to the night. He swung gently to and fro, his face purple, his neck stretched and his eyes bulging. His swollen tongue hung out of the side of his mouth. Cesari's pulse raced as he scanned back and forth looking for an enemy. He ran back to the desk and picked up the crowbar determined not to go down without a fight.

Back in the corridor, naked and armed with steel, he stepped cautiously toward the suspended corpulent corpse of the formerly living being known as Lou. As he closed in, he noted a pentagram drawn in blood on the floor below him. It was six feet wide in diameter and still wet. Just then Cesari noticed a drop of blood fall from Lou's left wrist. The pentagram was too neat. There were no smudges. Someone had slit his wrist after they hung him to use the blood as paint, but who could possibly have had the strength to hang a guy that size, and why were there no signs of a struggle? He had heard nothing.

A sound from behind caused him to turn around precipitously, raising the crowbar for combat. Brom came strolling out from the on-call room holding his duffle bag and stuffing his clothes inside. He finished and stood there staring coolly at Cesari. Dressed as Satan, he was hideous, frightening, and alarmingly self-confident, armed only with a wicked grin. Cesari stepped toward him, thinking of the best line of attack. He had made up his mind that if this was going to be his last night alive, it was going to be epic. Generations from now they would tell the tale of this clash of titans. He would be a modern Beowulf or Gilgamesh.

Ten feet from Brom he stopped and nodded at the duffle bag, "What are you going to do with my stuff, Brom? Bury them next to Pullman's?"

"Found that did you?" he snickered. "The thought had crossed my mind."

"What did you do to him anyway?"

"He's in hell where you will be soon too."

"But why? He didn't do anything to you."

Brom drew himself up and smiled. "You didn't do anything to me either…not really. He begged for his life. You should have seen him crying like a baby while he wrote Jasmine's goodbye letter. I would so much enjoy it if you would do the same."

"I wouldn't count on that, bee keeper."

Brom's eyes flashed angrily at the insult. "I would have loved to keep you around long enough to teach you some manners, but I have much bigger plans for you that just can't wait. You came along at just the right time, Doctor. You see, the coven hasn't had a good human sacrifice on Halloween in generations and the stars are in perfect alignment tonight for just such an event. I have no doubt the Master will be pleased with my offering. Unfortunately, you may be dead before he appears."

Cesari couldn't believe what he was hearing and said, "You're batshit crazy, aren't you?"

"My powers grow daily and when Satan bestows his grace on me tonight as reward for my obeisance, I will be the most powerful witch ever."

"Aren't you forgetting one thing?"

"Such as…?"

"I'm the one with the crowbar."

He chuckled. "Yes you are but I have him."

Cesari was momentarily confused and saw that Brom was looking past him so he turned around quickly. Horror and fright overwhelmed him as he shuddered and stepped back. A giant figure stood just three feet away towering seven feet high at the shoulders and four feet across in girth. He wore an eighteenth-century European military uniform;

dark green waistcoat with red trim, white pants and long black riding boots. His waist was as high as Cesari's chest and he had no head just a black hole. Raised high in the air in his right hand was a long, glimmering saber.

The Horseman!

Chapter 49

I am with Child

Cesari woke up shivering from cold, dazed and disoriented, his face hurt like hell, and he was naked buried beneath a massive, furry weight. As his mind focused, he remembered what had happened. The grisly sight of the Horseman had paralyzed him even as the monster swung his blade, but it wasn't a kill shot. The Horseman had punched him with his hilted hand, a hand the size of a brisket, and had knocked him unconscious. He tasted blood from a cracked lip and his left eye was swollen partially shut.

He didn't know what to think. If the Horseman was real, then Jasmine actually was a witch and everything she had told him about herself might be true. Stunned, he tried to absorb the significance of that thought. It was almost beyond the limits of his comprehension. He tried to rationalize it but couldn't nor did he have time to think it through fully at the moment.

His survival on the line, he forced his mind to clear and discovered his hands were free. That was good, and he probed the object on top of him realizing he was pinned beneath a dead animal, a very large dead animal...the black bear. With great effort, he pushed it out of the way and the light of a full moon suddenly lit up his surroundings. He was in the back of Sal's pickup but where?

Just as he wiggled free of the bear, a colossal hand reached over the side of the vehicle, grabbed him roughly and hoisted him out as if he weighed twenty-two ounces not two hundred and twenty pounds. The Horseman then threw him over his shoulder as if he were a rag doll, knocking both the wind and any idea about resisting right out of him. They were in the parking lot of Jasmine's church and heading toward the rear entrance in big lumbering steps. The pain and swelling on the left side of his face was excruciating as they bobbed along. He couldn't remember ever being hit that hard, but he supposed he was lucky. The Horseman could easily have cut off his head. Somehow Brom had mastered the art of controlling the Horseman, and Cesari guessed that years of practicing black magic had finally paid off. It must be a nice feeling to have a five-hundred-pound demon to do your bidding.

Approaching the door, Cesari spotted Ichabod hiding behind a garbage can watching the proceedings, his eyepatch and earring still in place. Suddenly, he ran off. Cesari didn't blame him. He knew a lost cause when he saw one. Inside the church, there were a group of hooded men, at least ten by Cesari's count, waiting by the wooden altar he had seen before. The rest of the meeting house was packed with the remaining members of the coven. He couldn't be sure but estimated there were several hundred witches crammed into the pews, and standing shoulder to shoulder in the aisles, sides, and back of the church. It looked like Christmas Eve mass in a Catholic Church except many were wearing Halloween costumes and he surmised they had just come from the gala on the other side of the lake.

He scanned around as best he could and was relieved he didn't see Jasmine or her parents. He didn't want to believe that they could be part of this. Candle light illuminated the room from multiple wall sconces and all the windows were shuttered to thwart prying eyes. Moonlight shone through the large stained-glass window behind the altar. The Horsemen brought him to the table and flung him down face up. Cesari's head slammed back hard, scrambling his brain even more, and he lay there motionless as several of the men stepped forward to tie his arms and legs spread-eagled with rope to the four legs of the table. Once he was restrained, Brom pulled his hood back and came forward to face the congregation. The Horseman and robed figures stood dutifully to the side.

Brom raised his arms over Cesari's naked form and invoked a higher authority in a language no longer spoken by men. The hooded acolytes chanted in practiced harmony. This went on for more than ten minutes as Cesari stared blankly at the ceiling resigned to his fate. There was not the slightest chance he could talk his way out of this and he resolved that under no circumstances would he beg for his life.

Brom then spoke to his people in the common tongue. "Brethren of the Order of Nine Angels, for generations have we watched our power wane and our blood diluted by the impure such as this blemish you see before you. For years have I yearned to bring our house back to the glory and might of ancient lore. In secret, I have practiced the black magic long forgotten by even the eldest present, and with each passing moon my powers, skills and knowledge have grown ever stronger."

He paused for effect and then said in a booming voice, "Behold the Horseman!"

All eyes turned toward the monstrosity of what was once a human being and a low murmur filled the room as those present acknowledged Brom's accomplishment. Brom continued, "I alone among you have the power to summon the beast. I alone among you command him to my will. I alone among you hold his loyalty and obedience."

Brom studied their faces and satisfied they were duly impressed, got right to the point. "Tonight I have summoned you here not to demonstrate my power. Tonight, we gather to do something far greater. Something that has not been done in more than two hundred years. Something that others have tried and failed, but tonight we will succeed. Tonight I, Brom Van Brunt, descended from the original Abraham Van Brunt, will summon the Dark Lord himself and offer him our lives and our souls to renew our faith. We offer him for the first time in a generation a human sacrifice as proof of our devotion. We ask him humbly to grace us with his presence and his trust and we shall promise to be ever faithful to him and never to stray again."

Cesari glanced around wondering if anybody was going to object. Apparently not. Suddenly the room went quiet as Brom reached into his robe and came out with a ten-inch long dagger and Cesari realized all was lost. The crazed and deranged look on Brom's face was enough to convince him that the man was much too far gone to reason with. Brom stepped close to the table and holding the dagger with both hands high over his head, he pointed it straight down at Cesari's heart. Cesari closed his eyes waiting for the inevitable wondering if it would be painful or if death would come so quickly, he wouldn't have time to register discomfort.

A loud noise from the church's front entrance caused him to open his eyes and look. The double doors had literally blown open on their hinges slamming against the walls behind them with a deafening clatter. Everyone flinched as fear and consternation rippled through the crowd at this new development. The mob of witches parted and Jasmine stormed in dressed as Katrina Van Tassel and she was boiling mad. Ichabod prowled at her side hissing.

Red faced with anger, she shouted, "Brom!"

He looked up, suddenly uncertain. Apparently, this wasn't in the script. He said, "No, Katrina, even you can't stop tonight."

She took a few more steps down the aisle and stopped. Her eyes narrowed as she zoomed in on the dagger. Her countenance was grave as she roared at him with determination, "This is folly, Brom, and I will not allow it."

Brom turned to the gathering. "Katrina has betrayed us. It has been her intention for many years to leave the coven. It is time we made a new pact with Hell and time for us to have a new leader. I, Brom, will guide the coven into greatness once again. I, Brom, will commune with the Master tonight. You will see. He will be pleased by this offering and favor us."

Katrina took another few steps toward him. "You will not summon him, Brom. I will not permit it."

Brom bellowed at her, "Come no further, Katrina. I do not wish to harm you."

Her eyes burned white hot with fury as she defied him and continued her path toward the altar. Brom glanced over at the Horseman and nodded. The leviathan sprang into action and marched down the center aisle to meet Jasmine head on. Cesari couldn't believe that Brom would purposefully hurt Jasmine but at this very moment in time all bets were off.

And then it happened. Instead of hesitating, Jasmine went straight for the Horseman, stretched her arms out in front of her with palms facing forward, and just a few feet away stopped and said, "You have no power over me, fiend so foul! For I am Jasmine, heir to Katrina, the most powerful of all witches who brought you forth from your ghastly lair. I am the Grand Mistress whom you must now obey. And I say be gone and return no more!"

With explosive force, the Horseman was thrown backward off his feet as if fired from a cannon. His body rocketed in the air over Cesari and Brom's heads and crashed through the stained-glass window in the back of the church into the parking lot and possibly as far as the lake a hundred yards away. Cesari couldn't be sure where he landed nor could he imagine the force required to do that to an object that weighed at least five hundred pounds. He held his breath and Brom started to sweat, but he held the knife steady pointing at Cesari's chest. He wasn't ready to give up.

Jasmine glared at Brom who seemed paralyzed from indecision. Her hands were back at her sides and she had a stern, serious expression on her face, but she was calm and very much in charge. The rest of the church had gone deadly quiet in anticipation of the coming confrontation.

"Put the knife down and release him," she commanded.

He vacillated but didn't move and said defiantly, "I won't let him or anyone else have you."

"It's too late, Brom. I am with child…his child."

Cesari looked at her and there was a collective gasp from the pews, but no one dared intervene. With tensions high, all waited anxiously for Brom's next move. He glowered at her with consternation on his face. That news sucked the oxygen right out of him and seemed to be the final straw. Then he looked at Cesari with an evil gleam in his eyes, and his features contorted with jealous rage. He raised the blade ever so slightly and with murderous intent plunged it downward at Cesari's exposed chest. With lightning alacrity, Jasmine flung her hands out at him causing the blade to arc backward. The tip grazed Cesari's skin drawing a trace of blood, and backed by the force of his own attack, the point plunged itself into Brom's heart. With a shocked look on his face he staggered backward and collapsed in a heap.

Everyone froze in place waiting. Jasmine turned to the hooded men and said, "Untie him and give him one of your robes to wear."

With unquestioning obedience they did as they were told. Jasmine turned and saw several members trying to scurry away without her permission and she raised her hands up. The front doors slammed shut and they meekly returned to their places.

She scolded them all as if they were children. "I have never been more ashamed of my people than I am at this moment. How could you have let Brom seduce you like this? We gave up the old ways for good reason so that we can live in peace amongst the others. There can be no benefit to revisiting the past and I will not be part of it. After tonight, we will no longer be welcome in Auburn and must relocate the coven. Those of you who wish to stay may do so, but those who choose to accompany me must agree to put aside Brom's quest. Now go to your homes and make your decisions by sun up."

The doors suddenly opened by themselves, and the members rapidly filed out. Cesari had donned one of the men's robes and walked up to Jasmine. She touched his swollen face gently. "I'm sorry, John."

"I'm sorry I didn't believe you. You really are…"

She nodded her head. "I really am."

"And not just an ordinary one…"

She smiled. "I tried to tell you."

They were alone now, and he sat down in one of the pews, fatigue suddenly overcoming him. He said, "How did you know where to find me?"

She sat next to him. "When I went to check on my parents, I noticed that all or most of the coven members had left the gala. It didn't strike me as too odd until I went back to the hospital to see you again. When I found the body hanging in the hallway and you were missing, I suspected the Horseman. I searched for you and was worried sick. Then Ichabod found me and brought me here. Until tonight, I hadn't thought anyone could control the Horseman the way Brom could. He must have worked hard at his art over the years."

"But you…? How did you…? I thought the Horseman was too powerful."

She held his hand. "The Horseman's only reason to exist was to protect the coven. Brom overplayed his hand tonight when he sent the Horseman at me… John, I am the coven, and even more importantly my children will be the future of our kind. The Horseman could no more hurt me than a kitten could hurt a lioness."

"I guess that makes sense… You said you're with child. How is that possible?"

She cocked her head. "How many times do I have to tell you?"

"Because you're a witch?"

Nodding she said, "I knew the second one of your guys landed on one of my guys."

"Exactly how many of my guys landed on how many of your guys?"

"Let's just say it was a good night for the home team."

Ichabod had come up to him and he reached down to pick him up. He held him on his lap and stroked him softly. "So I guess I owe you one, Ichabod?"

Ichabod purred softly and contentedly. Jasmine said, "He really likes you."

"And I really like you, Ichabod." He turned to Jasmine. "There's a lot of cleaning up to be done," he said nodding at Brom's body.

She nodded. "We'll take him with us."

"What about the Horseman?"

"He's gone… hopefully forever. Your friend hanging over the pentagram unfortunately is going to be a problem."

"And everyone knows I was up there tonight… Great," he said letting out a deep breath. "How am I going to explain that?"

She didn't say anything for what seemed like a long time. Finally, she caught his gaze. "You could always come with us."

He thought about that. "What would I do?"

Another big smile. "For starters, you could be a father. Twelve girls are going to be load for me."

"Twelve girls?"

She nodded. "I said it was a good night."

He said, "That's a lot of college tuition. I'm going to have to work long hours to pay for that."

"You don't have to. It was an invitation not an order."

"Are you sure we have to leave Auburn? I have a pretty good job here. If I leave in the middle of the night it may be a while before I'm employable again…if ever. Hospitals don't like unreliability."

"There are bodies all over the place and signs of witch-craft to go along with it. By morning there will be hysteria like it was 1692 all over again."

"Not necessarily. Let's think about this. We need a short-term plan and a long-term plan to dispose of the bodies; something to get us through the night and the next few days before deciding on the bigger strategy."

"You sound like you've done this before," she noted with a grin.

He smiled, "A couple of times… I was waiting for the right moment to tell you some disturbing news. I think this is the time… Jasmine, I found out what happened to Brom's parents."

"You did? Tell me."

"Brom murdered them. They're in that storage container in the basement of the honey-house. I got suspicious, went snooping around and discovered them."

She covered her mouth with her hand. "That's so horri-ble. Why would he do that? They were so good to him."

"It was probably over his determination to pursue black magic and conjure up Satan. They were opposed to it and may have been getting in the way. Maybe they threatened to expose him to the coven for his own good? It's hard to say.

Maybe they were the first victims of the Horseman as he practiced raising him and controlling him."

She thought about that for a long time before saying, "If his parents were the first victims, then the others…"

Cesari nodded. "Yes, it was Brom who conjured up the Horseman every time you got too involved with another man. It had nothing to do with the curse. I found Pullman's clothes and Mickey Mouse watch buried in the ground behind the honey-house and Brom admitted to me that he killed him after making him write you a 'Dear John' letter. We didn't get a chance to discuss what happened to the others, but I have no doubt Brom was behind them all."

She let out a deep breath. "And you found this all out how?"

"Some of it I deduced but a lot of it was with the help of Ichabod who pointed me in the right direction."

Ichabod meowed, and Jasmine frowned and then looked puzzled. "Why didn't you lead me in the right direction, Ichabod?"

No response.

Cesari defended him. "I thought about that. I think he was concerned for your safety or possibly the effect it might have had on you and your parents. Ichabod doesn't say much but he seems to be very intuitive. I like his style, and I'm assuming you've never displayed your power like that before, so he wouldn't have known that you were more than capable of handling Brom."

"I didn't know what I was capable of until tonight."

"I bet your parents knew. Last week when Brom threatened your parents in their house and you got mad. The whole building shook. Balthazar wrote it off to a tremor like a minor earthquake, but I could see in his face he was lying. That was you only you didn't know it. I could see that too. I looked it up in the library and on the internet. There has never been a recorded seismic event in this area of New York nor was one reported that day."

She thought that over as she rubbed her hand gently over Ichabod's head. "I guess I forgive you Ichabod, but we're going to have to talk about our future relationship." Ichabod seemed to agree, and she looked at Cesari. "So what now?"

"I suggest for tonight we put Brom in the honey vat with his parents. The same with the fat guy you found hanging in the hospital. We'll have plenty of time to clean up the Pentagram before morning. In any event, it's Sunday after the gala. The whole town will be hungover and there won't be many people snooping around. Organize the coven and have them patch up the back wall of the church first thing when the sun comes."

"All right... Who was that guy in the hospital anyway?"

"He was one of my friend Vito's traveling companions. Trust me, he was on the short list to disappear anyway His work ethic was questionable."

"One problem. I may have the strength of ten men when it comes to Headless Horsemen, but I don't think I'll be able to help you carry a morbidly obese guy out of a hospital."

"I'll get Vito and we'll take care of it. You go find the coven and tell them there's a new plan and that we're not going anywhere."

"You'll need some clothes."

"They brought me here in a pickup that's probably still out back. I'll bet they're in there. Speaking of having the strength of ten men… Do you think that's something you can turn on and off?"

"I don't know. I never had to that before. Why?"

"I'm thinking I'm never going to underestimate an angry woman again."

She smiled. "Or a mother protecting her children."

Chapter 50

Cover-ups Are My Specialty

"Lou, snap out of it. We got work to do," Vito growled at his nephew.

They were on the third floor of the old psychiatric hospital staring up at the other Lou dangling from the pipe and Vito was growing impatient. Lou was sobbing uncontrollably at the loss of his brother as he nibbled compulsively on a candy bar.

"But Uncle Vito, look at him," he sniffled. "We're never going to be able to share a pepperoni pizza again."

"C'mon be honest, Lou. You two never shared a pepperoni pizza in your life."

"You know what I mean. He would get one and I would get one."

"Lou, I'm sorry, but we're going to have to deal with your grief later, okay? Now put the candy bar away and hold his legs steady. I'll climb up on the chair and cut him loose. Cesari you got the stretcher stabilized?"

Cesari had borrowed an unused gurney from outside the emergency room with a couple of extra sheets. He braced it close to the body. If all went well, Vito would cut the rope and most of the weight would be passed on to his brother who was holding on tightly to the lower half. He would tilt the body toward the stretcher where Cesari would guide it into a lying position. Vito would do his best to hang on to his end of the rope, but he was in an awkward position and might have to let go.

Cesari said, "Let her rip."

Vito sliced through the rope with a five-inch switchblade he kept in the glove compartment of his car. The knife, along with the assault rifle, baseball bat, brass knuckles and various other weaponry for personal protection helped him relax when he was on the road. Unfortunately, the blade's edge only went halfway through on the first attempt but had damaged the rope's integrity enough for the dead Lou's enormous weight to cause the rest to snap. Three hundred and fifty pounds precipitously hurled downward. Living Lou wasn't the greatest athlete in the world and stumbled away from the gurney rather than toward it like he was supposed to. He tripped and fell backward onto the floor with his brother on top.

Crying and screaming he wiggled like a walrus trying to escape from a polar bear. Vito and Cesari pulled dead Lou off his brother with great effort, and then heaved the man up onto the stretcher while Lou sniveled on the floor.

Cesari and Vito rested against the stretcher for a few seconds after their exertion trying to catch their breath. Then Cesari covered the corpse from head to toe with the sheets he stole from the ER. Now they had a body that most hospital employees would just walk past with only minimal curiosity.

Vito said, "Lou, get yourself together and clean this pentagram up. Put the chair back in the on-call room and make sure you get rid of the rope. Cesari and I are going to put your brother in the pickup. Meet us downstairs in the parking lot and don't dawdle by the vending machines."

Cesari had gone to the maintenance closet and found a mop and cleaning fluid which he placed by Lou, who was struggling to his feet. As Lou started mopping the floor, tears streaming down his face, Cesari and Vito pushed the stretcher onto the elevator.

Cesari said, "You got your hands full with him."

"Yeah but look at the bright side. One down and one to go."

"Right."

"So Cesari, you going to tell me what's going on here?"

Cesari wasn't sure he should tell him the whole truth, so he kept it in simplified terms. "Brom made his play on me tonight. He killed Lou because he defended me. Lou fought like a tiger by the way. It took five guys to subdue him and they strung him up as a lesson because he was so heroic."

Vito's eyes went wide as they navigated the stretcher down the desolate main corridor to the front door. It was 2:00 a.m. and the gala was still in full swing. He was deeply skeptical. "Lou fought like a tiger? That's hard to believe."

"Well, he did. I saw it. He was like Beowulf and Gilgamesh."

"Who?"

"It doesn't matter. I think you should give his brother a chance. He's just grieving right now."

"I'll think about it. So what happened with Brom?"

"You'll see. He brought me to an old deserted church no one uses down the lake where he wanted to go one on one with me, mano a mano with knives. The church was abandoned. There's even a big hole in a stained-glass window in the back. So sure was he that he would kill me, he sent his men home. Can you believe that? The cocky bastard. Well, it didn't work out too well for him. We're going to pick him up after this and then dump them both in the honey vat."

"You sure bring out the worst in people Cesari. You need to work on that."

They reached the pickup and Cesari let the tailgate down. They looked around and saw no one, not even traffic on the road in the distance. They lifted the body and pushed it in albeit with great difficulty.

Vito squinted his eyes. Cesari had parked the truck in a remote section of the parking lot away from lights. "What's that thing?" he asked pointing at a dark lump in the back of the pickup.

"I think it's the bear we saw in the back of the inn last night."

"Jesus... Okay, so what happens after all the bodies are out of sight?"

"Not my problem."

"Isn't somebody eventually going to find them?"

"What do you care? If I were you, tomorrow I would clear out as fast as I could and don't look back. With your reputation and police record it wouldn't behoove you to be here when the shit hits the fan."

"Good point although I'll miss Abigail. She's a lot fun but I have to say, she's a little goofy like your girl, Jasmine. Get this...she got drunk tonight and told me she was a witch too and around midnight she ran out of the party to go to some big emergency witch meeting. Is everyone in this town nuts?"

"That's what it seems like."

"All right. Here comes Lou. Let's get rolling. What are we going to do with the bear?"

"We'll dump him on the side of the road somewhere. It'll look like roadkill."

****

After they hid the bodies in the honey vat, Vito packed his bags and left with Lou back to New York. He saw nothing to be gained by hanging around a murder scene with his prints all over it. Cesari went to his room and found Jasmine sitting on the sofa with Ichabod curled up on the bed. It was nearly 5:00 a.m. The window was wide open. He shook his head and closed it.

"I couldn't sleep. How'd it go?" she asked.

"Lou was upset about his brother but other than that it went about as smoothly as one could hope for. I don't think anyone saw us. What about you?"

"I didn't have time to speak to everyone personally, so I found the most important ones and explained the plan. Most of them don't want to move anyway and were willing to give it a chance. Several of them will be heading over there soon to patch up the wall. We'll need to explain to the community where Brom went in such a hurry."

Cesari sat down next to her. "I was just thinking about that when I was out in the honey-house dropping him in the tank. How's this sound? He received an urgent communication from the Brazilian government that they may have finally found his parents remains deep in the Amazon rain forest and requested he come down there as soon as possible to help identify the bodies and take them home. He became so excited that he took the first jet out of here and left you in charge of the inn. We're all so relieved for him to finally have resolution, etcetera, etcetera."

"That's a great story. What about when he doesn't return?"

"Unfortunately, he was in such a rush he didn't consult with his physicians about travelling to the Amazon and never received an anti-malarial vaccination or medications to take with him. Sadly, he passed away in a septic fever just two weeks after arriving."

"Man, you're good...and the bodies?"

"One step at a time. I just bought us at least a month and a half breathing room to think it over. The first thing is no more mead for a while, all right."

She nodded. "And the second thing?"

"Once things settle down, I'll dig a hole behind the honey-house. It's pretty deserted back there. I could dump Lou in it and we could put some new bee hives over the grave. That'll discourage visitors."

"That would work. What about Brom and his parents? I'd hate to do that to them."

"I don't think we'll have to. Nobody in this town was as close to Brom as you were so they will accept anything you tell them about his parents. The coven's on your side so they'll go along with your lead, right?"

"So far so good."

"Right, well it seems a reasonable thing that if Brom died in Brazil after identifying his parents' bodies that the authorities might reach out to you as the contact person. That would make sense. You pretend to have all the bodies shipped up here and we'll hold a funeral. It will be beautiful. Lots of flowers and stuff like that. The entire town will turn out. It would be great closure for everyone."

"Do I tell anyone in the coven where Brom's parents have been for the last ten years."

"Absolutely not, and if they were smart, they wouldn't want to know. The less said the better in these situations."

"In these situations?"

"You know your way around boiling cauldrons, and I know my way around cover-ups. In fact, cover-ups are my specialty. I would also start figuring out if Brom had a will and if he didn't how can we make one for him that would fly legally. There's no point in losing the property to government auction."

"Is that what would happen?"

"Yes, and it would be a shame. It's such a nice house and we're going to need the space."

"Yes, we will."

"Can't you just wiggle your nose and forge a will with his signature on it willing the property to you?"

"Wiggle my nose? Like on TV?" she said. "I could try that or I could have Kevin Barnes do it for me. He's an attorney in town. He's one of us."

The name sounded familiar and then it came to him. "Kevin Barnes? He was the ref at fight club. He's one of the coven?"

"Yes, he was there tonight at the church. I don't blame you for not recognizing him. After what happened, I'm sure he'll go along. He was no fan of Brom's anyway. In fact, they hated each other."

"He hated Brom but was going to let him stick a knife in me?"

"He was scared. They all were."

"Fine, I guess... Then we're all set for the moment. Little things are bound to come up but I think we've got a great start."

She touched his hand. "Are our girls going to be more like you or more like me?"

He thought about that, then said, "I hope they're more like you. Then I'll never have to worry about guys pushing them around. They could just fling them through a wall."

She liked that and laughed. "It figures that's the quality you would like most in a daughter... Well, I'm pretty tired. Are you going to invite me into your bed or not?"

"Since when do you need an invitation?"

Chapter 51

It's a Boy!

The room was dark and quiet. Cesari stood nervously watching the screen and holding Jasmine's hand as the technician scanned her lower abdomen. Jasmine wore a surgical gown which had been pulled up for the girl to work and a blanket covering her from the waist down. After a few minutes and with a startled look on her face the technician said, "I'm going to have to call the doctor."

She left and Cesari leaned down and kissed Jasmine. "It's fine," he said.

"I know it is," she countered confidently. "The lubrication is cold. I thought they warmed it up before they put it on you."

"Hang in there. It won't take too long."

It was now eight weeks since that fateful Halloween night and the ultrasound technician was out of her element. Brom and his parent's funerals behind them, they were now focused on Jasmine's health and transitioning the inn to her legally. Kevin Barnes had taken care of all the phony paperwork to the tune of ten years imprisonment for everybody involved if it ever came out, but all things considered that would have been a light sentence. Thankfully, Brom had no relatives to contest the will.

A very businesslike woman with short hair walked into the room with the technician close behind. She was forty and wore blue surgical scrubs beneath a white coat. She introduced herself to Cesari and Jasmine as the OB/Gyn on call. She didn't work for Auburn Memorial but was covering the hospital this weekend from Syracuse. They thanked her for seeing them on a Saturday morning.

She sat on a stool and placed the ultrasound probe on Jasmine's lower abdomen as she spoke. "Not a problem. I had to come in for another patient anyway. So what happened?"

"Nothing really," Jasmine explained. "I had a little cramping discomfort. It's already passed. John insisted we come in for a quick check. I think he overreacted. I'm sorry for bothering you."

"You don't have to be sorry. I agree with John. It can't hurt to be safe. So who's your regular OB?"

"I don't have one. I was going to use a midwife."

She moved the probe around deftly as she observed the screen while she spoke. "That's fine. Do you guys want to know what the sex is if I can tell?"

They both nodded their heads at the same time and said, "Sure."

"Great, that's always my favorite part. So Jasmine, I hear you're a nurse."

Jasmine said, "Yes, I am and John's a doctor. We both work here at the hospital."

"How nice. What kind of doctor?"

"A gastroenterologist… Is everything okay?" Cesari asked.

"So far so good. Are you taking your prenatal vitamins, Jasmine?"

"Yes."

"No spotting?"

"Everything's good. Like I said it was just a little discomfort. I think I was a little anxious this morning."

The doctor was quiet for what seemed like a long time before saying, "Do you two have any idea what I'm looking at right now?"

Cesari said, "Tell us."

She looked at him. "I'm looking at history in the making. That's what I'm looking at. I don't think I've ever heard of anything like this. One, two, three…" she counted under her breath for a few seconds. "There are twelve babies in there. I can't believe it, and it looks like they're all girls. You better start building extra bathrooms in your house. Are you on any medications or fertility drugs to promote gestation?"

Jasmine said, "No, I'm not."

"Well, this is just amazing."

Cesari said, "They're all fine?"

"They seem so. Hold it. What's that?"

She reached around Jasmine's significant baby bump and pressed the probe in a little deeper from an awkward angle. "Jesus," she whispered.

"Doctor, what is it?' Jasmine asked suddenly alarmed. Cesari gripped her hand tightly.

"There's a thirteenth. One, two, three…" she began the count again. "Yes, there are thirteen. The last one was hidden from view the first time I looked." She smiled at Jasmine and Cesari. "It's a little crowded in there, but he's in there all right. Getting pushed around by all the women but he's fine."

There's a boy in there?" Cesari asked.

"As far as I can tell, there are twelve girls and one boy, yes. Don't hold me to that, all right? It's still a little early and they're all moving around. How far along are you again? It said on the form you filled out that you're eight weeks, but I would have guessed twelve or fourteen at least by their size. Please don't take this the wrong way, but you definitely look more than eight weeks."

"Jasmine said, "I understand, but eight weeks is correct."

"Well, I wouldn't be shocked if you deliver earlier than planned. People are frequently off with dates. But everything looks fine so I'm letting you go. Keep up with the vitamins and keep the stress down. I hope to see you again some time and I encourage you to see an obstetrician. Midwives are great, and I believe in them but thirteen kids might present a problem for even the best of them. Heck, this would even present a problem for an obstetrician. The other reason to seek a higher level of care is that with so many babies you might well need a perinatologist around in case there's a problem. Well, I said my piece. Have a nice day and good luck."

"Thank you for your time and we'll consider it," Jasmine said.

"Was this your first ultrasound?"

"Yes, why do you ask?" Jasmine replied.

"Neither of you seem surprised to find out you're about to enter the Guinness Book of Records."

Cesari said, "We're very reserved people. This is about as excited we get."

"Well, I'm impressed. Most men pass out when they hear twins and I've never seen any standing upright after hearing triplets. The only quadruplets I've ever delivered sent the husband to the ER with chest pain."

"Not my John," smiled Jasmine. "He's very laid back… for an Italian."

Cesari laughed. "Thanks."

The doctor grinned. "That's good because with twelve girls you're going to have to be. Well, I am ecstatic for the both of you." She looked at Cesari's clothes with interest. "So what's with the tuxedo? I know it's New Year's Eve but it's not even noon yet."

"We were on our way to a wedding when Jasmine told me she wasn't feeling well so we detoured here but I now agree that it was just a little stress."

"A wedding. How nice. Well, have fun. Look, I'd like you to have my card if you change your mind." She reached into her lab coat and handed him her business card. "Call me for anything. This is a big deal. I'm going to research it later, but I really don't think there are any recorded cases like this. We could probably get you on TV."

Jasmine sat up and said, "We really appreciate that but to be honest, we are very private people, and would appreciate it if you kept this to yourself."

"Of course, I wouldn't dream of telling anyone without your consent. That would be a gross violation of your privacy. Have no fear about that… Well, happy New Year."

"Thank you and happy New Year to you too, Doctor."

She left and the technician offered to help Jasmine clean off the lubrication, but she waved her off. "Thank you but I can handle it."

"Both of you have a nice day," she said. "I think you know where the changing room is, Jasmine, and congratulations."

"I do and thank you."

When they were alone, she pushed him gently. "I told you it was nothing."

"Yeah, but I feel better now." Then he grinned and hugged her. "There's a boy in there."

She laughed. "I can't believe I didn't know about him."

"This witchery stuff is tricky business… Boy, that doctor got all excited. Could you imagine what she would have done if you told her a witch's gestational period is only seven months?"

"Oh my God. She would have passed out or called the newspapers."

"Do you want me to help you get dressed?"

"It would be better if you sent the girls in."

"I'll do that."

In the waiting room were three young women from the coven sitting with Vito. They wore beautiful full-length lavender colored bridesmaid dresses. Cesari sent them in to help Jasmine with her wedding gown. He sat next to Vito and propped his feet up on the table in front of them.

"How'd it go in there, Cesari?"

"Everything's fine. You look good in a tux, Vito, and thank you for being my best man. I really appreciate it."

"Are you kidding? I wouldn't have missed this for the world. It's not every day your best friend marries a crazy girl. You sure you want to go through with this?"

"What is love anyway, Vito, but a pleasant form of insanity."

"What the hell is that supposed to mean? Can I smoke in here?"

"No, you can't smoke in here and what it means is that we're all a little unbalanced when it comes to our emotions."

"Yeah, but she thinks she's a witch. What's your friend Mark have to say about all this?"

"You can ask him yourself. He'll be at the reception."

"I will. So do you know what you're having?"

Cesari hadn't told him that Jasmine really was a witch and pregnant with a dozen now thirteen children. He had only told him that she was pregnant, and that's why they were getting married. Vito was from a generation where that made sense and had no difficulty accepting that. He'd find out the truth about Jasmine one day but Cesari felt it would be best done in small increments, the same for Mark who had put his desire to analyze Jasmine on hold because of the complicated nature of the situation. Predictably, Mark had smacked him down with a blistering rebuke for sleeping with Jasmine despite his vehement warnings but after he settled down to a slow burn he wished him well and grudgingly admitted that he sort of, maybe, even admired him for taking on such a daunting responsibility given her mental state.

Cesari said, "Brace yourself, Vito."

"Why?"

"The doctor told us we're having a boy."

Vito smiled and exclaimed, "No way! Congratulations, Cesari! I'm really happy for you. Wow! You did it. You really did it. I'm proud of you. C'mon…c'mon, give Uncle Vito a hug."

They stood up and embraced. Cesari said, "Thanks, pal."

"You know what they say, Cesari?"

"What's that?"

"It takes a man to make a boy."

"That's me."

Chapter 52

St. Matt's

"It's a boy! It's a boy! It's a boy!" Cesari exclaimed over and over. His voice was hoarse and his mouth was dry. He sat up suddenly in the bed, confused and disoriented, and felt a sharp pain in the lower part of his abdomen. There was a tube coming out of his nose and he tried to pull it out.

Strong hands thwarted his intention and gripped his shoulders firmly pressing him back downward onto his pillow. Vito said, "Take it easy, big guy. Nurse! Somebody! Come quickly."

Cesari opened his eyes and saw a worried look on Vito's face as two nurses came hurriedly into the room, checked his monitors, and soothingly tucked him back under his sheets. He knew them. They were ICU nurses from Saint Matt's in Manhattan. What were they doing in Auburn?

He looked around. He was in an ICU bed with IVs in both arms and bags of antibiotics hanging from nearby poles. "Where am I, Linda?" he asked weakly.

She said, "You're in the ICU, Doctor."

"Yes, but where? What hospital?"

She glanced at the other nurse and then back at him. "You're in St. Matt's, Dr. Cesari…in Manhattan. You work here, remember?"

The other nurse checked his blood pressure and temperature. He was agitated. "Linda, what happened? Why am I in the ICU?"

She said soothingly. "You had your appendix out two days ago. Unfortunately it ruptured, and you developed peritonitis. You underwent emergency surgery with Dr. Pullman. The surgery went well, but you've had a high fever and have been in a lot of pain requiring high doses of narcotics. You've been delirious for the last day and a half. Otherwise you've been doing very well. It's good to have you back."

"Pullman operated on me?" he asked starting to calm down as the information slowly sank in through his morphine addled brain. "But I thought he was gone?"

"He was…for six whole weeks. Poor guy. Sitting alone in his apartment staring at the four walls. He just needed some time to get his life back together and put everything into proper perspective. It's not everyday you get dumped at the altar like that, but you should know how broken up he was. You were there. Anyway, he'll be around later. I'll call him now to let him know you're snapping out of it. He'll be very happy. Now please don't try to get out of bed or pull any tubes out, all right?"

He nodded, his memory sluggishly returning. "I won't."

Vito stepped forward as the nurses retreated from the room. "Hey pal. How're you doing?"

"Not so great. My stomach hurts like hell and I feel like I just fell through a black hole and landed in someone else's body. My brain has never been so muddled. Why are you here?"

Vito laughed. "Thanks. I save your life and all I get is a why are you here? Jesus, you're ungrateful."

"How did you save my life?"

"You really don't remember?"

Cesari rubbed his eyes and shook his head. "I have no idea what's going on. I can barely tell you my own name right now. My throat hurts."

"We went to a Halloween party on the West Side two nights ago, a club called Sal and Dicky's. Do you remember that?"

"Sal and Dicky's?" he repeated. "No, not really… maybe…vaguely. What happened there?"

"It was a big party. Your hospital sponsored it and spared no expense. I came as your guest. You weren't feeling great. You thought maybe you were coming down with a stomach bug or something, but it didn't slow you down too much. You were doing whiskey shots with a nurse you met there just before you went down for the count. You were probably trying to impress her."

Bits and pieces were coming back to him. "A Halloween party you say?"

"The mother of all Halloween parties, Cesari. There were at least a thousand people there. The place was rocking, and they went all out with the decorations. They even had a cauldron set up in the center of the room with dry ice. Anyway, you were pounding down the shots with this nurse who was dressed as a witch when suddenly you doubled over in pain and your legs gave out. I was standing right next to you and caught you before you hit the ground. I carried you outside, threw you in an Uber and brought you here. You actually diagnosed yourself on the way. I felt pretty smart when we got to the emergency department. I told the doctor, 'I think he's got appendicitis, pal. You better call a surgeon.'

And he did. And you've been babbling about witches and black cats ever since."

"Really? Well thanks, Vito. I appreciate your taking care of me even if I don't remember. You said I was trying to impress a nurse who was dressed as a witch?"

"Yeah, she's really cute too. She's been up to see you a few times, but you've been out of it. She's new here and works down in medical records or something like that. She feels terrible about what happened. Thinks maybe she stressed you out with some scary Halloween story she was telling you."

"A scary story?"

"Yeah, she's from the Tarrytown area just north of the city near a place called Sleepy Hollow which apparently is ground zero for spooky Halloween stories."

Cesari raised his eyebrows. "Is her name Jasmine?"

"No, who's Jasmine?"

"It doesn't matter."

"Her name's Katrina."

The End

Boo!

About the Author

John Avanzato grew up in the Bronx, New York. After receiving a bachelor's degree in biology from Fordham University, he went on to earn his medical degree at the State University of New York at Buffalo, School of Medicine. He is currently a board-certified gastroenterologist practicing in upstate, New York, where he lives with his wife of thirty years. Dr. Avanzato co-teaches a course on pulp fiction at Hobart and William Smith Colleges in Geneva, New York.

Inspired by authors like Tom Clancy, John Grisham, and Lee Child, Avanzato writes about strong but flawed heroes. His stories are fast-paced thrillers with larger than life characters and tongue-in-cheek humor.

His first eight novels, *Hostile Hospital, Prescription for Disaster, Temperature Rising, Claimed Denied, The Gas Man Cometh, Jailhouse Doc, Sea Sick,* and *Pace Yourself* have been received well.

Author's Note

Dear Reader,

    I hope you enjoyed reading *Night Nurse* as much as I enjoyed writing it. Please do me a favor and write a review for me on amazon. The reviews are important, and your support is greatly appreciated. I can be reached at johnavanzato59@gmail.com or Facebook for further discussion.

Thank you,

John Avanzato MD

Hostile Hospital

When former mob thug turned doctor, John Cesari, takes a job as a gastroenterologist at a small hospital in upstate New York, he assumes he's outrun his past and started life anew. But trouble has a way of finding the scrappy Bronx native.

Things go awry one night at a bar when he punches out an obnoxious drunk who won't leave his date alone. Unbeknownst to Dr. Cesari, that drunk is his date's stalker ex-boyfriend—and a crooked cop.

Over the course of several action-packed days, Cesari uncovers the dirty little secrets of a small-town hospital. As the bodies pile up, he is forced to confront his own bloody past.

Hostile Hospital is a fast-paced journey that is not only entertaining but maintains an interesting view on the philosophy of healthcare. If you aren't too scared after reading, get the sequel, *Prescription for Disaster*.

Prescription for Disaster

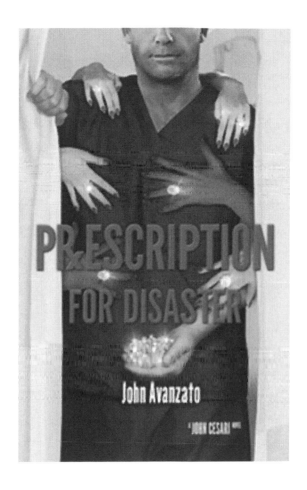

Dr. John Cesari is a gastroenterologist employed at Saint Matt's Hospital in Manhattan. He tries to escape his unsavory past on the Bronx streets by settling into a Greenwich Village apartment with his girlfriend, Kelly. After his adventures in Hostile Hospital, Cesari wants to stay under the radar of his many enemies.

Through no fault of his own, Cesari winds up in the wrong place at the wrong time. A chance encounter with a mugger turns on its head when Cesari watches his assailant get murdered right before his eyes.

After being framed for the crime, he attempts to unravel the mystery, propelling himself deeply into the world of international diamond smuggling. He is surrounded by bad guys at every turn and behind it all are Russian and Italian mobsters determined to ensure Cesari has an untimely and unpleasant demise.

His prescription is to beat them at their own game, but before he can do that he must deal with a corrupt boss and an environment filled with temptation and danger from all sides. Everywhere Cesari goes, someone is watching. The dramatic climax will leave you breathless and wanting more.

Temperature Rising

John Cesari is a gangster turned doctor living in Manhattan saving lives one colonoscopy at a time. While on a well-deserved vacation, he stumbles upon a murder scene and becomes embroiled in political intrigue involving the world's oldest profession.

His hot pursuit of the truth leads him to the highest levels of government, where individuals operate above the law. As always, girl trouble hounds him along the way making his already edgy life that much more complex.

The bad guys are ruthless, powerful, and nasty but they are no match for this tough, street-smart doctor from the Bronx who is as comfortable with a crowbar as he is with a stethoscope. Get ready for a wild ride in *Temperature Rising*. The exciting and unexpected conclusion will leave you on the edge of your seat.

Claim Denied

In Manhattan, a cancer ridden patient commits suicide rather than become a financial burden to his family. Accusations of malfeasance are leveled against his caregivers. Rogue gastroenterologist, part-time mobster, John Cesari, is tasked to look into the matter on behalf of St. Matt's hospital.

The chaos and inequities of a healthcare system run amok, driven by corporate greed and endless bureaucratic red tape, become all too apparent to him as his inquiry into this tragedy proceeds. On his way to interview the wife of the dead man, Cesari is the victim of seemingly random gun violence and finds himself on life support.

Recovering from his wounds, he finds that both he and his world are a very different place. His journey back to normalcy rouses in him a burning desire for justice, placing him in constant danger as evil forces conspire to keep him in the dark.

The Gas Man Cometh

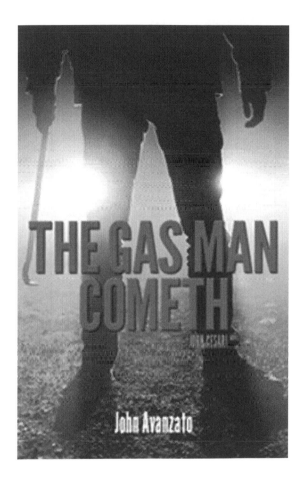

A deranged anesthesiologist with unnatural desires lures innocent women to his brownstone in a swank section of Manhattan. All was going well until John Cesari M.D. came along becoming a thorn in his side.

Known as The Gas Man, his hatred of Cesari reaches the boiling point. He plots to take him down once and for all turning an ordinary medical conference into a Las Vegas bloodbath.

Hungover and disoriented, Cesari awakens next to a mobster's dead girlfriend in a high-end brothel. Wanted dead or alive by more than a few people, Cesari is on the run with gangsters and the police hot on his trail.

There is never a dull moment in this new thriller as Cesari blazes a trail from Sin City to lower Manhattan desperately trying to stay one step ahead of The Gas Man.

Jailhouse Doc

Dr. John Cesari, former mobster turned gastroenterologist, finds himself on the wrong end of the law. A felony conviction lands him in Riker's Island, one of the country's most dangerous correctional facilities, doing community service.

Fighting to survive, he becomes trapped in the web of a vicious criminal gang dealing in drugs and human flesh.

A seemingly unrelated and mysterious death of a college student in Greenwich Village thrusts Cesari into the middle of the action and, forced to take sides, his options are to either cooperate or die. Which will it be?

Sea Sick

Recovering from a broken heart, John Cesari M.D. embarks on a Mediterranean cruise to unwind and clear his head. His goals are to see the sights, eat a lot, and most of all to stay away from women.

A chance encounter in a Venetian Bar with the lusty captain of the Croatian women's national volleyball team just before setting sail turns his plan on its head. When she tells him she is being sold into a forced marriage, he is thrust into the middle of a rollicking, ocean-going adventure to rescue her.

Murder on the high seas wasn't on the itinerary when he purchased his ticket, but in true Cesari fashion, he embraces his fate and dives in.

Pace Yourself

John Cesari's former lover Kelly and her children have gone missing and her husband is found dead in an underground garage. When law enforcement fails to act, Cesari launches his own investigation. He discovers their disappearance is linked to a shady company in Manhattan called EverBeat selling defective pacemakers to hospitals.

EverBeat has ties to both the Chinese military complex in Beijing and to the United States government. Trying to unravel the web of deceit one lie at a time leads to a trail of corpses throughout the city that never sleeps. Hunted by professional killers and thwarted by personal betrayal, his only goal is to save Kelly and her family.

KCM Publishing

a division of KCM Digital Media, LLC

50736169R00309

Made in the USA
Middletown, DE
27 June 2019